SMUGGLER'S DILEMMA

JAMIE McFARLANE

Cover Artwork: Sviatoslav Gerasymchuk

ISBN: 1508740496
ISBN-13: 978-1508740490

CONTENTS

ACKNOWLEDGMENTS

To Diane Greenwood Muir for excellence in editing and fine word-smithery. My wife, Janet, for carefully and kindly pointing out my poor grammatical habits. I cannot imagine working through these projects without you both.

To my beta readers: Nancy Higgins Quist, Dave Muir, Carol Greenwood, Kelli Whyte and Jeff Rothermel for wonderful and thoughtful suggestions.

PROLOGUE

Tradition calls for spacers to celebrate a voyage's mid-point. This crew was exhausted and beat up, but we'd managed to stay together and deliver the bad guys into custody. Those were all good reasons for a celebration.

The downside? Our flagship, the General Astral Cutter, *Sterra's Gift,* was completely wrecked. I'll admit it – mostly my fault. Ramming it into a frigate wasn't a choice most captains would make, but it was the only choice I had at the time. She'd never sail again and that fact alone was hard to accept. All the work we'd put into the ship… all of those hours scrubbing out the septic… all that investment… lay on the barge, not much more than broken pieces. In return, however, we'd captured a pirate frigate that was worth a small fortune.

Destroying the frigate's engines was great for capturing it, but it sure made moving it around difficult. In the end we finally just lashed it to one of the three loaded barges we were pushing back to Mars. We must have presented such a sight - two broken ships and a crap-tonne of ore.

Mid-way between the Jeratorn space station and Mars, we cut the tug's engines and were gliding without power. Ada Chen, an extraordinary heavy-freight pilot, was sailing our tug, named after her deceased mother, Adela Chen. She'd just finished sliding the tug out from one end of the string of three barges and had successfully mated back onto the opposite side. We'd have our equatorial celebration before she fired the tug's massive engines to decelerate us on our long approach to Mars.

The spread of food Nick and Marny laid out in the frigate's mess hall, looked better than anyone had reason to expect given that our pantry on *Sterra's Gift* had been destroyed by blaster fire.

"Is that chocolate cake?" I'd only recently been introduced to real chocolate and I'd have to say I'm a big fan.

"Aye, Cap. That it is," Marny's cheerful voice reassured me from around the corner in the galley.

"Are you sure you and Nick are solid? 'Cause if you're not, I might make a run at you myself," I said.

Nick's voice came from the same direction. "Hey, I heard that."

"I'm just saying. Treat her right." Like he had any choice. Nick weighed in at fifty kilograms if dunked in hydraulic fluid, and was one-point-seven meters tall - small, even for a spacer. Marny, on the other hand, was taller and outweighed us both at ninety kilograms. The size disparity didn't bother either of them.

"Keep it down or I'll tell Tabby," Nick entered the mess hall carrying a platter filled with thick, steaming slices of ham. His threat was good. Tabby was the jealous type and wouldn't like to hear about me flirting. I understood, though, it was hard on both of us with her at the Naval Academy, but we were figuring it out. Marny followed with another platter of fresh bread, something we didn't see very often.

Ada had disembarked from the tug and was already seated at the table along with our two passengers, Tali Liszt and Jordy Kelti, former military special operators we'd hired for the voyage out to Jeratorn Station.

I sat at the head of the table, reserved for the captain. I wasn't currently the captain of anything, other than two broken ships that sat atop a load of ore. Technically, the only captain in attendance was Ada, who'd removed the colorful beads from the tight curls on her head and was sporting four centimeters of what she called a 'fro.' She was one of the most naturally beautiful women I'd ever met, but lacked any self-awareness of that fact, something I found refreshing.

It seemed years ago when Captain Sterra had grabbed the attention of an entire table on the *Kuznetsov* by tapping the side of her glass with a fork. I tried the same, but since we didn't have any actual glass or crystal on board, all I got was a dull clacking sound. It was hard to feel sorry for myself when I looked around the table. As a group, we'd been through harrowing experiences, each contributing value in their own unique and critical way. I felt like I needed to say something, though.

"My dad was a man of few words. I've always believed it wasn't that he didn't have anything to say, rather he liked to make sure that when he said something, people understood it was important. One of the pieces of advice he gave me when I was younger was that 'It is the people in your life who are important, not the things.' Looking around this table, I can't imagine any truer words spoken. I'm better for having known you all."

The faces I looked into around the table smiled back at me. Inspiring words, to be sure, but there was hot food on the table, so I declared, "Now, let's eat!"

After we'd eaten and drunk our fill - and even sung a little, Ada and Jordy headed back to the tug to resume our journey.

"Do you think they're a thing?" I asked Tali, who was the oldest in our crew and leader of her small group of ex-special forces.

"Not sure. She's not the type he generally goes for."

"Pretty?"

"No, that he likes. More like smart and confident. He's a love 'em and leave 'em type."

"Interesting. Think she's in over her head?"

"Not at all. We talked. I didn't want any bad blood because of his commitment issues. She said he's been a perfect gentleman and they just enjoy hanging out and talking."

"Oh crap, he's in trouble," I said.

"That's kind of what I thought," Tali said. "What are you all doing next? I hope you're taking the Navy's warning about laying low seriously." She didn't have any commitment to me from here on out. Her team had done just what we hired them to do and done it well.

"I'm not sure," I said. "We're still trying to figure it out."

Nick slid into a chair opposite Tali. "I've got an idea. We should tear down that pirate compound we took from the Red Houzi and bring the loot back. There's got to be at least half a million still there, not to mention the stationary guns, warehouse and habitation domes."

Tali interrupted, "I'll leave you boys to it. This sounds interesting and all, but I've got an appointment to get beat up by your girlfriend." Tali and Marny regularly practiced their hand-to-hand combat skills together.

Nick nodded with a smile but didn't respond, focused on his current train of thought. "We should stop at home and visit. Mom's been wanting to meet Marny."

"We'll need to take the tug," I was still thinking about that pirate outpost. "There's no way we'll have a ship big enough to carry the outpost defensive guns and the buildings. The buildings will pack up pretty good, but the cannons and their generators will take space."

"We could rent a barge and run the tug out. It'd be a little sketchy if we ran into pirates, though," Nick was the most thoughtful person I knew. He needed time to work this out.

"No way. I'm not going back without serious firepower. I don't want to get trapped by Red Houzi again." Once we took the heavy station guns offline, we'd be vulnerable to whatever was in the neighborhood. I doubted Red Houzi would still hang around a base they'd lost control of, but I wasn't willing to risk it either.

"What are you thinking?" Nick asked.

"We've got to replace *Sterra's Gift*."

"As long as we have the hull, we have the ability to replicate all of the parts. That was the deal we made with the Navy. All we need to do is find another General Astral CA-12 and we're in business."

"I was also thinking we should cut Ada in on the company," I said. "I can't imagine a pilot I'd rather sail with. If we don't keep her, she'll just end up working for someone else and I don't want to sail a tug forever."

"A cut like we gave Marny?" Nick asked.

"Yes, that and a salary, but she'd get a captain's share if she's running the ship."

He nodded. "Sounds like we have a plan."

PUSKAR STELLAR

There were a half dozen shipyards near Puskar Stellar and Coolidge, the two cities where we spent the majority of our time. Like any large city on Mars, both had space elevators connected to large, public transportation terminals - in orbit and on the ground.

Contrary to what you might expect, finding a shipyard that would let you drop off a couple of derelict ships is difficult. Both of our ships, Sterra's Gift and the much larger frigate, had seen quite a bit of hostile action. None of the yards wanted to deal with anything that remotely looked like pirate activity. It took several hours to get someone from Mars Protectorate to acknowledge that we were indeed not pirates and had legal right to both craft.

Once we worked through the security issues, a shipyard over Puskar Stellar became quite helpful. Yard-hand semi-autonomous robots easily plucked the derelicts from the barges and placed both hulls in their designated spaces. They even conveniently stretched a catwalk between the frigate and their small station.

"I guess this is it." We'd called for a space taxi to take Tali and Jordy to the closest Puskar Stellar space station. From there, they'd catch the elevator down to the surface.

"Look us up next time you're in town. We'd like a rematch in the simulations." Tali's grin was more than a little mischievous.

Words couldn't adequately express how grateful I was for Tali and Jordy's help in getting us back alive, so I gave them each a heartfelt hug. If they found that weird they graciously kept it to themselves. Ada followed suit and I was surprised she didn't linger when she hugged Jordy. Nick and Marny bade them farewell and we all waved as they pulled away in their taxi.

"Let's deliver that ore, eh?" I said to lighten the mood. We had three barges filled with a spec-load of ore. Two weeks ago, we'd locked in a price and the gain looked good. Unfortunately, Nick and I had given our personal shares to Tali and Jordy to incent them to come on our last trip. It had been a good call - we wouldn't have survived otherwise.

"You didn't get many hours toward your master's license on the way back," Ada poked at me as the four of us walked toward a shuttle.

I was having none of that. "You and Jordy were getting along so well, I didn't want to get in the way." Marny's head swiveled toward Nick and I imagined her raised eyebrow.

"What?" Ada sputtered. "No... no... he just gets motion sick."

I wasn't finished, so I pushed. "So you're saying there's nothing going on between you two?"

She gave a little smirk and asked, "Jealous?"

Just in the nick of time the shuttle showed up to ferry us out to the waiting *Adela Chen*. Hopefully, my raised face-shield hid a rising blush and if I was lucky, the burning in my cheeks would dissipate before we boarded.

"You want to sail her, Liam?" Ada asked.

"I would. Nick, you and Marny are welcome to watch. There's a ledge right behind the stairs that isn't too uncomfortable, especially if I turn down the gravity." I followed Ada up the ladder into the cockpit. It was compact with two comfortable chairs sitting side by side. Like most tugs, the cockpit rotated a hundred and eighty degrees, allowing the captain a clear view forward or backwards depending on whether the ship was accelerating or decelerating.

Display Adela Chen pre-sail checklist, I commanded my AI (Artificial Intelligence). We punched through the items and I wasn't surprised to see all greens. Ada was an extremely precise captain and would have made sure things were ready to go before she disembarked to meet us in the shipyard.

"I show we're clear," she said. "I've set a course in to the refinery for you. Navigation Plan Alpha."

I reviewed the plan and ordered, *Engage Plan Alpha*. With Ada, a master pilot on board, I was within my legal right to take the flight sticks and manually sail the tug and its nine hundred meter long string of barges to the refinery. There were some captains who would do it, too, but the risk was too high. With my whole company aboard and a delivery to make, I preferred to allow the ship's AI handle the navigation.

It was a relief to finally release the barge string above the refinery. We waited for the customary inspection that would record our delivery. A small fleet of robots flitted about the surface of the barges and our wait was short.

Seven point five oh oh two kilo tonnes are accepted, the AI informed me. Good news. We'd contracted for exactly seven-point-five kilo-tonnes and the extra four hundred kilograms would go straight to the bottom line.

"Liam, you want me to find us a place to stay tonight? Ada, you need a room?" Nick asked.

"I'll probably go home," she answered. Her father's apartment was nearby and whenever she was here, she stayed with him.

"I see a suite with three bedrooms. Ada, you sure you don't want to at least hang out for one night?" Nick asked. "It's going to be 0200 local time when we get down there."

She thought about it for a minute then agreed. "Sure, that makes sense. No reason to wake up Dad."

The hotel Nick found in Puskar Stellar wasn't anywhere near as nice as the resort we'd stayed at in Coolidge. The beds, however, were comfortable. I'd brought my civvies along (clothing that didn't immediately brand me as a spacer) and threw them on the room's only chair. The hotel had a funny smell, like too much cleanser had been used, but I was worn out and fell asleep easily.

After I awoke, I sauntered out to the common room of the suite. Nick and Ada were seated on one of the two couches talking.

"Marny's still sleeping?" I asked, surprised.

"No, she took off about an hour ago. Wanted to get a run in," Nick explained. "Should be back shortly."

"You all get anything to eat yet?"

"We're waiting on you and Marny. Thought we'd go out. Ada knows some good restaurants."

I nodded. I was starving. But first, I needed to at least start the conversation. "Ada, I'm glad you're here. We'd like to talk to you about a business proposition."

"Sure, what's on your mind?"

"We'd like you to join our company. Full captain's share and some other perks."

Ada looked at the both of us in turn. "Are you serious? Why would you do that?"

"You're an excellent pilot, good in a pinch, people like you and we trust you," I'd anticipated her question and had the answer ready to go.

"That's flattering. What's the catch?" she asked. "You said there's more."

The door opened and Marny walked in, dressed in what I'd come to know as her running suit. Her well-defined, heavy, Earth-borne muscles showed the result of a strenuous workout and I had to be careful not to stare. It was incredible to me that she could be so powerfully built and still so attractive.

"You guys up for lunch?" Marny asked cheerfully. She winked at me when she saw me staring. "I just need a quick shower."

"Yup. We were just pitching Ada on the company," Nick said. He was staring too. That woman had grabbed his attention the first time he met her and he'd never gotten over it.

"Save it for lunch, I want to hear the rest." Marny reappeared five minutes later in her standard tight jeans and loose top.

"Let's eat. I'm starving," I said.

Ada had a restaurant she wanted to introduce us to and directed the cab to its location.

The Southern Garden's interior was brightly lit with high ceilings and white painted woodwork. Dark green vines had been encouraged to grow up the thick beams that appeared to hold up the roof and colorful flowers adorned each of the tables.

"It's one of my favorite places when I'm in this part of town," Ada said. "Everything on the menu is freshly made here in the restaurant." Her excitement was contagious. I had no idea what to order as I was generally satisfied with meal bars, but I looked over the menu nonetheless.

"Okay, spill. What other perks could you possibly offer me?" Ada asked conspiratorially, looking quickly from Marny to Nick and then to me with a slight grin.

A waiter appeared with water, coffee and fresh juice. I chose what Ada ordered and waited for him to leave. Ada looked back to me expectantly.

"The full offer is five percent of the company plus one hundred twenty percent of standard captain's salary and a captain's share on the loads you command."

"Am I in charge of setting up my own runs?" she asked.

Nick stepped in. "Not at first, because we'll fly as a fleet. But, we're open to the idea."

"That sounds fair. Can I have time to think about it? I'd like to talk it through with Dad," she said.

"Of course," I said. "How long do you think you'll need?"

"Three days. Dad's going to be a pain about everything, but eventually he'll settle down. The return on the ore-hauling put him in a good mood." Ada's dad had been an investor in our trip to Jeratorn. He was protective of his daughter after his wife's death, but the family still had to make a living.

The food arrived and for several minutes the table was quiet as we dug in.

Ada finally broke the silence. "So what are you going to do with all your busted up ships?"

"Look for a replacement. We're headed out this afternoon and tomorrow. Want to go along?" I asked.

She beamed, "What girl doesn't like shopping? But I promised Dad that I'd see him this afternoon, so how about tomorrow?"

"That works. I'm picking up Tabby at 1100 and expect to be space-side by 1300." I said.

"Great. See you tomorrow," Ada stood and we all stood with her as she handed out good-bye hugs.

"What's on the schedule for today?" I asked my compatriots.

"You need to do a little scouting to narrow down our ship choices," Nick told me. "I sent you a list of the ten CA-12s between Coolidge and Puskar Stellar. We won't know what we can afford until we sell the frigate, but you can at least see what the market has to offer."

It seemed like a fun way to spend the afternoon.

REUNION

Early the next morning, I found Nick at a desk in the common room of the suite - obviously working. I grabbed a cup of coffee and a meal bar.

"How'd it go yesterday?" he asked. "You didn't get back until late."

"Expensive." I figured that explained it. "Every ship was seven hundred thousand or better. Although I did choose to start at the top of the list. I wanted to see what a million got you in a CA-12. They're nice, but it doesn't seem worth it."

"*Sterra's Gift* was worth almost that much on our last run," Nick said.

"You mean before I ran it into the back of that frigate?"

"That certainly didn't help its value," he said. I couldn't tell if he was serious or not. "Keep your eye out for a second ship. Something with teeth. Maybe something we could lash to the tug and use if we get into trouble."

"With the prices I've been seeing, I don't know how possible it'll be," I knew I sounded frustrated, but yesterday was not as much fun as I'd hoped.

"Keep looking," he said. "You'll find better prices today. Remember we can make parts for it, so it can be a little beat up."

"You should have seen how crappy some of the ships were, though. Are you going with us today?" I asked.

"Nope, we're on a short timeframe. I'd like to get underway within a week. A ship surveyor is meeting me at the frigate at 1000." He paused and then said, "Oh, I also purchased a container so we can offload non-essentials. Think you could pick that up? I know you want to spend time with Tabby, but you'll be space-side anyway."

Nick was in full planning mode. The best thing I could do for him was take care of any details I could wrap my brain around.

"Roger that. So, three shipyards today. Give me numbers. What's my ballpark for the cutter and an attack craft?" I couldn't wait to check out the darts, although truth be told I didn't think they had enough teeth.

"Six to seven hundred for both. We've got one-ninety in the bank and should clear a million for the frigate."

I whistled, "That much?"

"It's worth at least one point two."

"Roger. I haven't seen even half of the CA-12s out there and I'll drop off the container, first thing."

If Nick heard me, he wasn't saying. He was back to gesturing in the air, dismissing virtual windows and scrolling virtual panes. I had three shipyards to visit. Brinkman's, Cintani's and I was saving Weird Wally's Bone Yard for last. It was three times the size of the other yards and his advertising was pasted all over the space station. Apparently, Wally's hook was that he was a little unstable and likely to cut you a good deal even if it wasn't a good deal for him. I didn't believe it for a minute, but if he had the ships, I was all in.

I had ninety minutes to make it from Puskar Stellar to the Naval Academy at Coolidge where I'd pick up Tabby. Nick had chosen a hotel close to the transportation terminal which doubled as the terminus for the space elevator as well as a stop for the mag-lev (MAG-L) train that joined many of the Martian cities. At the Coolidge terminal I caught a cab and gave it instructions to fly out to the Naval Academy.

The purple-hued Martian forest that had been planted centuries before was beautiful. Flying over it took my breath away. I recognized the landscape from the last time we'd stayed in Coolidge. Nick, Marny and I had really done it up by staying at a beautiful lakeside resort which sat on the same lake bordering the Naval Academy. When the taxi stopped, Tabby was standing outside of the visitor's center in her dress whites.

"Heya, hot-stuff," I said, opening the door. She jogged over to the cab.

"Privacy screen," she said as she jumped in, dropped her bag, and pulled the door closed. I raised my eyebrows, but wasn't left wondering very long as she launched herself on top of me. The model of cab I'd chosen was just a big circular couch with a hole in the middle to put your feet. I had made a good choice. She pushed me back into the cushion, straddled me and gave me a kiss that I'll never forget. After a few minutes of intense welcoming, she finally released me.

"Tell me you're making up for lost time and if we were together it wouldn't always be like that," I said, panting for breath. I was half joking, but wow, really only half.

She smiled wickedly and I took a moment to look her up and down. She'd let her hair grow out from the hard-core buzz-cut she'd given herself just before starting at the Academy. Her muscle tone had also significantly increased. When she held me down, I wasn't sure I'd have had an option to not comply.

"As if a rogue like you would ever settle down with a respectable woman." Tabby was looking at me playfully. I took advantage and pushed her over onto the opposite couch. Two could play at that game. Her lithe body wriggled beneath me and I enjoyed running my hands over the soft skin that covered those firm muscles.

Breathless, Tabby finally broke us apart and shifted so we were lying next to each other. "Jupiter, I miss having you around," she said. "Where are we going?"

It was a friendly reminder that we were still sitting next to the Naval Academy visitor's center. Our little display of affection would have been trouble for her if she hadn't requested the privacy screen.

Coolidge Terminal, I instructed the cab.

"You'll never guess who I ran into," she said, turning to face me. Her hands trailed along my chest.

My mind blanked. Having her this close to me was difficult enough, but I couldn't imagine who might have been on Mars that we'd both know. "No idea."

"Commander Sterra," she said. "She gave a lecture on ethics."

"Did you get a chance to meet her?"

"Of course, silly, why do you think I'd bring it up? She ate lunch with my whole class. Did you know she knew your dad?"

I just looked at her dumbfounded, "No…"

"When he and your mom were in the Amazonian conflict." I must have looked confused. She returned my perplexed look. "Are you serious? You didn't know they were in the war together?"

"Mom? I knew Dad was, but…"

"You Hoffens really need to talk more. So, guess what else?" she asked brightly.

I smiled. It was fun to see her so energetic. "What?"

"Guess," she repeated.

"Uh, you got a promotion?"

"Well, true, but that's only sort of it."

"You're… Frak, I don't know…"

"I got accepted to Space Combat School," she said.

"Doesn't that describe the Academy?"

She punched me, "No dumb-ass. Space Combat School means I'll fly a fighter, and I'm going to be assigned to a ship, probably a destroyer."

"No shite! That's amazing! When do you start?"

"At the end of this semester. I'll take a reduced load and start flying trainers right away."

"We need to celebrate," I said huskily. I wrapped my arms around her and pulled her tight "Can you stay at the hotel tonight?"

She kissed me, but before I could get serious, she stopped and said, "I've got until 1900 tomorrow. My time was extended since I was promoted to combat-school candidate."

I whistled, "Two whole extra hours. Big stuff."

Tabby slugged me in response. I preferred the kissing.

She sat up, grabbed her bag, and pulled her vac-suit out. "Look away," she demanded and started removing her dress whites. I made a half-hearted attempt to look away, but gave it up when I saw a number of bruises on her ribs and legs.

"What's all that about?" I asked, running my finger across her ribs.

Her eyes followed mine down to the bruises. "Oh, that's nothing to worry about. Hand-to-hand training. We're supposed to go half-speed, but sometimes it gets a little out of control." That made sense to me. The Tabby I knew didn't do anything halfway.

The cab arrived at the Coolidge main transport terminal. Waiting fifteen minutes for the next train was easy, I was spending time with Tabby. We grabbed meal bars and sat on a bench next to the track.

"What are we doing today?" she asked.

"Non-stop fun," I said, teasingly. "No, really. It's a big day. I rented a hauler so we can run a container over to the frigate we captured. We're moving all of our gear and supplies out."

"I didn't completely follow what happened to *Sterra's Gift*. Did you actually ram the back end of that frigate with your ship?"

"Yeah. We were desperate. That frigate wa-ay out gunned us, it was the only thing I could come up with," I said.

She nodded, as if seeing the action in her mind. "Do you have the combat data stream? We've been dissecting data streams in our fleet maneuvers class. I'd love to share it with my professors."

"Sure, later tonight we can run through some of it and see if it's something you're interested in."

We'd just stood to get on the train. Tabby was holding onto my arm with both of her hands and she gave me a squeeze. "I'm not sure I like that you keep getting into these scrapes."

"I think you don't like us getting into these scrapes without you. You gotta know that's why we're shopping for ships. We're upgrading our offense. I'm tired of getting kicked around."

"Can't you keep the frigate? That thing should be loaded for bear," she asked as we stepped into the train.

We sat and waited for it to start. "It totally is, but the cost to keep it running is incredible. It runs through more credits of ordinance in a minute than we could recover on most trips. We're better off selling it and stepping back. Besides, a frigate is a fleet vehicle and not really designed for one-on-one combat. It's all teeth."

She snuggled against me as the train sped toward Puskar Stellar. I wondered how we would ever make it as a couple. I felt so complete when we were together. It was as if she filled a hole in my life that I didn't know was there. I hated that we were always having to leave each other. Tabby must have been tired because she fell asleep against me. I wrapped my arm around her and enjoyed a quiet ride.

I pinged Ada on my HUD to let her know where we were. She was already at Puskar Stellar's space station.

Open comm, Ada Chen.

I smiled when I heard her cheerful voice. "Heyas, Liam. Are you guys getting close?"

"Yup. Sleepyhead and I are just getting off the train and we'll be on the elevator in a couple of minutes."

"Sounds great, see you in a few," Ada said and then cut the comm.

"Ada's coming?" Tabby asked.

"It was last minute, but Nick and I are trying to hire her. She's a killer pilot. I thought it'd be good to get her opinion about the ships we're looking at."

"Really?" Tabby raised her eyebrows and the look on her face confused me. We were heading for bad territory and I had no idea why.

"Okay, what?" I asked.

"You didn't think to mention that you were bringing your gorgeous pilot friend, who you just might be hiring, along on our day out?" She definitely seemed miffed.

I'd totally missed that angle and wasn't sure what I needed to do. "I don't think about her like that. She's just a friend."

"You should have seen your face when you were talking to her. You were all smiles."

The trap had been set. It was right in front of me, but I was completely unable to avoid it. "That's because she's always so upbeat."

Tabby closed her mouth and looked away, her lips so tightly pressed together they were white. We only had a couple of minutes before exiting the elevator and this wasn't how I wanted us to spend our day. There were things we had to do and I needed Tabby not to be grumpy. With our limited time together, fighting was a terrible waste of time.

"We've had this conversation, but just in case you forgot how I feel…" I grabbed her arm to turn her toward me. She held fast, but I didn't care. I moved around her and pulled her in close, kissing her face with small pecks. At first she was rigid, but she soon began to melt. Within moments she accepted, started giggling and finally returned my affection.

I pulled back, "I'm serious, Tabby. As long as you'll have me, I don't have eyes for anyone else." Apparently, this wasn't a bad thing to say because she pulled me back in for another long kiss. I could get used to this.

I heard clapping nearby and let go long enough to look up. To my dismay, the elevator had stopped and a small crowd of people who were waiting to enter, applauded our efforts. My cheeks burned and I grabbed Tabby's bag from the floor of the elevator as we slunk off. At least she was also blushing. Once we cleared the crowd, she gave me a quick poke with her fist.

"Tabby!" I heard Ada's voice from nearby. I thought it was odd that Ada called her by name since they hadn't actually met. I turned to see Ada in her vac-suit, approaching at a jog. "Liam said you'd be joining us today. I couldn't wait to meet you. The boys talk about you all the time." She didn't hesitate and pulled a slightly reluctant Tabby in for a hug.

In typical Ada-style she kept right on rolling. "Oh, my gosh! They totally were telling the truth too. You're gorgeous! Do you ever grow your hair out? I bet it's beautiful. But I suppose, as an officer you like to keep it short. It's great to finally meet you!"

"Liam neglected to tell me that I'd get to meet you today," Tabby said, not yet completely over it.

"Men. They're useless." She grabbed Tabby's hand, led her away and called over her shoulder. "Liam, did you rent that hauler?"

I trailed along behind them and Tabby glanced back apologetically. She now understood the enigma we all knew as Ada and was helplessly swept along in its wake.

HMS HOTSPUR

"You want to fly it?" I asked Tabby while we were standing next to the spindly legged container hauler. It reminded me of the ore-sled I used to fly for my dad on our mining claim.

"Absolutely," she said. We'd exchanged enough video messages where she lamented her lack of time in the pilot's chair, that I already knew the answer.

"Ada's probably better suited to helping you through traffic than I am."

Tabby nodded amiably. I popped the bat-wing door on the port side and climbed over the pilot's chair and onto a back bench. Tabby and Ada strapped into the two front seats and pressurized the cabin.

"First stop is to grab a container. Nick bought one from the yard where we stored the frigate. I just sent you the nav-plan, Tabby," I said.

"Got it."

She smoothly joined a stream of traffic exiting the controlled space around Puskar Stellar Space Station. I was surprised that she was stick flying. In heavy traffic, I preferred to let the AI do the work. In my defense, I'd always been sailing a much larger ship, but I didn't think for a moment it would have made any difference to Tabby.

"You're a natural," Ada said in her normal bubbly way. If I didn't know better, I'd have thought that she was sucking up to Tabby.

If Tabby thought anything of it she didn't give any clue, "Thanks. Liam gave me a nice wide nav-path."

It took twenty minutes of sailing, but Tabby didn't have any trouble. Once there, she hooked up to the empty container we'd purchased. Having grown up in a mining colony, it was old hat for her as much as it was for me.

As we sailed over to the frigate, I was pleased to discover that it was designed to receive cargo by placing the open end of a container next to the cargo elevator. Heavy clamps held the container in place and the elevator doubled as an air lock, pressurizing and depressurizing so cargo could be transferred quickly. All in all it was well thought out and it took us less than twenty minutes to secure the container and get going again.

The first shipyard, Brinkman's, was a bust. They had two beautifully maintained CA-12s but they were very proud of them and the price reflected it. The second yard had a single CA-12 that was a possibility, but still on the high end. I wouldn't rule it out. When we finally made it to Weird Wally's Bone Yard it was getting late. Fortunately, Weird Wally didn't mind that at all.

"So, you're looking for what exactly?" I hadn't expected to be meeting with Weird Wally himself, but there he was in a purple vac-suit covered by a white suit coat. We'd already sailed through the Bone Yard and seen his three CA-12s. From the outside, they'd seen a significant amount of use, but their prices were also the most competitive. Even so, the lowest price was half a million and we needed to fit repairs and another ship into my max budget of seven hundred thousand.

"We're looking for two ships. I need something with some real teeth and a General Astral CA-12." I had no idea how to negotiate with a ship salesman, so I just put it out there on the table.

"I see. What kind of budget do you have?" The four of us were seated at a clear glass table in his office. While he talked, Wally was gesturing, giving commands to his HUD. Three CA-12s emerged from the glowing, translucent blue table top, hovering in a line. They looked so lifelike that I couldn't help myself and reached out to touch one. It jumped to the center of the table, and grew in size to half a meter long and perfectly proportioned.

"Seven hundred thousand for both ships, fully functional," I said.

He nodded and flicked one of the CAs off of the table. It

tumbled and disappeared when it reached the edge. He lined up five smaller ships in front of the cutters. Two of them were the same arrowhead shaped darts that we'd come into contact with many times before. I wasn't impressed with their armor. Sure, a dart was fast, but we'd been able to take them out every time.

"Probably not the darts," I said.

"Good. Tell me why, it will help the search," he said.

"Too fragile. They've got speed, but missiles or even a good gunner takes 'em out too easily."

He considered what I said and nodded appreciatively. "That'd be quite a gunner, but I get your point. I don't get too many fighters in, so you'll understand that they come at a hefty price." He swept his hand across the entire lineup of fighters and sent them tumbling. "You've really got to have a CA-12?"

"Yes. Why?" I asked.

"It's killing your budget." He pushed the two remaining cutters off the board. "We'll get back to those. Like I was saying, the fighters are going to be the hardest to find and eliminating the dart class causes some problems. Let's be creative for a minute. Tell me why you need more than a dart. What are you kids getting into?" Ordinarily I'd have been offended by his use of the word kids, but he was such an odd character and he'd said it so earnestly that it didn't bother me.

"Loose Nuts is a shipping company, recently founded. The problem is we keep running into trouble and the equipment we're sailing gets beat to crap."

"You're smuggling?" he asked, completely unabashed.

"Not so far," I replied honestly.

Ada was scandalized by my comment and she gave me a one word correction. "Liam."

I looked at her and smiled. "Right. No, just problems with pirates."

"And the CA-12 isn't enough? Surprising, since that's the point of a cutter. Long range and teeth enough to defend itself. That Chrysler Frigate you brought back, did you take that down with your CA-12?"

I was shocked. How did he know about the frigate? I didn't even know that it was a Chrysler make.

"We got lucky and the CA-12 didn't survive."

"More than luck if you all made it back. That cutter isn't designed to take on warships. Let me take you out to the yard to look at something special. I don't even want to put it on the table. You've got to see it in person."

He had my attention. I knew I was being reeled in by a master salesman, but felt powerless. He'd shown aptitude, interest and even indirectly complimented me. I was trying to learn something from his salesmanship, but it was hard as I was the target of his not inconsiderable charm. I looked to Tabby and Ada for support, but they'd been drawn in too.

"Alright. We're game," I said.

"Perfect." He stood up and his vac-suit's hoodie deployed, face mask rising.

Comm channel request from Wenton Waldorf, my AI requested as the three of us followed suit.

"This way," he said. Wally placed a white top hat on his helmet and grabbed a long yellow cane. Past his desk, a door slid to the side revealing an airlock large enough to fit a dozen people. We cycled through the lock into a comfortable transport vehicle that resembled a large cab with plush cushioned chairs in rows facing forward. Wally perched himself on a stool at the head of the vehicle, centered in front of an expansive window.

"Sometimes when people come to me asking for one thing, I get a flash of inspiration that I just have to share with them. Often that inspiration turns out to be the ramblings of a madman, but sometimes - once in a blue moon - that inspiration changes the course of history," he said, waving his hands dramatically still holding his bright yellow cane. The vehicle slowly pulled away from the office.

"Today, I've had one of those flashes of brilliance. Pragmatically, you've been asking for ships with which you are familiar – with possible improvements here and there. I applaud you for that. I believe, however, that I can take you - not just to the next level - but that I can transport you to an entirely new, unmatched level."

I had to hand it to him. He might be full of crap, but he was totally committed to it. I certainly hoped he wasn't going nutty on us.

"Your problem is that you need to be able to sail cargo into hostile territory. You are smugglers - but you don't know it."

Ada gasped.

"No, my pretty little friend! I don't mean literal smugglers - although I don't think our friend Mr. Hoffen has completely ruled this out. I mean figuratively. You have the smuggler's dilemma. If you can't beat it, you need to be able to outrun it. In addition to this, you've got what I call Don Quixote syndrome."

He looked at us expectantly. I had no earthly idea what he was saying, but I loved his enthusiasm. "Oh, come on! Surely one of you has read the classic story?"

I shook my head negatively, but made a mental note to look up this Don Quixote later.

Wally sighed and pushed on. He was trying to fill time. It wasn't that I didn't appreciate his waxing on eloquently, but a literary reference might have been a little much for this group.

"You defend the defenseless. You come to the aid of the righteous. Am I right?"

I shrugged, but he'd caught a nerve with Ada, who responded, "Yes. That's right."

"Thank you, Ms. Chen. And we're here. Behind me is the starship *HMS Hotspur*. I've been holding onto her for several years, waiting for the right captain. And Mr. Hoffen, I believe that captain is you."

I looked through the glass behind him and couldn't see anything other than a dark space where something was blocking out the stars.

"I assure you it's there, my friends. The reason you're having trouble seeing the ship is because of its light-absorptive armor."

"You said starship. What do you mean?" I asked.

"Tut-tut. All in good time, Mr. Hoffen. The *HMS Hotspur* is a sloop class starship, weighing in at three hundred metric tonnes. Named after an ancient sailing vessel, the *Hotspur* was constructed over a century ago when gate travel was extremely dangerous, but also highly profitable. Have you ever considered gate travel, Mr. Hoffen?" I wasn't sure if he was asking a question or not, but he'd paused long enough that I recognized he was awaiting an answer.

"Yes. We're interested in gate travel."

"Interesting. You didn't mention that earlier, yet I *knew* this. We are simpatico, you and I, Mr. Hoffen." As if to emphasize the relationship, he gestured back and forth between us. I wasn't sure what to do with this, but it turned out he wasn't finished yet. "If I were in your position, I'd be looking at those gates jealously. At three hundred tonnes, she's twice as long as the CA-12 and three times as heavy, yet with a maximum crew compliment of ten, and that's if you hot bunk your crew. Any idea where all that weight shows up?"

"Armor?" I asked. It was the only thing I could come up with.

"Very good! And yes, almost entirely. She's also equipped with three laser blaster turrets, two forward missile tubes and something you won't find on most ships nowadays. Care to take a guess?" Wally stood up, pacing back and forth, unable to contain his excitement.

"I can't imagine," I said.

"An aft-facing cannon - and I'm not talking about your basic namby-pamby plinker here. This thing is so big that it can only be fired once every thirty seconds."

"Cargo?" I asked.

"Six hundred cubic meters."

I was impressed. "That's more than twice the CA-12."

Wally, not wanting to miss his moment, interjected, "All pressurized and easily accessed. There'll be no hauling cargo through the air locks and into bunk rooms."

"How much?" I asked.

"Not yet, Mr. Hoffen. So far you've only heard about it. Before we talk price, you need to experience it."

He gestured subtly and the transport moved forward. It wasn't until we were ten meters from the side of the ship that I was able to make out any details. The color was a dark grey with a matte finish. I'd never seen anything like it. The armored glass bridge appeared smaller than *Sterra's Gift* from the outside. Instead of taking up the entire ship's nose, it was five meters up from the sloped nose at the very top of the ship. I wondered why it sat so high, but there were a lot of possibilities.

We came along the top spine of the ship and ran across one of the three turrets. It had three squat, meter-long barrels configured in a triangular shape.

"The energy stores for the turrets are interlinked. In a crisis, one of the two main engines can be diverted to power the weaponry. While, of course this slows you down, sometimes you just want to lay it on heavily and the *Hotspur* will oblige you."

We arrived at the airlock. One of the two main engines was tucked under a curved wing, which started at the top of the ship, curling down around the engine. It wasn't something you saw in spaceships, since air-foils were only necessary for atmospheric ships. Nowadays that wasn't important, as ship's engines were more than powerful enough to overcome atmospheric entry.

"What's with the wings?" I asked.

"Beautiful and functional," Wally responded. "She's made for landing on high-g planets with thick atmospheres. Not only that, the armor surrounds the engines." He stabilized our shuttle and exhausted the atmosphere as the port airlock of the *Hotspur* opened. We followed Wally across and waited for him to cycle the doors.

Lights flooded the ten meter high, six meter across and eight meter long cargo space. Fairly close to the airlock was a door in the forward bulkhead leading to the crew spaces. It seemed like a deficiency that the airlock was open to the entire cargo space. In my experience, that meant we wouldn't be able to move between the living space and the mid-ship portside airlock when the hold wasn't pressurized. I started a mental checklist of issues. I would have loved to have had this much pressurized cargo space available on previous runs.

"The aft cargo ramp allows for the largest loads to be rolled right in," Wally explained. "But this little gem also has a belly loader."

"Belly loader?"

"That's not the technical term, mind you, but if you are so inclined, there's a bottom loading trap door, complete with winches and tackles. Let's you take on a load without actually touching down. You see it more with often with ships like this that have a military background."

I nodded, not sure why I cared, but it did seem like a nice option.

Wally led us forward through the tall bulkhead. "This is the berth deck. There are two cabins with bunks down here, so you can hold a total of eight if you're hot bunking on twelve hour shifts. Down the hall is the galley and mess."

I didn't much care for hot bunking, or hot racking, as some called it. It was the idea that while one shift was working, their beds could be used by another shift. It felt like he was over stating the ship's crew capacity by doubling up in this way.

I poked my head into one of the bunk rooms. It hadn't seen any attention in a number of years and had skeletal bunks and shelves for lockers. I suspected the bed frames were totally rotted through. It looked grim.

"Head?" I asked. No ship was fully functional without a working head – something that I'd learned the hard way.

"Second door, port side."

I walked down the hallway two meters and on the wall a straight ladder went up into the ceiling. It would be a hard climb with my prosthetic foot - another note. Past the ladder was a second door and beyond that the hallway opened into a large empty room. I looked into the 'head.' My mind immediately jumped back to the mess I'd dealt with when we'd taken over *Sterra's Gift*. I hadn't checked, but I hoped the small replicator had survived our encounter- more notes added.

"What's this open room," I asked. Wally didn't answer, but my

HUD lit up with a design that showed a long table with chairs around it on the starboard side and a galley built into the port side.

"Not in great shape down here, is it?" I observed.

"All cosmetics, my boy," Wally answered. "Everything you're interested in is on the next deck. You go first." He gestured grandly toward the ladder.

I obliged and climbed up through the hatch into a room that had armored glass windows on opposite sides. The windows followed the contour of the hull and rounded inward, toward the top. There was a lot of viewable glass. Under one window was a well-padded couch with a permanently attached table in front of it. Opposite the couch were two chairs that swiveled and slid over to workstations on the opposite wall. They were currently in position around the table.

A doorway opened to the aft. To the fore were steps leading up a meter and a half. I walked past the table and up the steps. Just as I suspected, it was the cockpit, about the same size as the *Adela Chen's*, just wide enough to hold two pilot's chairs and a number of vid-panel displays. I grabbed the overhead handle and slid down into the port-side chair, my hands coming to rest naturally on the control sticks. I was pleasantly surprised to see the wrap-around view available to the pilots. While seated at the highest point inside the ship, just beneath the spine, I had better than a hundred and eighty degrees of sight.

I heard Ada and Tabby whispering, but couldn't make out what was being said. Apparently, they'd made a decision about seating because Tabby slid into the starboard side pilot's chair next to me.

"What are you thinking?" Tabby asked.

"It's a hell of a view," I said.

"Built almost a century and a half ago by the Brits," Wally said, having climbed up the stairs behind us.

"I didn't think the Brits were that active in space," I said. I also thought he'd originally said it was a century old.

"Not as much today, but they had their time. This ship was a blockade runner. The Brits used it to transport supplies to their colonists on the other side of the Transloc Gates. Not much gets through this armor. Care to take it out for a test sail?"

"Sure. If you're okay with that," I said.

"The only way to truly understand the soul of a ship is to sail her," he replied.

After some gesturing on Wally's part, the cockpit came alive and the screens showed all green statuses. I wasn't getting my hopes up. No doubt he was only showing systems that were in good shape. The system map showed that Wally's Bone Yard was arranged on a plane, with nothing above or below. The easiest exit was to elevate the ship above the plane, which Wally instructed the AI to do.

A blue course appeared on the center console.

"Mr. Hoffen, the helm is yours. If you could stay within the blue corridor."

I didn't have any real feel for the ship so I took it easy as we left the shipyard's local space. I pushed forward on the stick that controlled thrust and appreciated how easily the ship accelerated. I'd expected a century and a half to be as hard on the engines as it had been on the interior, but this certainly wasn't the case.

"Surely you've got more in you than that," Wally chided.

"Just getting my bearings." I was uncomfortable putting a ship I didn't own through a full combat run.

"Don't be fooled by the rust. The Brits built her with an eye for longevity, the rest can be fixed with a little paint and pleather," he said. I wasn't sure what pleather was, but I got his point.

I pushed the stick down further and we accelerated smoothly. The gravity and inertial systems adjusted and I was again pleased with its performance, surprised that this large of a ship responded as nimbly as - or possibly even more so - than *Sterra's Gift*.

"Mr. Hoffen, I implore you to take off the kid gloves. The *Hotspur* deserves to be run like the thoroughbred she is." I knew Wally was taunting me, but I didn't need a lot of encouragement.

Tabby looked at me and said, "Don't get too crazy there, Buck Rogers."

I winked at her and then warned, "Hold on to something."

Combat controls, I commanded. My AI would now negotiate my commands to push the ship much closer to its limits. I pushed the stick down to about eighty-five percent wide open. The ship responded immediately, jumping forward and pressing my body back into the chair while the inertial systems caught up. We were accelerating much faster than *Sterra's Gift* ever could. It was a rush. I couldn't help myself and I jammed the thrust stick down to full. Frak, but this thing had some balls.

I backed off and tipped the stick that controlled our pitch and yaw, then barrel rolled through a turn and slid the back end around so that we were headed back on the path we'd just taken. As we rolled through the turn I punched the thrust up to a hundred percent again. It didn't take long to burn off the acceleration we'd gained heading away from the shipyard. I reduced our acceleration until we were gliding toward the yard relatively slowly.

"Take a turn, Tabby?" I asked.

"Sure. That okay?" she asked Wally.

"Yes ma'am, but let me make a small adjustment," he said. *Revoke control Hoffen. Initiate silent running. Grant Tabitha Masters pilot control.*

Tabby started working the controls and I noticed that we'd lost a significant amount of acceleration. The ship was still sailing smoothly, just not as performant as before.

"What's silent running?" I asked.

"That's part of being a blockade runner. The emissions from the engines and other systems have been reduced a hundred-fold under this mode. You're still visible, but nothing like before."

CRAZY LIKE A FOX

"One point one million." We'd caught up with Nick and Marny, who had been working on the frigate.

"That's a lot," Nick said. "Do you think it's a contender?"

"I do, but I want you and Marny to take a look at it."

Tabby's head whipped around in surprise and she couldn't contain herself, "Are you kidding me? That thing is the biggest piece of crap I've ever seen. I can't believe you're serious."

"No way! It's perfect," I said, not caring if Tabby lambasted me.

"You're crazy, Liam," Ada added. "There's a million things wrong with that ship. First, it smelled like a backed up septic field. Did you see all of the rust on everything? And the bunks were practically falling apart. You'd have to totally refit the entire interior."

"Speaking of crap, did you see the main head?" Tabby asked Ada.

"Yes. Looked like it hadn't been cleaned since the ship was commissioned. And that was what, a century and a half ago? When I sat in the couch on the bridge, I was nearly lost in the dust," Ada answered. Clearly the women weren't impressed.

"Didn't you see how it accelerated? Even though it's three times the size, it was faster and more agile than *Sterra's Gift*. It has a six-hundred cubic meter hold *AND* transloc engines, three turrets, a rear cannon, missile tubes and light absorptive armor."

Nick sighed, "Still, that's a lot. Did he have any cutters?"

"We saw several CA-12s today. His were the least expensive at five hundred thousand and the attack ships were all dart class. I just don't see that working for us."

"Frak, I was afraid of that. I'd have expected better prices this close to the core planets, but the demand must be too high. How many of the systems were working on the *Hotspur*?" Nick asked.

"I didn't have a chance to check them, but he certainly represented that they were working. He also knew about our frigate. Sounds like he might be interested. Did that guy come out and survey it?" I asked.

"Yup. He'll post it tomorrow. He brought quite a fleet of robots out with him and they scoured the entire ship."

"Will he set a price?" I asked.

"No, but he gives an inventory of all the systems, and what shape they're in. From that he'll be able to help us with any offers we receive."

"Do we have any?"

"Offers? Two, but they're lowballs. He said we should counter them."

"How do we get to a price?"

"It's not hard. Algorithms use the base survey data."

I just shook my head. "How about moving our supplies down to the frigate. We should get started."

"All done," Nick said. "I rented a pair of robots to do it. They inventoried it all and then packed it in sections. Neatest thing you ever saw. Marny and I cleared *Sterra's Gift* out too. The robots cost a thousand credits, but we'd have been at it for days otherwise."

"You don't have to sell me. I'm just glad I don't have to do it. Could you and Marny take a look at the *Hotspur* tomorrow? I'd like to know if you even think it's a possibility."

"Yup, we'll get on it first thing. Are you ready to get out of here?" Nick asked.

We all piled into the cargo hauler. It was tight, but we only had to make it to the Puskar Stellar Space Station.

"Ada, we're working on a load for Colony 40. You interested? There's a side trip in it too. Probably not the best pay on this one," Nick said.

"That doesn't sound like you guys. What's this about?" she asked.

"We're dismantling that pirate base. We can make it worth your time," he answered.

"I think so. Send me some details. I haven't forgotten about your offer either. I've been talking it over with Dad."

"How's that going?" I knew he wasn't happy with how dangerous our last trip had been.

She grimaced. "About like you'd expect. He wants me sailing for a larger company. More stability, less combat."

"Can't say there won't be issues with the run, since we took this base away from the Red Houzi. I'm sure they're still plenty annoyed," I answered.

"Let's touch base tomorrow, Ada," Nick said.

"Okay. It was sure nice to meet you finally, Tabby. I'll send you reports on Liam if he gets in trouble." She winked conspiratorially.

We'd arrived at the rental company dock. Ada gave each of us a hug goodbye after unloading from the hauler. I felt a little self-conscious with Tabby standing there, but figured that was just me being awkward.

"You guys want to join us for dinner tonight?" Marny asked. "We're going upscale tonight."

"I think we'll skip this time, if that's okay. We've got some talking to do," I said.

Tabby looped her arm around my own and stood closer, "Sounds interesting," she said in a husky voice. I really had meant we needed to talk, but now she had me thinking of other things.

"So what do you need to talk about?" Tabby asked once we found a place to sit. Neither of us liked fancy restaurants and found a burger joint. "Or was that code for snogging?"

"What's snogging?" I asked, I had a pretty good idea, but it wasn't a term I was familiar with.

"Here let me show you." She placed her hand behind my neck and pulled me in gently, kissing my face. She released me after a few short moments.

"Ooh. Yeah, that's a keeper. I like that," I said.

"Do I have anything to worry about between you and Ada?" Tabby asked. She'd taken me off guard with her approach and I was still reeling from her snogging lesson. Tabby was normally an attack-and-defend type of conversationalist. This new, softer side was surprising. It was a fair question, though I was certain I'd set her mind at ease earlier.

"How straight do you want it?" I asked.

"Lie to me and I'll know it and cut off your nuts."

Bingo. There's my girl.

"You're right. She's really pretty, extremely nice and I enjoy being around her."

"You really suck at this," Tabby said scooting away from me.

"That's also true about Marny and, with the exception of the pretty thing, it's true about Nick too. No, if you want rid of me, you'll have to do it yourself, 'cause I'm not going anywhere. Well, I suppose I am - but you get the idea." I put my hand out to pull her back. "Now, about this snogging thing…"

Sunday afternoon arrived much quicker than I'd hoped and it was a lonely ride back from Coolidge to Puskar Stellar. Nick had sent me directions to a pizzeria in the University Hills area. It seemed like an odd choice as it wasn't anywhere close to our hotel, but I was game.

When I entered the busy restaurant it wasn't hard to spot them. Marny was easy to find in a crowd. She was bigger than life and her distinctive voice carried across the room. I was surprised to see two extra people at the table, one of whom I'd only ever seen on a small vid screen.

The tall, red-blond haired, heavyset Bit Coffman caught my approach. She stood and held her hand out with a lopsided grin, "Captain Hoffen in the flesh."

"What a great surprise," I said and pulled the large woman in for a hug. I didn't know how she felt about such things, but to me she was family, even though we'd never met before in person. She'd had our backs when we needed it desperately in Jeratorn and I owed her a lot.

"Hoffen, I'd like to introduce you to one of my grad students, Jacob Berandor." She looked over to the thickset man who was seated at the table. When he stood, I was surprised to see that he was even taller than Bit. His giant hand all but enveloped my own when we shook.

"Pleased to meet you, Mr. Hoffen. Call me Jake," his deep voice rumbled. I had difficulty getting a read on his age, but he had a close-cut beard and bright blue eyes.

"Please, call me Liam. Nice to meet you too." I took the open chair next to him, looked around the table and noticed that Nick was giving me the, 'you're missing something' look. "So, what's going on?" I pulled a piece of pizza onto a clean plate. I was used to not catching everything.

"How bad do you want the *Hotspur*?" Nick asked. That got my attention. I was wondering what he and Marny thought about the ship after their visit.

"I think you know the answer to that," I said.

"You know it's beat to crap, right?" he asked.

"You're saying the hull and engines are junk?" I pushed back.

"No. Believe it or not, those appear to be in perfect order," he said. I couldn't put it all together. Why were we having this conversation with Bit and her student?

"Weapons?"

"Reasonable shape," he said.

"You just said it's beat to crap."

"You want to cover this, Bit?" Nick asked, confusing me even further.

"Wait, what do you know about the *Hotspur*?" I asked her.

"Oh, you're so cute. I love how you do that lost puppy thing, but I'll let Berandor handle this next," Bit answered. I was bewildered.

"Thank you, Professor Coffman," he said. "As you've already seen, the sloop *Hotspur* is a warship from a generation long past. It was originally commissioned the *HMS Hotspur*, one-hundred-eighty-two years ago in what most historians see as the golden age of galactic expansion. Basically, back when the Translocation Gates were first established. The designation HMS, standing for Her Majesty's Service, no longer applies since it isn't in the employ of the British."

"I thought that was more like four hundred years ago?" I asked.

"Good memory. And yes, the first gates were built three

hundred forty years ago, but travel through the gates was ridiculously expensive. The Anino engine, named after its inventor, Thomas Anino, changed all that using commonly available elements - well, common in the asteroid belts that is. After that, it was essentially a gold rush. The Brits were all in too, sending ten different colonizing missions through the Bethe Peieris gate to the planets of Curie and Bohr. In total, they sent more than fourteen thousand citizens."

"Didn't a lot of those colonists die?" I remembered something from a history class about this.

"That's right. A well-organized pirate organization - buccaneers really - disrupted the supply runs that the colonists had contracted and the British Navy had to step in to rescue its citizens."

"Buccaneers?" I asked.

"Sure, it wasn't a lot different from what the Spaniards and Brits ran into in ancient history when ships actually sailed the oceans on Earth. These weren't just random pirates, but groups with strong military organization," Jake explained.

"Okay, that's good information. But, I'm not sure how that relates to you and Bit," I said.

"Oh right, my specialization is in ship systems. I'm focused on propulsion, but I've got advanced degrees in communications and weapon systems as well."

"Now I get it. So, is it a piece of crap?" I asked.

"Hey, don't put words in my mouth," Nick said, chuckling. "I said it was beat to crap."

Jake looked between us and smiled, perhaps a little condescendingly, "I think that characterization is a little strong, but all of its systems are ancient by today's standards. That said, they don't make ships like the *Hotspur* today either. The engines were designed to last centuries and they have. The armor is difficult and expensive to replicate and can withstand both kinetic and energy weapons well beyond anything in use today, at least in the private sector."

"Great information." I said. There was something else going on and I wasn't sure what it was. I looked at Nick and said, "What? You've got that look."

He answered. "If we're going to buy that ship, we need someone who can help us bring it back to full function. Most of the internal systems need updating. This thing is a money pit, but Marny and I both see the value. We've never had the tactical advantages of speed and stealth."

I looked back to Jake, "Don't get me wrong, I definitely appreciate the information, but what's your interest in the *Hotspur* beyond the academic?"

Jake pushed his shirt sleeves up. "In short, if you're putting the *Hotspur* back into active service, I'd like to help. I think I'm asking for a job."

Nick stepped in, "*Hotspur's* first run probably won't be anything too exciting. I can't get into the details, though. We've had some run-ins with unsavory types and as a result we don't share our destinations outside of crew. We've got good reason to trust you two, but I don't see any reason to talk about it just yet. I've got a proposal for you though, Jake."

"No offense taken," Bit added. She sat with arms crossed, leaning back in her chair, clearly enjoying the conversation.

"What's your proposal?" Jake asked.

"We'll pay you a retainer of a thousand credits if you help us through the purchase of the *Hotspur* and get her ready to sail. If the deal falls through, the thousand credits are still yours. Either way, we'll all have a chance to work together and decide if this new team is a good fit."

"Hard to beat that," he said. "I'm in."

***

The next morning I was up early. I'd spent most of the last two days either shopping for a ship or hanging out with Tabby. I needed to turn my attention to finding a load for the tug and a freighter. If we stuck with the CA-12 we'd have two hundred cubic meters and if we got the *Hotspur* I'd need to fill six hundred.

Pulling up the TradeNet interface, I created two fleets. The first fleet was a CA-12 cutter and a four hundred meter T400 barge. The second was the *Hotspur* and a T400. I ran loads starting at one, two, three, and four weeks out, varied the burn plans and widened our arc through the solar system. There were so many variables that I couldn't fathom how I'd ever found work without TradeNet. The permutations seemed endless and I worked with it for a couple of hours until I heard a knock at my door.

"Come in," I said.

"Coffee?" Nick asked as he entered my hotel room. He handed the cup that he was carrying to me and sat. "I thought I heard you awake in here. What 'cha working on?"

"Just trying to find a load that will get us close to Colony 40 and the outpost," I said. "Paying for our own fuel sucks and the *Hotspur* really burns it up. I don't think the Brits considered that in their design."

Nick chuckled, "No, I don't suppose they did. Jake and I just finished reviewing a recent survey of the *Hotspur*."

"Jake's here?" I asked.

"Been here since 0600," Nick answered.

"What's the verdict?"

"We offered eight hundred thousand, contingent on the sale of the frigate."

"Did he take it?"

"There's more," Nick answered. "Weird Wally countered. Eight-fifty, with us selling him the frigate at nine hundred thousand, and that's where we stand at the moment." Jake had come to my bedroom door and leaned against the frame to listen to the conversation.

"That's not bad," I said. "We started at one hundred thousand apart, and he's at fifty. That's close. Send me a contract that has eight-fifty for the *Hotspur* and a million for the frigate. I'll get him to sign it," I said.

"You really think you can?" Nick asked.

"If I take Jake with me, we have a very good chance. Weird Wally wants to see this ship fly again. He's a romantic and knows this is a good price. He gets to trade out something he hasn't been able to sell in forever for a modern frigate worth a couple of million - once he fixes the engines. You up for a trip, Jake?" I asked.

"Let's do it," he answered.

I didn't even ping Wally. In my mind, if Weird Wally was one thing, he was passionate about life. His dramatic presentation of the ship, detailed stories and even his appeals to my sense of adventure were dead giveaways. I knew he was a shrewd business manager and was convinced he would have at least a hundred thousand credits of wiggle room. I just needed to get him to give it up.

"Mr. Berandor and Mr. Hoffen together. I suddenly feel outnumbered," he said with a smile when we strode into his office. I didn't believe for a moment that he was even remotely concerned. "How can I help you?"

I started out as professionally as I could. "Mr. Waldorf, I appreciate your willingness to meet with us on such short notice. I'm sure your time is valuable, but wanted to impress upon you just how seriously we are considering your offer by coming to see you personally. Before we get to that, however, I was wondering if you had a moment where I could show you a short video sequence?"

This got his attention. "What sort of video?"

"Well, I was putting myself in your shoes and thinking about what we could bring to the table to help you add value to the frigate," I said.

"That's a lot to ask from a video. But I do like your optimism." He gestured to the back wall. "Join me in my office, would you?"

He darkened the room and the three of us sat in chairs facing one of the blank office walls. A large vid-screen appeared, brightening the room.

"If a person is looking to purchase a frigate such as this, I believe they will want a demonstration as to its raw power. As you know, a frigate is most powerful when at broadside. There is also not very much video available from the perspective of the frigate's foe, because as you know, its wrath is complete in its destructive power." I was hamming it up, but it felt like a good story. "So, to the extent a picture is worth a thousand words, I'll let you be the judge of the value of this sequence."

The video started, showing Tali and me running pell-mell through the Jeratorn docking bay for *Sterra's Gift,* the nose of the frigate just entering into the picture from left to right through the end of the docking bay. I'd chosen some suspenseful music and flashed back to the engines of our ship starting to fire up, just about the same time the frigate started letting loose its terrible broadside. I followed *Sterra's Gift* out of the end of the docking bay, concentrating on the damage being done to the station. The video then showed two missiles being launched from *Sterra's Gift* streaking toward the frigate, contact imminent, when it activated its anti-missile counter measures, thwarting the missiles, leaving the frigate unscathed. I had spliced together an ending scene where *Sterra's Gift* was sent tumbling, broken, away from the frigate to end the piece.

Wally clapped his hands together as the lights came back up. "Oh what a wonderful piece of fiction you've assembled," he said.

He had me, I'd put in that last piece, but I felt like it was best not to show that we'd taken the frigate down by disabling its engines. "Okay, you've got me there. That last scene came at a different time, but everything up to that point, I can assure you, happened just as it was shown. That sequence was constructed from our actual combat data streams."

"You don't say. And you'd submit those streams for validation?" he asked.

"Of course. We earned 'em, might as well get something out of them," I answered.

"Excellent setting, my friend. I do love a showman. So what is your counter then?"

I pinched the contract that Nick had modified and flung it to him. "You do seem rather proud of your video, Mr. Hoffen. I'm not sure that's worth a hundred thousand."

"No, I don't suppose it is, but after talking with Jake, we've become aware of quite a few items that need to be addressed on the *Hotspur*. But before I bring these items to your attention, which, as you know, would legally obligate you to share them with all other interested buyers, I'd like you to consider the value of such a video."

"Ooh, you are a playful one, Mr. Hoffen." He was very much enjoying the conversation.

"To completely lay my cards on the table, Mr. Waldorf, you have treated me well and I'd rather not complete this deal if it would taint our relationship. That said, I believe our offer is more than generous, especially given the condition of many of the *Hotspur's* internal systems."

He grinned widely, almost manically, and stuck out his hand. "Mr. Hoffen, they don't call me Weird Wally for nothing. You have yourself a deal and if you ever get tired of chasing pirates, come look me up. I think you'd make an excellent ship salesman."

HOTSPUR DECK LAYOUTS

BERTH DECK

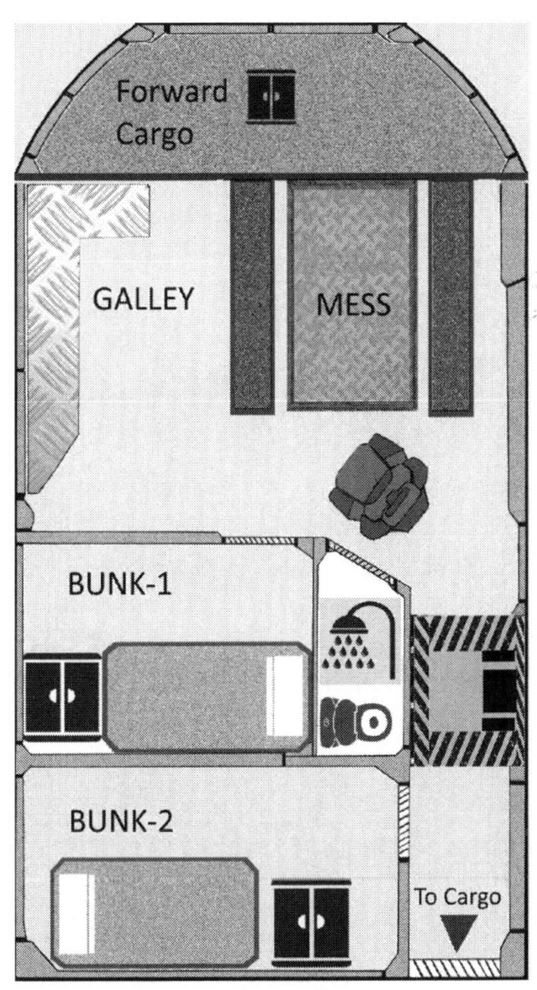

BRIDGE DECK

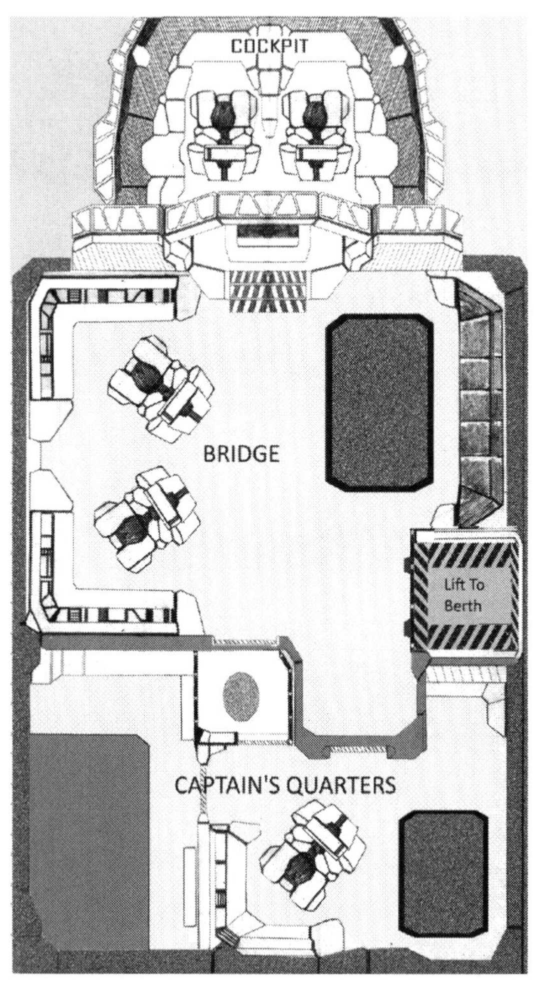

BUYER'S REMORSE

"Have you heard from Ada?" I asked Nick through the comm. We'd been working on the *Hotspur* since very early in the morning.

"She accepted our offer," he grunted back from the crawlspace between the two decks where he was working with Jake.

"Have you talked to Belcose about his comm gear?"

Lieutenant Gregor Belcose was our contact with Mars Protectorate Navy and currently assigned to the *Kuznetsov*. With the help of Bit Coffman, we'd discovered that the comm equipment they'd installed on *Sterra's Gift* was actually a quantum device that could communicate almost instantaneously over long distances. We'd also discovered that the device could be used to monitor our ship without our knowledge.

"Yes. He's got someone coming over at the end of the week to move it from *Sterra's Gift* into the office quarters. You good with that?" Nick asked.

"Sounds fine. At least this time, it's not in my bedroom. Not that anything happens in there."

Nick cut off a laugh. "Understood." Which was Nick speak for 'unless you have something important to say, I'm done talking.'

My job was to completely remove the entire septic system – from the fixtures in the head to the septic field in the bilge. I had finally resigned myself to being the resident expert in all things poop. Unlike when we'd taken over Sterra's Gift, the Hotspur's system was unrepairable. The septic field stretched out beneath the bottom (berth) deck and it had been patched, repaired and jury rigged what looked like hundreds of times. It would cost twenty thousand credits to replace the system, but remembering the nightmare of my septic repair while under sail on *Sterra's Gift,*

I'd decided this was my first priority while we were still docked.

"Are we going to see her today?" I asked.

"Ada? I sent her our location. Not sure," he said. He must have been lying on his stomach as it sounded like he was out of breath.

The top deck, which we were calling the bridge deck, had a small, fully functional four-piece head - that is a shower, sink, head and zero-grav head. The whole thing wasn't much bigger than the size of a closet. It was operational, but just barely, so it was a full gut. Not a single piece came out without a fight.

I piled the antique parts into a heavy plastic bag and lowered it down through the hatch at the back of the bridge, having yet to make friends with the ladder. It was the one thing I couldn't navigate well with my prosthetic foot, but Nick had agreed to run the grav generator at .4g instead of the normal .6g, making it easier for me to climb up and down. I had four hours to remove the entire system before the plumbing fitter showed up.

We'd rented a renovation robot and I was dying to try it out. This particular model was a meter tall and narrow with three spindly, articulated arms. We'd already scanned every room on the ship and sent the data to the fitter. The fitter had then sent back a program we could feed to the robot for each room. All I had to do was remove the fixtures and deploy the bot. According to the manufacturer's advertisement, when done, the room would be completely clean, rust ground down and metal built back up where necessary. All openings would be patched or precisely resized for the new equipment, and fresh paint would be applied.

Run Hotspur bridge-head program, I instructed my AI.

"*Exit bridge head and close door. Program will complete in thirty-four minutes.*" I was still experimenting with different voices and today's choice was that of a middle aged woman. It would do for now.

I exited the room and heard the machine start. It was expensive to rent, but if it could remodel that head in thirty-four minutes, it would be money well spent.

My next task was the main head, so I climbed down to the berth deck. This head had also seen decades of hard use and neglect and the fittings were just as frozen and just as hard to remove as those in the bridge head. Luckily, there's something about getting into a task; things that start off as difficult become easier as you get into a rhythm. Apparently, removing plumbing fittings was one of those things.

I was making good progress until I got to the toilet. In the bridge head I had to cut the fixture out and I didn't expect things to be any different here. Something most people don't know about a ship is that the septic system has to be very carefully designed to deal with pressure buildup. Since this system was barely functioning and hadn't been in service for more than a decade, I didn't think there could possibly be anything active left inside. That was a bad assumption to make. When I popped off the head, several liters of foul material suddenly exploded into the lower pressure environment. The half gas / half fetid material immediately filled the interior, coating every surface and occupant.

"Anybody home?" I heard Ada's familiar voice echo through the empty hallway.

"Down here," I answered ruefully. Of *course* she'd chosen this moment to show up.

"Oh my stars! What's that smell?" she asked as she turned the corner and looked into the head. "Is that...?" She couldn't finish the sentence.

"Ancient shite? Yes." I finished the sentence for her.

Save video from when I entered ship until now, Ada instructed.

"You rat!"

"I'm not done," she giggled. *Send video to Tabitha Masters.*

"Oh, you're dead."

"Let's not get all worked up. She requested recordings of our lighter moments. Apparently, all she's getting are your successes."

"But, that?"

"Frak, Cap. What's that smell?" Marny's voice filtered down.

"Nothing to be concerned about," I yelled back.

"How about you shut the door while you're in there?" she responded over the comm.

"That won't help," Ada joined the comm channel. "He's got it all over himself."

"Yeah, yeah. Marny, could you help me out by bringing the renobot down from the bridge head?"

"Aye, aye, Cap. It spun down about ten minutes ago. That little bugger did a nice job, it's the best looking room in the whole ship. I'll be down in a jiffy."

"Can't wait to see it. I'll be in the bilge. That guy's gonna be here in two hours," I said to Marny. "Ada, you feel like helping out with the septic field?" I was mostly joking and was surprised at her response.

"Sure. I'd like to see what this old tub's got down there," she said. "But, are you going to scrape some of that off first?" She waved her hand, gesturing to my suit.

The good news was that I'd already removed the remaining furniture from the berth deck and it was ready for the renobot. The bed frames had come off with the merest of tugs. I'd originally been concerned the structure of the ship would be in similar decay, but Jake assured me that the skeleton's stronger alloy was still in perfect shape.

The bad news was I'd not been able to save much. In several cases, the cutting torch was the only way to free up several of the access hatches, pretty much destroying them. I was starting to wonder just how expensive it might be to purchase the little robotic wonder that had so far only transformed the smallest space on our ship. At this rate I could keep it occupied full time.

The bilge was anywhere from one and a half to two meters deep and fixed between the hull and the berth deck. Three systems occupied the space - septic, water and atmospheric. Fortunately, the ship had been designed by naval engineers and everything had originally been very neatly laid out. That said, a hundred and fifty years of patches and work-arounds and we had a mess Mary Shelley would be proud of.

It would work out okay, though. The septic field was the only system on the port side. It was so much easier to remove a bunch of crap (in this case literally) than it was to maintain it. Ada and I worked out a system. I resorted to a long-bladed cutter and started hacking off half meter chunks of the system. I'd decided to start with the slimy end first, since I was already a mess. I packed it into bags and tossed the bags up on the deck. From there Ada carried them off to the hold.

"Cap. Your bot's in the main head. Door's closed. Need anything else?" Marny asked over the comm.

"Thanks, Marny. That's perfect." I was glad for her help. I remotely started the program already loaded for the main head. I think we all eagerly anticipated the sterilization that would occur.

Two hours later I finally threw the last bag up from a hatch in the aft-most bunk room. It's difficult to describe just how disgusting both Ada and I smelled. I'd originally thought she had been saved from the mess, but apparently at some point, she'd thrown a bag up onto her shoulder, mistakenly trusting the holding force of the clasp.

"Nick, you have a minute?" I asked over the comm.

"Yup."

"We may need to ask the fitter to come out another day. I can't possibly get all this cleaned up by the time he arrives. We've got all of the stuff out, but it's a mess," I said. I also knew there was no way the renobot would be able to negotiate the ribs of the hull that I'd been straddling for the last couple of hours.

"Too late. She's here," Nick said.

"Shite. Okay. I'll deal with it."

"*Incoming hail, Sparkles Aloft,*" my AI said.

Accept hail. "Liam Hoffen," I announced.

"Hi, Mr. Hoffen. Betty Sparkles. We're here to refit your septic system. If you could depressurize your cargo bay and open up, we'll bring in the fab shop."

"We might have a problem. Any chance you could come and do a quick inspection?"

"Time is money, Mr. Hoffen. And, I guarantee you don't have anything I haven't seen before," she said.

"Nick, you and Jake okay if I depressurize the cargo bay?"

"Yup. Marny's here with us too. Go ahead," he answered.

"Let's stand in the cargo bay while it depressurizes. I bet we can get rid of a bunch of this stuff that's on us," I said to Ada. She nodded and we sealed the door behind us. I instructed the ship to depressurize the bay.

I lowered the cargo bay ramp and a small vehicle glided in and settled down on the floor. After raising the ramp and starting the pressurization sequence again, I noticed that Ada had done a pretty good job of brushing the now crystalized crap from her suit, so I did the same.

A large woman - one who would give Marny a run for her money in the size department - walked around from the front of the vehicle. I extended my hand and we shook.

"Alright, Mr. Hoffen. Let's take a look at your emergency."

"Sorry, we need to equalize pressure with the interior," I said.

"I see. I'll set my shop up." She pulled the back doors open on the cargo vehicle. It was a cluttered mess with boxes of fittings everywhere. "Here, you can help. Put these boxes on the floor and keep 'em out of that crap you just dropped. The faster we get this done the sooner I'm outta here."

Not a real charmer, this one. Ada and I pulled all of the boxes out and dropped them in a line. As we did, I could see that her shop had two fairly obvious replicators and at least twenty different small robots with varying appendages. I was more than glad when the bay finally completed the pressurization cycle.

"Well. That couldn't have taken a lot longer," she grumbled. "So what's the drama you wanted to show me?" Her mood was clearly deteriorating.

I led her through the aft door to the berth deck and pointed at the open bilge hatch. "We haven't been able to clean up around the ribs. It's a real mess down there."

She jumped down into the pit, "Your grav generator's running low. Can you put it back up to .6g? Yeah, you left a right proper mess down here and that's not in our contract."

"We ran out of time," I said.

"If I leave now, you'll lose your fifteen hundred credit expedite fee," she said.

I was starting to get annoyed with her attitude and was surprised when Ada stepped in. "I bet you have a service for that. What's the up-charge for cleaning, repair and paint?" she asked.

"Not sure, wasn't in the contract. Give me a minute." She brushed past us on the way to her vehicle and returned after a few minutes with a fist sized robot and dropped it in the hole. It hovered, centering in the open space. She instructed the bot and it started traversing the bilge. "It already knows the project, but we only scanned the parts of the hull where we were going to put in the field. I need to fill in the details."

The bot returned after several minutes. Betty Sparkles gestured for several more minutes and finally appeared to have completed her assessment. "Twenty-three hundred credits and I'll throw in disposal of all of those bags you already pulled out."

"Deal," I said. As soon as I said it a contract showed up in my comm queue. I was suspicious that this was a more common event than she was letting on.

"I'll need you to keep clear of the aft hallway here while my boys get to work. The more you get in the way, the longer they'll take."

"Where's your crew?" I asked.

"You're standing in their way." She nodded behind me and I turned to see a hovering fleet of robots that had previously been dormant in her fabrication shop. They descended into the bilge one after another. The final robot in the armada flitted between the open hatches, closing them one by one. "I'll be back in four hours. They'll be done by then if you stay out of the way."

"You're not sticking around?" I asked. I was certainly not expecting her to leave, since it was illegal to leave an autonomous robot unaccompanied.

"It's all in your contract." She brushed past me and through the open door to the cargo bay.

***

Nick had left me with a budget of eighty thousand credits to fix the septic, water and atmospheric systems and as much interior work as possible. We'd gotten off to a bad start with the septic system and the atmospheric system was nearly as bad. We just weren't going to get everything and I needed to make some tradeoffs. I wasn't about to skimp on primary systems, so it was going to have to be the interior.

By late Thursday the interior, while a little short on amenities, had at least been thoroughly scrubbed and repainted. In addition to that, we had a new atmo scrubber complete with a full load of O2 crystals. I was amazed at just how cheery the ship looked with the grime and rust-laden metal gone.

"How much of the furniture are you replacing on the bridge deck?" Nick asked. The five of us had ended up back at the pizzeria in University Hills. It was out of the way, but the environment was right.

"The couch on the bridge will be fine, but pilot's chairs are shot. I'm re-using the Captain's Quarter's furniture from *Sterra's Gift*. I'm also bringing over some of the galley equipment and the screens from the engine room," I answered. "What have you guys been working on? You've been awful busy in the tween deck."

"The batteries for the turrets are shot," Marny said.

"I thought we inspected those," I interrupted her.

"We did. They inspect okay, they just aren't up to combat use. If we hit 'em hard, they'll deplete and we'll just be plinking away. Jake here thought he could get 'em repaired, but it's not going to work."

"How much will that set us back," I asked.

Nick answered, "One hundred-fifty."

"Frak. Where's that put us?"

"We won't be able to afford any missiles, but we'll be okay. We pulled the bridge holo-projectors and navigation system over from *Sterra's Gift,* and most of the other systems are in good shape. When are you thinking it will be livable? Not that we don't appreciate the heads working."

"Saturday morning Ada and I will be done with the interior. We've got it all planned out. You and Marny are in the forward bunk on berth deck. The rear bunk will be set up with stacking singles. The top bunk will fold up when it isn't needed. All the rooms will be pretty spartan. Nothing on the floors, but the beds should be comfortable."

"Galley?" Marny asked.

"Roger that. Coffee brewer and Galley-Pro on *Sterra's Gift* were salvaged but the refrigeration was holed, so we need a new one."

"Any progress on getting us a load yet?" Nick asked. He had a crappy grin on his face, knowing it was an unfair question.

"Yes." The boy should know better than to set me up. "It's better than you think. Thanks to Lieutenant Belcose, we're lined up to deliver heavy equipment to the Valhalla Platform and I've got a line on nearly a full load to Terrence." I said.

"Who's Lieutenant Belcose?" Jake asked.

"Yeah, sorry. We're talking out of turn here Jake," Nick said. "We shouldn't be quite so free with our information until you're crew. You understand, I'm sure. Have you given any thought to joining our little fleet?" I was pleased to hear that Nick was ready to hire him. I had a feeling Jake would fit in, but Nick was the one who'd been working with him all week.

"I'm not sure," he said. "I've only heard bits and pieces of your story and from what I can tell, you all get into it pretty deep. I know you're concerned about security, but I need more details before I can answer. Ultimately I'm interested, but I want to know what I'm signing up for."

"Fair enough," Nick said, "Your word that you won't share what we're about to tell you?"

"You've got it." Jake nodded in agreement.

"Marny?" Nick asked. In normal Nick style, he'd expected to have this conversation and had pre-arranged something with Marny.

"As the security officer for our corporation, I've executed a public records search and looked into your background. You've led an interesting life, but from my perspective you pose no security threat to the company. I'll send you the results of the research I've done. Please understand, that information will remain confidential between you and me," Marny said.

"Thank you," Jake looked at all of us, perplexed. "Why are you telling me this?"

"It's part of who we are and who we want to be. You need to know that we care enough to look into your background and that we don't hide important information. It is all about trust. We get in enough scrapes that we can't afford to be questioning each other."

"I can work with that. So what would I be signing up for?" Jake asked.

"Our primary goal is to be traders, but we've been mostly operating as freight haulers," Nick started. "As crew, that difference isn't huge. As owners, the real money is in speculative runs. Secondarily, we have the designation from Mars Protectorate as Privateers. We carry a Letter of Marque that entitles us to defend ourselves and more importantly lay claim to sundered enemy assets. So far, the vast majority of our net worth has been derived from our secondary activities as Privateers."

"That's where you got the frigate?" Jake asked.

"The frigate, *Sterra's Gift* and even the *Adela Chen*," I added.

"So, let me get this straight. You've made most of your money by plundering pirates. Doesn't that make for enemies?"

"No doubt it does, although it's not like these guys are friendly towards anyone. So far, we haven't been targeted and we certainly aren't looking for trouble. It's just that trouble seems to find us and we have a hard time turning our backs on it," I said. That felt like the understatement of the century.

"So what does your next run look like?"

"We have an outpost in Indian space. It's one we took from the Red Houzi. We're going to work our way out there, dismantle it and bring it back to Mars. We'll stop by Colony 40 on the way back, which is where Liam and I come from," Nick answered. "Liam is lining up cargo deliveries along the way."

"Unmanned base? Why haven't they taken it back?" Jake asked.

"The base is heavily defended and they know we pulled two cutters worth of cargo out. Our experience with pirates is that they understand value, probably more than most. They're happy to take big risks as long as the reward is even bigger. The equipment they'd need to take down the base would likely destroy it, leaving them with nothing for their efforts. That's my best guess," Nick answered.

Jake nodded thoughtfully. "Why me? I've got no experience trading… or fighting pirates for that matter."

"We're dismantling the base and going to need help with the weapon systems. Your expertise would be valuable. We also always seem to be refitting ships. A real engineer would be a good addition," Nick answered.

"Not to be too mercenary, but what's my cut?"

"Two things. First you'd get an officer's share of each trip you participate in. Second, you get standard officer salary. This particular trip should be a good one. We consider the loot at the base to be at significant risk. Whatever goods are recovered will be included in your share with only fuel, O2 and food discounted. The recovered structures wouldn't be included. They're considered assets of the corporation since they're currently protecting the goods," Nick said.

"How about crew allowance for cargo? What if I want to do some of my own trading?" Jake asked.

It was the first time I'd ever seen Nick stumped, although it didn't last long.

"Sure. We don't currently have an allowance for that, but that's mainly because I hadn't thought of it yet. Off the cuff I'd say that I'm okay with it. There would be two classes. First is cargo loaded last minute, after we've finalized our load. I'd be good with one-hundred fifty percent fuel cost. Second would be regularly scheduled cargo. We'll give you five cubic meters and up to five hundred kilograms. In both cases, we'll assume no risk and require a bill of lading."

That was the Nick I knew - ready with a detailed answer in the space of a heartbeat.

"I'm in." Jake held his hand out across the table to Nick. They shook.

PACKING UP

I eagerly awaited Tabby's arrival at the shipyard. The fitters had finished up with the pilot's chairs and I couldn't have been happier. They were just as nice as what Ada had on the *Adela Chen*. I would have liked another twenty thousand to spend on interior upgrades, but everything we'd done so far was high quality, if a bit sparse.

I was seated at the desk in the captain's quarters working on scheduling our trip when I heard the now familiar chime of the airlock.

Show airlock, I requested. Tabby waved at the camera.

I ran out and hopped onto the grav-lift Nick had thoughtfully installed. His argument at the time had been safety. He didn't want a hole in the floor of the bridge that people could fall through. I knew him well enough to know he'd put it in for me. I wasn't sure what my problem with ladders was - I didn't have trouble with most other activities - but ladders caused me no end of troubles.

"I hope you didn't mind me sending a cab. I had to babysit a work crew. Want to check out all the changes?" I asked.

"What's that?" Tabby pointed to the ceiling of the cargo hold. I looked up and saw a white square platform pushed up against the ceiling. I didn't recognize it, nor had it been there a couple days ago when I'd been cleaning.

"Frak, no idea," I shrugged. It was a five meter flat square with posts in each corner that stood around one-point-five meters tall.

"Looks like a boxing ring," she offered.

"What would you know about that?"

"It's popular at the Academy. Turns out I'm pretty good at it too, for someone who hasn't boxed that is. You should see this kid, Glori. She's smaller than me… quiet… you wouldn't expect much, but she's a killer. I can barely lay a glove on her. Does Marny box?"

"I have no idea. Remind me to ask when Nick and Marny get back." I said.

"Where are they?" she asked as I led her around the berth deck.

"Puskar Stellar, they're grabbing a quiet dinner together. We've been working pretty hard to get things shipshape."

"I think you were successful. Everything looks so clean, I can't tell we're even in the same ship," she said.

"You're almost not. We've had every surface ground down, filled in and repainted. The only remaining furniture is the table and couch in the main bridge and if we'd had enough money, we'd have replaced those too."

"It's awesome. It feels less cramped than your last ship," she said. I agreed, but the mention of *Sterra's Gift* made me feel homesick.

"I'm just finishing our schedule for the next run. It'll only take me a few minutes. Check out the bridge while I finish, then I'm all yours."

We rode the lift up to the bridge deck and I sat back at my desk and got to work.

After a few minutes, Tabby lost interest and walked into my small bedroom, which had little more than a bed and shelving that served as a footlocker. I heard her flop on the bed.

Forty minutes later I finished, happy with my progress.

"Are you up for a ride?" I asked, standing in the doorway to the bedroom.

"Where we going?"

I jumped on the bed next to her and pulled her into a hug. She initially resisted, letting me know she didn't appreciate being ignored. We wrestled for a few minutes and ended up making out. I wasn't so sure I liked her provincial rules about how far we could go, but I was willing to live with it.

"You didn't answer me. Where're we going?"

"Other side of Mars. City called Deivid."

"What's there?" she asked.

"Three hundred fifty cubic meters of equipment."

"Where is that going?" she asked

"Can't say. If I told you, what's to prevent you from telling your friends at the Academy, who will tell their friends? Eventually, pirates hear about it and then I'm handing over my load to some crazy warlord." I tickled her as I talked.

"You don't trust me?"

"You gonna keep it to yourself?"

She gave me pouty lips and I figured I'd driven my point home well enough. I wasn't specifically worried that she'd say anything, but I felt like I needed to make sure she understood.

"Yes," she relented.

"We're taking off tomorrow for the Valhalla Platform. First shift, Ada's headed to the Navy yard to pick up a load of unnamed cargo with the tug. It must be heavy, because they're giving us an extra fuel allowance. We're not getting a lot for that load, otherwise. But it'll cover fuel out to Colony 40 and back."

"Is that where the Deivid equipment is headed? Valhalla Platform?" she asked.

"Nope, that's going to Terrence." I didn't need to explain where that was since we'd both grown up on Colony 40 and Terrence was the second closest colony to our home.

Tabby sprung over the top of me and landed neatly next to the bed. "Let's go, old man. I want to see this thing under sail."

To say I was a little apprehensive about landing the *Hotspur* on Mars was an understatement. I knew the ship handled well and that all her systems had been thoroughly checked. I'd felt no hesitation when bringing *Sterra's Gift* down through the atmosphere. For some reason, this flight made me nervous. Tabby was all business when I showed her our checklist and we ran through the systems one by one, seeing green light after green light.

"External inspection?" she asked.

"I'm not following?"

"Probably applies to fighters more than bigger ships, but we have to do a visual inspection. I wouldn't mind seeing this old girl up-front and personal though," Tabby said. I didn't think it was necessary, but I was game for an EVA.

Tabby and I jetted around the ship. I was glad I'd taken her advice. We didn't find anything wrong, but with all of the activity going on inside, I hadn't had much chance to appreciate the unique design of this ship. Floating back, looking at her straight on, I took in my new ship. I liked the stubby, curved wings. They made me think of a falcon, diving after its prey. She'd have to prove herself to me, but she sure looked good, sitting here at rest.

"That's one gorgeous ship," I said to Tabby once we were back in the airlock.

"Careful, Hoffen. I'm the jealous type," she replied.

I sank back into the pilot's chair. It was a little stiffer than I liked, but the fitter told me we'd break it in over the first year. I pulled on the battle harness, more because I was curious than worried, but Tabby followed suit. Generally, the gravity and inertial systems would keep the ship smooth, even during an atmospheric entry.

"You ready for this?" I asked.

"Hit it."

It would have been a lot more dramatic if we hadn't been sailing through Puskar Stellar local space. There were too many ships around and we all had to stick to a narrow corridor of travel. The constraints took away that sense of freedom I so enjoyed while sailing. Fortunately, we broke free of the traffic after half an hour and I cranked up the throttle.

"Faster," Tabby demanded.

"Grab the stick, Tabs. It's all yours," I said. I didn't have to say it twice and was glad I hadn't engaged the combat override as she pushed it up to a hundred percent.

"Whoo hoo!" she screamed, every bit the fighter jock.

We arrived in orbit over Deivid more quickly than I'd planned, but I didn't think it'd be a problem.

"I'm going to take control back, Tabs," I said.

"What a rush. I love this beast," she answered.

"Do I have anything to worry about?" She just smiled back at me. I already knew the answer. Once she was given her own fighter, I wouldn't be able to compete with it. That was okay, because I also knew her ship wouldn't be able to love her back.

Once we were within Mars's atmosphere, I discovered the joy of flying a ship with wings. Initially it took some getting used to, but the AI easily made up the difference. The dynamics of actual flight were much different from simply having to overpower gravity. The wings provided no small amount of lift at the speed we were going.

"*Urgent hail from Deivid Air Defense,*" my AI announced.

Accept comm. "*Hotspur*, go ahead," I answered.

"You've entered Deivid Air Defense controlled air space. State your business."

"We're a commercial ship, picking up a load of equipment from the Wellington factory," I responded.

"Maintain altitude and bearing. Wait One."

"Roger." I pulled back on the stick, slowed our speed and stopped descending.

"*Hotspur,* you're early. Proceed on transmitted course." My HUD showed a tight navigation path that ended at the factory.

"Roger," I replied.

"Not extra friendly, are they?" Tabby acknowledged.

"I guess not."

The setting sun glinted off a tall white wall that surrounded the entire city of Deivid. I'd never seen a walled city before and wondered how effective it could be when arc-jet technology was so prevalent.

"What do you suppose that wall is about?" I asked Tabby as we flew over the top. We could see gun emplacements built into the top of the wall.

"Has to be to keep out raiders. Those walls are at least a hundred meters tall so arc-jets wouldn't lift anything real heavy over them. They must have some unhappy neighbors. Kind of explains our reception."

I nodded, noting that I needed to pay better attention to things like this. I'd just blithely assumed that all of Mars was completely civilized. This place looked more like a fort than a city.

We soon came upon the Wellington factory, a kilometer long building that was well marked on the map I'd pushed up to the forward holo display. A factory communique had instructed us not to land. We'd be picking up the cargo without touching down, pulling the cargo up with old fashioned cables.

My AI caught movement to the aft of the ship. Two armed men rose up through the floor of the bay we were hovering over.

"Greetings, Captain. We'll be ready to load in ten minutes." His voice was friendly enough.

"Roger that," I answered. *Close comm.*

"They look like they mean business," Tabby observed.

"You want to stay on the bridge? I have to oversee this from the hold and I'm changing into my armored suit first."

"No way. I'm not missing this."

"We've got extra armor, want to put one on?" I asked. "There's one your size that's never been worn."

"Frak, yah I do," she answered.

We hustled back to the hold and opened the container holding our armor and weapons. Marny had done a nice job welding in shelves, blaster chargers and suit hangers. Everything we needed was here, so we changed in the newly outfitted armory. I was glad to find my Ruger F0C heavy flechette, already loaded, in the rack. I snapped it into a holster that crossed in front of my chest. It didn't look as cool as the hip or thigh holsters, but it was a lot easier to access.

When I turned to look at Tabby, my breath caught in my throat. Something about a shapely woman in armor just got me fired up. "You're hot." I said, almost involuntarily.

"Back at you. That's quite a gun you have there," she said.

"Marny picked it up for me. She thinks I need to use a flechette and not a blaster. Are you allowed to carry when you're not at the Academy?"

"Nothing specifically prevents it. I'd prefer not to get into any trouble, though. I don't need that kind of attention."

I plucked a heavy blaster from the rack and handed it to her.

"Ultimately, I just need you to stand with me and keep your eyes out for anything suspicious. Nothing's going to happen, though. If it does, just take cover," I said. "Ready?" I turned to walk out of the container.

"I feel bad ass," she said and slapped my butt.

It's hard not to strut a little with that type of encouragement and I was feeling pretty big while we watched the floor drop out of the bottom of the hold.

Finally, an unarmed man rose into the cargo bay below just behind the two guards. He arc-jetted into the hold with a friendly hand extended. I stepped forward and shook it. He held up a reading pad with a familiar cargo program running on it, touching it to my pad. Working with union stevedores had made loading old-hat and I was happy to see that Wellington followed the same conventions. With his list loaded on my reading pad, I waited for the first crate to rise up into the hold so I could add it to my bill of lading. Each of the crates were at least ten cubic meters and we loaded all twenty-eight in two hours.

It felt good to have the hold almost two-thirds full. I'd chosen to stack from bottom to top, leaving a small corridor around the outside of the crates.

"Sign here," the corporate representative requested. I did and he left the way he came, sinking down through the landing pad. I wasn't surprised to see that the two guards remained. They weren't leaving until we did.

"Ready to get out of here?" I asked Tabby, once again distracted by her in the armored suit.

"Let's do it," she answered.

Close cargo bay, I instructed.

Back in the cockpit, I hailed Deivid's Air Defense and asked for permission to leave. They sounded a little surprised that I'd asked and provided a much wider corridor for our departure. Apparently, they weren't as picky about people leaving the city.

Escaping the gravity of Mars takes work when near the surface. Fortunately, the Wellington factory had figured out that ships didn't need modified gravity (typically .8g for most habitation zones) and left the landing pads at Mars natural .38g. It made for an easier lift-off.

I preferred to be outside of Deivid's walls as quickly as possible. I didn't like the less than warm welcome we'd originally been given. Once we cleared, I pulled back on the stick and forward on the thrust. We would use a fair bit of fuel escaping the atmosphere, but that had been factored into the price of delivering the equipment. I took it easy, knowing that I was saving money by doing so.

"What's that?" Tabby asked as two blinking lights showed up on the center display.

Ships approaching on intercept course, the AI announced in the cockpit.

"Don't know and I don't want to." I pushed the throttle down to a hundred percent which sat us back in our seats. I hadn't engaged combat controls but the Hotspur had some serious nuts and we accelerated fast. I was disappointed to see that the two ships continued to close the distance between us, albeit not as quickly as they had been.

Hail ships that are approaching and get an ident scan on them.

Ships are not registered, the AI replied. Frak.

"Pull on your combat harness and take the helm," I said to Tabby.

"Got it," she said after buckling in. I followed suit.

Bring turrets online, track incoming ships with auto-targeting, I instructed. There was a good chance they thought we were an unarmed freighter and a simple target lock would be enough to scare them off. Unfortunately, that didn't seem to be the case.

Broadcast a message to unknown ships, I instructed. "Unidentified ships. Please know that we're armed and will take defensive measures to protect both our crew and cargo."

They continued to close on us while the *Hotspur* struggled against Mars gravity.

Fire across their bows using top turrets, three second burst. Muted thup-thup-thup sounds resonated through the ship as the blasters fired. My HUD immediately displayed the main battery's energy reserve which dipped to ninety-six percent and then recharged. Fortunately, it was enough. The ships peeled away from their pursuit just as we came free of the atmosphere.

Send data-stream to Deivid Air Defense. I didn't know if they cared, but it was their neighborhood.

"You think they're done?" Tabby asked.

Engage silent running. The lights in the cockpit turned off and the vid screens dulled to their minimum display levels. Our rate of acceleration slowed considerably but according to Wally and Jake, we were now emitting less than a hundredth of our previous signature. If someone wanted to find us, they'd have to work really hard at it.

Engage navigation plan 'quiet-night,' I instructed after we'd sailed clear for twenty minutes.

"What's quiet night?" she asked.

"I don't like sitting in port with a full load, so I find a quiet location and heave-to until we're ready to get going," I said.

"You're making this up," she said. "Did you pay those guys to chase us?"

I laughed. She was giving me entirely too much credit.

"Want to get something to eat? Marny said she left a surprise for us," I said.

Tabby unbuckled her combat harness and allowed it to spool into the back of the seat. She reached over, unclipped my harness and climbed onto my lap. Dressed in our armored vac-suits it turned out to be a little clumsy, but I wasn't about to complain. She grabbed the back of my head and pulled me in for a long kiss. "I think we need to get out of these suits," she said.

And just like that, I was unable to think of just about anything else. To say it was confusing would be an understatement. We'd made a commitment not to go too far, but here we were alone on a darkened ship with my girlfriend wanting to get me undressed. We ended up on the couch of the bridge, just down from the cockpit. We had a beautiful view of Mars - when we thought enough to look out at it.

As normally happened, we ended up in a snuggling position on the couch. It wasn't overly comfortable but neither of us wanted to spoil it. It was well after 2300 when Tabby finally suggested we find out what Marny had left for us. The ship had reached its destination and we were hove-to for the night.

"Are you kidding me? There are chocolate cupcakes with sprinkles on them in here," Tabby exclaimed from the open door of the new refrigerator unit. "And something called calzones. Sounds Italian. Here, throw them in the Galley-Pro." She handed me two plates that would stack neatly in the food preparation device. "Do you like Corona? Looks like beer." She didn't wait for my answer and handed me a transparent bottle of light golden liquid.

I'd have to remember to thank Marny as the food was beyond delicious. Being able to share it with Tabby was everything I wanted in life. At 0100 we were back in the bed in the captain's quarters. Tabby lay in the crook of my arm and my eyes drooped, finally shutting. It had been a perfect night.

The peace didn't last long. Something in Tabby's bag started whooping and flashing brightly. She awoke immediately at the sound. "Frak, that's the Academy."

"You're not late," I said, defensively.

"No. That's the emergency signal. Quiet for a minute. I need to call in," she said. I watched as she gestured and listened, finally replying, "Aye, aye, ma'am. I'll be right there." She terminated the call.

"What's that about?" I asked.

"I've been assigned to the *Theodore Dunham* and I'm shipping out tomorrow," she said.

"Wait, what? You said you were going to finish the semester," I said.

"Welcome to the Navy. But I'm to take every precaution getting back," she said.

"What does that mean?"

"We're on an alert status. Can you take me to Coolidge Space Station?" she asked.

"Of course," I said. "I'll get us going and you take a shower and pack up."

"Thanks." She gave me a peck and hopped out of bed, stripping off her vac-suit. I wasn't about to turn away without being asked and was pleased that she didn't. Once she closed the door, I tossed her suit-liner into the suit freshener and headed for the cockpit.

Navigate to Coolidge Space Station, negotiate closest, temporary berth to elevator.

I slid into my chair and did a quick systems check. As expected, everything was green. We weren't too far out and would be there in thirty-five minutes. Ten minutes later, Tabby slid into the chair next to me in her dress-whites.

"Sorry it's got to be like this," she said.

"Whatever it takes," I patted her leg. "And I had an awesome night."

"Yeah, not exactly what everyone else talks about on their dates, but I wouldn't have it any other way."

TAKE ME HOME

It was hard to let her go, but if I was honest, it was getting easier. We were in a good place.

I had two low priority comms in my queue, one from Nick and the other from Jake. It was 0530 and I'd only had a couple hours of sleep. I had three more hours in the temporary slip so I set an alarm for 0800 and lay back in the chair. I swear, no sooner had my head hit the back of the chair than that frakking alarm went off.

With only a few minutes before I had to push off, I took the lift down to the berth deck and started a fresh pot of coffee. I sat at the long table Ada and I had installed for the mess, waiting for the coffee to finish and pulling up Nick's comm. It was short and to the point: he and Marny would be ready to go any time after 0800. It wasn't surprising, we often used 0800 as start of the day's business. The comm from Jake was asking how much room we had available to Terrence.

Open comm, Jake Berandor.

"Good morning, Captain." Jake's deep voice reverberated in my ears.

"We've got almost two hundred fifty meters open. I can send you the geometry," I answered. I directed my AI to send the ship's cargo hold current cargo layout.

"I don't need anywhere near that much. Can I speak for fifteen cubic meters? I'll need it to Terrence."

"Sure can. I'm in Coolidge right now, about to head to Puskar Stellar. Where's your load?"

"I'll send you the contact. It's a beer distributor in orbit over Puskar Stellar. Are you willing to pick it up on your way back?"

"Roger that, just as long as you don't have me doing an

atmospheric entry," I said. "Meet at Puskar Stellar Space Station, 0930?"

"I'll be there. Berandor out." He closed the channel.

Open comm, Ada Chen, I requested.

"Hiyas, Liam," she said. "You ready to get going? I'm already loaded and clear of traffic." It was hard not to smile when talking with Ada. I wondered if I'd awakened her. It was impossible to tell as her hair didn't seem to moosh down like everyone else's when she slept - or she was quick to brush it out.

"Hi, Ada. I've got one more pickup and we'll be ready for burn by 1000. Why don't you start your burn for Valhalla and we'll catch up."

"Yes, sir. See you later, alligator." Ada closed the comm channel.

Send comm Nick James.

Pulling out of Coolidge station right now. Have one pickup for Jake and then I'm headed for Puskar Stellar station. I'm estimating 0930. Let me know if that will cause a problem.

By the time I got to the cockpit, Jake had sent me the coordinates of the distributor's space-side warehouse.

Navigate to Mid-Mars Distribution warehouse. Request space loading bay.

I sat back and allowed the AI to pick its way through the congested Coolidge traffic. Twenty minutes later my HUD highlighted the Mid-Mars Distribution platform. It looked straightforward enough and when I got closer a glow appeared around my designated landing pad.

Incoming hail from Mid-Mars Distribution, my AI intoned.

Accept. "Captain Hoffen, Loose Nuts Corporation," I answered.

"Greetings, Captain. We've got twenty five crates of our finest ale, ready to go."

"Roger that. Down in a minute." I cut the comm, not a big fan of idle chatter. I pulled on my armored vac-suit, pushed my Ruger flechette into the holster and waited for the AI to complete the landing and depressurize the hold.

A single man waited as I lowered the loading ramp onto the landing pad. He waved when he caught my eye.

"That's a beautiful ship, Captain."

I approached him and he bumped our reading pads. The expected fifteen crates showed up on my list.

"Thanks. We're proud of her."

Three bots appeared, loaded with the crates. I wasn't sure what a pale ale might be, but it looked like Jake was getting quite a bit. I want to talk to him about how he set the deal up - maybe I could learn something.

Twenty minutes later, I was sealing up the loading ramp and re-pressurizing the cargo bay. I didn't like our current configuration. The starboard entrance hatch was the only airlock on the ship. The door between the living space and the cargo bay didn't have its own airlock. I was spending too much time waiting for the entire bay to pressurize before I could open the door to the rest of the ship. I hoped we'd never get holed like we had on *Sterra's Gift*. Without that separating airlock, we'd have fewer options if the hold lost pressure.

Hail Nick James, I instructed as I slid back into the pilot's chair.

"Where are you?" he asked.

"Just taking off from a beer distributor platform. I should be at the station in less than ten minutes."

"Great. We met up with Jake and have breakfast for you."

"Roger that," I answered and closed comm.

It wasn't difficult to find an open slip and I transmitted the location to Nick. I nosed in and saw three suited figures waiting for me. I took the lift down to the berth deck and waited for them to cycle through.

Jake was first through the door. "Whoa, what's with the armor?" he asked.

"Our security officer requires us to be armored when we take on cargo," I answered.

"Darn right I do and don't you forget it." Marny handed me a cup and a bag that smelled of fresh pastry.

"You're an angel, Marny," I wrapped my free arm around her in a quick hug. We took the lift up and I sat at the table in the bridge, pulling out a cylindrical pastry with almonds and glaze on top. When I bit down, there was a sweet filling inside.

"Are you ready to roll?" Nick asked.

"Roger that," I answered trying to enunciate around a mouth full of deliciousness.

Establish navigation plan to overtake the Adela Chen in no more than ninety minutes.

"So what happened last night? Did you guys get in a fight?" Marny asked, once we were cruising along.

"Nothing like that. Tabby was called back to the Academy in the middle of the night. Said she was being deployed," I said. "She didn't really know what was going on. Any ideas on that?"

"Hard to tell. An elevated security status could be issued for a number of reasons," she said. "It's probably not a big deal unless you happen to be wherever the action is. The Navy just doesn't want the cadets getting into trouble and pulls them all back from leave."

"Do you think it has anything to do with those ships which chased us when we left Deivid?" I asked.

"You were chased?" Marny asked. I'd surprised her, which she didn't like, especially when the topic involved crew safety.

"Yeah, two ships tried to intercept us while we were burning for orbit."

"What'd you do?" Marny asked. I definitely had everyone's attention.

"I tried to talk 'em out of it and when they wouldn't turn away, I lobbed a three-second volley across their bows. That made them scurry," I said.

"That's a pretty wild part of Mars. I shouldn't have let you go by yourself. Even so, I can't imagine that has any relationship to the recall. Let me do some checking. Most of the time there's news about that sort of thing," Marny said.

"By the way, thanks for the goodies," I said. "Those cupcakes were amazing."

"What'd you think of the Corona?" she asked.

"A little easier to drink than Guinness. We liked it."

"Doesn't really go with cupcakes, but I had limited time, so I had to improvise," Marny said.

"It was excellent. Thanks again." I appreciated that she was looking out for me, like the big sister I'd never had. I got up and slid into the pilot's chair.

Engage navigation plan, I directed. The ship slowly backed out of the slip, turned and accelerated into a stream of traffic leading away from Puskar Stellar.

Ninety minutes later - almost to the second - we pulled up on the *Adela Chen*.

"Knock, knock," I said after opening a comm channel with Ada.

"Who's there," she played along.

"Can you cut your burn, please?" I asked.

"Can you cut your burn, please, who?" she asked.

"What? Oh... uh, sorry, I don't know any knock, knock jokes," I said.

"You're hopeless," she said. The tug's engines shut down.

"Anything to report?" Nick asked. It was the formal opening to our shift change routine. We'd agreed that I'd sail the tug out with Ada to the Valhalla Platform, which was a quick three days out. My responsibility, after being asked for a report, was to point out any significant changes to ship or navigation status.

"Negative. All systems are green. The *Adela Chen* and *Hotspur* are both gliding with zero Delta-V and both ships report no burn."

"I relieve you," Nick said.

"I stand relieved. See you guys in a couple of days."

"Aye, aye, Cap," Marny said. "I'll see you out."

I already had my pack ready to go. I clipped it onto my chest and slid my AGBs (arc-jet gloves and boots) over my vac-suit. "Here's hoping for a quiet ride," I said to Marny as I stepped into the air lock.

"Always the dreamer, eh Cap?" she said as the door closed.

I looked back at the *Hotspur* as I arc-jetted between the two ships. I wished I could stay and pilot her, but I wasn't about to separate Nick and Marny just because I liked the ship better. Moreover, Nick didn't have any real experience with the tug. I cycled through the *Adela Chen's* airlock and walked to the base of the ladder leading to the cockpit.

"You need coffee?" I said into my comm.

"Got one," Ada's cheery voice replied. I grabbed a cup for myself, took the lift up to the cockpit, and slid into the open chair.

"Ready?" Ada asked.

"Not quite," I said. "Ever heard of John Denver?"

Ada groaned.

Open comm with Hotspur bridge. Cue playlist 1.

...Country roads take me home
to the place, where I belong...

PASSAGE TO VALHALLA

Ada and I fell into a comfortable rhythm of shifts. At first we were both working to catch up on lost sleep, but by the time we'd flipped around on approach to the Valhalla Platform, we were back to hanging out and chatting during the day cycles.

"Are you making any progress on your master's license?" she asked.

"Nothing more than time in the seat." I hated to admit this to her. She was going to push me now. "I bought the course, I just haven't started it yet."

"Let's get going on it so I'm not the only who can move this tub," she said.

"What would you think about training Nick on the tug? He's probably got as much time with a dual stick system as I do, albeit much smaller craft."

"Sure, why not?"

"Heh, I'm not sure he'll like that I sicced you on him. To your point though, we need more than a couple of people who can sail this rig if it's going to be part of our fleet," I said.

"That sounds good, but you're not changing the subject. Pull your course up and let's work through the first section."

I sighed, obviously unsuccessful in derailing her interest in getting me back into the course. I tossed the chapter outline onto the center vid screen.

"Propulsion Dynamics," I said, reading off the first section heading. I wanted to bang my head into the console. It wasn't that I couldn't do the math, but it was going to be laborious.

"Ooh, this is a fun one..." Ada clapped her hands excitedly.

After a couple of back-to-back shifts of coursework, Ada finally relented and allowed us to limit the amount of time spent studying and testing. With her help the material went quickly, but even so, I estimated there were at least a hundred hours of work left in the first of three sections. I'd be at this for the rest of my life - or at least the foreseeable future. I was learning things about navigation, fuel consumption, electrical systems and many other useful subjects, so I wasn't sure why I resisted so hard.

After seventy-five hours of sailing we dropped out of hard-burn. The protocols for entering the perimeter Mars Navy had established around Valhalla were strict and we had no interest in breaking them.

Establish comm with Nick. I'd learned from my current coursework that the AI had to work through several systems to get me in contact with Nick on another ship.

"What's up?" he asked.

"Would you like to handle docking the *Adela Chen*? It's a good opportunity to get comfortable with it," I said.

"I could do that," he answered. I couldn't tell if he thought it was a good idea or not.

"Let's go to zero-burn and I'll pop over?"

"Yup, that makes sense," Nick said. We hadn't had a lot of time to plan out all of the details of our trip. I shouldn't have been surprised by the additional work caused by having extra crew and multiple ships, but I was. When it had just been Nick and me on *Sterra's Gift*, we just did the next necessary thing without a lot of planning.

I waved to Nick as we passed each other, arc-jetting between the ships. Once I was through the airlock I took the lift from the berth deck up to bridge deck. Jake was currently sailing the ship. It gave me a little pause, since I knew he didn't have much experience. But, we all had to start somewhere and the AI pretty much did everything needed. The coursework I'd been taking had made me more aware of the gross details of that work and caused me to rethink some of my assumptions.

Marny was seated on the couch in the main bridge-area on the starboard side. I slid one of the two chairs from the port side over to the table.

"You guys look pretty serious," I said. Marny had the far-off look of someone who was reading through news listings or comms on their HUD. She blinked and then focused on me.

"You get any word from Tabby?" she asked.

"I haven't checked, why?" I squinted my eyes, indicating to my AI my request to see prioritized comms. Sure enough I had a low priority comm from Tabby. "Hold on a sec," I said.

Liam – I'm sorry I had to take off so quickly. I miss you already. Give a hug to your mom and dad for me, as well as Wendy and Jack. I wish I could say more or send video but we are about to go on a complete lockdown. –Tabby

"They're going on lockdown," I said. "It feels like something's going on. Any ideas?"

"Maybe. There are unofficial reports - nothing specific - of Anaimalai getting raided by Red Houzi," Marny said.

"Where's that?" I asked.

"Indian space. Not all that far away from Baru Manush. It's a big colony too, about the same size as Colony 40. Thing is, the colony has gone completely dark, the only reports were right before the attack," she answered.

"What do you think we should do?" I asked.

"Nothing we can do," she said. "The Indian government has all but given up on asteroid mining in this system."

I had a sinking feeling in my stomach, but she was right. Moreover, we had business that needed attending to.

"Guys," Jake's voice sounded stressed "We've got a visitor, destroyer class. They're hailing us."

Identify ship. Accept hail. "*Hotspur,* Captain Liam Hoffen." I identified myself and jumped into the pilot's seat next to Jake. The center console showed the large ship approaching us, a ship identified as the *Walter Sydney Adams*. I engaged the video portion of the comm system.

"Greetings, Captain Hoffen. Commander Joe Alto of the *Walter Sydney Adams*. Please state your business." I recognized the middle aged officer from our last visit.

"We've got a barge full of equipment to deliver. I'm transmitting our bill of lading." I answered.

"Thank you, Captain. Stand by," he said, blanking the video.

I waited several minutes until he finally re-appeared. "Captain, we're currently operating at an increased security level. We're requesting that your sloop conduct a stand-off of twenty thousand kilometers. Are you able to comply?" It was a provocative request, but I didn't see any reason to take issue with it.

"Roger that, Commander. We'll comply. Is there anything you can share with us regarding the security condition?" I asked.

"I'm sorry, Captain. No information available at this time. That said, where are you headed?"

"Next stop is Terrence," I said.

"I've no reports of criminal activity in that sector," he answered. "Alto out."

"That is a giant ship," Jake said after Commander Alto terminated the comms.

"Too bad they didn't let us accompany Nick and Ada in. Last time we were here, we saw a battleship. If you liked that destroyer, you'd really love to see that," I said.

Open comm with Nick.

"What was that all about?" Nick asked. He couldn't possibly have missed the destroyer.

"They've asked us to keep the Hotspur at twenty thousand kilometers," I said.

"Understood. See you on the other side," Nick replied.

"Roger that," I closed the comm. "Mr. Berandor, have you worked much with the navigation system?"

"Only in theory, but I think I've got the basic idea. Where would you like to go?" he asked.

On cockpit holo, show remaining original navigation plan to Terrence. Show all intersections at twenty thousand kilometers distance from Valhalla. I said.

The *Hotspur*, Valhalla station and several structures I presumed were Terrence popped up in front of us, larger than would be a true representation of scale. A blue line was drawn from the Hotspur, to Valhalla, and then on to Terrence.

I pointed to where the line intersected the twenty thousand kilometer stand-off zone between Valhalla and Terrence. "We need to go there," I said. "But make sure we don't get inside the boundary Commander Alto requested. It will take Ada and Nick at least two hours to unload, so we aren't in any hurry."

"Got it," Jake worked with the AI for a few minutes and finally pushed his results back up onto the holo projection.

"Perfect. The helm is still yours," I said.

Navigation plan update has been requested. Do you approve? I was surprised to hear my AI requesting the permission. Apparently, Nick had added a security feature. *Approved,* I answered. The *Hotspur's* engines spun up and we gently turned away from our original path.

"Looks like we have a couple of hours to kill," I said to Marny as I sat back down across from her. She was laying back on the couch, reading something on her HUD.

"Have you been working out?" she asked.

"Not as much as I'd like, but I've been getting to my yoga every twenty-four or so." I was stretching the truth with that. I had done the stretches but hadn't pushed it too hard.

"Follow me, Liam. Jake, I'm going to show Liam our new toy." She got off the couch and waited on the lift for me.

"Gotcha," Jake called from the cockpit.

"Where we going?" I asked. Marny didn't answer, but gave me a smirk I had come to know well. This was likely to be good for me, if not specifically fun.

She led me into the cargo hold and jumped up on top of one crate after another. I noticed right away that someone had turned the gravity down in the hold, which made following her that much easier. Once she got to the top crate, she jumped over and grabbed one of the outer ribs of the hull and crawled hand over hand until she was at the ceiling. I couldn't help but notice that she ended up very close to the large white platform I'd seen earlier.

"What's that?" I called from the highest crate. I hadn't started crawling up the wall yet and wasn't sure how that was going to go. With the gravity down, I suspected I could make it.

"Come on up. The gravity is reversed up here."

She didn't need to say that last part, as I could see she was now standing upside down on the platform. As a spacer, I was used to seeing people in different orientations, so it didn't give me too much pause. I jumped for the same rib Marny had climbed and pulled myself up. The transition in gravity toward the top was gradual, finally allowing me to stand on the hull and walk onto the platform.

"So, really, what is this?" I asked. The gravity was heavy, at least 1g if not more.

"Mostly, it's a boxing ring. But it also has grav-weights, bench and a track." Marny opened a locker next to the platform and pulled out some equipment. She handed me a pair of gloves and a padded helmet.

"You want me to box?" I asked.

"It's a better workout than you think. Krav Maga is good, but we need to mix things up. Don't worry, I'll take it easy on you," she said.

"Are you boxing with Nick?" I asked, surprised.

"I'm teaching him, but I wouldn't call what we're doing boxing," she said.

"No. I wouldn't either," I said and raised my eyebrows.

"I didn't mean that." Marny's face flushed but she pushed on. "First, we need to warm up. You've already learned about hitting techniques, but boxing is more than punching someone."

She showed me how to turn on the running track and while she jumped rope, I ran on the stationary track built into the floor of the ring. It felt good to run. I hadn't been on a track since I'd lost my foot and was surprised at how little the prosthetic bothered me. Running was definitely an easier motion than climbing a ladder. After twenty minutes I was more than warmed up, but I wasn't about to admit it, especially after watching Marny effortlessly jump rope next to me. I was satisfied, however, to see that she was sweating heavily once we stopped.

"Stretch it out now that we're nice and warmed up. We don't want to cool off, but we don't need to be straining anything either," she directed.

We stretched for several minutes and she finally popped up and grabbed two sets of gloves. One set looked like it was really flattened out and the other looked like what I'd come to expect from boxing gloves. Marny threw me the normal looking gloves and pulled on the flattened pair. It took me a few minutes to pull them on, but the auto-synching mechanism finally closed comfortably around my wrists.

"A boxer has to remain light on their feet," Marny started, fully in instructor mode. "At the same time, a lot of the power you need for a big hit is translated from the ground, through your legs, and into your target. So it's important to spend some time on your footwork."

We'd spent a good deal of time working out together in the past, so it was easy for me to figure out what she was communicating.

"I'm wearing focus mitts. When I flash a mitt, you're going to respond to it. Initially, if you see my left mitt, you jab with your left. If you see my right mitt, hit with your right. Also, keep your stance like we worked on and rotate with me," she continued.

It was an interesting dance we performed. I wasn't particularly light on my feet but Marny didn't seem to mind. Each time I thought I was getting somewhere, she'd introduce a new twist. By the end of the session I was completely beat, to the point of not being able to lift my arms. I finally held up my left glove, knelt down and rolled onto my back.

"When did you box?" I asked.

"Navy," Marny said, lying down next to me. "I wasn't that good, but I got along."

"I have a hard time believing that," I said.

"Nah, I started too late and I'm too heavy. It's a helluva workout though, don't you think?"

"I'm dead. I don't think I can lift my arms."

"Yeah, you're going to feel it. You should work out with Jake. He competed in Golden Gloves back on Earth," she said.

"Golden Gloves?"

"Amateur boxing league."

"Can you take him?"

"Jake gave it up once he started school, but he's got a hook that you don't want to ignore. His knowledge of form is excellent. I'm learning a lot from him."

"You didn't answer my question," I said, although I knew the answer.

"You want to lie here or grab the shower first?" She wasn't about to answer me.

I didn't think I could get up if I wanted. "How about I'll hang out for a few."

About an hour later I slid into the cockpit next Jake. My arms trembled when I pushed against the chair to adjust my position.

"You ready to take a break?" I asked. I had no intention of going anywhere for quite a while.

"Sure. Did you actually spar with her?" Jake asked.

"She wore flat gloves and made me hit them," I said.

"They're called focus mitts. If you keep that up for a couple of weeks you'll be ready to do some sparring. Just focus on your form and footwork, don't worry about trying to hit hard. There's too much to think about initially."

"I can barely lift my arms," I said.

"Yeah, right there with you. I haven't hurt this bad for a long time. I'm kind of glad you showed up. You think she'll give me a break now that you're here?" Jake said.

"I wouldn't count on it. Any news from Nick?" I asked.

"He's half an hour out. Are we still planning to have the *Adela Chen* transport the *Hotspur* on the barge?" Jake asked.

"Roger that. Would you like me to take the helm for that?" I asked.

"No, but maybe you could stick around. I'd like to get some experience with the stick."

"Good. Then let's line up with the Adela Chen so we're

matching speed when they get here."

Create navigation plan to synchronize speed with Adela Chen.

Identify optimization parameters; time or fuel efficiency, the AI requested.

Optimize fuel efficiency to schedule c. Report time required, Jake answered.

Forty-eight minutes.

"Captain?" Jake asked.

Approved. The ship's engines spun up in response to the new plan.

"How will we do shift changes once we're on the barge?" Jake asked.

He was every bit a greenie - interested in every aspect of ship life. At some point he'd be more comfortable with the routine. "We'll do twenty-four hour rotations with four hour watches and shut the engines down every rotation so we can transfer people between ships. With five people, everyone will get more than sufficient rest," I outlined.

"I volunteer to take every other rotation. I'd like to get the hours in," he said.

"Careful about talking like that in front of Ada. She'll have you working on your Master's license."

"That's a great idea," he said.

TRADING 101

By the time we were a day from Terrence station, my body had started to recover from Marny and Jake's near daily pounding. Two weeks wasn't enough time to become even a junior boxer, but I'd grown to appreciate the sport. There was a period of time in the past, where boxing had all but disappeared. Medical science hadn't been able to repair the damage inflicted to the brain and elite boxers suffered greatly as they aged. Now, it simply required a medical patch.

Terrence was a relatively new mining colony when compared to Colony 40. The founders of Colony 40 had ignored Terrence's location due to a lower mineral density. Colony 40 had been settled eighty years ago, but Terrence was half that age and its founders were aggressively working through the nearby material.

The main station of Terrence was well designed with a large tube-shaped central core and five round tower pods attached to the outer rim. The entire bottom section of the central core consisted of stacked landing bays that could accommodate a multitude of different size ships. If we cared to, we could have docked the tug and barge at a nearby mooring. They came equipped with an automated tender to run passengers back and forth to the station. I'd set the rotation schedule so that Jake, Marny and I were on the *Hotspur* on approach. Nick and Ada would set course to our captured pirate outpost and we'd catch up after finishing the delivery.

"How is your beer selling?" I asked Jake. I had the helm, but he wanted to watch the approach to the station.

"I've got all but two crates sold," he said. "Didn't make as much as I'd like to, but I'll clear ten percent even if I don't sell the last two cases. I'm kicking myself for not trying to sell it to the Navy."

"I'd be surprised if you can't move it on Colony 40," I said.

"More fuel cost, but if I get a decent price, it'll be worth it."

"We didn't get fresh beer out there very often. I like your chances."

Hail Terrence. Request docking permission.

"Welcome, *Hotspur*. You are cleared on pad Twenty-A. Please transmit your bill of lading for our customs office and we request a turret lockout at five hundred kilometers." Video of a spacer woman in her mid-thirties showed on my screen.

"Roger that. Captain Hoffen out."

Transmit bill of lading. Negotiate navigation plan with Terrence Station to pad Twenty-A. Terminate comm, I directed.

On the cockpit's HUD a wide blue line cut a swath through space to the station that I hadn't been able to pick out of the blackness in front of us. I accelerated along the path and, sure enough, at five hundred meters we received the request, *Terrence requests turret lockdown override for five hundred kilometer perimeter.*

Approved, I responded. I hadn't yet picked out where their defensive guns were, but I'd been shot at enough that I preferred to avoid any conflict. Then it occurred to me that I was awfully young to have experience with being shot at by defensive guns. I gave a small chuckle and decided that even being shot at was better than a life of hauling ore. Jake gave me an odd look and I got my head back in the game.

For some reason, I always thought a station looked more alive through the armored glass of a cockpit than it did through the vid screen's magnified display. I made sure to keep us lined up so that both Jake and I could get a good view of Terrence. It was a busy station with lots of small ships coming and going, not unlike Colony 40. I idly wondered how far off the refining platform was. I'd heard this colony had the ability to manufacture their own variety of low-grade nano-crystalized steel. It was something the co-op back home had considered many times.

The approach from the bottom of the station was busy, but nowhere near as crazy as the traffic on Mars. I'd considered letting the AI bring us in, but the docking bay they'd assigned us was large and would be easy to land in. I considered letting Jake bring us in, but figured he could watch this first time. Although I was sitting up higher on the *Hotspur* than I was used to with *Sterra's Gift*, the controls felt tighter and the process was a breeze.

Incoming hail from bay service, the ship's AI informed us.

"Captain Hoffen. Go ahead," I answered.

"Greetings, Captain. Sissy Stein here. Will you need any fuel, O2 or waste service? You should have received a price list with the hail." It was the same woman I'd just talked to.

My AI, overhearing the conversation, showed our fuel, O2 levels and their prices. We were fine for O2, but could use fuel. Prices were better than we were likely to see once we got home. "Hi, Sissy. Could you top us off on fuel? I think we're in good shape otherwise," I said.

"Will do," she said and closed the comm.

Jake sat back in his chair and asked, "How do you contact the receivers?"

"Let's talk to Marny. She likes to handle this, especially when we're out here in the wild."

I pulled myself out of the chair and smiled as I saw that Marny was already dressed in her armored vac-suit. She had draped my suit and one for Jake on the bridge's meeting table. Since I was wearing a liner, I didn't bother to look for a private place to change.

"What's with the armor?" he asked.

I just grinned and gestured to Marny, who obliged. "It keeps people from getting funny ideas. You never know who might be skulking around. You should ask the Cap about that though, because there's a reason I kick his ass every time I get the chance."

"I'm not sure I see the logic in that, Marny. I think you just said you kick my ass so other people don't have to," I complained.

"No. I think you've got it," Marny answered me and then said to Jake, "You don't have to carry a gun, but while that cargo bay is open, I'll be standing by with a blaster rifle. Just don't ever open that bay without me around, especially if there's cargo in it, 'cause you'll have hell to pay if you do."

Jake looked at me to see if Marny was serious. I nodded and pushed my Ruger Flechette into the chest holster. "Marny, have you made contact with the stevedore's union?"

"Aye, Cap. They're waiting for us. Jake's beer is unloading first, followed by the mining equipment."

"What's the security status like here?" I asked. "Should we call Nick and Ada in for a break?"

"I'm uneasy, Cap. I'd like to drop and run if it's all the same to you. I've been reading reports of Houzi activity in the Indian sector. Nothing official, but given we're headed in that direction and all..."

I knew that sector, so I asked, "Baru Manush?"

"Negative. I contacted my old deputy, Barney, and he said there've been rumors, but so far everything's quiet."

"Then it's your ex-captain who bothers me." I exchanged a look with Marny, who also knew about Tabby's cryptic message and the Navy's heightened alert status.

"I never could quite figure him out. You ready to go, there, Mr. Berandor?" Marny changed the subject.

"What kind of gun do I get?" he asked.

Marny handed him a flechette. It was a smaller model, but it'd do the job against non-armored suits. He looked a little disappointed, but I think he understood.

I picked up a reading pad and handed it to Jake. "I'll let you do the check-off for your crates, so you get used to the drill. Also, take this program, you'll want it for managing freight in the future. It's not at all complex," I bumped his pad with one that I'd picked up. "We scan the crates as they leave and make sure that everything gets crossed off. Stevedores will do the same thing. Ready?"

"Sure," he said.

Marny waited for us to join her on the lift down, blaster rifle in hand. Three of us in armored suits made for a tight squeeze. We waited to cycle the air out of the cargo bay and I made another mental note to get an air lock installed between the living space and the cargo bay.

When the loading ramp was finally on the ground, I was surprised to see two people waiting for us. In front was the small woman, Sissy Stein, who I'd talked with several times. I held out my hand and she shook it with a friendly smile.

"We do things a little differently here. We've had problems with smuggling, so we scan all cargo that's delivered," she said.

"Sounds reasonable," I said.

"Brad? Let's get this rolling?" Her voice changed from friendly greeting to sharp command and the taller figure behind her stepped forward immediately.

He stuck his hand out nervously and I shook it. "Brad Stein, local stevedore's union." At least I understood why he'd responded so quickly. Most likely, Sissy was his wife. After we shook, he held out a reading pad.

"Transfer your bill to Mr. Stein," I said to Jake, who was prepared for my request and bumped Brad's pad.

"Ten crates of Pale Ale from Mars," Brad announced.

An hour later we'd worked through both the beer and the mining equipment without incident.

"You all going to join the Mrs. and me for a drink?" Brad asked.

"No can do this time. We're on a tight schedule," Marny answered. "I think we're just waiting for a delivery from Magee's."

"I'm sure they'll be here shortly. Shame what happened there," he said.

"Terrible," Marny agreed. "Thanks for the help. Mr. Stein, Mrs. Stein."

When we were back in the ship with the cargo bay's loading ramp closing I finally asked, "What happened? What was terrible?"

"Magee's is the restaurant where Celina worked before she got captured by the Red Houzi. The pirate Boyarov tortured the owner, Magee, trying to get Celina's location. I didn't think you wanted to get involved in that conversation. You know how rumors go," Marny explained.

"Roger that. So what kind of food did you order?" I asked as we sat down around the table in the bridge.

"They have a great selection of fresh baked items, so I got several days' worth of bread and muffins," she said. "And, speak of the devil, they're here." Marny got up, jumped on the lift and disappeared.

"We should settle up," I said to Jake. "You don't owe docking fees since we were coming here already. You had ninety-six hundred kilograms, which is eighty-six hundred over your allotment. We calculate fuel at the destination price. I'll give you a break going forward on your remaining crates - you're still six hundred kilograms over, but we'll be sailing empty, so let's call that even." I sent him the calculations that I'd worked out. "Let me know if that works for you and I'll transfer the money."

Jake looked at the information for a few minutes. "That looks fair. I hope I can move the last two crates, they represent almost all of my profit."

"You clear twenty percent?" I asked.

"If I'd sold everything it would have been twenty one."

"Not bad. You tied up your money for two weeks for a twenty percent profit. I'd do that anytime I could." It reminded me that I hadn't done a single speculative load yet. That said, we didn't have any cash reserves, either. Everything we had went directly back into the corporation.

"Keeping them could be a mistake. I bet I could have sold the last two crates right here if I discounted them," he said.

"It sounds like you have your investment back, so it doesn't sound very risky," I said.

I smelled Marny's arrival before I actually heard her walk up behind me. I'd learned what fresh baked bread smelled like and loved it. I swiveled my chair and was delighted to see her holding a small plate with three golden rolls on it.

"We might need to invest in an oven," she said. "This stuff isn't that hard to make and it's amazing. Go ahead, dig in," she said pulling one of the rolls off.

I stood up and grabbed a roll, it was warm to the touch. She might have warmed it up for us, but I preferred to think it was just that fresh. "Marny, we'll get underway in a few minutes, anything to report?"

"No. We're clear," she answered.

I punched up our checklist. One by one, I rolled through the systems.

Hail Adela Chen.

"Hiyas, Liam," Ada answered. "What's shaking?"

"We're done here and headed your way," I said. "Any updates on navigation?"

"Transmitting now," she replied.

"Roger that," I said. "Marny's got a surprise for you when we get back together."

TARGET PRACTICE

We declared the rendezvous near Terrence as our voyage's mid-point. After we landed the *Hotspur* on the barge, Nick and Ada joined us in the combined galley / mess of the ship. It had become Marny's signature to set an elaborate table with the best food and drink she could get her hands on. We all pitched in to set up, but Marny was definitely the one in charge and handed out orders with military efficiency.

Toward the end of the feast, I raised my clear cup, which was half full of sparkling wine. "I'd like to toast our good fortune. Never have we travelled so far without a single incident involving pirates. To a safe journey," I said with flourish and took a big drink.

Marny took a drink and then chastised, "Cap, I think you'd best be careful tempting fate like that."

"I can feel it, Marny. Lady Fortuna is on our side in this journey," I said.

"So what's the basic plan? I know we're headed for that outpost you all took over, but what are we doing once we get there?" Jake asked.

"We're going to pack it all up and bring it with us," Nick said. "Since the Red Houzi know its location, it isn't useful to us. It's only a matter of time before they either destroy it or figure out a way to subvert it. We've leased a construction bot and a cargo bot. I think we can be in and out in under a week, maybe sooner."

"Fair enough," Jake replied.

"I've posted the new rotation and we only have ten days on this leg," I said. "Jake and I are next up, so unless we have anything else, I say we get going."

For the next nine days we sailed in the comfortable routine

we'd established. Marny's crazy workouts seemed less intimidating and I was starting to feel more confident in my boxing. I understood that I hadn't scratched the surface of the sport, but every once in a while, a combo would go my way and it was exhilarating. Boxing seemed to be as much about defense as offense. If you want to get your bell rung, all you needed to do was drop your mitts for half a second. I wasn't in either Jake's or Marny's league, but the skills were definitely something I felt could be useful in the future.

Our last day of the journey came and I'd arranged the rotation so Ada and Jake ended up on the *Adela Chen*.

Open comm, Ada Chen.

"Hiyas, Liam," she answered.

"I've uploaded a nav-plan for your approach. I'm giving the *Hotspur* a few hours at the outpost before you arrive just in case there's any funny business. Copy?"

"Copy that," Ada said.

"If you could cut your engines, we'll separate."

"Safe travels, Liam," she replied and then seconds later spooled down the tug's engines.

"Roger that. You too, Ada. We'll see you on the other side. Hoffen out."

All sections report status, I requested.

"All green," I heard from Marny and then from Nick.

I lifted the *Hotspur* from the deck of the barge. It was good to be sailing under our own power, as opposed to riding along like so much freight.

Nick slid into the pilot's chair next to me. "You ready for this?" he asked.

"Sure am. It seems awful quiet out here, though," I said.

"Don't spook yourself. Red Houzi picked this spot because it's out of the way. You'd expect it to be quiet," Nick said.

"Well still, I'll feel better when we're burning our way outta here."

Nick nodded at the console. "I'm uploading a plan that will have us orbit the cluster of asteroids around the outpost. It'll give us a good look before we commit to landing,"

"Might as well get your armored vac-suit on now, Cap. You probably won't want to take the time once we get closer," Marny was sitting at the top of the short flight of stairs that led down to the bridge from the cockpit. It would take the *Adela Chen* sixteen hours to arrive at the outpost, but we'd be there in less than five. "And I've placed blaster rifles for you and Nick next to the airlock. I don't want either of you more than a meter away from your rifle at any time once we're on the ground."

I knew better than to argue with Marny. Her approach was to plan for the worst and expect things to degrade from there. "Take the helm for a few, Nick?" I asked.

"Yup."

My first stop was the galley for a fresh cup of coffee and then I went for my armored vac-suit. It was bulkier than I liked if I had to take the *Hotspur* into combat maneuvers, but it would absorb not only quite a bit of shock, but any shrapnel that my normal suit couldn't. I figured it was a reasonable trade off.

"Have you done any live fire testing, Marny?" I asked, sliding into the pilot's chair.

"You're reading my mind, Cap. Maybe you could give me a few minutes of combat simulations when we get into the asteroids and Nick can light up some targets for us," she said.

"Happy to oblige."

"Your turn, Nicholas. Your suit's in our room on the bed," Marny said.

"So how'd we end up with all the extra arms and suits?" I asked. "I thought we were supposed to return those to the Navy."

"Just as soon as they request it," Marny said. Considering the equipment had come from a Navy ship that had been destroyed, I suspected the request would never come.

On course for the outpost, we chatted some, but mostly sat for long spells in amicable silence, lost in our own thoughts. We had finally reached the edge of Mars Protectorate territory and were moving into Indian controlled space. Perhaps we were all a bit apprehensive. On our last trip through the area, we'd seen firsthand how neither Mars Protectorate nor the Indian government had any interest in getting involved in issues this far out. If we got into trouble, we were less than a day from Baru Manush. Colony 40 would be safer, but it would take us a week to get there on hard burn, longer if we had to accompany the tug.

"I've got a full linkup with the outpost," Nick said at thirty minutes out when we cut the hard burn and flipped back over.

"How good are the sensors, do they see us yet?" I asked.

Show sensor net from outpost on forward holo, Nick requested.

The magnified display in front of us showed three long-range, asteroid mounted cannons, along with the actual outpost sitting on its asteroid in the center of the three weapons. A short, dark green line, cut into the blue oval sensor net.

"That's us, dropping into their range while still under hard-burn. You can see our progress since hard burn just on the end." Nick explained as he pointed to the dark green line that pierced the edge of the slightly pancaked sphere. I hadn't initially seen it, but there was a smaller light green stub growing out of the end of the dark green line.

"Why doesn't it show our ship?" I asked.

"This ship's registration isn't in the outpost's database. One sec," Nick said. He typed on a virtual keyboard that I couldn't see. A moment later, a tiny image of the *Hotspur* popped up on the holo field.

"So, green is good?" I asked.

"Yup. Red would be real bad. Yellow would give you a few minutes of warning, unless you got too close," Nick explained.

"What's the firing range of those cannons?"

Show outpost cannon effective range, Nick said.

Three translucent orange spheres popped onto the display and centered on the cannon emplacements. The intensity of the color changed in bands as you got closer to each gun. It also showed where the physical asteroid got in the way of the cannon's ability to effectively fire. Each of the guns, however, had been placed in such a way that they overlapped and covered each other's blind spots.

"We're going to be at our most vulnerable when we start dismantling the cannons," Nick said. "We'll want to have everything else packed and ready to go before we start on that. My best guess is we'll be open for six hours - the time it takes to dismantle the command portion of the outpost and take down the last gun."

"So, we'll want to have the *Hotspur* on patrol at that point, I'd guess," I said.

"Yup."

"Marny, you ready to break some rocks?" I asked.

"Aye, aye, Cap."

"Alright, get strapped in. Nick, you want to give us a few targets?" I pulled my combat harness over my shoulders.

"Targets are programmed in and should be popping up shortly," he said.

Engage combat controls, I said.

Attacking asteroids wasn't a fair fight for a couple of reasons. First, they didn't move. Second, they didn't fire back. Even so, it would allow Marny and me to work on our coordination. The first asteroid showed blue and I pushed the stick over instinctively to give Marny a better shot with the top mounted turrets.

Marny waited for us to get closer and then sprayed the asteroid from one turret before locking on with the second. I watched as the battery levels dipped and charged back up. She wasn't the sort to lay it on thick, but rather used a pulsing style of fire. Marny easily hit the target, although I'd have been surprised if she hadn't.

The next two targets were ahead of us and I sailed over the top of them so Marny would be forced to use the bottom turret. As expected, she had no problems with it.

"You're going to need to make this harder, Cap," she taunted.

"Roger that." There were three targets coming up and I had an idea. "I'm going to twist through these, try to use a different turret for each target."

"Aye," she replied.

Game on, I thought. I pushed the flight stick forward and

flipped the ship end-for-end, then pulled back on the throttle. Like *Sterra's Gift,* we had a limited amount of forward thrusters available and I accelerated, sailing backwards through Nick's course. I'd lined up the center-most target with the ship and sailed at high-speed directly at it.

When we were within a kilometer, I hit the bow thrusters at the same time that I reversed the engines, causing us to do a slow cartwheel around the target. I also introduced a little twist so that Marny's turrets wouldn't immediately be lined up with the other two targets. She'd have only a few moments to shoot as we spun. I wasn't giving her an easy line on the third, either, aligning it with the tail of the ship.

I heard two turrets burp a stream of blaster fire when the targeting window opened and I watched as the battery drained, predictably, a couple of percentage points. I was about to twist around to give her a short moment of alignment on the aft target when I heard a fah-whump and saw the battery drop twenty five percent. I grabbed at the aft view screen and tossed it up to the forward holo projector. The top third of the asteroid, which was roughly the size of a barge, had splintered apart from the rest of its mass.

Roll back ten seconds, I said and watched as a large blaster round exited the back of our ship and struck the asteroid.

"Is that what you were looking for?" Marny asked, her voice unusually excited. When the battle was real, Marny was stone cold serious.

"No," I admitted. "I'd forgotten about the aft cannon. I was about to spin around to give you a shot."

"Cap. There might be such a thing as being too honest," she said, laughing. "Give me a slow pass on this last group."

I wasn't sure what she had in mind, but I was game. She made it easy for me to feel like we were peers and that my sailing skill matched her combat or gunnery skills, but it just wasn't the case. Marny substantially outclassed me and I always needed to bring my A-Game to live up to the trust she placed in me.

I lined the *Hotspur* up on the next set of targets and slowly sailed beneath the first two. Instead of a short burp, Marny poured a constant stream of blaster fire into each of them. I spun the ship over slowly so she could get the third turret involved and watched as the battery level dropped off quickly and the asteroids took a substantial beating.

Switch port engine to energy regeneration, I ordered. The battery usage levelled off and even started to gain slightly. Marny must have finally seen what she wanted.

"Nice job, Cap," she said. "I was wondering how well that generator would do. That's a frak-tonne of firepower. I'm glad we never ran into a ship like this when we were in *Sterra's Gift*. Although, somehow I think you'd have come out on top even so."

"Nick, are you satisfied?" I asked. "Or do you want us to work through your last targets?"

"I'm good. I didn't know how much work you guys wanted." He slid a look at me. "And for the record, I was running the belly turret."

"Nice job," I said and then gave him a grin. "Don't get cocky."

LIFE FINDS A WAY

The asteroid at the center of the outpost had a large shelf that had obviously been created by mining equipment. For someone who'd grown up in a mining colony it was easy to pick out the tell-tale drill holes and loose piles of scree. The work had been hastily accomplished by amateurs, but they'd gotten the job done.

The amount of litter around the buildings told me that the pirates had been in this location for at least a few years. Marny had once told me that outlaws liked to leave litter outside their buildings as a poor-man's alarm system. With the low gravity of the asteroid, the litter didn't necessarily lie on the ground, but it also didn't simply fly off without an external force. Moving debris was a dead giveaway that someone was intruding.

Our plan wasn't complex. Secure the area first and then the buildings. Ada and Jake would be coming along in the barge in a few hours. While connected to the barge, the tug was a sitting duck, so we needed to make sure there weren't any problems. Now that we'd confirmed our control of the cannons and made sure there were no baddies in the neighborhood, the tug would be safe once they were inside the compound's perimeter.

The buildings were arranged so that the front side of the large warehouse was clear. It was surrounded on the other three sides by clusters of habitation domes. The basic design of a habitation dome is a four meter square room that is three meters tall. It's considered enough room for four people. Maybe that's true for survival, but for long term living that would be extremely cramped. The great thing about these domes, however, was that they were designed to be ganged together on any of their six sides.

In all, there were twelve domes arranged in three groups of

four. The left quad was closest to the front, connected to the side of the warehouse by an airlock and tucked under the narrow, raised control center. When Marny and I had infiltrated the compound several months ago, we'd blown its connecting airlock.

"On me," Marny said through the comm. We were standing outside the main entrance of the warehouse. We weren't expecting to find anyone, but she wasn't willing to take any chances. It was deja-vu for me, but my understanding of room clearing techniques was much better than the last time we'd been here.

Our first target was the control center just inside the front door and up a heavy set of metal stairs. Marny left me on the lower level while she and Nick cleared the narrow room that was just a long, countertop with vid screens, an empty gun locker and a couple of uncomfortable chairs.

"Clear," she announced.

I felt a hand tap my shoulder and recognized the transfer of point from her to me. The rest of the warehouse was a single large room, twenty meters square and ten meters tall. Eight rows of shelves with wide walkways filled the open space. Marny had prepared the walkthrough before we'd arrived. My job was to take one aisle and Nick the adjacent one, while Marny covered us from the end. When we got to the end, I'd check both new aisles while Nick covered me. We moved through the warehouse quickly, ignoring the airlocks until it was completely clear.

Since the airlock leading to the left-most habitation quad was disabled, we planned to save that for last. The rear quad was arranged in a square. Given that it was still pressurized, we passed through the inert airlock quickly. One of the domes was set up as a seating area and the other three had bunks to hold nine people. Grime covered every surface and junk was strewn about the entire space. I couldn't imagine living like that.

Other than being t-shaped, the right quad was more of the same - junk everywhere, but otherwise empty. To get to the final quad of habitation domes we had to go around the outside. It was all part of Marny's plan, however, so we exited the right quad onto the asteroid surface. I had another flashback to our incursion.

Back then, Marny and I had approached the complex from this side first and then set explosives on the right-side dome before going around to enter from the left.

Defensively, we leap-frogged around the back and over to the left side, using the buildings for cover. In the process, we came upon the main power plant. Marny and I took up defensive positions to allow Nick a chance to inspect the unit.

"All's good," Nick said. "It's not a new unit, but its output is probably double what they needed."

"Aye. Move out," Marny was all business when dealing with security. We continued our leap-frog to the final quad. "Freeze," Marny said. "I've got movement."

Nick and I crouched down next to the building and scanned our designated zones. I knew Marny would be working with her AI to replay the movement that she'd detected and attempt to get a read on it.

"There's movement in the final quad. Not enough detail to make it out. We're going to have to take it hard," she said.

Taking a space without ruining the airlock would be a difficult task, but we'd brought along a tool specifically for this purpose. Marny unfolded the thick, transparent riot shield and handed it to me. The shield was a meter and a half tall and half a meter wide. My job was to hold it in front of me and deflect any fire we might take once the door was opened.

Marny placed her hand on my shoulder to let me know she was behind me. Nick wouldn't be coming through with us. There was enough room, but we didn't want to put all of our eggs in one basket. I palmed the lock's panel. The green color drained from the vertical indicator bars and orange filled in. There were a few different animations on airlocks, but in all cases, green was good and orange was vacuum.

I didn't have the capability to hold both the shield and my blaster rifle, so I slung the rifle over my shoulder and held the shield with two hands. Worst case was that we'd get pinned in the lock and I'd have to threaten the inhabitants with blowing the dome. I looked through the transparent part of the door while we waited for the lock to pressurize and was unable to see anything moving. I didn't have a great view of the entire space and my heart was pounding.

If something was going to happen, it would most likely be right here when we were nicely pinned down. Finally, the orange bars turned to green indicating that the pressure of the lock was equalized with that of the interior. I palmed the security panel and hunkered down behind the shield. The door swung open. Not seeing anything dangerous, I pushed into the room, visually scanning from right to left.

"Contact left," I said, sounding much calmer than I felt. My AI had registered movement, but was still unable to provide any details.

"I got it too, Cap," Marny said. "Whoever it is, they don't have comms and I'm not getting a weapon signature."

"I'm going non-lethal." I leaned the shield against the wall and pulled my flechette pistol from its chest holster. As point person, it was my call to make and I knew Marny would back me up.

"Careful, Cap," she warned.

Where the first two quads had been set up as barracks, this quad was broken into two different types of spaces. The area we'd initially entered was a galley and pantry and it was completely trashed, with foodstuffs and debris spread everywhere. I didn't think we'd recover anything that I'd be willing to eat. In order to track down the movement, we would have to clear what I knew to be a common living space. Through that room was the base commander's suite, where my AI had tracked the movement.

Marny and I cleared the corner, sweeping visually, trying to locate whatever was moving. Still nothing. I moved quickly to the door frame leading into the commander's quarters. Whoever was playing with us had to have ended up in there. I covered the opposite side of the door while Marny pie'd the corner, which was simply a movement where she gained visibility into the space a small slice at a time.

"Frak, Cap. What the heck is that?"

Her question surprised me. She was always so professional and in command. I had expected to hear her require the inhabitant to surrender, fire at some baddie or announce that we were clear. I was unprepared for questions.

"Are we clear?" I asked.

"Aye, Cap. We're clear," she said and lowered her blaster rifle.

I wasn't as convinced as she was and kept my pistol at the ready as I swung into the room. I stood, flatfooted as I finally found the source of the movement. Huddled in a pile of debris were two small cats - kittens I supposed. I didn't have any experience with small animals, but couldn't imagine how they could look much worse than they did. Their fur was patchy and missing in some places and they were unhealthily gaunt.

"How did these get here?" I asked and knelt next to them. They were mewing quietly.

Provide medical analysis, I asked my AI. I didn't have any instruments, but my AI would be able to get a lot of information from the video feed.

Dehydration, malnutrition, evidence of parasites, respiration and pulse below expected norms, body temperature…

Prioritize treatment, I interrupted the litany. Immediately my HUD showed a water pouch the AI had seen in the common room.

"What are you doing, Cap? Are you sure you want to get involved with this?" Marny asked.

"What's going on?" Nick had been monitoring us on the comms.

"Cap found a couple of nearly dead kittens. I think he's going to try to fix 'em," Marny answered for me.

"Oh," Nick said, nonplussed. "So we're clear?"

"Aye, we're clear."

"Nick, I need a way to move these little guys to the ship and keep them at thirty-eight degrees. They're freezing." I'd located the water pouch and was back to tending the emaciated little critters. The AI instructed me to feed them only a small amount of water. One kitten responded to my offering, lapping the water up. Its sibling was too weak to show any interest.

"For real?" Nick asked.

"I can't just leave them here. That'd be cruel." I'd never taken care of an animal before, but it wasn't about that for me. These pirates had no respect for life and I'd be damned if that's who I became. Life was important and I'd do what I could for these kittens.

To Nick's credit, that was all he needed to know - that I was serious. "Easy enough. There are several small crates with atmo seals. They'll stay warm long enough to transport to the *Hotspur*. We've been gone for months though. Where could kittens come from?"

"It's not as crazy as you think," Marny answered. "You bring in enough cargo, you'll get rats. Two adult cats would handle that – they're probably around here somewhere."

"How'd we miss that?" I asked.

"We weren't looking for it," she said. "Last time we were here, we were struggling just to stay alive. With all the gun fire, those animals would have hidden."

Nick arrived with a small crate. He put it down carefully next to where I sat cradling the two animals in my lap.

I saw the soft material he'd placed inside it and looked up at him with gratitude. "Thanks. I know I'm being nutty about this. I just can't kill 'em though. They're innocents."

He put his hand on my shoulder. "I get it, Liam. I'm glad you care."

I placed the tiny orange animals into the crate. Neither made any attempt to move. I felt bad sealing the top, but there was no helping it. I carried the crate back to my quarters on the ship and opened it back up.

When people got sick, it was common to apply a small adhesive discs to their skin to monitor health. While treating animals in space wasn't particularly common, medical data was easily accessible and I found a feline monitoring disc pattern for the replicator. It cost me a hundred credits, but I was all in by now.

As much as I wanted to save these little guys, it wasn't lost on me that they might have some ugly bugs that I wouldn't want in my bed. I manufactured a couple soft towels, placed them on the bottom of the crate and gently transferred the kittens onto them. The smaller kitten wasn't moving at all when I applied the diagnostic disc to its stomach. It was still alive, but barely. Its brother had the energy to complain slightly about the disc's application.

The AI's diagnosis was immediate and followed by a prescription which included manufacturing an appliance that clipped on a front leg and a medical blanket that would treat the parasites and provide an appropriate level of warmth.

I found it difficult to walk away, but we were in a dangerous place and there was little more I could do. I carved off a small spot in my HUD to constantly show a view of the kittens and caught up to Nick and Marny, who were still searching the base commander's suite.

Marny acknowledged my return. "What are you going to call them?"

"No idea. I've never had pets before," I said.

They had assembled several two cubic meter crates and were throwing items into them in a way that looked haphazard. Nick pinched and tossed a subroutine at me.

"What's that?" I asked.

"Run it and then just pick up anything. Your AI will tell you which crate to put it in," Nick answered.

"Even the junk?" I asked.

"We'll pack that last, but the salvage is worth more than the fuel to transport it. By the way, we found the mother cat and the rest of the litter." Nick gave a small sigh.

"Dead?" I asked.

"Yeah, sorry."

There wasn't much to say. I wasn't particularly upset by the news, but it did put me in a funky mood. I decided the best course of action was to get to the work at hand. Nick's subroutine was pretty well designed. As soon as I picked up something, my HUD displayed an outline around the appropriate crate and directed me on how to orient the items as I put them in. Two hours later, we had picked up and crated everything as directed.

"I'd say we get some dinner," Marny said. "I'm starving."

"I'll program the construction bot to take down these domes and we can stack the full crates," Nick said.

"How many bots did you bring?" I asked.

"Just two. You can't believe how much security deposit they wanted," Nick said. "I had to tie up over a hundred thousand of our bond just for these. Apparently, we're considered a high risk."

I guffawed, "I can't imagine why. Do you need my help? I'd like to go back and check on the kittens. One of them isn't moving much and isn't responding to the medical cuff."

"No problem. Would you take the half-loaded crates into the next quad for when we start back up? The construction bot will need a few hours to take down this side and get it crated up."

"Do we have enough room to haul everything?" I asked.

"I think so. I haven't been able to get a full list yet, but my estimates are that we have more than enough room. Even so, I'm stacking the junk crates to the side. I wish we had a reclaimer, but they're just not practical to haul around. I'd love to have all the raw materials from this junk."

"Once we get to Colony 40 we can use the big reclaimer in the down-under," I reminded him.

The down-under referred to the bottom side of the main station of Colony 40, which was called P-Zero (Perth Zero). P-Zero had been carved out of a large, watermelon shaped asteroid. Anything below the equator was called the down-under and it was where most of the industrial type activities took place. It was also where the more unsavory types could be found, which I'd had more than enough experience with.

"Yup." Nick answered. I knew enough about his responses to know that he'd already thought it through.

I entered my quarters and sat on the floor next to the box where the two kittens lay. I'd been watching their progress from my HUD and knew that the littlest one didn't stand much of a chance. Its vitals had declined even with the help of the cuff.

"How are they doing?" Marny asked from the doorway, holding out a cup of coffee.

"Oh, you are my favorite person," I said, gratefully taking the cup. "The little one isn't responding to the cuff."

"How about the other?"

"He's getting stronger. I hope they make it," I said.

FILBERT

"Where are the kitties?" Ada burst into the mess/galley. Nick, Marny and I had gathered around the long table, waiting expectantly for her to arrive with Jake. Marny had been ordering Nick and me around for the last thirty minutes in preparation for one of her signature feasts.

I pointed up. "In my room."

"We've got to go see 'em. Marny said one is really sick. Is he going to make it? Can I hold them?" Ada fired off rapidly.

"Neither is doing very well. I've got a video channel, here…" I pinched the channel from my HUD and flicked it at her. "How about after dinner we go up and look at them?" I glanced at Marny, not wanting to ruin her dinner plans.

"Don't be silly, Cap," Marny said, "We can wait to eat."

Jake entered from the direction of the cargo hold and looked confused to find us lined up waiting to step onto the lift. To his credit he just lifted an eyebrow and watched as Ada and I disappeared.

"They're tiny," Ada whispered, looking into the box. "Can I hold them? They look so lonely." I started to suggest that it might not be a good idea, but Ada had apparently already decided. She reached into the box and lifted the blanket containing the two tiny felines and cradled them against her chest. "You can't just leave them in there, they need to know that someone loves them."

"You want to eat up here?" I asked, knowing better than to argue.

"No. They can come down with me." She smiled, turned and walked out of the room. We rejoined the crew at the mess table where Marny gave me what I could only guess was an 'I told you so' look.

"How can we help pack up?" Jake asked after we sat down.

"Inventory," Nick said. "I've sent everyone a subroutine that will scan the contents of a crate and create a bill of lading. We have to assume that everything in here has been stolen, there's a good chance that some of it is also illegal. We'll send a list of it to Mars Protectorate and see what they want us to do with it."

"We're in Indian space. Any legal problems with bringing this stuff into Mars space?" Jake asked.

"Already cleared it," Nick said.

"What'd that cost?" I asked. I'd started to realize that Mars Navy gifts never came without a price.

"They want our scans of the cargo. I'm sure they want to track the stolen goods."

"Why wouldn't they just confiscate it all?" Jake asked.

Marny took that one. "They don't care about the stuff, they just want to track Red Houzi's movements. If they start seizing our plunder, then we might just decide to start hiding things from them. It's a symbiotic relationship."

"I like it," Jake said, nodding.

"Marny, how do you want to run security while we're here? Do we need to have shifts on both ships?" I asked.

"We'll maintain a watch on the *Hotspur*. Nick has it connected to the command center so one person can easily cover both."

Ada spoke immediately. "I volunteer."

"You want first watch?" I asked.

"I'll take 'em all, that way I can watch the kitties. Any problem if I snooze, Marny? " she asked.

Marny shrugged her shoulders. "I don't think so. We're not expecting trouble and the ship will certainly wake you if there's a problem."

"Good. It's settled then," Ada said triumphantly. I'd never seen her so excited about anything before.

"Perfect," Nick interrupted and drew everyone's attention back. "I know everyone's tired, so the first order of business is sleep. We won't set a specific schedule, just work your way to the warehouse whenever you're ready. The two things we need to focus on are organizing the junk in the two remaining quads and completing the inventory of the warehouse. It's 2200 now. I plan to start at 0600 tomorrow morning, join me when you can."

It didn't take long for us to break up. Everyone was exhausted. We'd been pushing hard and the tension of being in enemy territory weighed on us all. I walked Ada up to the cockpit and sat next to her.

"You need to hold them, Liam," she said and pushed the warm bundle into my arms. They were so small, I couldn't imagine how they'd survived to this point.

"Do you think they'll live?" I asked.

"You have to have faith, Liam."

"I hope you're right." I leaned back in the pilot's chair, surprised at how attached to these little guys I'd become in such a short period of time. I heard a tiny fluttering sound from the blankets. "I think one of them is having trouble breathing," I said quietly, more than a little concerned.

"No, he just likes you, that's a happy sound he makes," Ada whispered.

I must have fallen asleep. The next thing I knew, I woke up with the kittens still on my chest. I checked the medical display and was sorry to see that sometime in the night the smaller of the two had passed away. I looked over to Ada, who was awake and looking at me. She held her finger up to her mouth and I saw tears in her eyes.

"He passed half an hour ago," she whispered, "and there was nothing we could do for him."

It was almost 0500 and I'd been asleep for over six hours. "I think he should be buried with the rest of his litter," I said.

Ada held out her arms and I handed the blankets to her and stood up. I leaned over and gave her a hug then wrapped the deceased kitten carefully in one of the blankets. I felt a strong responsibility to take him back to his family.

I didn't have any trouble locating the small mound of rocks where Nick and Marny had buried the small family of cats. I removed a few of the rocks and placed his body next to his mother and then covered them all back up.

"Don't worry," I said before leaving. "We'll take care of him." I felt a little self-conscious talking to the dead, but it didn't stop me.

I wasn't surprised when I entered the galley and found Marny standing in front of the coffee maker. I suspected she'd already talked to Ada since she just nodded and handed me a cup of coffee.

"You know, it's why people are drawn to you, Cap," she said.

"What's that?" I asked.

"You care," she said. "The universe is full of people who are just out for themselves, but you make people feel like they're part of something bigger because you care."

I took a deep breath. "Well, it kind of sucks today."

"Aye, Cap. Some days it sure does."

"Where's Nick?" I asked.

"He's working on getting the first quad packed onto the barge," she said. "He's pushing hard."

"I feel it too. This place gives me the creeps and I don't want to be here any longer than I have to. Are you ready to head over?"

She nodded in agreement. "Might as well. It's all got to get done."

A couple of hours later Jake joined us in packing up the two remaining quads and by the end of the day we were finished with both of them. It had been a long day, but we'd accomplished a lot. At dinner, Nick informed us that the construction bot estimated its completion by 1000 the next morning. It was quicker than we'd need, since it would take us all of the next day to inventory the crates in the warehouse.

Ada brought the kitten down to dinner. She looked tired and I knew it was because she hadn't slept much the night before. We hadn't talked about it yet and I wondered if we ever would.

"Liam, I think it's up to you to give him a name," she said.

"Are you sure?" I asked.

"Of course. I might be caring for him, but he's your cat."

Everyone looked at me expectantly.

"Filbert," I said. I got more than a few questioning eyebrows.

"It's what I thought about when I first saw him. He looked like a little hazelnut curled up next to his brother."

Marny let loose a small laugh. "When have you ever had a hazelnut?"

"Sometimes we'd get hazelnuts when the family traders docked on Colony 40. It seems fitting," I said.

Ada handed me the bundle. "Well, Filbert, you need to go to Liam because Auntie Ada needs a few minutes to get cleaned up."

"It seems like he's responding to the cuff," I said, looking down at him. He still looked pretty bad with the large tufts of missing fur.

"AI says all the parasites are gone and he's gained fifty grams today, mostly fluid," Ada said. She continued to fill us in on all of the minute details of Filbert's day. If anyone thought it was annoying they sure didn't let on. I, for one, found it interesting.

"I found a pattern for a gravity box," Ada finally said after recounting the day. "You should manufacture two and install one in the cockpit and one in your quarters."

I'd heard of a gravity box, although I'd never seen a reason to have one before. Ultimately, it created a stable gravitational field in a very small area. If we could train Filbert to rest in the gravity box during combat maneuvers or when we dropped out of hard burn, he'd be a lot more comfortable. I looked at the plan Ada had sent and noticed she'd found one designed by spacers. In addition to being able to plug into the gravitational system, it also maintained heat, pressure, atmo and had cartridges for water and food. The cost of the pattern was two hundred credits for a single use, but it was perfect, so I shipped the pattern to our replicator. At two hours construction time for each unit, I set the priority to low, so Nick's packing supplies would get completed first.

"That thing's perfect," I said. "Do you think he'd wear a vac-suit?"

"It's been done," Ada said, "but I don't think it's very common. The reading I did today says that if you give them experience in zero gravity as babies, they are really natural at it."

"What about septic?" I asked.

"That's a bit harder," she answered. "Turns out some people teach them to use the head. I've found instructional videos you can watch. It's a lot of work, but then as spacers, we tend to have a lot of free time."

"Kind of sounds fun," I said.

"For now, this little guy just needs sleep. I hope he'll be off the cuff by the time we leave this rock," she said. "Did you find any kitty food on the base? He's a little young to be weaned, but according to everything I've read, he should be able to eat solid food."

Nick put up his hand. "I know where there's some cat food. There was a bunch in their pantry. I'll make sure that crate is on top."

I spent the night in the pilot's chair next to Ada again and she let me keep Filbert on my chest. She had to keep reassuring me that his purr, which sounded more like a piece of loose metal rattling, was him expressing happiness.

JUST BECAUSE YOU'RE PARANOID

Nick assured us that we could get through the crates in one day, even though we were to inventory each of them thoroughly. I didn't have any reason to doubt him, but it was a lot of work to handle every item in each crate. He'd made it easier by having the stevedore bot bring us a crate and place it on a platform so that we didn't need to bend much. Once we'd sifted through the crate we repacked it, recorded its serial number and the stevedore bot moved it out of the way.

"Cap, Nick, you're going to want to see this," Marny said.

She'd opened one of the larger crates. We had to stand on ladders to look down into it. I hoped she'd found missiles. I wasn't expecting trouble, but you could bet we would eventually find a use for them. What I saw in the crate confused me, though. It was some sort of vac-suit made of a very heavy, armored material.

"What the frak is that?" I asked.

"Mechanized infantry suit," Jake said. "Talk about contraband."

I looked at Marny. "Is he right?" It certainly lined up with what I thought a mechanized suit would look like.

"On both counts," she said. "It doesn't get a lot more illegal than one of these. I bet the Navy will change their mind about our agreement when they see these bad boys."

"How many are there?" I asked.

"Three," she said.

I couldn't believe our luck. "Are they operational?"

"They operate on ship fuel, although their batteries are probably low. Maybe have Jake check 'em out - they're right up his alley." Marny said.

"I've never seen one, but I bet I can figure it out." Jake had come over, interested in what we'd found. He bent over the crate and touched the suit. "Want me to spend time with 'em?"

"It'd be worth a look," Marny said. "I'd like to know if they have ammo. But it's not like any of us could use it."

"Why's that?" I asked.

"Training for a suit like this takes almost three or four months," she said. "They're super sensitive. We could walk around with it, but if you did something wrong, you could punch through the side of the ship in a heartbeat."

"Is there more than one kind of mechanized infantry?" I asked.

"Not sure what you mean," she responded.

"Well, my dad said he was mechanized infantry," I said. "Do you think he had a suit like this?"

"No idea. Was he Mars?"

"Nope, North American," I said. "Beginning of the Amazonian war."

"Really?" Marny asked. "That was my war. You're making me feel old. But if he said mechanized, he could have been an engineer or some sort of support staff. These are the suits they used. Did he see action?"

"I think so, he didn't talk about it much. You have to know Big Pete. He's not really a talker, especially about himself."

"Did he ever call someone a squishy?" she asked.

"Hah! Yes. If he got pissed at someone, he'd call 'em that, like he couldn't think of a worse insult."

"Aye, that sounds about right. They called everyone that wasn't wearing one of these suits a squishy. We'll have to charge 'em up, maybe he can take it out for a ride before M-Pro (Mars Protectorate) shows up to confiscate them."

"I'll let you know what I can figure out. It can't be that complex. Most military gear is simplified so people who are under stress can still make sense of it," Jake said. "We actually have a maximum complexity calculation we use when designing interfaces for field use."

"Cool, love to see what you come up with," I said.

By the end of the day, we'd gotten through all of the crates, not finding anything else anywhere near as interesting as the mechanized infantry suits.

***

At dinner that night, Jake had more information for us. "On the black market, each of those suits is worth at least a million. Maybe a million and a half."

"That's more than the entire rest of the load. Each," Nick said, sounding thoroughly impressed.

"Really?" Jake asked. "You feel like we've got a million in the rest of that?"

"Might be closer to eight hundred, but yeah, it's a good load," Nick said. "Better yet, the stevedore bot has been packing the ship all afternoon. The construction bot is tearing down the shelving and will work on the warehouse while we sleep. By 1200 tomorrow, the only thing left on the asteroid will be the control center and power generator. We're about twenty hours ahead of schedule."

"How's Filbert?" Marny asked before I could.

"If he has another day like today, we'll take the medical cuff off the day after tomorrow. He gained another fifty grams and he's a lot more active. I just hope his hair grows back." Ada laid the blanket down on the table and pulled it back, exposing the scraggly kitten. He stood up and walked across to where Nick sat and batted at a reflection on the surface of the table.

"He's a lot more active," I said. "Did any of the gravity boxes get manufactured today?"

"They both did," Nick said. "I pushed up their priority. I don't need the stuff I had in the queue until tomorrow. Tell me where you want them, and I'll install them. I won't have much to do until the warehouse is disassembled and packed up."

I turned to Ada and asked, "Think he's ready to sleep on my bed?"

"I wouldn't," she said. "I manufactured a litter box for him to start training on, but he might make a mess on your bed, he's not real good with that yet."

"What else did you find out about the suits?" I turned back to Jake, remembering that we'd been talking about those before we got distracted by the fur ball.

Jake was ready to talk about his discoveries. "I woke 'em up and they automatically found the power grid and topped off their emergency batteries. They've got fuel and are half loaded with ordinance. They're amazing. Each suit manufactures ammunition on the fly. It runs on normal ship fuel, oxy crystals and recycled water. Basically, they're mini one-person ships and as far as I can tell, they've never been used."

"Too bad we'll never get to play with them." I turned my attention to Nick. "Speaking of, when will we send the bill of lading to Belcose?"

"Belcose?" Jake asked.

"We talked about him back on Mars. Remember?" Nick responded. "Lieutenant Gregor Belcose is our Navy contact and I figured we'd send him an update once we're in Mars space."

"Why wouldn't we sell the suits outside of Mars jurisdiction?" Jake asked. "It feels like you're giving away a pile of credits, and that affects all of us."

"We made a promise to M-Pro that we'd give them the scans of the cargo. I can't go back on that without risking our reputation," Nick explained.

"We're not even in their space, I don't see the big deal. I'm not crazy about leaving that kind of money on the table." Jake didn't have the relationship that I did with Nick. He also didn't know about our background with the Navy. I got all that and breathed deep so I wouldn't get confrontational with him.

Nick looked at me, clearly hoping I'd pick up the conversation. I did.

"It's a judgment call. From our perspective the Letter of Marque, which gives us our privateer status, is worth a lot more than the suits. We also don't know that Belcose will confiscate them. We'd be acting in bad faith if we didn't send him the scans or if we sold them before we made contact," I said.

"That's a pretty big loss you're asking us stakeholders to take," Jake said.

I studied his face. He wasn't angry, but he wasn't backing down either.

"How about this. If they decide to confiscate, we'll counter with a negotiation for missiles, fuel or something of value. If that works, the corporation will pay out based on the value of the trade," I said.

"That's a lot of ifs," he replied.

I nodded at him. "Agreed. And, at this point, we have no idea if the Navy will confiscate them. So let's table the conversation for now. Until we get off this rock, there's not much we can do about it."

"Understood," Jake said, a bit sullenly.

"Anyone else?" I asked.

"We have one more night on the asteroid," Marny said. "Nick and Jake will disassemble the first stationary gun tomorrow afternoon. Two stationary guns are reasonable protection out here, but once we power down number two, the *Hotspur* will need to be on patrol."

Marny, Nick and I had already been through this, but I appreciated her help in disseminating that information to the rest of the group.

She continued, "Nick and Jake, you'll sail the barge to Colony 40. It won't be full, but the Hotspur will escort anyway. I don't want to be strapped to the barge on the way over. We're not expecting trouble, but it's what you're not expecting that typically ruins your day. Liam, how many days travel are we looking at?"

I acknowledged her question. "*Hotspur* could do it with a Schedule-B burn plan in five days. With the tug, we'll go slower and get there in six. Tonight Ada, Marny and I will start rotating watches on the *Hotspur*. We'll leave Jake and Nick out of the rotation since they'll have a couple of long days working on the stationary guns."

"How about a load from Colony 40 back to Mars? Any thoughts on that?" Jake asked.

I didn't mind answering the question, but it felt like he was starting to second guess our planning.

"Once we offload the recyclables on P-Zero we'll have a hundred twenty cubic meters free. I'll be working on filling that tomorrow morning. You're welcome to join me if you'd like to see how we work with TradeNet." I hoped that being more transparent would help him trust the process more. "Have you lined up a buyer for your beer? We know the guy who runs one of the more popular diners called the Gravel Pit."

"I'll take you up on both of those ideas. And no, I haven't found a buyer yet, so the introduction might be helpful," Jake answered.

"Would you like me to take Filbert for a while?" I asked Ada. During our conversation he'd been exploring the top of the table and jumping at anything that moved. Clearly he was feeling much better and I hoped to spend some time with him.

"I wouldn't mind a shower and a few hours of sleep on a flat surface." Ada had been sleeping in the pilot's chairs in the cockpit and while they were very comfortable, they didn't allow you to stretch out.

"I'll take the next watch," I offered.

It was 2200 and we were all exhausted from the day. Dinner broke up without much more conversation and I picked up the squirming little Filbert and carried him to the bridge. I marveled at his transformation from nearly dead to unable to sit still. I put him down on the bridge's new carpet and walked toward the cockpit to start my watch. Clumsily he followed, his claws grabbing the carpet at inopportune moments, causing him to plant his face on more than one occasion. I took pity on him once we reached the stairs separating the cockpit from the bridge. For now, he was too small to get into much trouble, even in the cockpit.

At 0200 I heard someone arrive on the lift at the back of the bridge. Filbert had been asleep for an hour and I'd been looking for cargo contracts between Colony 40, Delta, Terrence and Mars in just about any combination that ended at Mars. There was no lack of possibilities, but many of the cargos were small enough that dragging both ships along didn't make much sense.

"Cap, we might have a problem," Marny said sitting on the arm of the other pilot's chair.

"All's quiet here, what's going on?"

Our sensors and those on the station certainly hadn't detected any problems. I noticed that Nick had taken a seat on the bridge's couch, his long dark hair a mess. I carefully lowered Filbert into his box and followed Marny down to the bridge's main level to join Nick.

"Not here. Remember when I told you that there might be a problem at the Indian Colony Anaimalai? Well it's official. They were hit a week ago by a fleet of Red Houzi," Marny said.

I didn't think it was that far from where we were.

Show Anaimalai in relationship to us on bridge holo.

I swiveled my chair for a better view. A familiar solar system map appeared, highlighting the different colonies that I was familiar with including Baru Manush, only four hours away. I was startled to discover that Anaimalai was only six days past that.

"How big of a fleet?" I asked.

"It's not clear. Anaimalai is big, five thousand souls. So far, they can only account for two hundred survivors," she explained.

"Frak. They killed all those people?" It was about the worst case you could imagine for a colony. It was one thing to be hit by a rogue asteroid, but a fleet of warships bent on destruction would be terrifying.

"No doubt they murdered a lot of them. Some would have been pressed into service," Marny said soberly.

"Anything we can do about it?" I asked.

"No. The fight's over and relief is on the way. The thing is, the Indians don't have a strong enough presence to actually do anything and clearly the Red Houzi know it."

"Do you still have decent contacts at Baru Manush?" I asked.

"We'll monitor channels, but I can't risk sending a comm. If that fleet is anywhere near us, they'd be able to track back on us and I'm not about to announce our location," Marny said.

"You think they're coming this way?" I asked.

"It follows that they'd move on to Baru Manush," she said. "If the Indian government can't protect Anaimalai, what hope would Baru Manush have?"

"Are you worried that Captain Stabos is already part of it?" I asked. Last time we'd been to Baru Manush we'd had a run in with the head of station security.

"I know we had problems with him, but I'm not sure he's Red Houzi. More likely, he's just dirty. He's got family on that station," Marny said. She didn't sound overly convinced.

"You want to cut our losses?" I asked.

"Not yet. This outpost is small potatoes compared to Anaimalai. It'd be too expensive for them to bring the whole fleet. At best they'd send a raiding party."

"I'm not sure we want to run into a raiding party," I said.

"We only need twenty more hours. Everything we do out here is a risk, I don't want to run unless the threat is real," Nick said.

I didn't want to make this decision without more input. "Marny?"

"There's no real threat right now, so I don't see a problem with staying. I'd like to have the *Hotspur* on patrol first thing in the morning, though, which means you need to get some sleep."

Nick relieved me from the watch. I didn't think I'd be able to get to sleep, but the next thing I knew, Marny was trying to wake me up and I was annoyed that I didn't feel rested at all.

"Anything new?" I asked, noting that it was 0800, which meant I'd actually gotten five and a half hours of sleep.

"A little more news on the attack on Anaimalai, but nothing that affects us. I'm asking everyone to wear armored suits today," she answered.

I sighed and started changing. "Have you talked with Jake and Ada yet?"

"Aye. Nick and I briefed 'em this morning," she answered.

"Any issues?" I wondered how Jake would handle the stressful environment.

"Yeah. Ada was concerned that Nick didn't have the gravity boxes installed for Filbert. I think she's anticipating problems."

I smiled at this. She'd learned about a pirate fleet in the neighborhood and her primary concern was that the kitten would be taken care of.

Marny continued, "Nick installed one box behind the starboard pilot's chair and said he would install the other one later. He and Jake have already disembarked and I've got coffee and a meal bar in the cockpit for you."

"You're ready to get going," I said.

She was apologetic. "I let you sleep as long as I could."

I followed her out of my quarters and slid into the pilot seat next to Ada.

"Anything to report?" I asked, starting our watch change ritual.

Ada responded with her report. "All systems are green. Nick and Jake are onboard the *Adela Chen*. Marny is reporting that we are secure."

"I relieve you," I finished.

"I stand relieved," Ada answered.

Display preflight checklist. The center console displayed a list of items we needed to work through. Ada and I efficiently checked them off. We'd worked together so much in the last several weeks that we were able to anticipate each other.

"All sections report status for immediate departure," I announced over the ship wide communication. I knew Marny was the only other person on board but we had a discipline that I preferred to observe. A green indicator on my console showed that Marny had responded positively to my query.

Engage silent running, I directed and pushed the throttle handle forward gently. We slid gracefully through the piles of trash and lifted from the asteroid's surface. I rolled onto our side and caught a glimpse of the construction robot working on the skeletal warehouse.

I set a course for Baru Manush on a lower schedule burn plan. I had no intention of actually going to the colony that orbited the planetoid Ceres, but wanted to focus much of our patrol in that direction. I broadened our navigational path in a widening oval spiral that started well within the sensor range of the outpost and skewed toward Baru Manush. Each revolution would bring us closer to Baru Manush, but would also keep us from straying too far from the outpost. On our final revolution in sixteen hours, we'd be within two hours of Baru Manush.

To say that the day dragged on would be an understatement. For me, the idea of a patrol was mind numbingly dull. We weren't trying to go somewhere, we were just sailing around in one of the most desolate areas of the solar system with a slim possibility of running into trouble. I'm not sure why I found it so much harder than sailing toward a destination, but it was.

Finally, at the end of my second shift, we turned away from Ceres and Baru Manush for the last time and sailed for the asteroid. By the time we got there, Nick and Jake should have everything packed and ready to go. We'd agreed not to send comms while on patrol, since military craft would be able to pinpoint our location if we did. Had we run into something dangerous, we could have sent a warning, but letting Nick know we were on our way back wasn't considered important enough for the additional risk. I blithely recited an old saying in my head, 'just because you're paranoid doesn't mean they're not after you.' We were taking an awful lot of precautions for an enemy that we'd had no contact with.

CAT AND MOUSE

When we arrived back at the outpost it was abandoned. The *Adela Chen* was nowhere to be found.

"Marny, you seeing this?" I asked.

"Aye, Cap."

"Any thoughts?"

"I think we should go to high resolution on our sensor package," she said.

I ended silent running, allowing our sensors to actively scan the area. I sailed up to the outpost's main asteroid and observed that, other than trash, it was completely clear.

"Anything?" I asked.

"The last stationary gun is still there," Marny said. She'd sent me a view of the asteroid that held the final gun.

"Frak. Something got past us," I said.

"Maybe," she said, "but if they were under attack, we'd be hearing about it. The only reason to keep comm silence is because they haven't been discovered."

"And the only reason to abandon the outpost is because they saw something and bugged out," I finished her thought and re-engaged the ship's silent running mode. If there was something out here, there was no reason to poke the bear. I pushed the throttle down and burned away from the outpost. Stealth would do us no good if we were sitting next to an obvious landmark.

"Any thoughts on where they might have gone?" I asked.

"You're not going to outrun anyone in a tug," Ada chimed in. "If it were me and I didn't want to be seen, I'd find the biggest rock I could and shut down behind it."

Map all asteroids within a thousand kilometers greater than four hundred meters across, I said. The holo displayed ten large asteroids all significantly larger than four hundred meters. The AI predicted my next request and displayed a navigational path that would allow us to inspect each of them, in turn. I pushed the throttle handle forward and started maneuvering around each of the large asteroids. It would take thirty minutes to finish the passes.

I shouldn't have been surprised when lights around the ceiling started pulsing red and the warning klaxon sounded, but we'd been sailing quietly for hours with an expectation of trouble and hadn't run into anything. In our attempt to locate Nick and Jake, we'd actually found someone else, hiding amongst the asteroids, and they had seen us.

Combat controls. End silent running, I said as calmly as I could manage. The *Hotspur* lurched to the side as we took a fusillade to the aft, on the starboard side. I mashed the throttle stick down. I had no idea what we were facing, but I knew that we certainly didn't want to be sitting still when we did.

With our sensors turned back on, the AI was able to display the three ships that were pursuing us. There were two smaller cutters and a frigate. We certainly couldn't expect to stand and deliver with this group. I'd be willing to take on the cutters, but not the frigate.

While the frigate was a fearsome combatant, it wasn't particularly well suited for chasing down prey. It had only a few of its weapons available when behind an opponent. The cutters, however, didn't have that problem and directed their single turrets at us. One advantage we had was that we were faster than the frigate and at least on par with the cutters.

I decided to gamble that they wouldn't split up and burned as hard as we could stand away from them. We took some hits on our aft, but so far the heavy armor was holding up well. It didn't take long to get out of range of our pursuer's guns. I backed off on our acceleration, not allowing them to close in, but keeping out of their turret's range.

"What's your plan, Cap?" Marny asked.

"Split them up. That frigate could be the end of us if we get in too close," I said.

She agreed with me. "Aye. Doesn't look like they're biting."

"I'm good with it as long as we keep dragging them away from where we found 'em. They were hunting for Nick and Jake."

"The thought crossed my mind," she said.

We ran like this for almost thirty minutes, but the cutters were disciplined and stayed close in with the frigate. Finally, they broke off their pursuit and turned back toward the outpost's location, which I assumed was where the *Adela Chen* was also located. I backed off on our acceleration and allowed them to slip out of sensor range.

Engage silent running. I turned the ship on a lazy arc and accelerated back toward the outpost.

"They saw us before, don't you think they'll see us again?" Ada asked.

"I think they saw us when we were inspecting the outpost and were lying in wait," I said. "If we can sneak up on them, we might be able to free Nick and Jake."

"Worth a try," she agreed.

It didn't take long to get back to where we'd started, but this time I sailed in uncomfortably close to the asteroids. They'd fooled us once, I wasn't getting sucked in again. I felt like I could sense their presence even though they weren't visible, either through the cockpit or from our passive sensors. Two could play at this game, however, so I stayed close in on one of the larger asteroids and waited, slowly orbiting as closely as possible. It was a tense game of cat and mouse, especially since I wasn't sure who was the cat and who was the mouse.

"Movement off the starboard bow," Marny said quietly, as if they might pick up our internal ship communications. I understood. She dialed our external video sensor package onto the location she'd highlighted on the tactical holo. The AI picked up on it and painted one of the cutters moving among the asteroids, hunting.

"They must have seen Nick and Jake but lost 'em," I said. "You ready for this?"

"Aye."

I waited for the cutter to pass behind an asteroid and took off, following around the back side. We crept silently around in pursuit, my heart hammering with anticipation. I hoped the frigate wasn't waiting for us on the other side.

"Everything you've got, Marny," I said once the smaller ship came into view. Simultaneously, I switched into combat burn and shut down silent running. The frigate would know right where we were, but it would give us significantly more acceleration. It's not like once we started firing, they'd have any trouble locating us anyway.

We flew past the side of the cutter and all three of our turrets raked its side, mercilessly tearing through its armor. In a single pass we'd wounded it critically, but to my disappointment we hadn't put it down. I doubted we'd get a second chance.

"Give me aft cannon," Marny requested.

It was brilliant. We'd just raked its side and were pulling away from it. I swung the nose of the ship over using the arc-jet thrusters and accelerated as hard as I could. We'd end up passing closer to the frigate than I'd like, but it was a gambit that made sense. Our weapon batteries dropped thirty percent with that single shot but the cutter exploded violently.

I dodged down, away from the frigate, trying to locate the other cutter. Two on one was a game we might have a chance of winning if we could stay away from the frigate's broadside. I found the other cutter racing toward the frigate, its captain understanding that they couldn't hope to survive if they were separated.

Our gun batteries had been depleted to forty percent. I was shocked to see how much we'd used in such a short period of time. I closed the distance, careful not to overshoot it too far and rolled onto our side as we passed so Marny could use all three turrets. The cutter returned fire but its smaller blasters did very little against our military grade armor. Marny attempted an aft cannon shot as we passed and unfortunately missed.

I spun around and executed a combat burn to catch the fleeing ship. We'd wounded it, but not put it down. It was a devil's choice. If we continued to chase it, we'd come within range of the frigate's guns. If we let it go, we'd be back to stalemate. For me, stalemate put Nick and Jake at considerable risk.

"We're going in," I said. We'd damaged the cutter's engines and overtook it easily. Our batteries were empty and Marny was unable to do more than plink at it with a single shot.

Maximum combat battery regeneration, I said.

The cutter pulled away toward the frigate and I pushed the throttle handle to maximum. We'd lost one engine to weapons power generation. At maximum thrust we were losing ground, but more importantly the batteries were filling back up.

The *Hotspur's* guns thrummed back into life and ripped into the smaller craft that hadn't yet escaped our reach. It didn't explode as spectacularly as its predecessor, but we'd finished it all the same.

Restore engines to normal operation, I demanded, then pushed over the stick and accelerated hard toward the approaching frigate. I'd had enough experience with the angelfish-shaped ship to know that it had little weaponry along its center line. We were still far enough away that it had a clear lane to pound away at our armor though. By sailing directly at it I would be able to use its acceleration and our own, since they were in opposite directions, to put significant distance between us once we passed. It was down to a game of chicken again.

Marny didn't waste any time and blasted away with the remaining energy we had in our batteries. I sure wished we had enough left to leave 'em with a taste of our aft cannon, but I'd be satisfied to just get away from the physically superior ship.

We squirted out the other side and I turned sharply to the port. I'd correctly anticipated that the frigate also had an aft cannon and would try to get a shot on us as soon as we came into range. The frigate turned to pursue but lacked the speed to run us down. Once out of range of its guns, I started turning. With our superior mobility, I believed we'd be able to circle around on its aft and pick it apart over time. It might take a few hours but I had to free up Nick and Jake.

We spent the next ten minutes lining up on the ship. Before we could move closer to attack, the captain must have figured out what I had in mind. He or she had obviously analyzed the situation the way I had and realized, at a minimum, they were in for a lot of harassment. The frigate ran. For the next two hours we chased them, staying far enough back to avoid any chance they might have with their rear cannon but close enough for them to know we were serious and there to stay.

"Marny, what do you think about sending an encoded message to Nick. If he could see where we're at, he might be able to get rolling," I asked.

"I'll send him the combat data streams too," she said.

I slowly allowed the frigate to pull away and move out of sensor range. If they were willing to leave the area and cease hostilities, we'd be just fine with that. I reengaged silent running and turned back toward the outpost.

"I've got confirmation from Nick," Marny said. "You're going to have to decode it for us though."

"Ada, you have the helm," I said. I needed to stand and move a little.

"Roger, Captain. I have the helm," she replied formally.

I heard something odd in Ada's voice and turned to see that she'd been crying. It was a confusing moment for me. I felt like I needed to work on this coded message, but I was also concerned about what Ada was going through. In the end, compassion won out. I reached down and unlocked the grav box where Filbert lay stretched out on his warm blanket. I extracted him with the blanket and handed the bundle to Ada.

"Want to talk about it?" I asked.

"What?" she asked.

"That was pretty stressful, are you doing okay?" I asked.

"Oh," she said and wiped her eyes. "It just makes me so mad. They take what they want and don't care about anyone else. You and Marny handle it so easily and it doesn't seem to get to you. I'd have never been able to do all that."

"Don't count yourself out yet. I've seen you execute maneuvers that I still can't understand. And don't think for a minute that I wasn't scared out of my mind. All I could think was that Nick and Jake were doomed if we couldn't run those guys outta there."

"I suppose. It's just such a waste." Filbert sprang from her arms and fell none too gently on the floor. He dodged my clumsy attempts to catch him, sprinting down the stairs onto the bridge.

I looked at Ada who smiled at his antics. "I guess he didn't like being cooped up." I said.

"I'm okay, Liam. And I don't want you to think I'm weak. It's just hard," she said.

"It is hard and it's important to talk through it. Marny has to talk me off the ledge all the time," I said.

"Cap, you coming?" Marny called from below. "I think you might have an escapee down here."

"I'm coming," I said. I patted Ada on the arm and tried to smile reassuringly.

When I got to Marny she was holding the tiny, squirming Filbert. "He's sure got a lot of piss and vinegar in him for having such a rough start in life."

I laughed. "What's the message?"

"It just says East Bound and Down plus one sixty," Marny explained.

"Oh, that's easy."

Look up navigation path that Sterra's Gift took from Colony 40 to Baru Manush. Plot course to the point where Sterra's Gift was at one hundred sixty hours.

"How'd you figure that out?" Marny asked.

I gave her a wicked grin.

Play East Bound and Down over ship's public address.

Once again Jerry Reed's twangy voice started singing… *East Bound and Down…*

INVASION

"I'm going to grab some coffee and a meal bar. Either of you want anything?" I asked. Marny and Ada were both within earshot.

"Hold on, Cap. I'm starving and was thinking about making something more substantial. Can you make it for a few minutes?" Marny asked.

"Sure. I'm game." Marny handed me the still squirming Filbert. I didn't see any reason not to let him roam, so I put him on the floor. I was amused to see that he followed me to the stairs leading up to the cockpit. I gave him a lift up and over the obstacle.

"I've got some work to do," I said to Ada. "How about I take the first shift. Can you rest?"

"What? Now you think I'm weak?" she asked.

I wasn't prepared for the question and didn't know how to answer it. "Uh, no. I really have work to do."

"Just because I cried doesn't mean I can't handle it, Liam. Don't treat me like I'm fragile."

I had no idea where this was coming from. Worse yet, I had even less of an idea how to diffuse the situation. "Would you like to take the first shift?" I asked.

"You bet I would," she answered.

"Okay, the helm is yours." I skipped the normal watch change procedure, in a hurry to get out of there.

I caught up with Marny on the lift and followed her into the galley. "Can I help?" I asked.

Marny didn't turn around, but she said, "I'll talk to her."

"About what?"

"Well, she opened up to you about how the pirates made her feel and you didn't respond. The next time you talked to her, you suggested she needed to rest. I'm guessing she doesn't have a lot of experience around men."

"I didn't mean…"

Marny cut me off. "No. You didn't and she'll figure that out. It's just post combat stress. Give her space for a couple of hours and she'll work through it. You have to be careful not to make decisions based on her showing vulnerability."

"You think I would?" I asked.

"Aye. That you would, Cap. You're a decent person and want to protect your friends, but there's a balance to find."

"What could I have done differently?" I asked.

"If you'd given her the option to take this watch or the next then you'd have avoided the entire thing, instead of just assuming that she'd like the first break. Don't let it mess with you too much, you can take it too far. Welcome to leadership."

Marny handed me a plate with a good looking sandwich on it. I was both starved and exhausted. I wolfed down the sandwich and retired to my quarters, setting my alarm for three hours. That was a good length for a nap and I woke easily to the alarm. I changed suit liners, took a shower and felt about a hundred times better.

"How's it going up here?" I asked, noticing too late that Filbert was asleep in Ada's lap.

"All's quiet. Would you mind putting him in his box?"

I accepted the small bundle and placed him in the grav-box behind my chair.

"Sorry about before. I just don't want you thinking I can't pull my weight. My dad still treats me like a little girl," she said.

"I'll get better at this, Ada," I said. "Anything to report?"

"All systems are green. No sign of any hostiles - or friendlies, for that matter. We're three hours from our destination."

"You are relieved," I said.

"I stand relieved," she answered.

"I'll wake you if we have any contact. I'm hoping that we'll beat the *Adela Chen* to the rendezvous by a few hours. I'd like to scout it out."

"That shouldn't be a problem. Nick would have to push it pretty hard to get there in front of us given the burn you've set," she said.

"That's what I'm hoping."

Ada leaned over on the way out of the cockpit and gave me a quick hug. I knew it was her way of letting me know that we were okay. It wasn't exactly military protocol, but it worked for me.

Two hours into my watch I switched to silent running. Nick and Jake would have a harder time seeing us, but if I was going to scout out the area, I might as well not announce our presence. Fortunately, I found nothing as I made a nice wide sweep.

Meeting up with someone in the deep dark of space is a pretty good trick. The concept of speed out in space is really just a relationship between two different objects, because everything's moving. I had to make a guess that when Nick indicated one hundred sixty hours from Colony 40, he meant that we should expect to be at that point, with a zero relative speed to Colony 40, neither moving toward or away from the colony. You might think that sitting still would put us in a defenseless position, and it would if someone were able to somehow guess our exact location. That was the genius of a random spot in space. I turned off our silent running to make us more visible to the *Adela Chen*. I wasn't sure when they'd be arriving and didn't want to miss them.

On the outside, we could have been as many as ten hours ahead of the *Adela Chen*, although four or five hours was more likely. Marny and Ada were on the couch in the bridge, chatting, when I got a sensor contact. Something big was coming through our space at a high Delta-V - that is, we weren't even close in relative speed and direction.

"Marny, Ada, you might want to look at this." I tossed the sensor tracking onto both the bridge and the forward cockpit holo. At the extreme range of our sensors we couldn't yet tell what it was, other than to see that it was very large, likely multiple ships, and that they were still accelerating.

Calculate trajectory for new ships. I directed

Colony 40 in one hundred thirty hours, the ship's AI calculated.

"Cap. That looks like a big fleet," Marny said. As we watched the signature of the ships grew larger and larger.

"And they're moving fast," I said. Understanding hit me like a brick.

Send sensor data stream to Lieutenant Belcose, Pete Hoffen, and Wendy James. Send message to Pete Hoffen, Wendy James: large fleet of unknown intent one hundred thirty hours from your location, take precaution.

"Cap. They've seen us," Marny said.

"How do you know?"

"They dropped a comm disrupter," Marny said with a sigh. "I don't know if your message got out or not."

"What's that?" I asked.

"It's bad news Cap. We're done talking to the rest of the solar system and it confirms they're hostiles. A comm disrupter like that is highly illegal for civilian use."

"Can we shoot it down?" I asked. We had to get word out to our family.

"Not possible, it's not a single thing. Think of it as a spray they're releasing. It fouls the area for hundreds of thousands of kilometers with a disruptive radiation. It's not much different from what happens when we're on hard burn - the same sort of interference."

Calculate minimum arrival time at max burn to Colony 40. I instructed. If I could beat them there, I'd tell them myself.

One hundred fifty hours on combat burn, the AI informed. *Frak.* We were starting from zero relative speed. The fleet had thirty plus hours of acceleration on us. We couldn't overtake them. I hoped my message had gotten through, it was their only hope. I couldn't very well leave without communicating with Nick and with those frakking comm disrupters, I wouldn't be able to tell him what was going on.

"Are they sending anything else our way?" Ada asked.

"I don't see anything. With their current speed I'm not sure what they could do." I knew I was right, but frustration caused me to spit out my words. Even with the short period of time we'd seen them, they were almost out of our sensor range. There was no chance they'd slow down and come after us as it would take days of deceleration to zero out our Delta-V.

Display makeup of hostile fleet on forward holo, I instructed.

"Cap, I've got it down here already," Marny said.

"Can you take the helm, Ada?"

"Got it."

I didn't think we'd be getting into any immediate trouble, but I also wanted someone ready to move the ship if there was.

"What do we have?" I asked, standing behind Marny's shoulder.

"Not good, Cap. They're rolling two destroyers, four frigates and I'm not sure of the count on the cutters. We counted ten, but I think there might be more. No doubt they've got a handful of darts in there too," she said.

"What, no corvettes?" I quipped. My heart sank. We could barely hold our own against a frigate, which out massed us by forty percent. My mind raced back to the first time I'd seen a destroyer sidle up to us on our way to the Valhalla Platform. A single destroyer out massed us by ten or twenty times and was a hundred forty meters longer.

"I didn't see any," Marny answered.

"How long before we're clear of the comm disrupters?"

"Ten hours, but believe it or not, we've already helped. The Navy will become aware of the comm disrupters at least within that time frame and they'll put two and two together," she answered.

"We could burn hard and send a warning," I was desperate to come up with any plan that might help.

"I think it's a better than good guess that comms are being disrupted on Colony 40 too. Although with the firepower they're rolling in with, they'll just roll over the top of whatever defenses are there."

"Even the stationary guns?" I asked. I already knew the answer but I had to hope.

"Stationary guns will ding up a destroyer, but they aren't going to stop one, much less two."

"Ada, can you join us?" She'd overheard the entire conversation, but I needed her to be part of the next decision.

"The way I see it, we have a decision to make. That fleet is headed toward Colony 40, which can't possibly defend itself against so much firepower. We can't do anything to stop that. What we can do is get clear of this communication disruption and get a message to the Mars Protectorate Navy," I started.

"I'm not sure what the decision is," Ada said.

"If we're not here when Nick and Jake arrive, they could decide to keep going to Colony 40," Marny filled in.

"They'd sail right into the fight if we did that. They'd never survive," Ada said.

"Right. The flip side of that is, the sooner we tell the Navy, the sooner they'll arrive and that could save people's lives." I was sick to my stomach at the idea of leaving Nick and Jake behind, the danger to them was outrageous, but the moral dilemma made my head spin.

"If the *Adela Chen* were here right now, what would you do?" Marny asked.

That was an easy decision. "Send the tug back to Mars and I'd go to Colony 40."

Ada was horrified, tears once again forming in her eyes. "You can't, Liam. Red Houzi would most certainly murder you."

"It's my family, Ada. I can't just leave them," I answered.

She nodded her head, understanding. "I'll go with you," she said quietly and reached over to hold my hand. The touching move exemplified what I loved about her.

"That's right, Cap," Marny said. "There's nothing we can do that will stop that fleet from busting up your home, but if we take off right now, we'll lose ten hours on our trip to Colony 40. Sometimes holding tight is the right thing to do, even though it sucks. We need to wait for Nick and Jake, then we can split up."

It took an excruciating ninety minutes for the *Adela Chen* to finally show up on our sensors.

"Ada, can you line up on them while I talk to Nick?"

"Will do."

Hail *Adela Chen*, I said.

"What's the sit-rep, Liam," Nick asked. The communication disruption weapon caused his face to blink in and out on my HUD, but we were close enough to overcome full communication lockdown.

"I'll come alongside. We need both you and Jake onboard to talk this through. Ninety minutes ago a large fleet passed within ten thousand kilometers of our current location, headed to Colony 40," I said.

"Understood," Nick answered. Ada hadn't wasted any time and was neatly pulling us up parallel to the *Adela Chen*. He closed the comm and within a few minutes we were all seated around the table on the bridge.

"Did you get any communications off to Colony 40?" Nick asked.

"We don't know," I shook my head in frustration. "I sent something about the same time they dropped the communication disruption weapon."

"What's the plan?"

"I'd like to send the *Adela Chen* back to Mars. It has no business in a war zone. Whoever goes can relay our combat data stream and try to warn Colony 40. Marny estimates that they should be able to clear the comm dead-zone in ten hours, which would still be a hundred and ten hours before that fleet reaches home."

"What about the *Hotspur*?"

"I want to take it home and look for survivors - do whatever we can to help," I said. "They had two destroyers, it's not going to be good, Nick. Honestly, I'd like all of you to go back on the tug."

"We can talk about that, but, did you use the Navy's comm set?" Nick asked. He was referring to the communications gear the Navy had installed on *Sterra's Gift* and that we'd moved over to the *Hotspur*.

"Communications are blacked out," I said, knowing that I was missing something.

"Shouldn't affect a quantum device," Jake said.

"I'm not following."

"It's a quantum communication device. It will work for the same reason it communicates almost instantly. It's not sending a wave out from our ship like normal communications. There are crystals in the device that operate on a quantum level. When you stimulate the crystals on this side, their matching crystals get vibrated pretty much wherever they're located," Jake explained.

The explanation didn't do anything for me, but if it shortened our contact by ten hours I didn't much care. I jumped up, ran to my quarters, pulled the comm set out from the wall and opened the box. I'd wondered why it took up so much space as just about anything digital was always microscopic.

"Mayday, Mayday, Mayday. This is *Hotspur*. We've just witnessed a large, hostile fleet en route from Baru Manush to Colony 40. Estimated arrival in one hundred twenty six hours." I waited ten seconds and repeated the message. On my fourth iteration a voice broke in.

"Belcose here. Message received. Please identify yourself," he said.

"Captain Hoffen," I answered.

"Captain, there's a small, clear stick in a pouch on the top of the box lid that this comm device came in. Do you see it?" Belcose asked.

I looked at the box top and found a sleeve that had a dozen finger-long, clear, thin tubes. I pulled one out. "Roger that, Lieutenant. I've extracted one and am holding it."

"This is going to pinch a little, I need you to remove your glove and poke the sharp end of that into your finger. Once you do that, slide the stick into the small hole on top of the handset you're holding."

The rest of the crew was standing in the room watching the exchange. Marny helped me understand by explaining, "It will transmit your identity after doing an analysis."

I raised my eyebrows at the suggestion. I trusted Belcose to do the right thing for Mars Protectorate, which most often lined up with what I cared about. Sure, he'd spied on us, put us in some bad spots and skimped on the sharing of information, but mostly he was looking out for the greater good. I did as he suggested and stabbed my finger, probably more vigorously than needed. The clear tube turned red and I withdrew it from my finger and slid it into the end of the handset.

"Thank you, Captain Hoffen. We can't be too careful with this kind of information. We're reading that you're feeling a substantial amount of stress, but we don't get any indication that you are currently under duress. Are you able to speak freely?" he asked.

I had difficulty believing that he could tell all that from the phial of blood, but then I suppose the entire box could have been designed to gather information that I didn't know was getting transmitted. It certainly wouldn't be the first time for this device.

"I've got my crew in here. We're not currently under duress. We don't have any mechanism for transmitting a data stream to you, but we got a decent look at the fleet. Any suggestions?"

"Have your AI repeat the data stream information using a Morse encoded protocol. We'll have an AI on this side receive and decode it," he instructed.

I conveyed his instructions to the ship's AI and it started beeping a monotone signal at high speed. Within three minutes it appeared to be complete.

"What are your plans now, Captain?" Belcose asked.

"I'm not sure how secure this channel is Lieutenant, so I won't be sharing that information," I answered. I looked at Nick who nodded his head in agreement.

"Look, Liam. I know you have family back there, but you need to stay clear," Belcose said.

"Understood. Hoffen out," I said.

"*Kuznetsov* out," he responded.

BEACHHEAD

"I intend to take the *Hotspur* on to Colony 40. The tug needs to head back to Mars." I wasn't sure we'd be coming back from this one.

"I'm in," Nick said, without hesitation.

"Try to stop me," Marny said.

"Count me in," Ada answered.

"You all are nuts," Jake said defensively.

"That's the first sane thing I've heard," I said to Jake. "I don't like our odds on this one. I also don't think it's safe to just send Jake back alone."

"Please don't ask me to go back," Ada said. "You were there when Mom needed you." Ugh, I could see her logic.

Jake responded, "I can handle the tug as long as I arrange for a master pilot when I get into Mars space."

"Ada, I can't change your mind on this?" I asked. "It would be safer for Jake if you went with him."

"Liam, you can order me to do this. I will respect your position. But if you're asking, then I'm staying."

"I won't order you. Nick, can you punch up orders for Jake so he knows what to do with the cargo upon arriving? Ada, will you head over with Jake and do a systems check and help him lay out a navigation path?"

"Any stops?" Ada asked.

"No. Not solo, especially with all the crap that's going on right now. Jake, you should be safe, mostly because you're taking off from a random point in space. I doubt anyone could estimate where you're coming from."

"Agreed," he said soberly.

"If we don't come back or make contact within ninety days, I'm transferring ownership of the *Adela Chen* to you, Jake," Nick said. "Otherwise, I'm bumping you to a captain's share for the return leg."

"That's more than fair. Good luck to you all," he said.

Ada followed him to the lift and looked over at me before it dropped. "Don't even think about locking me out. You gave me your word." The lift dropped out of sight. I thought back to the conversation and didn't recall giving her my word. But, I wasn't about to lock her out either.

Thirty minutes later we were burning hard for Colony 40. We'd burned through quite a bit of fuel scuffling with the frigate and I was thankful we'd topped off in Terrence. As it was, we were going to need every last kilogram of fuel.

At one hundred fifty hours out - just over six days - the pirate fleet would arrive a day before we would. Whatever resistance the colony put up would be crushed within a couple of hours. I hoped Dad hadn't decided to make a stand. Colony 40 wouldn't stand a chance this time with the firepower sailing toward them. My mind raced with the rumors I'd heard about how pirates treated their captives and made it impossible to sleep more than a few hours every twenty four.

When we were a day out, I knew the fleet would have arrived by now. I was unable to stop my mind from inventing all sorts of awful things that might be occurring. Ada slid into the other pilot's chair even though it wasn't her watch.

"You can't do that to yourself," she said.

I wasn't ready to be honest about my inner turmoil. "What's that?"

"I can see it in your face."

"The waiting is impossible," I said.

"Let's think of something more constructive. What's the plan?" she asked.

"It depends mostly on what we run into. I'd like to locate our families and get them out safely. We can't possibly stand up to these guys," I said.

"Why's that?" she asked. "You've certainly gone up against bad odds in the past."

I shook my head in confusion. "You know why. Two destroyers, four frigates. No way could we take on a group of that size."

"Geez, the way I heard it, you and Marny took out an entire outpost with two blaster rifles and some flash-bangs. And who's saying you need to stand toe-to-toe? Like you said, we need to find your people and get 'em out. It's just a bonus if we take out the baddies in the process. Think audaciously, Liam. You're shutting down because of the stakes. They can only kill us one time and we've certainly been up against that before." She smiled at me after delivering her lecture.

I smiled for the first time in several days. Ada's attitude was infectious. Oh, I thought she was nuts, but a little swagger at this point was worth a lot. She was right, too. I needed to start thinking like someone who was going to come out on top.

"The first step is to find our family and I have an idea about that," I said.

"Great, what's your idea?"

"Let's get Marny and Nick and we'll talk it through," I said. "And, thanks for the pep talk. I needed it."

"I was going to kick your ass if that didn't work, so you're lucky." She was still smiling. I was shocked, I'd never heard her say anything remotely like cussing.

Nick and Marny were on the couch with the bridge holo showing what I recognized as the collection of asteroids that made up Colony 40. If you backed off far enough, you saw that the claims around Colony 40 were shaped like a crescent, with P-Zero at the center.

"Any thoughts?" Nick asked as we approached.

"I've nudged us downward so we'll end below the ecliptic at ten thousand kilometers as we pass under P-Zero," I said.

"I think our best shot is to try Big Pete's claim first. It should be quieter out there. After that we work our way in and try to get whatever information we can. It really depends on how much they've spread the fleet out," Nick said.

"If we can derive anything from their previous occupations, they stay in the area for a maximum of five days," Marny said. "If people outlast them, they should be in the clear."

"Haven't they been blowing the stations on the way out?" Nick asked. I understood his concern. His mother Wendy and brother Jack lived on the station, as did Tabby's dad.

"From what I can tell, P-Zero is a completely different type of station for them. It's not a totally man-made structure, but a hollowed out, primarily iron asteroid. They could cause a lot of destruction, but they'd have a hard time completely blowing it up," Marny said.

"My point is, whoever we don't find by the time these guys move on will be in immense peril," Nick said.

"Aye, that is certain. I also think it's fair to say they'll focus much of the looting to the station and the refinery," Marny said. "Individual claims probably don't hold enough value for any specific fleet action."

"Shouldn't we try to get to your mom and Jack first?" I asked.

Marny obviously had something to say but waited for Nick to speak.

"If Mom and Jack are on station, they'll already have had to deal with the invasion for twenty hours. It's not like we're going to sail up to the station, get out and go look for them. We should start at your dad's claim. I think the risk is worth it. If your parents are there, it would give us a beachhead - a place to start," Nick said.

It had taken us an additional five hours to arrive at the outer edge of the colony. It was a sure bet that a hard-burn deceleration would have been picked up by the attacking force, so we'd played it safe. I wished we could just run in, guns blazing, but the destroyers eliminated that as a possibility.

We changed into armored vac-suits and strapped into our chairs - Marny and Nick at the two bridge stations and Ada and me in the pilot's chairs. I felt a swell of pride when I thought about the crew and I couldn't help saying something.

"I want you guys to know, I couldn't be prouder than I am

right now to be sailing with you all," I said over the comm channel.

"Aye," Marny replied. It meant a lot to me, coming from her as she'd seen more than her share of combat and was a decorated veteran of the Amazonian war.

I'd slowed our speed to nearly a crawl, working under the understanding that our ship's largest signature was the engines.

"Are you seeing this, Cap?" Marny asked. The forward holo showed our ship approaching the asteroid which held my parent's claim. A cutter popped onto the display, sailing directly at us. Its current trajectory would take it over us at less than a hundred meters distance.

Extinguish all light on bridge and cockpit, I directed. We were already running in a low-light environment, but this shut down all of the holographic images and vid-screens. The likelihood of the glow being detected by a ship moving at forty meters a second was very low, but detection would be bad. I held my breath as the ship passed above us. It was a small cutter, one we wouldn't have much trouble dealing with if we had to. I waited for a count of twenty before restoring our low-light configuration.

"Frak, that was close. Good catch, Marny. Was that a ship we've seen?" I asked.

"Aye, it's one of the ten the AI detected."

"What do you think they'd do if we took it out?" I asked.

"They'd send a large group out to discover what happened. We should avoid that if we can," she said.

"That's what I figured too," I said. "But, I have to say, that was almost too tempting."

"Provocative actions draw attention," she said.

Slowly we closed in on the asteroid that my parents had been living on for the last three years. Something was definitely off. There was no equipment to be seen anywhere. It wasn't that it had been attacked and destroyed, rather, it just wasn't there. Something else was off, but I couldn't place it.

"That's odd," I said.

"What?" Ada asked.

"The asteroid is barren. There should be a habitation dome, generator and an ore-sled or two," Nick answered for me. "Wait. Didn't you guys dig your domes in? I'm not seeing where that was. Are you sure you have the right asteroid?"

"Dig in?" Marny asked.

"That's it," I said with relief. "He got the message. There's no reason they'd clean the asteroid off like this unless they'd gotten the message."

Outline where the habitation dome was originally located. My AI had a perfect recall of how the asteroid had been laid out. My HUD showed a small swale where we'd originally dug into the asteroid to provide protection for our habitation dome.

"You see that, Nick?" I asked.

"Yup. There'd be no reason to push rock back into the hollow where your dome had been," Nick answered. I heard the excitement in his voice.

"Cap. There's another cutter - another one from the original fleet. I bet they're trying to find your family's claim. There's no other reason for two ships to pass this close." She was right. There were hundreds of thousands of asteroids of all sizes in the ten thousand kilometers that made up the colony. The odds of two ships, or one fifth of their cutters, being in the same area at the same time seemed pretty far out without another reason.

We were almost on top of the asteroid. If we stayed put, the pirate ship would pass just about as close as the other had. I blacked us out and nudged the *Hotspur* around so we weren't on the same side of the asteroid.

"I'd like to EVA," I said. "I bet they're dug in and holding those rocks in with a gravity generator. Otherwise why would the rocks be there?"

"They could be hiding the equipment," Nick said.

"We'll never know if I don't get a good look," I said.

"Yup, I'll go with you," he said.

"That works. Ada and I can play patty cake with the cutters," Marny said. I wasn't sure how good Ada would be in combat, but I had no doubt about her ship handling skills.

Nick and I picked up our blaster rifles, still hanging by the cargo bay, thanks to Marny. Somehow, in the excitement, Filbert had found his way down to the lower level and was sitting by the back door.

"I'm sorry, little man. You need to stay here." He complained and tried to wriggle free when I picked him up. I took the lift back to the bridge and placed him in the grav-box. We didn't need the distraction.

Nick and I entered the cargo bay and exited through the airlock. We'd set the suits to communicate over a very low-power, line-of-site band. We couldn't afford to have a ship pick up our location.

The asteroid had no discernable gravity, but we hugged the surface anyway, snaking our way back around to where the habitation dome had been. I saw tell-tale signs of our operation, but nothing that could be identified easily from a ship. Someone had done a masterful job of removing all evidence of a habitation.

"Take cover!" Nick's voice exploded in my ear.

I lit the arc-jets on both my boots and gloves and jumped to the side. Something impacted my shoulder and since I wasn't in contact with the asteroid, I spun over in an awkward barrel roll. I fought against the induced spin and dove down to the asteroid.

"I'm pinned down," Nick said.

"Are you hit?" I asked.

"No, but there's fire coming from the swale," he said. I'd found a large boulder and was currently doing okay. But like Nick, I was pinned down by blaster fire. If it hadn't been for my armored vac-suit I'd likely be dead.

"I think it's your parents, Liam. They don't know who we are," Nick said.

It made sense but I didn't have any idea how to get in contact with them. If we transmitted over an open comm channel we'd attract even more attention than the blaster fire. I imagined Dad had decided we were part of the raiding party and was making his last stand.

"I'm going to have to go on open channel. Those cutters will definitely see the blaster fire," I said.

"Agreed. It's a good chance they've already picked up on it."

Establish comm on Hoffen Channel One. I assumed that my parents hadn't kicked me out of our family's comm channel.

"Mom. Dad. Stop shooting. I'm dropping the comm channel, there are hostiles nearby," I said.

Terminate all comms. Re-establish line of sight comm with Nick, Big Pete and Mom.

The blaster fire immediately ceased. I hoped that it wasn't a coincidence. I raised my hands over my head, illuminated my face within my helmet and slowly peeked around the crag which I was hiding behind.

"Liam?" Mom's voice came over the comm. "What are you doing here?"

I doused my helmet's light.

"There are pirate ships nearby. We could be in danger," I said. "I had to transmit on a comm channel and they're likely tracking those."

"Right, but we were blasting away at you and Nick. They'd see that just as soon," Big Pete said.

Blaster fire lanced across the ground where we'd been hiding just moments ago. Some ship, probably one of the cutters, had clearly locked onto our comm signal. Luckily, the ships were having a hard time distinguishing our suits from the rocky surface and would need to illuminate the area to find us.

"We gotta get out of here. Follow me. That fire came from the same direction as our ship. Make sure your arc-jets are aimed directly behind you. They won't be able to pick that up," I said.

"Why aren't they firing at your ship?" Big Pete asked.

"You'll see. Let's move and keep your jets to a minimum," I said. I popped my glove's arc-jets in the direction of the *Hotspur*.

"We can hunker down. We've got cover," Mom said. Blaster fire continued to rip up the surface of the asteroid, but fortunately we were moving away from it.

"I wouldn't count on that, Mrs. Hoffen," Nick warned. "We've seen two cutters buzz this asteroid in the last twenty minutes.

They're clearly looking for something."

We didn't have time for argument. "I need you to trust me right now. We have a ship, but we're risking my crew by staying here."

"You want us to come with you?" Dad asked.

"Yes. Trust me, Dad," I said. "If you don't like what you see, then you can come back."

"What's your play here?" Big Pete asked.

"We came for you and Mom," I said. "These guys aren't taking prisoners and they're destroying everything they come into contact with. If you're found, it will be bad for you and worse for Mom."

That got his attention. "You have a ship?"

"That's what I said."

A second cutter pulled up alongside the first. It was creepy that they were within two hundred meters of the *Hotspur* but appeared to have absolutely no idea we were there. Bright spotlights shown down on the surface. Their ship's AIs apparently were able to identify something that was off, as they started blasting away at the location where our home had been. It was heartbreaking, but the distraction was probably saving our lives.

"Nick, you and Mom go first. Dad and I will wait until you've cycled through the airlock," I said.

He didn't respond other than to slowly glide to our ship, Mom following closely. It seemed like a lifetime as they cycled into the lock. I felt like the security panel of the lock was a flashing strobe when Nick touched it. Dad and I lifted off and reached the door just as it opened. Nick had thoughtfully evacuated the atmo and opened the lock behind him so that Dad and I could enter without waiting.

"Ada, we're all on board. Can you get us out of here?"

"Happy to, Captain. I'll have to take it slow, a third cutter just showed up. Crap, Liam. I think he saw us. Get up here!" I heard the panic in her voice and took off at a dead run.

HIDE 'N SEEK

"Shut down engines, full dark," I told her. Ada had the helm and would have to give the instructions. I jumped on to the lift and left my bewildered parents on the berth deck without any explanation. If not for my HUD projecting the outline of the bridge onto my eye I would have no doubt fallen on my face in my race to the cockpit.

Once I'd landed in the chair I saw what Ada was talking about. A brightly lit medium sized cutter was sailing directly at us. No doubt the cutter had caught our engines lighting up as we pushed away from the asteroid. If they knew exactly where we were, or what we were, there'd be a lot more activity than them just moving toward us. Without our engines running and with our light absorptive armor, however, they were simply moving toward what, for them, would have been a flash of light. I imagined the captain of the cutter replaying the video stream of whatever the sensors had caught.

"What do you have?"

Big Pete had found his way to the cockpit and was kneeling on the steps between the pilot's chairs. He was still talking over the line of sight communications channel we'd established on the asteroid.

Add Pete and Silver Hoffen as bridge crew. By adding them to the crew their AI would be able to show them what we were all seeing - which was a twenty-five meter long ship that we could crush in an instant, but that would alert the big boys to our presence.

"If I don't move, they'll run right into us," I said.

The AI showed the path the cutter was on and it would graze the belly of our ship if I didn't adjust our position. I tapped the arc-jets ever so gently. Unlike our engines, the arc-jets were shielded with long cowls that blocked the visible light from escaping in all but the direction of thrust.

The *Hotspur* rolled gently out of the path of the oncoming cutter, which passed beneath us by no more than fifteen meters.

We sat quietly for five minutes when Big Pete finally broke the silence. "How is it they didn't pick us up?"

"Ship's designed to run quiet, but we're not out of this yet," I said.

I pumped the arc-jets so that we moved away on a perpendicular path. The two cutters who had been focused on the surface turned, coming toward us and spreading out to form a wide noose. The AIs were just too intelligent and would be able to predict where we were going or at least how best to pen us in.

"Nick, can you help Mom and Big Pete find a place to strap in? This might get dicey. Marny, did they drop a comm disrupter?" I hadn't seen any updated comms, but we'd also been pretty busy.

"Aye, Cap," she replied.

"How far can those cutters communicate?"

"Line of sight, just like us," she answered.

Engage combat controls, I directed.

"What are you doing, Liam," Dad asked.

"Keep comm clear, Dad," I said. I hoped he wouldn't challenge me on this. "And get strapped in. The grav generator is good, but this baby… aah frak! Incoming."

Disengage silent running. I jammed the throttle stick forward and tipped the directional stick over to the port side at forty-five degrees.

"Liam, don't be crazy…" Big Pete started.

Lock out Big Pete from combat comm, I commanded. On second thought I added, *allow him to monitor*.

The forward holo jumped to life and the cutters all swung around to orient on me. They were spaced less than three hundred meters apart and were acting like wolves who had picked up the scent of their prey. 'Careful what you wish for,' I thought, wryly. I spun around and accelerated madly between the first two that had been closest to the asteroid.

"Nick, track the third one. We can't afford to let any of them get away," I said.

"Taking fire, port side," Ada said.

I could hear the thrapping of blaster fire against the hull. Hide and seek had once again turned into a game of chicken. We might have been outmatched and outgunned in the entire combat arena, but right here, right now, we were the big boys on the block.

Before I saw anything, I heard the familiar burping sound of our three turrets. From the sound of it, Marny wasn't leaving anything to chance and was pouring a full stream of fire into both ships. Once we were within a hundred meters, I flipped the *Hotspur* over and accelerated in-line with their trajectory. I wanted to give Marny as much time as possible in the *Hotspur's* turret range.

We slid between the two cutters and I watched the energy in the batteries spin down below fifty percent. Our hunters - turned quarry - must have realized the danger they were in as they were now accelerating on combat burn to get away. Marny continued to pour on the fire and I accelerated hard to keep up with them. We were pinned back in our seats, the gravity generators unable to keep up with the demands of the burn. I hoped Mom and Dad had locked in.

"Number three's making a run for P-Zero," Nick said. I glanced up and saw the ship exiting the area. I knew it had originally burned toward us to participate in the takedown, but at some point the captain had changed his mind. "We've got to get him before he calls in reinforcements."

"Marny? How long on these two?" I asked.

"Ten seconds, Cap," she answered. As if in response, one of the two cutters exploded. Marny directed all three turrets onto the second damaged ship which, in turn, exploded.

"Nice shooting." I flipped the *Hotspur* over so that we lined up on the fleeing ship.

How long before we overtake? I asked.

Twelve hundred kilometers. The AI could be frustrating when it randomly chose to take me literally. I really wanted to know how much time, but on quick reflection I realized that the distance was more relevant. We'd started at twenty-three hundred kilometers out and the AI was letting us know that we'd almost be back to the Colony's core by the time we caught up with it.

"Frak. We've got to get him," I said, uselessly. *Emergency burn one hundred ten percent.*

"Let him go, Liam," Mom's voice came over the comm. I really didn't want to mute her too. "Listen to me. Use this time to regain your cover. It's not like they aren't going to figure out what happened."

"I agree," Nick said. I pulled back on the throttle stick and veered off.

Engage silent running, take us out of combat. I briefly considered how we'd evolved to such a spot where I'd do what Nick said without question, but not my mom.

I tipped the directional stick to the side and continued to accelerate at a thirty percent burn. We'd skim past on the outside of the colony's main core. I wasn't ready to test if the *Hotspur* would be picked up by the colony's sensor array. Not yet, at least. I laid in a course to take us out an hour away from Colony 40.

"We're going to heave-to and let things settle down. You should be okay to take off the combat harnesses," I announced.

"I got up and walked back to the bridge stations where Nick and Marny were still seated.

"Nick, how bad does our armor look?" I asked.

"We took some hits, but it's holding okay."

"Marny, weapon systems?"

"All green," she answered.

I turned to where Big Pete and Silver were still both seated on the bridge couch. "Are you guys alright?" I asked. "I'm sorry I cut you off before, Dad."

"Had to be done. You put me in my place and good, son. But if you thought that'd piss me off, you'd be wrong. I had no business interrupting your chain of command." He held his hand out to me to shake. I took it and pulled him in for an embrace.

Mom gave me a hug. "It's good to see you, Liam." She let me go and then pulled Nick in for a hug.

"Silver, Pete, I'd like to introduce you to our security officer, Marny Bertrand," I said. Marny had walked up behind Nick.

"Good to meet you, ma'am, sir," Marny said, extending her hand.

"Call me Pete. I work for a living," Pete shook her hand, responding with a twinkle in his eye. I'd never seen him respond to anyone like that before.

"And pilot, Ada Chen," I said before Marny could say anything.

Ada stepped forward and hugged a surprised Big Pete and then Mom, in turn.

"Let's head down to the mess," I said. "There's plenty of room to sit and I bet you're hungry, living down in that hole."

"I've got a clean suit liner that I bet would fit you, Mrs. Hoffen. And the head has a wonderful new shower in it," Ada said, walking next to my mom, behind me.

"Please call me Silver, and that sounds wonderful. We've been in these suits since we got Liam's message," she answered.

Marny had engaged Dad. "Mr. Hoffen. Liam tells me you were active in the Amazonian war."

"Both of us were. I don't think Liam knows it, but that's where Silver and I met. She was a combat drop pilot. You carry yourself like you served. Am I right?"

My mind was blown. Who was this guy? He was positively chatty.

"Aye, that I did. Five years on the ground in Africa," she said.

Pete shook his head. "I don't miss that place."

Once in the mess, I pulled two cups, filled them with coffee, and handed them to my parents.

"How long are we hunkering down, Cap?" Marny asked.

"Nick?" I wasn't the right person for that question. In the heat of the moment, we typically leaned on my tactical skills, but for long term strategy Nick was often thinking well ahead of me.

"Not sure. Did you get any word from my family, Mr. Hoffen?" Nick asked.

"Five days back, after we got your message, we ran to P-Zero and talked to several people. We'd thought to pick up supplies, but once communications were down, all of the supplies evaporated," Mom said. "We asked Wendy and Jack to come out to the claim with us and hide, but Wendy said she had a plan."

"Any idea what that plan was?" Nick sounded a little better knowing that his Mom was aware of what was coming.

"She said they were getting off the station, but she didn't say where to," Mom answered.

"How about, Mr. Masters? Tabby's dad," I asked.

"He was on one of the ships that got out. At least that was the plan. We've been in the dark for a few days," Mom stared at the table. The stress of the last several days was evident.

"Mrs. Hoffen, there's nothing you could have done. It's an impossible situation and we're lucky to have found you alive," Ada said. "You can't feel guilty for that. These pirates killed my mom, but her last act was to save me. Not a day goes by where I don't think about it. I know my mom wouldn't want me to feel like I'd failed because I lived."

"And we're not giving up," Marny interjected. "We've got something these pirates have trouble understanding and that's purpose."

"Thank you," Mom said quietly. Big Pete slid an arm around her and pulled her in close. It made me think of Tabby.

"I've got bad news on your home, Mr. Hoffen," Nick said. Pete and Mom looked at him and he continued, "I replayed what the *Hotspur* recorded, those cutters broke through your rock wall. It looks like they pretty well destroyed everything. I sent the video over to your queue."

"Thank you, Nick," Mom reached out and patted his arm. "There's not much that can be done."

Marny stepped up beside Nick and changed the conversation, "It will take fifteen minutes to get something worth eating down here - and that's if I have help. Liam, go to the armory and get an armored suit for Silver and Pete. I noticed that Silver's packing a laser pistol. Pete you have anything?"

"I don't," he said. I found that unusual. Last time I'd seen him, he was packing.

She pointed at the door. "Take Big Pete with you, Liam. He no doubt knows his way around an armory. Everyone needs to be armed at all times. I don't think we'll get boarded, but if it were ever going to happen, this would be the place for it."

Ada had disappeared and returned holding a suit liner. She handed it to my mom. "There's a head on both decks. The door right behind us is the main head. I'll show you where the suit freshener is when you get out."

Dad followed me out to the cargo bay. I led him through a small maze that ended in the doors to the container we'd welded to the floor of the cargo bay.

"Where'd you learn to sail like that?"

"It's not a lot different than an ore-sled, just bigger," I said.

"You must have gotten that from your mom."

"I didn't know you guys met in the service. For that matter, I didn't know Mom had seen active duty." I turned up the lights in the container. "What do you think?" There was a row of pistols, both laser and flechette, blaster rifles, grenade marbles, flash bang discs and several things I didn't recognize.

"Where'd you get your hands on all of this?" he asked.

"Last mission. We borrowed it all from the Navy. It's possible we left them with the impression that it had all been destroyed when the pirates blew up our ship. About Mom. You tell complete strangers how you met her, but not me. Don't you find that weird?"

"It never seemed that important before. Besides, your mom says I need to open up more, that maybe you'd have stayed closer if I had. You don't buy that, do you?" he asked.

"Dad. How about you pick out a suit and weapon and I'll get one for Mom. She's the same size as Tabby or at least pretty close."

"I see you've upgraded your flechette. You have another Ruger like the one you're packing?"

"I think so. They're on the left," I said.

He looked over the selections and asked, "Do you have a plan?"

"Communications being down is making it hard. We were lucky that you hunkered down and were out on the edge. We couldn't have pulled that off if you'd been on station," I said. "We'll talk it through and come up with something, though."

"Count me in," he said selecting a pistol, which he handed to me. He then grabbed an armored vac-suit.

"We've got a second head on the bridge deck. Can you shower in five minutes? You don't want to be late for dinner," I said.

"That Marny runs a pretty tight ship," he said.

"You have no idea." I handed him the flechette he'd selected and led him back into the berth deck. We took the lift up and I showed him the head. "We'll be in the mess when you're ready. There's a suit freshener just outside the door."

It occurred to me that I'd left Filbert locked in the grav-box for the last several hours. When I opened the door, he looked up at me lazily and stretched a small arm up. I slid my hands under his blanket and pulled him out. When I got back to the mess, I handed him to Ada.

How Marny always seemed to come up with an amazing meal continued to surprise me. Somewhere she'd hidden a large sim-beef roast, which she and Nick presented with steaming potatoes and a thick brown gravy. She poured two large carafes full of a pinkish wine.

"I didn't think we were probably strong wine connoisseurs and decided to play it safe with a blush," she said almost apologetically.

"It looks delicious. Do you always eat this well?" Silver asked.

"Only on special occasions, which today certainly is. War is uncertain. We have to celebrate our victories when we have them. Today we recovered family and kept them safe from pirates. I'd say that qualifies," I added.

My dad looked at me, "Hear, hear." He raised his glass and drank deeply from it. "You've only been gone several months, but you talk of war like a veteran. I'd hoped you wouldn't have to go down that path."

"I'm sorry, Mr. Hoffen," Marny said, a little proudly, I thought.

"But our dear Captain Liam has already seen more combat than most maggots will for their entire career - Amazonian deployments excepted, that is."

"It's not hard to see it in his eyes. War takes a toll on good people," Mom said.

I needed to stop this. "We only do what we have to do. We aren't fighting a war, we're just trying to keep our heads above water."

"You have a real problem keeping your nose out of other people's trouble, though," Ada said. "And I, for one, am grateful."

I raised my glass and nodded my head appreciatively to Ada. Somehow she'd become the sister I'd never known I needed, but she was as much family to me as my parents, Nick, Tabby or Marny.

"So, Pete. From what I've heard, you were a cage monkey," Marny said.

"Cage monkey?" I asked.

"Guilty as charged. Three tours," he said.

Marny smiled in my direction. "Mechanized Infantry, Liam. Us squishies referred to the mechs as cage monkeys because they were all locked up in their cages. Navy used to hang 'em from rails in the drop ships like so much laundry, hung out to dry. I thought we talked about this."

"We talked about mechanized infantry and squishies. We never talked about monkeys," I said.

"How did you and Pete meet, Silver?" Ada asked.

"I was a Marine drop pilot," Mom said, smiling at Pete. "He actually rescued me when we got shot down."

Big Pete cleared his throat, "Didn't actually work like that. I agree, it was my plan to rescue her, but in the end she was the one doing all the rescuing. If I'd just left her alone, we'd both have been home and in bed a lot earlier."

"But, we'd never have met. I'd like to think that fate was on our side that day," Mom rested her head against his shoulder.

"Then you'll never believe what we picked up," Marny said.

Pete just stared at her, not really being the twenty questions type of guy.

"A suit. Well, actually three of them. Brand new, still in the box," she said.

"Well, that's illegal. Where'd you find them?" Pete asked.

"The Red Houzi outpost we sacked. We'll probably have to give them back to M-Pro, but they're in the hold at the moment," I answered.

"I'd like to see that," he said.

Marny winked. "I thought you might."

For the next forty-five minutes we continued to chat and it felt almost like old times, like we were sitting around the table after a long shift of mining. The main difference was that Dad was chatty. Something about Marny caused him to open up. Maybe he saw a kindred spirit in her.

After dinner, while cleaning off the table, an idea struck me. "Nick, I was thinking. If the comm device in my quarters is quantum, I bet it can't be tracked. We should have the ability to talk to Belcose."

"You're right on both counts," he said.

"If they're willing to put one of these devices on our ship, what are the odds that there's another one, maybe on the station," I asked.

"You think the Navy has a contact on Colony 40?" Pete asked.

"Wouldn't have to be a spy. Probably not the local sheriff, given how well that worked out. But, it could just be someone they trust," Marny said.

"It's worth a shot," Nick said.

With Mom and Dad comfortable on the bridge couch and Ada at the helm, Nick, Marny and I sat around the small office room next to my sleeping quarters. I pulled the communications device off the shelf and assembled it, placing an energy crystal into the device. On a previous journey, we'd learned that the Navy had been using the device to spy on our activities. It wasn't completely unwarranted, but I guess I just didn't like not having a say in it.

"Belcose, you there? Over," I said. He didn't answer right away, but that was to be expected. I waited thirty seconds and repeated the call. It took five tries, but finally he answered.

"Lieutenant Belcose here. Please identify yourself," his familiar voice responded.

"Liam Hoffen, Gregor. Can you validate that this signal can't be tracked?" I asked. "We're transmitting behind enemy lines."

"Affirmative. The quantum crystals have no signature. Please advise on your location," he said.

"Colony 40," I said. "We're trying to locate Nick's mom and brother. Do you have any information?"

"I can't share that information," Belcose answered.

"Don't be like that, Lieutenant," I said evenly. "We need to find them, these guys are animals."

"Wait one," he responded.

We waited uncomfortably for Belcose to respond.

"What do you think he's doing?" Ada asked.

Before I could answer we heard a woman's voice. "Captain Hoffen?"

"Yes, this is Liam Hoffen," I said.

"Commander Sterra here. It is good to hear your voice, Captain. We'd heard a report of a ship being destroyed." she asked.

"I can confirm that report. We were flushed out by a trio of cutters. We destroyed two of them."

"Captain," she started and then said a little more softly, "Liam, you're in grave danger. Enemy contact is not advised."

"We have a lot of friends and family on the station. Do you have any information?"

"Several hours ago the Red Houzi pirate clan raided the station, killing most of the inhabitants. So far, their mode of operation would suggest that anyone left behind, undiscovered, is murdered when they blow up the station. The only reason I'm telling you what I am is to convince you to move out of that area. I cannot stress enough how dangerous of a position you are in."

"What would you have us do? That's our family."

"We all do what we must, Captain. Sterra out."

PEAS IN A POD

I took a deep breath and looked around the table. "What's your take?"

"Sterra's holding something back," Marny said.

I was at a loss here. "There could be as many as a two thousand people on that station."

"Everyone who had a ship took off. You saved a lot of people with your warning, but there are probably a few hundred left on the station," Dad said from the door. I hadn't noticed that he'd been listening to our conversation.

I looked back at him to include him in the conversation. "I'd like to get closer and see how tight their security is. They can't be monitoring all of the bays. Maybe we could sneak into one."

"They'll be looking for us," Nick said.

"Let them look. Let's go find out what's happening down there." Everyone nodded. For once, we had home field advantage.

All sections report, I requested. I was seated in the cockpit, ready to go.

"Weapons are green," Marny replied.

"Bridge is secure. All passengers and crew are strapped in," Nick replied.

"You ready for this, Ada?" I asked. She sat next to me in the cockpit.

"It's been an honor sailing with you, Liam."

It was hard to keep from approaching too fast. I had no idea if the pirates had co-opted the sensor net. It had been tuned to look for potential asteroid collisions with critical structures. I'd hoped, by sailing dark, that if the sensor net detected us, it would see us as an asteroid and by sailing in on a non-direct path we wouldn't raise collision alarms.

"Ship on starboard," Ada said quietly.

A cutter passed beneath us at a distance of forty kilometers.

"Think they're still looking for us?" I asked.

"Aye. That they are, Cap," Marny answered. "I doubt they're very happy about losing those ships."

"We're closing in on the edge of the sensor net," I said. As we'd gotten closer I'd picked out a path that I knew well and slowed the *Hotspur* down to the speed of a local ore sled. The AI was projecting an estimated sensor strength of the net on my HUD. I watched a thermometer-styled gauge as it grew from nothing, ticked up rapidly and then showed a full bar. I'd been holding my breath.

"Port side, Cap. Ten degrees declination," Marny broke the silence.

I hadn't had to think about degrees in quite a while, but Marny's AI saved me the work by communicating what she was looking at. It was one of the frigates. If they'd seen us, they were doing a really good job of not tipping their hand. We sailed along quietly and I had no doubt that all six of us were tracking the frigate as we passed by.

Finally, we'd reached the asteroid I'd been looking for. Using nothing but arc-jets, I slowed us down and swung the ship around, sliding into a tunnel through the asteroid that I knew stretched two hundred meters to the other side.

"Frak!" I exclaimed. I had to hit the throttle to abruptly bleed off our remaining forward momentum. The tunnel that I'd planned on using to cloak our ship was occupied. A powder blue runabout sat in the tunnel.

"Nick, you seeing this?" I asked.

"Cap, Nick's gone. He jumped on the lift," Marny said.

"Marny, go! Dad, take the gunnery station. Ada, you have the helm. If you have to leave us to protect the ship, do it," I said.

I jumped from my seat and sprinted to the lift, using my arc-jets as I fell through the hole - Marny had already lowered the lift. I landed hard next to her but didn't think twice about it. Once through the door to the cargo bay, Marny grabbed the two blaster rifles that she'd strategically positioned. Nick had already cycled through the lock. I wished he'd given us even a second to catch up with him. I jammed my hand on the security panel to refill the lock with atmo.

"That's his mom's runabout," I explained.

"Aye. I figured it had to be something like that," Marny said as we cycled through the lock and into the tunnel. There was virtually no light and we'd been lucky that, in the enclosed space, the passive sensors of the *Hotspur* had picked up on the small structure of the vehicle.

We arc-jetted past the nose of the *Hotspur*. My AI had perfect recollection of this tunnel's interior. We'd spent quite a bit of time in it several months ago, scraping the broken remains of my ore-sled from one of the walls. I recalled the chase where Tabby had clipped the back of my sled, sending me careening into the wall. So much had changed since then.

A dim light glowed from within the runabout. Someone had cycled the atmo and I could make out figures standing next to the vehicle. My heart leapt as I caught a familiar shock of red hair. We'd found Jack, Nick's brother.

Initially, I thought that they were just embracing so that their helmets would make contact. As I got closer I could see that Nick's shoulders had sagged and that he was patting Jack's back.

"Let's secure the area, Marny."

I wasn't really that worried about the area as much as I wanted to give the two brothers a few moments of privacy. Marny didn't question it and swept wide of the craft. Once on the backside I dared to look into the rear of the vehicle, only to see the deceased body of Nick and Jack's mother, Wendy.

I caught Marny's attention and pointed my fingers at my eyes then into the back of the runabout. Even through her face plate I watched her jaw muscles contract. We walked back around to the other side. Nick and Jack had separated.

Add Jack James to line of sight comm channel.

Stress was evident in Jack's drawn face. I wrapped my arms around him, "I'm sorry, Jack." His return embrace was stronger than I'd expected.

After a few moments I felt it was necessary to move out. "It's not safe here," I said. "What can we take back to the ship?"

"Jack and I will bring Mom," Nick said.

After Jack and Nick extracted Wendy's body from the vehicle, I searched for anything that Jack might have left behind. We wouldn't have enough room to bring the vehicle with us, but if I was careful, the *Hotspur* would be able to scootch over the top. With our AI's record of their position, it shouldn't be overly difficult.

Back on the ship, Nick pulled out a large black sack. It was the reality of spaceflight that traveling with a body bag was important. Wendy had been a second mother to me while growing up. I'd spent almost as much time around her as I had my own mother. My throat constricted and I wanted to scream in frustration.

Marny and I helped Nick and Jack situate Wendy in the bag and strapped it into an open space on the hull wall. It was so final and cold. The woman that I'd grown up with was now dead and I was having difficulty thinking past this moment.

"Mom, would you come down? We found Jack."

"What about Wendy?" she asked.

"She didn't make it, Mom."

Her breath caught and she said, "I'll be right there."

I pulled Jack in for another hug. I wanted to ask what had happened and how he'd been able to escape, but I knew it was too early for him. When we'd put Wendy into the bag, scorch marks had been evident on her abdomen. The suit had clearly staunched the blood, but a suit could only do so much. I was proud that Jack remembered the tunnel in the asteroid. It was an excellent hiding place and had allowed us to find him. Whatever happened, I worried that the trauma would worsen his nearly speechless existence.

"Jack. You did good. No matter what happened, you did what Wendy would have wanted. You survived and that was what she wanted. From now on, you're part of the crew." I didn't want to let go of him. "I need to go take care of the ship and get us out of here, okay?"

I pulled back and looked at Jack. His face was grimy and tearstained, but he nodded, he understood.

Mom had entered the hold while I'd been talking. "Let's get you cleaned up," she said softly. Jack nodded again and followed her out.

I turned to Nick and my heart broke. His Dad had died years ago and Wendy and Jack were his entire family. I knew him well enough to know that he'd be feeling guilty about not being around when things had gone bad. He allowed me to hug him. I also knew there wasn't much I could say to him at the moment, he'd need to process it.

"Marny, take care of my buddy, will you? We'll hole up here for a while, we have some time."

I left the two of them alone in the hold. Nick would need time to say goodbye to his mom. I found my dad in the mess just staring at the table, a cup of coffee in front of him.

"Dad, how comfortable are you with turrets?" I asked.

"I'm rusty, but they'd be familiar enough."

"I'll take that. If we have to fight our way out of here, we sure could use a steady hand."

"I'll do my best," he said. I could tell he was relieved to have something to do. As a rule, we Hoffens weren't much for sharing emotions and this was the equivalent of a lifeline.

He followed me and I checked him into the forward bridge station. I watched as he registered with the guns and I suspected he'd be more than competent at the job. I slid into my pilot's chair next to Ada.

"What happened?" she asked on a cockpit only channel.

As I filled Ada in on what we'd discovered, her jaw went slack and her eyes filled with tears.

"Mom's taking care of Jack. Marny and Nick are having some quiet time," I finished.

"It's too much. They take too much," Ada said and I knew she was talking about her own mother.

I was beyond grief at this point. Too many good people had died for greed or simple political gain or whatever it was these pirates were after. I wanted to make them pay dearly. I also knew that I needed to keep my head clear. We'd be in danger if I started getting reckless out of a desire for revenge.

"We have to focus on getting out of here alive," I said.

Ada nodded her agreement.

"I think you have enough room to clear the runabout. Can you take us to the end of the tunnel, but stay back ten meters?"

"Can do, Captain," Ada said. Somewhere along the line I'd become Captain to her, no longer just Liam.

She expertly lifted us over the runabout and we slid down to the end of the tunnel. I'd chosen this asteroid because I knew we could hide inside while getting a clean view of P-Zero, the colony's main station. It had been a tight squeeze for the *Hotspur*, but it felt like a safe spot.

With the enhanced vision of the ship's passive sensors, we finally saw the two large destroyers orbiting P-Zero. I counted three of the frigates and four of the cutters as well. That left a single frigate and up to four cutters that could be running around looking for us.

We would observe the main station and come up with a plan based on what we found. For me, everything changed once we'd located Jack and Wendy. I felt a pang of guilt. No doubt there were people on the station suffering, but we had no chance against the force we were looking at.

"Pull back ten meters, arc-jets only," I said. I probably didn't need to say the latter, but in that situation, being too clear was forgivable. "Let's hold here for now and record the activity. I'd like to figure out what they're up to."

A huge freighter was docked next to the refinery. The refined ore, was the majority of the colony's wealth. It made sense that most of the pirate's efforts would be devoted to its removal. Over a period of a couple of hours we were able to account for all but two cutters.

"They'll open fire on the station once they're done at the

refinery. A good number of people escaped because of your warning. Wendy thought that she and Jack had a good spot to hide. The pirates must have found them," Dad said. He was kneeling on the steps between Ada and me, looking through the cockpit glass.

"I don't see a single move we could make that would help," I said.

"Then don't move. Sometimes the best action is to stay put," he said. "Your warning gave us time to work out a plan and get people to refuge. We sent the young families away first. You wouldn't believe how tough those old miners were, refusing to take a transport spot, even though they knew what was coming. You think you know people, but the only ones who stayed to defend Colony 40 were the crusty old bastards who'd used up their lives on these rocks."

I looked over my shoulder and noticed that the bridge had filled with all of my family. I needed to deal with it. It was easy to feel safe inside our little cocoon, but I knew that could change instantly. It would be dangerous for everyone to be milling around.

"Jack, I've got a job for you," I said. I pulled Filbert out of the grav-box and handed him to Jack. "Mom, Dad, I bet you're exhausted. You take my room. Jack, you and I will hot-bunk in the aft bunk room with Ada. Ada, you have the helm. If anything changes, call me right away."

I placed my arm around Jack's shoulders and led him to the lift, dropping through the floor to the berth deck. "Jack," I started, "Filbert is a survivor, but needs someone to look after him. There's a grav-box that we haven't had a chance to install yet. Take the top bunk and I'll bring the box in for you and you can mount it to the wall." We were standing just outside of the aft bunk room. Jack nodded his agreement. He was in much better shape once Mom had made him shower and clean his suit.

I found the grav-box and tools and dropped them in Jack's room. He was enthralled with Filbert, for which I was thankful. I closed the door and hopped on the lift.

"So, we wait?" Marny asked. She'd reclaimed her chair from Big Pete and slid it over to the table where I was seated.

"What else can we do?" I asked.

"If those destroyers have fighters on board, we wouldn't last long."

"You know that's what Tabby's been called up for. She's training to fly fighters," I said. "I'm not sure they'd let her fly one yet, though."

"That's how they train 'em, Cap. Baptism by fire. They'll have her flying a fighter within six months. Not in combat, mind you, but patrols can get dicey. Not everyone is happy to see the Navy show up."

"Liam, you better get up here," Ada called over the comm.

I ran to the cockpit and slid into my seat.

"Marny, you seeing this?" I asked.

The two destroyers had stopped their orbit around the station and come alongside each other with a frigate above and below each of them. The cutters had also moved in next to the destroyers. It was definitely some sort of formation.

"I thought maybe they were going to dock with each other, but I think something else is going on," Ada said.

"Something's in the system," Marny said. "That's a combat spread."

The destroyers were steaming forward, away from the station, as if it was all but forgotten. The problem was they were heading directly at us.

WAR

"Ada, I want you to back us up out of this asteroid as quietly as you possibly can. If you see a place to turn around, do it." Ada had a much finer touch on the controls and I needed time to think.

"I've got it," she responded.

"Marny, do you think they saw us?" I asked.

"No. I know it looks like that, but that's a crazy response," she said. "We're just not that big of a threat."

Ada gently spun us around in a spot I wouldn't have thought possible and we approached the other entrance.

"All crew, please take a seat. The Red Houzi fleet is on the move and we appear to be in their path," I announced. "Ada, take us out and poke us up above the horizon so we can see their approach."

We were still running dark and our sensors weren't at their best, but it wasn't difficult to see the approaching fleet of sixteen warships.

Calculate trajectory for the enemy fleet. Plot on forward holo.

I reasoned that if they were coming for us, the additional light of the holo wasn't going to tell them anything new. If they were focused on something else I'd think the same would be true. The holo displayed P-Zero, and the nearby larger asteroids along with the ships. A cylinder of translucent blue predicted their navigational path. They would pass above our asteroid at five kilometers. I sighed with relief, knowing they weren't coming directly for us.

"Nick, Marny, any ideas about what's going on?"

"It has to be Mars Protectorate," Marny said. "It's the only reason they'd form up so tightly."

I wanted to cheer. If the Navy was here, this fight was about to be over. I was surprised that the Red Houzi Fleet hadn't simply fled from the threat. Surely they couldn't stand against the Navy.

"Why wouldn't they flee?" I asked.

"Good question. M-Pro knows the size of this fleet. They certainly wouldn't be here without knowing they could win the fight."

"This might be our opportunity to rescue survivors from the station," I said. "Ada, sail us around on the opposite side of the asteroid as the fleet sails over the top of us."

I hastily drew a navigation path that would keep us behind asteroids on our way over to P-Zero. "Once they're past, take this route. It should keep us well out of their line of site."

I got up from my chair and walked through the bridge back to my office. Nick joined me as he saw me pass. I pulled out the communications box and picked up the handset.

"*Kuznetsov*, come in, this is *Hotspur*," I said.

I wasn't surprised that he answered immediately. "Belcose here."

"Red Houzi fleet is formed up and moving. I believe they are anticipating the arrival of a fleet," I said.

"Roger that. Can you transmit their current location and trajectory?"

Nick fired up the Morse protocol and a series of fast beeps could be heard.

"Thank you, Captain," he said. "Is there anything else?"

"Is your contact still on the station?" I asked.

"Yes."

"We're going to land in docking bay twelve, green level. We'd like to take as many survivors off as possible. I don't want to be on station for more than a few minutes. Can you get that word over to them? Do you have a head count?"

"Twenty-five souls. And I'll get word over to them. Belcose out," he said.

I'd been expecting hundreds. It must have been a massacre. I wondered how many people I'd grown up with were now dead at the hands of these murderers.

"We need to dump the containers that just have rubbish in them," Nick said. We'd originally planned to recycle the materials, but they were taking up much needed room.

"How long will O2 hold out with twenty-five additional?" I asked.

"It will stretch us, but we should be okay. I'm more worried about the septic," Nick answered.

"Crap, why is it always that?" I asked, flinching at my use of that curse word. "Hopefully, this is temporary and M-Pro will take them off our hands."

"Dad, can you meet me in the hold?" I asked, jumping on the lift. For a moment it refused to drop. He must have been passing beneath me.

I found him in the hold, waiting expectantly. "What's up?"

"We're going to land in docking bay twelve on the green level and I need you to dump the following crates out when we do." I pinched the list of junk crates from my HUD and tossed it at him.

"What's in the crates?" he asked.

"Just junk, we were going to run it through the reclaimer. Can you unload these in less than ten minutes?"

"You've got forty crates on here. It's not possible."

"I didn't tell you the best part." I lifted the top off the large crate that held the new mechanized infantry suit we'd taken from the outpost. "Could you do it in this?" I gestured dramatically like a game vid host.

"Right. If it has fuel and power, I sure can," he said, running his hands along the armor that was lying flat in the box.

"What do we need to do to get you in it?" I asked.

A moment later Dad had peeled off his vac-suit and was leaning over the crate, opening the mechanized suit's helmet. "We're in luck. It isn't registered. I suppose it would be hard to sell if it was all locked up." He placed his palm on a panel at the back of the neck. It was weird to see a suit that actually kept most of its shape while unoccupied. The joints moved slightly in response to startup and Dad brought his hand down the side of the chest, pulling it open. He perched on the side of the box, swung his legs around and slid them down into the suit. He lay back carefully into the open chest cavity and threaded his arms into the suit's arms. The suit did the rest, closing the chest and helmet sections with a series of mechanical clanks.

"I've missed this," he said. Rear arc-jets fired from his shoulders and he stood up. He was now a little over three meters tall and a meter and a half wide. "I've got half a load of ordinance and I'm fueled up. I'd say I can easily remove your crates."

"Good, I'm headed back to the bridge. I'll let you know when we're ready," I said. I watched for a moment as he flexed the suit around him. If he weren't my dad, I'd have been nervous to be this close to the man-machine combination.

"Cap, the M-Pro fleet has arrived and they're lighting it up, if we're going to do this, the time is now," Marny said.

"Ada. Punch it," I said. We could move at about sixty percent and stay dark. Fleet combat could take a few minutes or stretch out for hours. It depended a lot on how poorly balanced the fight was. The fact that the Red Houzi was headed out to meet them still confused me.

The *Hotspur* accelerated and the inertial system and gravity generator kicked in to make up for the rapid change.

"Mom, when we get there, can you help people onto the ship? We can't hold all twenty-five people in the main living space, but Dad's making room in the hold. I'm locking out the lift from all non-crew personnel," I said.

"Just let us know when," my mom replied.

"Liam, we're here," Ada said over the comm. "I'll have us down in sixty seconds."

Marny came down on the lift and followed me back out to the hold. I'd been transmitting all of my conversations to Nick and Marny so they knew what we were up to. I picked up a blaster rifle and handed one to Marny.

"You're terrifying, Pete," she said, admiring the unblemished, mechanized suit.

"Your captain has me working as a stevedore," he replied, amused.

Mom entered the hold as I locked the door and hit the atmo recycler. I would like to have timed it better so that we could have immediately opened the rear loading ramp when Ada came to a stop, but it took a full five minutes to remove the atmo. That seemed plenty fast under normal circumstances.

"We've got company, Cap," Marny said. She'd been monitoring the exterior video.

"Patch me in," Big Pete requested. After reviewing he said, "Looks like they left a squad of squishies behind. Let me clear the deck before you come out."

"Aye. You've got tactical control of the deck, Pete," Marny said. It was unusual for her to share tactical command with anyone, although it wasn't common for her to have someone around who was capable either, I supposed.

"Lower the ramp and stay back. This should only take a moment," he said.

I hit the button to lower the ramp and loaded a view screen in my HUD that showed what he was looking at. I wouldn't get all of the rich information he was receiving, but at least I would be able to see what had his direct attention.

The enemy squad had taken a position inside the open bay door. They clearly didn't want to come into range of the ship's turrets. I doubted those pirates had any idea we had a mechanized Marine, however. Pete exited the ship and bounded across the bay, immediately taking fire. I watched, through his HUD, as red target outlines jumped from one hostile to another. Instead of backing out or taking cover, Pete lobbed a grenade at the squad and charged forward, wading into the middle of a confused group, swinging his arms like giant clubs.

From my experience, it was the shortest combat I'd ever been involved in. An entire squad, taken out in less than thirty seconds.

"Do you think there are any more?" I asked Marny.

"Better than fair odds," she said.

"Okay, I'll go with Dad. Can you work on getting those crates outta there?" I tossed her the list.

"Aye. Just stay behind your dad's armor, Cap. That's what it's for."

"Nick, can you hear me? We don't have contact with the survivors. Can you establish communication with the station?" I asked.

"Yup. Working on it," he said.

We rounded a corner and saw an old man peering out from a doorway. Dad had also seen him as evidenced by a yellow outline highlighting the man's face.

"Red, you old scoundrel. This is your lucky day," Dad said. "You have the whole crew?"

The outline in my HUD changed from yellow to green.

"Pete?" The old miner asked. Red, I assumed.

"That's right. We're on a bit of a short leash here, Red. How many you have with you?"

"Everyone who's left. But there's several squads running around. You need to be careful." Red stepped into the hallway. I heard a thwap-thwap of blaster fire hitting the wall. I ducked down and lined up on where the fire was coming from. Red slumped over, falling toward me. His face shield had been pierced and he was obviously dead.

"Get down!" Dad ordered and as he spun to the left, fire erupted from both of his hands in short bursts. This squad was more careful and decided to duck behind a corner. I looked back to the man called Red. It was too awful to describe.

"Liam, get the rest of these people and make a run for the ship. This area is too open to defend." Dad's voice was calm but firm. It was the voice he used when he wanted me to do what he was saying and not argue.

I stepped into the room and had the AI do a quick head count. Twenty three. According to Belcose we should have one more.

"Listen up. We don't have far to go. We're just headed down to bay twelve. Big Pete can hold the hallway, but we have to move, now!" I said over an open comm. "I said MOVE." I pulled the first person out of the door and slowly got the group to start moving.

I grabbed the last person, looking at her through her helmet. It was Belta Goise. She wasn't a miner anymore, but did odd jobs around the station. "There should be one more, do you know who we're missing?"

"Austin Blathers. He's gone. Dead," she said.

"What happened?" I asked.

"Mouthed off one too many times. Couldn't figure out they were just going to kill us anyway. I think he thought they'd want to keep him alive," she explained. I remembered Austin. He wasn't that old, but had been injured in a mining accident where he'd lost his right arm.

"We're clear, Dad," I said as I helped Belta down the hallway. We were moving too slowly, but I had to remind myself that we were escorting a group of older people. I could cut them some slack, they had all given up their escape so that others could go.

Pete didn't turn around, but asked, "How's our count?"

"Got 'em all," I said.

He launched a fusillade of grenades at the end of the hallway and turned to follow us out. When we finally made it to the docking bay and closed the door, I breathed a sigh of relief.

"Ada, we're in, let's get out of here," I said and started filling the hold with atmo. Then I spoke out loud to the group. "I need you all to listen up. We're not really set up for a large number of guests, but Silver will organize care for you all. If you need something, please talk to her." I seriously couldn't get out of that hold quickly enough.

"Chicken," Marny said as she joined me on the lift.

"Any status?" I asked Nick.

"The main fight is taking place three thousand kilometers out. Best I can tell, M-Pro showed up with two corvettes and three destroyers. Red Houzi is getting thrashed," he answered.

"It's about time," I said. "Which destroyers? I wondered if Tabby was in the area and if I'd ever know."

"*Walter Sydney Adams, Theodore Dunham,* and the *Hipparchus,*" Nick replied.

"Tabby's on the *Dunham.*"

"They launched fighters about five minutes ago."

"Let's bring up full sensors."

"Agreed," Nick answered and we dropped out of silent running mode. It felt weird to see screens with data being displayed.

"Ahead slow, Ada. Let's not get in this, but we need to know how it's going to end."

With a full sensor package running, the holos displayed the battle in front of us and it was going very poorly for the Red Houzi. Their destroyers were all that remained and they were holding off the Navy fleet primarily because the Navy hadn't fully opened up on them. Maybe the Navy was attempting to negotiate a surrender instead of outright destroying them.

"What could they be thinking? Pirates aren't normally suicidal are they?" I asked.

"It is strange behavior," Marny acknowledge. "Something else is going on."

It was then that Ada saved all of us. *Emergency combat burn,* she yelled and pushed the throttle forward fully and pulled the flight stick up. I was grateful to have been seated as the g-force in the cockpit exceeded four gs for a moment and my vision started to grey out.

Something struck the starboard side of the ship and we violently cartwheeled. I hadn't pulled my combat harness on and was thrown into the ceiling. Between the grey out and contact, I lost consciousness, coming to as the gravity generator restored the .6g we were accustomed to and Ada corrected our spin.

"Status," I grunted, crumpled on the stairs. My head was spinning. We'd struck something large and it seemed like Ada had run into it with a combat maneuver.

"We've restored stable flight but the starboard engine is not responding. We've got damage to a number of systems, and we're sailing dark again," Ada said.

"Starboard wing and engine have been ripped off, along with the top turrets," Nick reported.

"What the frak happened?" I asked pulling on the combat harness that would have saved me so much pain only a few minutes before.

Ada pointed out the cockpit window. "That," she said.

A giant warship sailed in front of us on our starboard side.

"What the frak is that?" I asked. It was bigger even than the battleship we'd seen.

Titan class dreadnaught, my AI responded.

"That's why those destroyers were holding out," Marny said. "M-Pro needs to get out of there, they could be in trouble."

"They can't. The *Adams* has taken too much damage. If the others take off, it'll be a sitting duck," Nick said.

I cheered silently as one of the Red Houzi destroyers exploded. The gloves were off and time for negotiations had ended. The wounded *Walter Sydney Adams* with its limited mobility pushed toward the final destroyer and opened up. It was obvious that Commander Alto meant to eliminate that enemy before the dreadnaught came into range. With the concentrated firepower of the five ships the pirate's final destroyer sagged, then tore apart as the *Adams* plowed through the very center of it.

The small Navy fleet consisting of three destroyers and two corvettes formed up and prepared to meet the dreadnaught. From our range it was difficult to track the squadrons of fighters orbiting the intrepid fleet, but it was clear when the order to attack came. From fifty different points in space, brilliant blue streamers could be seen as the fighters mounted their opening gambit, streaking into combat. To me it appeared that it was an all-in approach, to pour all possible fire onto the behemoth before it started trading salvos with the smaller, but determined ships.

A burst of unhelpful adrenaline soured my stomach as we helplessly watched squadron after squadron of fighters pour out from the pirate's ship. Even with the dreadnaught in my sight, I'd underestimated the scope of the Red Houzi's resources. To date, we'd only run into comparatively pathetic teams, sailing beat up old warships. It was unimaginable to me that pirates could field this many ships.

When the two groups of fighters met in the middle, it was a slaughterhouse. Red Houzi fighters were blinking out of existence at an incredible rate. The difference in the fighter's skills was apparent. Every Navy fighter obliterated at least five pirates before succumbing to the horde. Even so, the mismatch in numbers took its toll and the Navy had to pull their fighters back as more and more pirates slipped past them, harrying the corvettes.

The pirate's strategy became clear - take out the corvettes with fighters and have the dreadnaught duke it out with the destroyers.

"We need to take cover," Marny said, breaking my reverie.

"What?" I asked.

"Those destroyers are going to be launching some big rounds. If just one of them comes our way, we're done. You need to get behind something big," she said.

I felt guilty hiding. Tabby might be on one of those ships and it went against my being to turn away from the fight. Marny was right, though, we had nothing to contribute.

"Understood." I grudgingly swung the ship around and sailed toward a large asteroid that would provide more than sufficient shield.

Just as we dropped out of visual sensor contact, I saw the *Theodore Dunham* explode under a heavy fusillade. I felt like someone had ripped my heart from my chest and I gasped. Tabby couldn't be on that ship. Surely there wasn't enough time for her to have transferred from Mars to the ship. It was horrific, but Tabby would be okay.

We sat behind the asteroid in stunned silence trying to process what we'd just seen. I thought I might throw up. I'd seen a lot of bad things in the last months, but we'd just witnessed the lives of several thousand people end in the blink of an eye. I shut down all but essential power and we quietly sat next to the asteroid. My mind reeled with the events we'd just witnessed, I fought the urge to scream. I'd never felt so helpless.

"Enemy vessel off port side," Nick said.

The dreadnaught was sailing past us slowly, close enough that if it could distinguish us from the asteroid, and if it had any desire, it could end us without a second thought. I should have run - we weren't on the winning side. Battle scars were evident as it sailed past. Large gashes had been rent from its side and a trail of debris marked its path. The only positive that I could see was that it was burning on a heading that wouldn't take it past the station. They would leave the station alone for now.

I waited half an hour for the ship to sail out of range and then slowly pulled out of our hiding spot. As the sensors gathered information on the debris field, the finality of the battle became clear. Not a single ship remained in any recognizable form. It had been a complete rout.

"Liam, I've got a fix on our wing and engine. I know it's hard to think about but I think we should recover them," Nick said.

My mind flashed back to Tabby. What if she was on that ship? She'd be gone.

"Liam?" Nick pushed. I ignored him and half walked, half jogged back to the office and sat down.

"*Kuznetsov*, this is *Hotspur*, please answer," I said. I could barely breathe.

"Captain. Where are you?" It was Sterra's voice.

"They're all gone," I said.

"Who's gone?"

"All of them," I replied.

"Liam focus. Get hold of yourself. I need you to be more specific. Please describe what you saw," she said.

"Was Tabby on the *Dunham*? Tell me she wasn't on the ship." I pled.

"Cadet Tabitha Masters? Your friend. Yes, Liam. Tell me what happened," she said.

"Was she on it?" I needed to know, nothing else mattered.

"Yes, Liam, she was on the *Theodore Dunham*."

The rushing sound in my ears grew to the point where I couldn't hear anything else and sweat broke out on my forehead. I stumbled to the head and threw up. Nothing mattered. I heard Nick enter the room and pick up the receiver.

STAY IN THE MOMENT

"Cap..."

"Cap..."

I felt Marny's strong hands pull me off the floor.

"She was on the ship, Marny," I said. Grief threatened to overwhelm me, I could barely get my legs underneath me.

"Sac up, Hoffen, you've got a ship full of people who are depending on you. We're deep in enemy territory. Do you want the same to happen to your Mom, your Dad?"

I closed my eyes, I knew what she was saying made sense, but I didn't know how to get it together.

"You've got to put that feeling in a deep dark place and get in the moment. The hold door is jammed and your parents were in there when that ship ran over the top of us."

"Shite!" I tried to pull away but she held on.

"Hold on." She ran some water in the sink and brushed off the front of my suit.

I looked down. I was a mess.

"You have a concussion from getting thrown around in the cockpit. Change into your normal vac-suit. If we get that dreadnaught's attention we won't need the armor," she said.

I nodded grimly and pulled off the suit I was wearing. My mind started clearing as the reality of our collision-induced tumble started to filter in.

"Frak. The crates were loose in the hold!" I said.

"Nick's working on getting the door open," Marny answered.

"What about the dreadnaught?" I asked. "Is it still local?"

"We could catch it, but it's on a burn for the outer reaches." The outer reaches was spacer talk for beyond the main asteroid belt.

"Ada, set a course for the wreckage. We're looking for

survivors," I said.

"Aye," she responded over the comm.

Track wreckage of all Mars Protectorate Fighter craft. Search for survivors.

"Nick, what is M-Pro's ETA?" I asked over the comm.

"Thirty five hours for fast response from Terrence," he said.

I stepped off of the lift onto the berth deck. Nick had the door open but crates were blocking our way in.

"Mom? Dad?" I said. They'd been agonizingly quiet.

"We're here, Liam. Jack is fine, but we've got injured and casualties. Did we hit something?" Mom asked.

I couldn't begin to describe what had just happened, so I simply answered, "Yes."

"You locked us out of the command channel once you engaged the combat controls."

She was right, we'd made the change when we brought the survivors in from the station.

Just then an idea struck me hard and I knew I had to act. "Ada, burn as hard as you can for the station."

"Dad, what shape are you in?" I asked.

"Fully functional, why? What's changed?"

Grant access to external video feeds to all occupants of ship.

"Everything. Too much to explain, I'll summarize. Both fleets have been destroyed. Hostile dreadnaught is outbound. We need to search for survivors. You have access to the video," I said.

"Got it. Good plan," he said.

All ship announcement, "We'll be landing at P-Zero in a few minutes. There are still hostiles on station and Big Pete will be securing it. If you are able bodied, we need your help. When we land, we need to unload all crates into the docking bay to make room for survivors. If you want to participate in search and rescue, we'd welcome your help. But know this, the debris field is not secure."

"Did I miss anything?" I asked Nick.

"I don't know," he said. It was an odd response for him and I noticed that he was favoring his right arm.

"What's going on with that?" I pointed at his arm.

"I think it's broken. There's more pressing issues."

"Adrenaline will only get you so far, Nick," Marny said from around the corner. She was apparently in the galley.

He slumped against the wall and slid down, his eyes fluttering. I leaned over and picked him up, he wasn't heavy in the .6g environment. His weight caused me to wonder why we weren't running at 1g, which was normal for a hard burn, until I realized we were down to a single engine.

"Marny. Nick's down, I'm going to the forward bunk with him."

I slung his legs through the door and laid him gently on the bed. Marny sat a medical kit next to him.

"Help me get his vac-suit off. Nick, if you can hear me, I'm going to give you a mild sedative. We've got to take off your suit and I have no idea where your wounds are."

He must have hit something incredibly hard to have overcome the suit's ability to absorb damage. I placed a small disc on his neck. It would knock him out for a few minutes. With his suit off, I placed diagnostic discs onto skin where the AI directed. My HUD showed that his right arm had multiple fractures, starting at his wrist. He must have reached out to stop his impact with something. He also had a tear in his gluteus medius.

"He'll be fine, Marny." Saying it mostly to reassure myself.

"Captain, we're sixty seconds out," Ada broke in.

"Roger that, Ada."

I left Marny to look after Nick. Now that we were at the station, the most important thing was to gain control of the medical facilities. If Nick's injuries were any indication, the old timers would be in bad shape. I needed to be in the hold to drop the loading ramp. Fortunately, Dad had prioritized clearing the crates blocking the rear door.

I wasn't prepared for what I walked into. It looked like a horror scene from a vid. People had been crushed by crates and in some cases lost limbs. Mom had found the emergency med kit we had in the hold, but it was woefully inadequate.

"Mom, can we seal those suits long enough to get the injured into the station?" I asked.

The ship's hold was probably the worst place for the severely wounded to be. If I'd thought my mom couldn't handle this kind of stress, I'd have been wrong. She took in the information and then spat out orders to the group around her.

"We'll manage," she said.

"Ada, once they've unloaded the cargo, I need you to bring the *Hotspur* out to the debris field and coordinate the search and retrieval efforts. M-Pro is thirty-five hours out."

Thirty-five hours was literally a lifetime for someone stranded in a suit. Most only had enough reserves to last fifteen hours at the max.

"Can do, Captain. Are you leaving the ship?"

"Yes," I said simply.

Download all fighter ship trajectories from Theodore Dunham. I cycled into the air lock.

Mom's voice came over the comm. "Liam, where are you going?"

"Tabby's out there. I'm going to find her," I said. I knew it was nuts, but I reasoned that she could have been in one of the fighters when the destroyer blew up. I wasn't about to give up on her.

Once outside the ship, I fired my arc-jets. The green level docking bays were just under the equator and I was headed to the top of the station where the James' Rental Shop was located. I'd helped Wendy for enough years to know she'd have a few haulers clamped to the station.

I crested the top and looked across. I wasn't particularly surprised to see scorching and deep gashes where the security tower had once been tethered to the station. The destroyers would have taken it out first to stop the defensive guns from pounding away at their armor. I hoped the rental shop's equipment yard hadn't received collateral damage, as it was only two hundred and fifty meters away.

I'd been jetting around with a vac-suit since I was very young. I didn't even think about it as I flew across the pockmarked surface as fast as I could and pulled up hard at the rental shop. I was in luck and Wendy's best hauler was still in the yard and undamaged. It had the largest pressurized hold, having been used to transport both equipment and people out to the claims before she'd purchased it.

Vent atmo, open port door, disengage docking clamps. My HUD showed the controls for the hauler. I laughed to myself as I climbed into the ship. I used to consider this type of craft a large vehicle and it now seemed tiny. The single vid screen in the center console lit up, showing a full load of fuel and O2. I marveled at the simplicity of the machine.

The hauler didn't have physical flight sticks but my AI knew to project a throttle and flight stick virtually onto my HUD. I grabbed the t-handled throttle and pushed it forward hard and lifted from the surface of the station. I reveled in the instant acceleration of the small ship.

It took thirty minutes to arrive at the edge of the battle's debris field. The first ship I came to was one of the pirate's destroyers. In my mind it deserved no name, and the survivors, if they were to be found, would not receive any priority from me. I'd plotted a course that would lead me across the hundreds of kilometers of continually expanding battlefield. The torn hunks of the derelict ships sailed along their final trajectories, at least until they collided with something else.

I'd hoped that the Navy's destroyers would have some remaining structure where survivors might be able to band together and seek shelter. A normal vac-suit had limited propulsion available, but it should be enough to allow survivors to hold on long enough for rescue. The destroyer's remains in no way resembled the once proud warship. Shredded husks were all that remained and my heart sank as I found no sign of life.

I knew it was unlikely that Tabby would have been in one of the fighters, but I held out hope and raced after the closest. I had to move fast as several of the fighters had been going at high speed when the dreadnaught shot them down. Two of the ten fighters with wreckage big enough to track were already far enough away that I would never be able to reach them. The farthest was a full twenty hours away in my current craft.

After a hard burn - at least as much as this hauler had to give - I caught the first craft. Before I even arrived at the ship, I knew there would be no survivors. A large hole had been punched through the cockpit, removing the entire passenger compartment. I forced myself to look hard, but didn't see anything too awful.

This went on for a few hours. The ship debris drifted further and further apart and I could find no sign of survivors. I'd been hopeful a couple of times. The fighters had some sort of protective foam that filled the cabin when the ship took significant damage. In all the ships I'd found like that, the pilots were damaged beyond the point where I could even recognize them as human. A sense of hopelessness filled me as I reached the final ship, once again, finding nothing.

Ada had set up in the middle of the debris field and was organizing the search efforts, using the hold of the *Hotspur* as a triage center. Apparently, I'd been too hasty when inspecting the debris field. Ada and her group were finding survivors, many of whom were inside the undamaged sections of the larger ships. Many had only slight injuries and were joining the recovery effort.

"Ada, did you find her?" I asked impatiently when I got close enough for a line of sight communication. The comm disruptors the pirates had left were still making it impossible to communicate over any distance.

"I'm sorry, Liam. No," she answered.

"How many survivors?" I asked.

"A hundred forty-five so far," she said. "I need you to make a run back to the station. We're getting full."

"Okay," I said. Darkness threatened to overtake me again.

I pulled alongside the *Hotspur* and helped people I didn't recognize, wearing naval uniforms, load the injured into the hauler. Once loaded, I sailed back to P-Zero. We were met by even more people I didn't recognize, many obviously injured, pulling the wounded out of my craft and carrying them into the station. I felt ashamed at my greedy, self-interested actions, wasting valuable time on a fruitless search.

I vowed not to make the same mistake again nor to continue wallowing in my grief. I'd have plenty of time for that later. These people, Tabby included, had sailed into harm's way to protect my family and they deserved my best efforts.

For thirty hours we searched and ferried survivors, Navy and pirate alike, back to the station. There's one thing that's never in short supply with the military; people wanting to take charge. Probably the biggest upside to that was the fact that most are competent to do so.

"Captain Hoffen, you need to land that bird," a voice I didn't recognize came over my headset. I was exhausted and wondered if I was making it all up.

"Sure, just one more trip," I said.

"Negatory, Captain. The fast response unit from Terrence has just arrived and they'll be taking over the mission now. You all have born enough of that burden. The Navy thanks you for your service, but you need to land that bird and get some shut-eye. You understand, son?"

He didn't need to push at that point, as I was having a difficult time keeping my eyes open.

"Is the *Hotspur* in?" I asked.

"She's in bay four, same level, Captain," he said.

I landed the hauler in the bay next to the *Hotspur*, arc-jetted over and cycled through the airlock and into the hold. I saw the end of the wing and the missing engine laying in the now, otherwise empty hold. The berth deck was empty, although the first bunk room door was closed. I took the lift up and stepped into my quarters. Nick and Marny lay on the bed. Marny started to rise, but I held my hand up to stop her and exited the room. I pulled a blanket out from under the couch and lay down. It wasn't the first time I'd slept on the couch and just stretching out meant the world to me.

"Cap, sorry. The other rooms are all taken," she said.

"It's okay, Marny. That's how we arranged it. I'd just forgotten. Go back to sleep," I said.

"Did you find her?"

"No." There was nothing more to say. I allowed the tears to flow.

"I'm sorry, Cap," she said quietly. Marny sat down on the couch next to me and stroked my hair. Mercifully, sleep found me.

When I finally woke up, I found myself in my bed. I was disoriented and for a moment I didn't remember the horrible battle or that Tabby had been lost. When reality struck home, a fresh wave of intense sadness crushed me and I slumped back into the bed, willing myself back to sleep.

Sometime later, I heard knocking at the door. I didn't care. I had nothing to say to anyone.

"Liam. Cover up, I'm coming in." It was Mom. I had nothing to cover up; I was still in my vac-suit. She handed me a cup of coffee, which I drank automatically. I was extremely thirsty, but couldn't drink too fast because the coffee was so hot. "I need to talk to you," she continued.

"Mom, I don't think I'm ready for this," I said. I wasn't about to listen to a lecture. I just didn't care.

She sat down beside me and put her hand on my leg. "No dear, we found Tabby."

My heart leapt. "Where? I've got to see her," I pushed the blanket away and tried to sit up. Mom stood and held out her hand.

"Liam, she's hurt and it's bad. She was trapped in the wreckage. When she was freed... well... she's barely alive and might not make it."

"I have to see her," I said. "Take me."

I stood and walked to the door. Mom hurried to keep up with me. I didn't know where we were going, but I knew it was off the ship.

"She's in a tank on the *Hope*. The Navy brought out a hospital ship. They'll shuttle you out, but you have to listen to them," she said to my back.

"Sure, of course," I said.

We wound our way through the interior of the station. Signs of life had already started to appear. As promised, a shuttle waited in one of the docking bays. The shuttle was painted bright white and the interior was spotless. We approached the destroyer-sized hospital ship and plunged through a translucent orange pressure barrier.

A man in a light blue vac-suit met us as we disembarked down the small ramp extending from the shuttle.

"Jon Bentcourt. I've been looking after Tabitha." He was an average looking man, spacer build. I found it odd that he wasn't wearing a helmet, given only a pressure barrier separated us from vacuum.

"Liam Hoffen," I said. I shook his proffered hand.

"There are some things you need to be aware of, Mr. Hoffen. Tabitha…"

"Tabby," I corrected.

"Right. You have been identified as Tabitha's next of kin."

I looked dumbly at him. It was weird. "What about her father?"

"He has been contacted, but you are her primary contact. The Navy is very good about keeping these types of records and Tabitha has specifically identified you as such."

"Okay. I'm not sure why you're telling me this."

"I wouldn't be able to share her condition with you if this weren't the case. As for Tabitha, her body has been subjected to extraordinary trauma. There's no good way to say this, but she's lost both of her legs, several ribs on her right side and her right arm. She's also suffered substantial burns to her abdomen. Of a more minor nature are the multitude of lacerations and contusions over what remains of her body. In short, she's alive, but barely."

I swallowed hard. It was a lot to take in.

BEGINS WITH THE FIRST STEP

Bentcourt led me into a long room with tall silver oval cylinders lined up against the wall. Each cylinder was almost a meter in diameter. I recognized them as medical tanks, having spent time in one when I'd received an upgrade for my prosthetic foot.

He pressed his hand on a cylinder's access pad and it slid down, allowing us a view through the clear, top third. Tabby was suspended in a pale yellow liquid. Tubes ran into virtually every part of her body. Bentcourt had warned me of her missing limbs, but seeing her like this was difficult. Her normally smooth skin was gouged, scraped, and black and blue over every square centimeter. A modesty shield had been applied to her torso and my eyes searched for her missing arm. Tears streamed down my cheeks as I forced myself to take it all in.

"When will you start reconstructing her limbs?" I asked.

"We've already inserted temporary ribs. It will be up to Tabitha's civilian doctors to work on any reconstruction. We will, however, fit her with a fantastic prosthetic arm, most people won't even be aware that it is not her own. Her legs are, unfortunately, beyond prosthetics, but you should see what they're doing with arc-jet chairs," he said.

"You have to make her whole," I insisted. "She's one of yours."

"Mr. Hoffen, surely you understand that's not my decision to make. This is a combat triage hospital. According to this chart, Tabitha will be honorably discharged with a Comet of Valorous Service. She's a hero and will receive the best medical care available on Mars."

I felt he was saying two things. "But you won't make her whole? I know it's possible, you can replace bones and regrow muscles."

"That is true, Mr. Hoffen, but that technology is well beyond what a government is able to pay for. The surgery you describe costs tens of millions of credits. Tabitha knew the risks when she signed up. We all know those risks, but *we* signed up anyway. I understand that you would like to be angry with me, but your anger is misplaced. It was pirates that hurt our young Tabitha."

Mom gently rested her hand on my arm. She could tell I was getting riled up. His simplistic argument made me want to scream. "Liam, he's doing his job looking after Tabby."

"When will she be conscious?" I asked.

"Let me be clear. There is no guarantee that she will regain consciousness. Her body must accept its new configuration. That said, she is strong, no doubt a fighter," he said flatly.

I wondered how many patients a person had to lose before they built up a wall like this guy had.

"Can I stay with her for a while?" I asked.

"Certainly. You can even talk to her. We've found that in some cases it's soothing to them. Although mostly, it's helpful for the visitors." He pulled a chair out from the wall. I decided I didn't like him.

"Mom, I need to stay for a while," I said.

"I understand. Stay as long as you need."

For the next few days I spent all of my waking moments next to Tabby's tank. It was oddly comforting to sit in the quiet room. A few sailors visited, stopping to look in on friends. There were twenty-four medical tanks in the room. When I wasn't talking to Tabby, telling her of Nick, Marny and my adventures, I was wondering about the background of the other sailors in the tanks. It was the highlight of my day when a tank would be lowered and a person would emerge. Sometimes they were almost a hundred percent recovered, although many were missing limbs.

On the fifth day, a Navy lieutenant showed up to tell me that I had to disembark; the *Hope* was setting sail for Mars. Tabby had crossed the threshold from grave to critical and Bentcourt - whom I had not become more fond of - felt that she would be upgraded to serious within the next few days. Small steps on a long journey.

I'd lost track of normal time and when I got back to the *Hotspur* it was 0200. I found it odd to see that the hold was once again full of crates and I wondered where the wing and engine had gone. That answer would have to wait until tomorrow.

I hadn't been showering regularly, and wasn't sure what the sleeping arrangements were, so I stripped and tossed my suit liner into the freshener and jumped into the main head on the berth deck. I risked the momentary nakedness, not wanting to wake whoever was in the captain's quarters.

The hot spray was luxurious and I felt like I was coming out of a long foggy sleep. Time on the hospital ship seemed to be nonexistent. Shifts would change, but nothing else. I'd been ignoring everything and everyone around me, completely wrapped up in my own thoughts. It was time to rejoin my crew. I shaved my scraggly beard and used a barber brush to cut my hair back to a manageable length.

Without the shower heating the room, it was chilly. I walked out of the head and to the end of the galley where the freshener sat. My suit liner lay neatly folded on top and my vac-suit was now in the machine. Since I hadn't been the one to load my vac-suit, I knew I'd been busted. With the unmistakable feeling of someone's eyes on me, I spun around to see who might be in the room with me.

"Cap, I have to say you put on a good show," Marny said, leaning back in a chair, with her feet on the mess table.

I grabbed my liner and scampered back to the head, trying to retrieve whatever dignity might be left for me. I re-emerged a few minutes later.

"What are you doing up?" I asked.

"Well, as head of security, I like to know who is coming and going on the ship at all hours. I'm glad to see you remember where your home is."

"They kicked me out. The *Hope* is headed for Mars," I said.

Nick walked out of the forward bunk room. As usual, when awakened in the night, his hair was mashed against one side of his head.

"Is she conscious?" Nick asked.

"No, she might wake up while they're en route, though. Did you know they're kicking her out of the Navy?"

"SOP," Marny said.

"Weren't you pretty badly injured? And didn't they fix you up?" I asked.

"Different scope of injuries and wrong country. I just had a messed up jaw, mostly. I hear you though, it's frakked up."

"What's been going on around here?"

"Mom's rental business got completely cleaned out," Nick said.

"That sucks," I said.

I heard the lift drop from the bridge deck.

"What? You're having a party without me?" Dad asked.

"Have you been out to your claim?" I asked, looking at him.

He sat at the mess table where Nick, Marny and I had been chatting. "It's not good, they pretty well wiped us out."

"Were you insured?" I asked. I knew the answer by the look on his face.

"Thirty percent. It's better than nothing. There's not much insurance available for miners, especially if you're not within a security perimeter."

"What will you do?"

"Silver and I wanted talk to you about booking passage back to Mars," he said.

That was Big Pete. Even with his own son he wouldn't presume to ask for a ride. It was somewhere between pride and idiocy.

"We've been running short-handed," I said. Nick gave me an almost imperceptible affirmative nod. "We'd love to have Mom join the watch rotation. That'd be more than enough to cover passage to Mars. Think she'd be in for that?"

"So you're going to finally let me sail this bird?" Mom approached the table and sat on Dad's lap.

"Don't you people ever sleep?" Ada was right behind Mom. She leaned over and gave me a hug as she passed by.

All we were missing was Jack. I hadn't intended on waking everyone. I'd just wanted to get cleaned up.

"So, I have a question. Where'd the engine go? I didn't see it in the hold." I said.

"A bunch of Navy engineers came by and re-attached it. It was their way of saying thank you for our help in the rescue," Marny said.

I raised both eyebrows questioningly. If they didn't attach it expertly, it might get ripped off during burn, possibly causing more damage.

Nick sensed my concern and preemptively answered my question. "It isn't pretty, but I scanned it and the AI is more than happy with the repairs. We'll have to do some cosmetics once we get back to Mars."

"So… I'm not sure how to say this, but thank you all for not pushing on me over the last several days," I said. "I know there's a lot going on and I haven't been any help."

"That's what family does," Marny said. She caught me off guard with her comment.

"You all really are my family. I don't know what I'd do without you," I said.

"What's next?" Big Pete asked. I suspect we'd crossed whatever threshold he set for sharing.

"I think we need to get to Mars," Nick said.

That was something I could do. "I'll work on the watch schedule right away."

Mom pinched some content and tossed it at me. A list showed up on my HUD and I opened it. She'd created a four, four, six rotation with her, Ada and myself. I was interested to see that she had given me the first shift. She knew me better than I'd expected. She'd also attached a navigation and burn schedule that would run us through Terrence. We were scheduled to sail at 0600, or in three hours.

"Hope you don't mind," she said, looking a little guilty.

"Looks good. Two questions; why Terrence and why the Class-D burn schedule?" She'd chosen a very conservative burn rate.

"Same answer for both. We're low on fuel," she said.

"None to buy here?" I asked.

"Some, but it's outrageously priced."

"Anyone see an issue with us getting underway for Terrence at 0600? And just as a reminder, please don't discuss our departure time or destination with anyone. We're sailing without our top turrets and I'm not all that crazy about trying a combat burn with the way that engine's sitting on there. If there are no objections, I'm going to get a few hours of sack time."

I hadn't spent much time in the aft bunkroom, but I found the bed to be quite welcoming. Ada joined me and took the top bunk. Filbert's second grav-box was installed within easy reach of her bunk. I suspected that Jack and Ada had worked something out between the two of them.

I woke to the smell of strong coffee and the noise of movement outside the bunk room. I quietly got out of bed and set the covers straight. A curious Filbert peered out at me from the bunk where Ada was sleeping soundly. His fur was starting to grow back and he was at least twice as big as when we'd first found him. I picked him up and held him against my chest. As quietly as I could, I exited the room.

Big Pete and Marny were in the galley with Nick and Jack seated at the mess table. I handed Filbert to Jack, whose eyes lit up. Dad was serving scrambled eggs, so I sat down. A few minutes later he wordlessly handed me a cup of coffee and a plate of food.

"Where'd you learn to cook?" I asked. We'd never had fresh food on the claim, so it was surprising to see him getting after it.

"Something you learn in the service; an army travels on its stomach. Eat up, you have ten minutes before your watch."

I didn't need to be prompted further. I hadn't been doing a good job of eating regularly and it smelled delicious.

"I'm going to do a quick exterior inspection and then we'll get underway if everyone's settled." I said after finishing my eggs.

"Aye. I'll come with you," Marny said.

I nodded and stood up, heading toward the cargo hold.

"Cap. You'll be putting on your armored suit, I assume," she said.

I looked back, saw my dad's raised eyebrows and knew I had no chance of winning this conversation.

"Right, my mistake." What a captain puts up with to stay in his crew's good graces.

I found my armored suit in our makeshift armory. Marny stood by and watched approvingly as I holstered my flechette. It seemed like a waste of time, what with the Navy still hanging around, but I knew what she would say - expect the worst.

I was particularly interested in the repairs to the wing and engine. From my perspective, it looked like crap, although I trusted Nick's assessment. The engineers had strapped the wing on and welded the frak out of it. Fortunately, aerodynamics weren't important for this trip.

Back in the ship, I settled into the pilot's chair. *All sections report,* I requested, pulling up my checklist. Several systems were no longer in the green. One of the laterals in the septic system had failed and was seeping. I'd need to get to it after my shift. I knew better than to think I could successfully delegate that job.

"We're secure and all passengers accounted for," Marny responded.

"All systems are operational. We're low on O2 crystals, but our algae system is okay," Nick said across the comm. "The collision knocked it about, but we'll make it to Mars."

"Roger that."

All ship announcement. "Welcome aboard, everyone. We're pushing off now. Prepare for hard burn in twenty minutes. Jack, you might consider coming up to the cockpit. It's quite a view."

I lifted the ship off the floor of the docking bay and slowly sailed forward. Jack came up between the two chairs and looked out the window with a big grin on his face.

"Sit in the chair. You might as well be comfortable," I said.

Nimbly, Jack swung into the chair. I'd forgotten how elegant his movements were. Filbert poked his head out of the crook of his arm and stretched his claws lazily onto Jack's chest. For a kid whose life was just turned upside down, Jack seemed surprisingly content.

"Is Tabby going to live?" Jack's question caught me completely off guard. Jack and Tabby had a special relationship. If you wanted to mess with Jack, you got Tabby - and no one in their right mind wanted a piece of Tabby. Their relationship had begun when we'd formed a team to play pod-ball together. Perhaps the most shocking part of Jack's question was that he had spoken. It happened so rarely that the very act was significant.

"Sure is, buddy. She's headed to Mars right now and we're going there to meet her. I'll make sure you get to see her, okay?"

Jack just smiled back at me and nodded his head. For whatever reason, speech was difficult for him. A lot of people thought he was simple, but it wasn't specifically that. He just didn't seem to prioritize things the same way everyone else did.

I sailed around the station once. I figured several people on the ship would appreciate a last look at Colony 40 before we left it behind, probably for good. Twenty minutes later we were burning hard for Terrence.

"Ever thought about boxing?" I asked Jack.

He looked at me like I'd grown a third eye.

"It's a type of fighting, but we use it for training. Marny's pretty good. She'll train you, if you want. I box with her all the time," I said.

His horrified look was comical. He and I were about the same height and build and I knew from experience that Marny out massed me by a whole lot.

"How about you watch me, then decide if you want to try it?" I said, which restored his affable smile.

By the time we reached Terrence, Jack had become relentless in the ring. I wasn't surprised that he was almost immediately better than me. He'd never be a great boxer, but that was more about the fact that Jack wasn't particularly aggressive. His punches quite often landed, but they lacked any real sting. Hitting him, however, was next to impossible. He would drive opponents crazy by avoiding every punch, scoring tons of points and smiling the whole time.

CENSORED

"Liam, you're going to want to look at this," Nick said.

I was hanging out at the table on the bridge. Jack and I had discovered that Filbert would chase just about anything that moved and we were taunting him with whatever we could find.

"What's up?" I asked and tipped back my head, a motion my AI knew was a request to bring up my communications HUD. We'd exited hard burn to Terrence and were coasting. We didn't have enough fuel to burn all the way until we flipped over to decelerate and, as a result, it was taking us four extra days to get there. A full message queue indicated that we'd finally escaped the influence of the communication disruption weapon.

At the top of the queue was an ultra-urgent message from Mars Protectorate. "I see it," I said. I'd never received anything with this level of urgency. I opened the message which was addressed to our corporation, as well as to Nick and myself. An overlay popped up and informed me that my receipt of the message had been recorded. The text was legalese that I had a hard time understanding. My AI could translate it for me, but I knew that Nick had already read it.

"So what's it all about?" I asked.

"M-Pro is declaring the incident at Colony 40 to be a national secret and is seizing our data streams and sensor logs. If we share the electronic record, we can be arrested for treason," Nick said soberly.

"That's crazy," I said. I scanned the text and found a reference to treason in the otherwise undecipherable text.

"It turns out we're not restricted from talking about it, we just can't put it into any digital communications."

"What do you think that's all about?" I asked.

"There's a news article that outlines how the Navy repelled a pirate attack at Colony 40 and destroyed the attacking fleet. There's no mention of the dreadnaught or the Navy fleet being destroyed."

"That's a pretty optimistic view of events," I said.

"We need to warn the others. M-Pro sounds serious about this," Nick said.

"They're going to cover it up?"

"How do you think people would react if they found out that the Red Houzi had a dreadnaught and taken out a fleet?" Nick asked.

"Panic, I suppose. I'm not sure how it's going to play that a fleet of Red Houzi pillaged four colonies," I said.

"That's the beauty of their message though, M-Pro did stop the original Red Houzi fleet. Their message is all true. It's just incomplete. When the full truth finally comes out, they won't have lied. What they've done is buy time. Time to find that Red Houzi base," he said.

"That's right. That's what Qiu Loo was doing at Jeratorn, she was trying to find the location of the Red Houzi base," I said.

"If they knew where the base was, you'd think they'd go out and destroy it," Nick said. It was a conversation we'd had before.

I shrugged, there wasn't much to be done about it. It wasn't like I produced a news feed and I had no intention of talking to anyone about the events. That said, I didn't like the implied threat. I checked the remaining messages. I saw several from Ada's dad. Not surprising, Sam was upset that he couldn't reach her. I imagined she was dealing with that, so I pushed them off to the side.

The only other message of significance was from Jake Berandor. He'd arrived safely at Mars and had unloaded the barge into the warehouse Nick had contracted with. He also mentioned that he had a proposition for us once we were back. I smiled, Jake wasn't someone to be underestimated.

A few days later, we stopped for a few hours in Terrence.

The coroner at Terrence met us when we docked. We offloaded

Wendy's body and an hour later he returned with her ashes in a small, sealed cylinder. We'd already had a nice memorial on the second day out of Colony 40. It was surreal to me how life just kept on going.

On a positive note, Jake had arranged to sell his remaining beer to a supplier on the station for a significant discount. It was a smart move. He wouldn't have been able to sell it on Mars without competing with the distributor he'd purchased it from, something he was contractually forbidden to do.

Big Pete and Marny had overseen the unloading of the crates of beer and headed into the station to find fresh supplies for the remainder of the trip. We could make it back with what we had in the pantry, but we'd been down to meal bars for the last day or two. I didn't really mind, but meals on the ship were more than just nutrition, they were a way to bring us together.

With the ship at rest, I crawled down into the bilge. The collision with the dreadnaught had unseated several of the couplings that connected the lateral water reclaimers to the bacteria field. Over the last few days nasty sludge had been seeping out and dropping onto the floor of my previously immaculate bilge. To say that I was disheartened was an understatement. I scraped as much up as I possibly could and even swabbed it clean, but the area had lost the sparkle of fresh paint we'd had for the start of the journey. The repair wasn't particularly difficult, however.

"You've developed a bit of a smell, Liam," Ada said, sitting in a chair in the aft bunk room, looking up from her reading pad. I'd entered the bilge from an access hatch in the small room.

"Yes, sorry. Some pieces got knocked loose. Made quite a mess." I lifted three buckets of unmentionable slime onto the deck which was about shoulder height from where I stood in the bilge on one of the ribs of the ship's skeleton.

"I see you've found the reality of owning your own business," she said.

I hoisted myself up onto the deck. "Which reality is that?"

"You get to do all of the dirty jobs. Can I help with those?"

"Nah. No reason for anyone else to get mixed up with this. I'll dump them and take a shower. Well, there is one thing you could do."

"What's that?" she asked, amused.

"Once I get into the shower, could you toss a fresh suit liner into the head? I don't want to touch anything clean right now."

She laughed. "Of course."

I wondered if the bilge would always be my lot in life.

By the time I'd cleaned the buckets and showered, Big Pete and Marny had returned with two full crates of supplies. We'd held off dinner, with the expectation that Marny and Dad would find something better than our dwindling supplies.

We'd been on hard burn for about an hour when Nick finally called us all down for dinner. It was well worth the wait. The smell of garlic wafted up as Jack and I descended on the lift to the berth deck. The table was filled with fresh bread, salad greens and pasta with meat sauce.

"Did you reach your dad, Ada?" I asked between bites.

"Yeah, sorry about that. He kind of freaked out," she answered.

"I've got something interesting for you all to think about," Nick said. He wasn't normally very chatty, so his announcement quieted the table. Seeing that he had everyone's attention, he continued, "I've been thinking about where everyone is going to stay once we get to Mars. I talked to a friend who offered to let us lease a part of her land to put up habitation domes."

"Tali?" I asked. Nick nodded affirmatively.

Mom jumped in. "Who's Tali?"

"Long story. Let's just say you won't have to worry about burglars," I said.

"Where are we talking about?" Dad asked.

"Just outside Puskar Stellar, which is generally our base of operation. That's mostly because of the free trade zone, but also because it was convenient when Tabby was in the Academy." Nick attempted to choke off the last, but his mouth had outpaced his mind.

I ignored it, "Coolidge is only a hundred fifty kilometers from

Puskar Stellar and the Academy is maybe twenty five kilometers out of Coolidge, which also happens to be where Tabby will be starting her rehab. So, that would work out really well."

Dad was shaking his head. "Our hab-domes were destroyed by the pirates. I'm not sure we can afford any right now."

"We've actually got an inventory of them. They're in bad need of a cleaning bot, but I can't see why we wouldn't use them. We can even look for a more permanent location if we plan to stay long. That's pretty nice of Tali," I said.

Nick nodded. "It is. But don't be too enamored, we're paying a competitive rate for the lease."

"Yeah, but she didn't need to offer," I said.

"On another subject. Loose Nuts has some job openings," Nick said. I raised my eyebrows. Two surprises in one dinner. He continued, "I think you'll be okay with it, Liam."

I shrugged. He knew me better than I knew myself most of the time.

"When we get to Mars, Liam will be tied up with Tabby, but we can't afford to let the *Adela Chen* sit idle. We have another crewman, but he's let me know that he won't be sailing with us anymore."

"Jake quit?" I asked.

"Sort of, you probably haven't read his message yet," Nick said. He was right, I hadn't paid attention to my queued messages.

I'd been ignoring a number of things lately and Nick had been picking up the slack. "Sorry."

"Don't be. We're all worried about her," Nick said and it made me wonder when he'd done so much growing up. "The point is, we could use a licensed pilot if you'd be up for that, Mrs. Hoffen. Ultimately, we have temporary work for everyone. Most of the jobs will probably only last for a few months, but it might help you get your feet on the ground. So think about it. If you're interested, talk to me or Liam."

I nodded in agreement. With two busted ships, a hold full of pirate loot and a tug that needed scheduling, we had a lot to get done in the next few months. I felt like I was letting Nick down. I had to get my head in the game.

After dinner, I found Nick and Marny on the bridge in their normal spots. Nick liked the aft work station and Marny the forward. The stations were lined up on the port side of the bridge. The chairs were both on tracks that allowed them to slide over to the round table that sat in front of the couch on the starboard side. Instead of making them slide over to the table, I plopped down between their workstations with my back against the hull.

"So, what's the deal with Jake?" I asked.

To Nick's credit, he didn't show any annoyance that I hadn't read Jake's comm.

"He doesn't want to be part of the crew, but has a business idea he wants to pass by us," Nick said.

"I'm not sure what that means. Any idea what he wants?" I asked.

"I have a guess. I'm not sure it's real important. He didn't include any specifics, other than he wasn't available as crew," Nick said.

"I think we should keep the *Adela Chen* in close. We won't make as much money, but it would be a lot safer," I said.

"Aye. If Silver will take the gig, I'd feel better about things. Her military instincts would be valuable. We need to be vigilant. Otherwise, I'll want to go along," Marny said.

"I'll talk to her," I said.

"Any word on Tabby?" Nick asked.

"I keep checking, but there's no information. I can't even get an estimate on when the *Hope* will arrive at the Coolidge Orbital station."

"Any chance her family will pay for the reconstructive surgery?" Nick asked.

"I don't think so. I know they have money, but I don't think it's that kind of money," I said.

"What kind of money are we talking about?" Nick asked.

"I've done a bunch of research, but there are so many variables it's hard to know. I saw a guy who replaced an arm, cost about seven million credits," I said.

Nick whistled.

"Yeah. It's incredible though. They were able to manufacture skin and regrow his muscles. That's why Tabby has temporary ribs right now. The Navy will fix anything internal, so they're probably growing or manufacturing her ribs right now," I said.

"There's a choice?" Nick asked.

"Aye, that there is," Marny said. "It's more expensive to regrow them and it takes longer. They can manufacture replacements with nano-manufactured alloys. The cost is close enough that they can afford to let the patient choose."

"Did you get to choose?" I asked.

"Aye. I went with the alloy. The alloy was considerably stronger than the regrown bone and I'd had my jaw broken so many times that it was an easy call."

"How much was replaced?" I asked.

"In total, about a third of my skull and both jaws," she answered.

It was hard to imagine. If she hadn't said anything, I'd have had no idea. "I'm sorry, Marny. That must have been awful."

"I was unconscious for most of it. It took six weeks and they kept me under. I get some weird flashbacks once in a while, but they tell me that's because they had to mess with my optic nerve," she said.

"What happened?" I couldn't resist. I'd avoided asking her about injuries previously.

"Blaster round to the face. I was lucky, it should have killed me."

"Glad it didn't," Nick said.

We continued to chat until it was time for me to take a watch. Somewhere along the line I'd become withdrawn and had been ignoring my friends. It felt good to just hang out.

Growing up on Colony 40, we were used to being able to visually locate Mars, but it was always a tiny spec. By the time we'd crossed a million kilometers, it had grown to the size of a large green pea to our unaided eyes. I knew from that point forward, however, it would grow quickly, as we'd cover the remaining distance within the next two days.

I was in the captain's office, working on scheduling the tug. Margins on close haul sailing were very tight and I was having a hard time coming to grips with the idea of only clearing a couple of thousand credits on each round trip.

"Liam, we're receiving a hail," Ada called from the cockpit.

Identify source.

Naval cutter, Penderghast, my AI announced.

Accept hail. "Captain Liam Hoffen. How can I help?"

I was surprised that a signal had been able to cut through the interference caused by our engines as we decelerated. Then again, it was the Navy.

"Captain Hoffen, this is Lieutenant Aiden Feldman. Please heave-to for an inspection."

The signal wasn't good enough for video, but he sounded young.

"Roger that, Lieutenant. I assume that it will be acceptable to cut our engines?" I wasn't sure what heave-to meant to Lieutenant Feldman. We were currently hurtling toward Mars and the term normally referred to staying at rest.

"That is correct, Captain," he replied curtly.

"Will do. Hoffen out." *Terminate comms.*

"Ada, cut engines. There's a Navy cutter, *Penderghast,* which will be coming along side."

"What's up, Captain?" she asked.

"Not sure. He said he was performing an inspection," I answered. "Nick, Marny, to the bridge, please."

I could have saved my request, as Ada spinning down the engines would have gotten their attention just as fast.

"What's going on?" Nick asked.

"Navy requested that we heave-to. They're doing an inspection," I said.

"That's not good," Marny said.

"How do you want to handle it?" I asked.

"I'll make an announcement, but you should probably meet them at the air lock," Nick said.

"Roger that. Can you validate their transponder?" I asked.

"Yup," Nick said.

I waited as two burly Marines in armored vac-suits cycled through the airlock first. Lieutenant Feldman followed. He was taller than most spacers and I caught a flash of red hair through his helmet.

"Welcome aboard, Lieutenant." I offered my hand which he accepted.

"Thank you, Captain."

"How can I help?"

"Under the orders of the Mars Protectorate Judiciary, I've been tasked with seizing all electronic records of the events for the dates 498.12.14 through 498.12.16. Will you comply?" He asked.

"If we refuse?" I asked.

"I'm under orders to seize your ship in that case and take you and your crew into custody." He visibly stiffened, although the Marines didn't change their stance.

"How do you propose to execute your task?" I asked. The idea that he could simply remove three full days of ships logs was a task I couldn't fathom. The information was stored on literally millions of devices throughout the ship.

"I'm to release a virus into your ship's systems. It will first extract the information and then delete it. It will also spread to all personal networks and remove the same," he said.

"And this is legal? You can just decide to wipe our systems?"

"Actually, the choice is yours," he said.

"Give me a minute?" I said.

"Not possible. You might attempt to transmit the data, which I feel compelled to tell you would be prosecuted as an act of treason," he said.

I breathed through my nose, trying to avoid fury. "Well, this just gets better and better."

"Mars Protectorate is at war, Captain Hoffen. I'll need your answer," he said impatiently.

"Very well. We'll comply."

NEW BEGINNINGS

It didn't take Lieutenant Feldman more than twenty minutes to plant the virus and be on his way. To say that it didn't sit well with everyone was something of an understatement.

Over the next day and a half, Mars grew to fill our view screen. The *Hotspur,* unlike *Sterra's Gift,* had engines that performed symmetrically, both providing acceleration and deceleration along the same axis. While I preferred this ship's design, where the cockpit view was always what we were approaching, it was hard not to miss our first ship.

"I've rented a pod-jumper for a week," Nick said as he sat down in a chair next to my desk.

"Glad you're making progress. I couldn't be more tired of working on loads. I'll tell you, I'm about fed up with these short hauls. We barely cover fuel, salaries and insurance. I can't imagine if someone had to buy a ship," I said.

"Show me," Nick said.

"Please. This is driving me nuts." I ran him through the different loads I'd been looking at. Initially, the numbers looked good if you just paid attention to the revenues.

"That's okay with me. Right now, we just need to break even for a while. If we can pay salaries and maintenance on the tug, that's worth a lot. You'll clear enough to cover our living expenses on the ground. We're not going to get rich, but at least people have something productive to do. You're doing the right things. Have you talked with Sam Chen about helping set up runs?" Nick asked, referring to Ada's dad.

"I'm not sure he'd return my pings. I finally listened to his comms. He has a temper."

"Maybe not, then. If it helps, I don't think you're doing

anything wrong," Nick said.

"I talked to Mom. She's in."

"Great, when will you get them started?"

"She wants to recertify her master's license, which I didn't even know she had."

"She's qualified on tugs?"

"Not specifically, but her flight hours from the service are all transferable. She was qualified to sail huge ships, although she mostly flew troop transports. According to Ada, Mom just needs to complete a series of tests and then take an instructor out for a sail. She could have it all done in a few weeks. Frankly, I'm glad to get Ada on someone else's tail," I said.

"No kidding. We should pay for the testing. It's a reasonable expense."

"That works. I got a consensus about shore leave. We'll schedule forty hours. I think Mom and Dad want to get out and see the sights. It's been a long time since they've been planet-side."

"Did you guys ever go to Mars when you were a kid?" Nick asked.

"Not that I recall," I responded, my mind unable to focus on the past with all that we had coming up. "What are you going to have Jack doing?"

"I've scheduled the *Hotspur* for dry-dock at Coolidge. We just need to unload it into the warehouse we rented and Jack can help with that. I was thinking we'd bring him on full time as crew."

"Absolutely. So did M-Pro say anything about the mech suits?"

"Not yet. I'm guessing that whoever was in charge of the review got busy with other things. I wouldn't feel good about selling them. But, I'm not handing them over if they don't ask."

"Agreed." After watching Dad in a mech suit, I hated the idea of losing them. "We should drop Mom, Dad and Ada off at Puskar Stellar orbital platform so they can start their shore-leave. The rest of us can deal with stowing cargo and setting up the habitation domes."

"Jack and I will bring the pod-jumper over to the warehouse and load the domes. We'll take Marny with us," Nick said.

"Tali know we're coming? I'd hate to surprise her," I said.

Nick chuckled. "She knows we're coming. We won't even be able to see her house from where we'll be sitting. She has a large plot of land."

"Likes her privacy, I guess."

"She gave me the choice. I thought we might be noisy neighbors and it would be better if we weren't too close."

"How long do you think we'll be there?"

"I told Tali we'd stay a maximum of three months and then find a more permanent location. We might be better renting apartments in Puskar or Coolidge. At least this way we have time to figure things out," he said.

I realized the thing we needed to figure out was about Tabby. Nick would never say it directly, but he knew our business was on hold until we knew what was happening with her. I'd successfully been able to get her condition out of my head for several days, knowing that there was nothing I could do. A cold lump in the pit of my stomach was my only reminder.

The energy level on the ship was high as I dropped everyone but Marny off at the platform. Nick had manufactured a portable grav-box for the cat. Filbert was Jack's responsibility and he wasn't letting him go anytime soon.

All of us would stay in the hotel until we got the habitation domes set up. I wished I could be there today when Jack experienced his first set of civilian clothes and walked around without his vac-suit. I hoped it would bring a smile to his face as he took in the sights. Both he and Nick had been slowly recovering from the death of their mother and today would be a healthy diversion from the grief.

The warehouse was fairly close to the orbital platform above Puskar Stellar. It wasn't anything more complex than a grid of rectangular steel boxes, although there were thousands of them. The facility was protected by a security patrol and, no doubt, other less obvious measures. This close in, however, Mars Protectorate could be expected to respond quickly if security problems arose.

I checked in with the security patrol and they cleared our approach. The warehouse had a convenient platform we could request be moved in front of our unit. It would give us positive surface onto which we could lock the aft section of the ship. We didn't need to worry about the ship drifting in space, but moving cargo would be enough to dislodge it if we weren't well tied in.

I pulled on my armored vac-suit and met Marny in the cargo hold. She gave me an approving look.

The warehouse had a full time stevedore supervisor and we were lucky she was available right away. It cost extra to use this warehouse service, but moving three hundred fifty cubic meters of crates was more work than we were interested in doing without help. Nick arrived a few minutes after the bots had started and we stood together, waiting for them to finish.

"I'll run the *Hotspur* over to Coolidge. See you in a few hours? I'll probably stop at the Veteran's hospital and see if I can get an update on the *Hope's* arrival," I said.

"Good luck," Marny said and clapped me on the back as I turned to go.

Set course for Coolidge Dry Dock. Negotiate arrival schedule, I instructed as I slid into my pilot's chair. It turned out there were three ship manufacturing plants in orbit above Coolidge, in addition to the Navy's own shipyard. Fortunately, my AI knew which one we were scheduled for. I certainly wouldn't have been able to find it on my own.

Thirty minutes later, I slid through a blue energy field and onto the deck of a hangar that could accommodate a ship at least twice the size of the *Hotspur*. I dropped the small backpack that contained my civvies by the air lock door and met a brown-skinned spacer on the scarred deck of the bay.

"Priyanka Lanka." He offered his hand.

"Liam Hoffen," I shook his hand.

"What are we working on today?"

I was sure that Nick had sent him a list of repairs, but I didn't mind answering his question.

"We had a collision with another craft and it ripped off the starboard wing and engine."

"An old British sloop like this is a real piece of history, such a beauty. Let's take a look," he said.

His arc-jets lifted him easily from the deck and I followed him up to the wing. Even though there were bright lights in the bay, the armor's absorptive skin made it difficult to make out the details. The Naval engineer's field patch stood out against the otherwise sleek lines. After flitting around the wing, he pulled up and sat on the edge of it.

"It's a shame we can't manufacture the old girl's armor. We can make her look good, but you'll be able to see the scar. On the positive side, it was a clean break. The impact must have been incredible to sheer this wing off. Mind telling me how she got this way?"

"We got run over by a much larger ship. My co-pilot saw it just seconds before it happened. If not for her quick action, we'd have been completely crushed," I said.

"Sounds like a heck of a ride. I didn't think that was even possible with transponders. Do you need us to inspect your electronics?"

"Won't be necessary," I said.

He gave me a quizzical smile but didn't push further. He hopped off the wing and jetted to the top to inspect the twin turrets that had been rendered inoperable by the collision.

"It could be worse. The turrets are easily manufactured. The cowls that covered them have been lost and without access to the materials for the armor, there's no good reason to replace them," he said.

I wondered how much less effective our stealth would be without the cowls.

"We've already provided an estimate for the interior work. Should I contact your partner, Nick James, once I work the numbers up?" Priyanka asked.

I wasn't sure what interior work he was talking about, so I touched the side of my earwig to engage my HUD projector without verbal direction. The AI had been listening to our conversation and understood I wanted to see the plans for the work he was referring to. A drawing popped up showing a new, narrow separation that had been added between the berth deck and the hold. On the port side was a permanent armory and on the other, a hallway that led to the ship's only airlock. A new airlock door had been added between the hallway and the hold, in effect extending the living quarters to include the side exit and the armory. It was a nice upgrade. We would now be able to walk from the berth deck over to the starboard airlock or into the cargo bay without having to depressurize the entire hold.

"Sorry, I needed to review something. And yes, definitely contact Nick with the estimates. He'll copy me on them," I said.

"Excellent. Can I give you a ride over to the platform?"

"I'd appreciate it."

I grabbed my bag and we loaded into a highly polished, bright red passenger vehicle. I'd never sat in a vehicle as richly appointed and wondered how much it must have cost. Priyanka was solicitous, offering me a variety of drinks from his well-stocked bar and suggesting that he could arrange for entertainment planet-side. I turned him down, mostly because I didn't have a lot of experience with that sort of thing and didn't want to embarrass myself. While I was grateful for the ride, I was just as glad to be out of the vehicle and standing on the orbital platform.

I took the space-elevator down to the surface and changed into my jeans and blazer. I mostly wore the blazer to hide the fact that I was packing a flechette in a shoulder holster. It was completely legal on Mars, but I'd received funny looks in the past when I'd worn it on my belt.

Veteran's Hospital, I directed the cab I'd jumped into.

Downtown Coolidge was smaller than Puskar Stellar but its layout belied its founder's roots in the naval hierarchy. All of the buildings were neatly organized and spotlessly clean. Some sort of central planning board had probably made sure all buildings met the standard. The white structures with large glass panels were separated by well-manicured green spaces. For someone who had spent most of their time in space, it was as impressive as it was beautiful.

The cab dropped me in front of one of the buildings. I pushed my way through a swinging door and walked up to an information console.

I need information on Tabitha Masters. She should be arriving on the hospital ship, Hope.

I probably didn't need to stand at the console. My other option was to stand in the atrium talking to myself.

Liam Hoffen, access granted. Tabitha Masters arrived forty hours ago having been transferred from the Hope, my AI informed.

Locate Tabby, I want to see her, I said.

A translucent blue vapor trail led to a bank of elevators. My heart raced, she hadn't contacted me. Did that mean she hadn't regained consciousness, or did she not want to see me for some reason? I steeled myself. We'd get through this no matter what.

As I exited the elevators, I was intercepted by a middle-aged woman in a naval uniform.

"Mr. Hoffen?" she asked politely. She had, no doubt, been alerted to my presence when I signed into the information console.

"Yes, I'm here to see Tabby Masters," I said. *Duh,* I thought to myself. It's not like I was here to deliver pizza.

"I'm Sonia Lemaigre, I've been caring for Tabitha. I'm glad to have been here when you arrived. Could we talk?"

I accepted her offered hand. I recognized the golden comet pin on the collar of her grey shirt, which designated her as Lieutenant Commander.

"Certainly, Commander, and please call me Liam." I'd learned that it was appropriate to shorten titles in greetings.

She led me into a small room with several comfortable chairs. She sat on the edge of one and gave me an earnest look, then laid her hand on my knee.

"Liam. Tabitha is at the beginning of a very long journey. A journey that can be made easier with friends." She stumbled over what sounded like rehearsed lines. "May I speak plainly?"

"Please," I encouraged her.

"I understand that you and she are very close. We have a lot of experience with recovering veterans. Tabitha's personality profile tells us that she will adapt to her body's new configuration over time. What she will struggle with the most is rejection from her family group. Fair or not, Mr. Hoffen, your response is critical. To say it more plainly; if you're not in this for the long haul, it would be better if you simply turned around and left right now."

Blood rushed to my face and I started to stand involuntarily. Commander Lemaigre didn't rise with me, but sat, passively watching. For reasons not entirely clear to me, I wanted to punch her.

"I want to see Tabby," I said through clenched teeth. Annoyingly, she returned my stare with that same passive expression. I felt like she was studying me.

"Your anger is understandable, Mr. Hoffen. What happened to Tabitha is a tragedy. Please understand, you and I need to make sure we don't compound that tragedy. Perhaps you should take a few days to think about this. We have counseling available to help you. I'm not sure you're in any state to see her yet."

I found it hard to hear her words through the rushing sound in my ears, but I now recognized that she stood between me and Tabby. I needed to get hold of myself or I'd be locked out. I exhaled, sat back in the chair and focused on relaxing my hands.

After a few minutes I felt like I had recovered enough to speak. "I do not need a couple of days to figure out who Tabby is to me." I was surprised at how angry I sounded.

"Who is that, Mr. Hoffen?" she asked.

She had me there. I didn't have a word or single phrase that would adequately describe how I felt about Tabby. "Look. I don't know what you're looking for here. I don't have everything worked out, but if I know one thing, it's that I will not abandon Tabby."

"For her sake, I hope that's the case. By stepping back into her life right now, you are in a unique position to help her through this transition. If you get cold feet and abandon her, it will have a devastating impact on her life," she said.

"Will you let me see her now?"

"Yes, of course. She is currently asleep, but she has been asking about you."

It peeved me to learn that my attempts to contact Tabby had been blocked, but Lieutenant Commander Lemaigre was up and moving. I wasn't about to say something that could jeopardize me being able to see Tabby.

"She's right in here," she said, gesturing to a room with a wide door that was mostly closed. She stood back, making no effort to enter the room. If she thought I was lacking courage, she was nuts. I'd spent several days with Tabby while she was in the tank.

I pushed the door open and slipped into the room. I'd expected to see tubes and vid screens everywhere, but instead there was just Tabby, lying under covers, slightly elevated, with her head on a pillow. If not for her bald head that was just now growing a fine layer of fuzz, I could easily imagine that nothing had happened.

I took off my coat and holster, laying them on a chair. I kicked off my shoes and removed my prosthetic foot. From experience, I knew that her stumps would be almost fully healed at this point. They might be tender if she'd started working with a prosthetic, but I knew what I needed to do. I hopped to the side of her bed and lay on top of the covers, on her right side, where her arm was missing.

She stirred, but didn't awaken. I snuggled in next to her and laid my arm across her chest, like I'd done so often before. Unconsciously, she tipped her head toward mine and I felt the anxiety of the last several weeks finally start to drain from my body.

LEVELING THE FIELD

"Hoffen, wake up. You're drooling on me." Tabby's voice was raspy, like a loud whisper.

The smell of the hospital's sanitizer struck me first and then her face came into view. My back hurt from lying in a single, uncomfortable position all night. As soon as I adjusted slightly, I rolled off the bed and landed on the floor.

"Frak," I said. The pain helped my head clear and I picked myself up off the floor, grabbing my prosthetic. "How long have you been awake?"

"A couple of hours," she said. She was studying my face. "Did you really mean what you said to Sonia?"

I was sure I'd never heard that name before. "Who's Sonia?"

"Doctor Lemaigre."

"How do you know what we talked about?" I said.

"It's part of my therapy. She recorded your conversation."

"That doesn't sound legal."

"She said that I was going to have a hard enough time dealing with my condition and I needed to know who was in my corner. You don't need to stay, Liam. I'd like more for your life than spending it taking care of me."

"That one was free, Tabby. You won't get another one," I said.

"What was free?"

"Don't play dumb, Masters. I don't want you questioning me on this. I'm here. You need to deal with it."

"Do you know what's weird?" she asked in a softer voice.

"Tell me."

"I knew you'd come."

I nodded. I didn't know what to say.

"Where are you with rehabilitation?" When I lost my foot,

they'd given me a small amount of instruction and a subroutine for my AI. Otherwise, I'd been left entirely on my own.

"I spend a few hours a day with a prosthetic arm. It's hard to control and of course I can't feel anything, but they say I'll be able to pick things up once I get the hang of it."

"Any word from your family?" I asked. Something in the back of my mind suggested that her grandfather lived on Mars. I had an ulterior motive. Her family had real money and I hoped there was some possibility they'd pay for at least one of the optional surgeries.

"I've been exchanging comms with Dad. He's talking about making a trip out here," she said.

"I'd heard your Dad had holed up with a bunch of the refinery staff. Is he doing all right?"

"Yes. He wanted me to pass along his thanks for the warning."

"We got lucky," I said.

"You make luck, Hoffen." She smiled at me and it melted my heart. "But you have weird pillow talk."

"Yeah, sorry."

"So, I'm sure you already know that I've been discharged from the service," she said.

"That's the rumor."

"And that the Navy won't pay for reconstructive surgeries?" she asked.

"I'd heard that."

"Well, if you're thinking my family will come up with the money, you'd be wrong there. My dad would, if he actually had money, but Grandpa still owns the corporation and there's no way that's going to happen."

I nodded. I wasn't sure where she was going with all of this.

"And you're good with this?" she asked, deliberately forcing me to look down at her. "We can't have a normal relationship. Best case is me in an arc-jet chair with one good arm."

"Are you going Dr. Jekyll and Mr. Hyde on me?" I asked. If there was something I recognized, it was when she was feeling insecure.

"What?"

"You heard me." I was surprised at how instantly pissed off I'd become.

"How sweet. Your first quarrel." A heavyset, older woman entered the room. "No doubt you were about to work out your angst about living together with long-term disabilities. Let's just put a pin in that and do something useful. For that, I need this one to leave and not come back until after 1800." She jabbed a finger at my chest.

I looked at Tabby questioningly, whose eyebrows were raised and whose mouth formed a perfect 'O.'

"Off with you. You can come back at dinner and get all self-righteous and ignore the reality of your new lives together. Or, maybe you'll figure it out and go back to making googly faces," she continued. "And if this one gets to work, maybe she can pick up a cup and show you what a good girl she is."

I must have given some clue that I was about to go off on this little goblin, because Tabby stopped me.

"Go, Liam. I've got this," she said.

I leaned in and gave Tabby a long kiss. When we separated, I gave Ms. Troll a once over and stalked out of the room. Surprisingly, she didn't toss any new jabs my way, so I was able to shrug it off by the time I made it to street level.

One of the advantages of the highly structured downtown was access to mass transit. I had taken a cab from the MAG-L terminal to arrive here and when I asked for another, my AI recognized my mistake and projected a path to a public transportation hub. It was a fifty meter walk from the hospital's front door to the pickup point of a four-seater arc-jet ground vehicle. I waited less than thirty seconds for the shiny, blue translucent vehicle to arrive. I sat down next to a Navy Lieutenant, no doubt on her way to the terminal on assignment. In the city, people didn't make small talk while on the public transit system, so we exchanged smiles and then politely ignored each other.

The four-seater dropped us at the main terminal, which served both the space elevator and the MAG-L system. After a short twenty-minute wait, I boarded the train destined for Puskar Stellar.

"Nick, I'm free for a few hours and headed back to Puskar," I said. He wouldn't answer if he was busy.

A short communications delay alerted me to the fact that Nick was likely up at the warehouse.

"Jack and I are on our way back with the second load of domes. Can we pick you up on our way through?" he asked.

"Sure," I said. "I'm going to run by Ballance Electronics first. Tabby doesn't have her earwig anymore."

"That works. I need to rent a couple of bots. I'll find someone close to where you're going. How's she doing?"

"Pretty much what you'd expect. She's trying to drive me off, but I know she doesn't mean it."

"Do you think she'd mind if Jack and I came by?" Nick asked.

"I think she'd like that. I'll talk to her. It might be easier when she gets her chair. She has a hard time moving around right now."

"Understood. See you in forty minutes or so," he said.

I picked up the highest quality earwig the store sold. I hoped she'd like it. The only difference between this earwig and her previous one was the ability to change the color of the small band that ran from her ear along her cheekbone to project the HUD on her retina. She could select any color or pattern, including chameleon mode, which would mimic her skin color and make it virtually invisible.

I caught up with Jack and Nick at the rental store. They'd rented a maid-bot and a construction bot that was considerably smaller than the one we'd needed to take apart the warehouse. It was a tight squeeze for the three of us in the front of the pod-jumper, but it felt reminiscent of so many deliveries we'd made back at Colony 40.

"We'll finish this so we can head back to University Hills. We're meeting with Jake at Megliano's for a late lunch," Nick said as we landed in a wide open field of rugged vegetation.

From the air, I'd been able to pick out Tali's old homestead house easily. On the ground, the terrain made it so we couldn't see any part of it. Marny waved as we jumped out of the vehicle. I, for one, was glad to have enough room for my shoulders to operate freely. The pod-jumper was clearly designed for two people, not three.

"Have you seen Tali?" I asked.

Nick nodded and said, "Yup. She came out and walked us around. Jenny seemed pretty excited to have a neighbor."

"Celina and Jenny are still living with her?" Celina Dontal had moved into Tali's home after Tali and her special ops group had helped rescue Celina's sister, Jenny, from slavers - which was, of course, an interesting story all on its own.

"Tali was asking about Tabby. If you recall, Tali had quite a bit of reconstructive surgery after her service," Nick said.

"That might be helpful." I knew everyone meant well, but wasn't sure Tabby was in any shape to have a lot of people visiting.

The bots were just being unloaded when a very thin girl came running over the rise separating our construction site from Tali's home. The long black hair streaming behind gave her away as Jenny. Next to her ran a giant orange tabby cat named Godzilla. That monstrosity weighed in at twenty kilos and his shoulders came up to my knee. I'm not ashamed to admit that Godzilla made me nervous, but Jack took a couple of steps forward and waved them over.

"Did I mention that Jack and Jenny like to hang out?" Nick asked.

"Seriously?" I asked. "They just barely met."

"You'll see. They clicked," Nick said.

I didn't need a long explanation, it made sense to me. Jenny and Jack had both survived traumatic experiences but still needed contact with someone their own age. My heart nearly stopped as Godzilla launched himself at Jack. Even more surprising was Jack's response, which was to hurl himself at the huge cat. They fell on the ground and wrestled roughly.

"Is he okay?" I looked to Nick for cues on how to respond.

"Yup. Let's get the bots running," Nick said.

The pod-jumper's payload was carried in a seven meter long 'short' container. Nick opened it and delivered programming instructions to the construction bot. He and Jack had already delivered two habitation domes and the pile of supporting machinery.

Nick's plan was to connect four domes in a T shape. A central dome with galley and mess and three attached domes with sleeping quarters.

The construction bot started by leveling a small patch of ground. Having come from asteroid mining, the concept of moving dirt around was foreign to me. Nick and I sat back on the hill and watched with rapt interest as the fine material was scraped and flattened into a perfect surface that could never be achieved on an asteroid.

"Where'd Jack go?" I asked. He and Jenny had disappeared.

"Probably up to the house, although they're safe wherever they go. Tali has surveillance on the entire lot," Nick said.

"I bet she has more than surveillance." If pushed, Tali referred to herself as ex-special forces, a description that undersold her capabilities. I suspected she also had an active component to her security. I wondered what form that might take, but suspected it was probably some sort of turret.

I took advantage of the quiet and finalized the first load that Ada and Mom would take out on the *Adela Chen*. I'd set up three legs that would take them from Mars over to two Indian space-borne factories. I was jealous that they'd pass close enough to Earth to be able to see the blue planet unaided - granted, it would be about the size of the end of my thumb, held out at arm's length.

The route would take ten days. They'd pick up a full load of metal products from a General Astral forge orbiting Mars above the city of Elysium. I discovered the route purely by accident, but felt foolish for not putting it together previously. Mars had better access to the asteroids than Earth corporations, but Earth factories had tremendous manufacturing output. We wouldn't get rich, but we could keep the *Adela Chen* employed for the foreseeable future. I signed the contracts and sent the information out.

Two hours later the construction bot finished and loaded itself back into the container beneath the pod-jumper. Nick programmed the maid-bot and set it loose in the grimy domes. Compared to the construction bot, it was inexpensive to rent and we could afford to leave it onsite. The construction bot, on the other hand, needed to be returned today.

"I talked to Lena. She's happy to have Jack hang out with them, but we're on the hook to bring back pizza," Nick said.

"Where's Marny?" I asked.

"She and Tali have a workout date. I'm just happy she didn't make me go along," he said.

It was 1430 by the time we'd dropped off the construction bot. We walked into Megliano's and found Jake already seated. He was gesturing subtly, obviously working through something on his HUD. As he saw us approach, Jake stood and offered his hand. It swallowed mine; the handshake firm, but not crushing.

"Thanks for meeting with me today," he said as we sat down.

"You definitely know how to pique our curiosity," I said.

"Hopefully, I wasn't overly dramatic, but I felt it would be better for us to discuss my proposal in person. You mind if I dive right in?"

Ironically, a server showed up just then. Nick rattled off what had become our standard order; double crust, pepperoni, cream-cheese pizza with a Guinness for me and a Phantom Citrus Berry Ale for him.

When the server left, Jake jumped back in. "I appreciate the offer to be part of your crew, but I just don't think that's where I want to go - long term," he said. "That said, I've got an idea that I think would benefit all of us and I'd like to get your take on it."

"Shoot," Nick said.

"If I understand correctly, Loose Nuts Corporation has an unlimited license to the General Astral CA-12 cutter's intellectual property for replicating parts for as long as you own the ship, *Sterra's Gift*." Jake paused and looked to Nick for confirmation. Nick nodded and Jake shifted in his chair as if it were uncomfortable. Our server showed up at that moment to deliver our drinks and seeing a lag in the conversation, asked how we were all doing. I knew he was just being friendly, but could see a flash of impatience on Jake's face.

"What I'd like to do," Jake said, once the server had moved on, "is create a sub-corporation to Loose Nuts dedicated to buying and selling CA-12s. I'd find junkers, manufacture necessary parts and restore them."

"How do you see ownership working out?" Nick asked.

"Loose Nuts retains ten percent, I keep ninety," he said.

I was curious. "Do you think you can find enough CA-12s?"

"I've done some research. I've found ten around Mars I think I could work with," he said.

"Do you have enough capital to make that work?" Nick asked.

"Well. That's the other part of it. I've got sixty thousand credits, which isn't enough. I need at least an additional hundred and fifty thousand credits." He sat back in his chair. This was what he deemed to be the biggest stumbling block.

"I'll bet you already have a ship lined up. What's your timeline on return of that capital and at what rate?" Nick asked.

Jake sat forward again. We hadn't balked. "Ten weeks and I'd pay back at ten percent."

"I don't think that works for us," Nick laid out a different arrangement.

I was having a hard time keeping up with Nick. The best I could determine, he'd countered a ten percent ownership with a seventy percent ownership and allowed Jake to buy us down to twenty-five percent. The two negotiated for a few minutes while I tried to stay engaged.

"I think we have an agreement," Jake finally said.

"You good with all this?" Nick asked me.

If I were honest, I'd have told Nick I was barely holding on. But, bottom line, I trusted him.

"Works for me," I said.

DROPPING IN ON A FRIEND

It was 1900 by the time I made it back to Tabby's room. She was sitting up in bed with a blanket pulled to her waist and she was wearing a vac-suit liner. For a moment, I didn't even notice that she must be wearing her prosthetic arm, as it looked much like her original. It was only her stiff movement of it that brought me back to reality.

"What do you think?" she asked hopefully.

I grinned and glanced down at my foot. "You know you yelled at me in a similar circumstance, right?"

She raised her eyebrows and pinched her cheeks together pushing her lips forward. The phrase 'disapproving school-marm' popped into my mind.

"What I meant, was, I didn't even notice it when I came through the door," I said.

"That's better. Seriously, it looks okay?" It was weird to have her show any insecurity.

"Yup, better than okay. It's really hard to tell the difference - maybe a little, when you move around, but I bet that's more about you getting used to it. So was it really horrible with troll breath?" I asked. I still hadn't forgotten how we'd been treated by the physical therapist this morning.

Tabby giggled at my name for the woman. "She's not that bad. Well, she is, but she's really dedicated, just not good with people. She only left about twenty minutes ago,"

"How much therapy will you have?"

"Two weeks. It'd be longer but..." she looked down at her missing legs and tears formed in her eyes.

I sat on the bed next to her, careful to choose the side with her good arm.

"We'll get through it, Tabby."

"Change the subject."

"Right. Oh, I got you an earwig today," I pulled the new device from my pocket and handed it to her.

"It's beautiful," she said. "Did it cost too much?"

"Not hardly! I need to be able to talk to you. I've had enough of passing messages through the hospital," I said.

"I love it. What else did you do today?" She placed the earwig into her ear and it expanded, leaving the opening intact and attaching itself to the ear canal's outer wall. It then extended along her cheek bone.

I told her about Jack and Jenny and setting up the habitation domes. She was interested in the route we'd created for Mom and Ada, so I showed her all of that too.

Once we got through all of my news, I finally broached the next difficult thing. "Nick said that Tali wanted to know if she could visit."

"Why?" Tabby creased her forehead. She wasn't ready for this.

I pressed forward quickly. "She's been through a similar experience, not as extensive, but she lost most of her right side and had it replaced, including part of her spine."

Tabby's eyes grew wide. "That's a lot."

"I don't think Marny would mind me telling you, but she also had extensive reconstructive surgery on her jaw. A good portion of her face is synthetic skin," I said.

"I never knew," Tabby still had that crease in her forehead, but she was softening.

"That's kind of my point. Whatever it takes, we'll figure it out," I said.

The next morning I left before the troll arrived, having no desire to mix it up with her. I suspected that was her goal.

Mom and Ada were leaving this morning and I wanted to be there to see them off. We'd agreed to meet in a restaurant that overlooked traffic sailing in and out of Puskar's space side terminal. I arrived early, ordered coffee and sat at the bar. It was enjoyable to watch the ships arriving and departing and I didn't notice when Marny, Ada, Mom, Dad and Nick showed up as a group.

Ada caught my attention and when I turned, I saw Mom and Dad holding hands, something I don't think I'd ever seen before.

***

"So what are we going to do while Ada and Silver are gone?" Dad asked.

"We need to sort through the crates. I promised a load to an auctioneer. Would love to have your help," Nick said.

"I was thinking we should make Dad show us how to operate those mech suits," I said.

Marny swiveled her head toward me and smiled. "That something you'd be willing to do, Pete?"

"Why not?" He shrugged his shoulders. "We can start in the warehouse and use them to load the crates."

"I thought it took months to train on a suit," Nick's voice was a little higher than normal.

"Every maggot starts somewhere. We'll set me up as squad commander, that way I can dial 'em back so you're not wrecking things," Pete said with a grin.

We piled into the pod-jumper and sailed to the warehouse. The front of each bay was designed to accept a standard container and provided a locking mechanism. Dad and I had ridden over in the container, since there was only room for two and a half in the cab of the pod-jumper. The back of the container finally opened and we piled out into our bay in the warehouse.

"It's a good thing we didn't wear our armored suits," Dad said, "The mechanized infantry suits have a lot of adjustment in them, but they can't accommodate the heavier, less flexible armor. Most of the time you'd only wear a suit-liner inside one of these things. Since the container isn't pressurized, we'll have to keep the vac-suits on. I've already configured one, so I'll start with it and get a command channel set up. Unpack the other two and figure out who's going first," he said.

"Don't worry about me," Nick said. "I'm not getting in one of those."

"Are you kidding?" I asked.

"No. The whole idea makes me feel claustrophobic," he said.

"It's just a big vac-suit," I said.

"Yeah, whatever," he said, brushing me off. "I can't get past the idea that I'm climbing into the solar system's smallest spaceship and I'll be trapped in one spot."

I shrugged, recognizing that he was probably serious. I didn't want to make a big deal about it, so I pulled off my ABGs and stashed them in the cab of the pod-jumper. I'd want them back, but they'd just get in the way inside the mechanized infantry suit.

"The suits aren't currently keyed. All you need to do is place the palm of your hand into the back of the helm," Dad instructed.

I ran my hand along the thigh of the suit, just to get a feel for it. The metal was smooth to the touch and had no give. Even our armored vac-suits had some give, if you touched them lightly. Since the suits had never been worn and weren't keyed to anyone else, they opened easily. I found a security plate about the size of a human hand just where Dad said it would be and pressed my hand into it. The suit split vertically along the entire length of the chest. I sat back into the cavity and slid my feet into the legs of the suit.

"That's right. Sit there until Marny catches up. Don't put your arms into the sleeves yet," Dad said.

We'd turned the gravity in our bay of the warehouse up to .6g, standard for most space operations. Nick sat on the pile of crates, waiting patiently, wearing a bemused grin. I smiled back at him, excited.

"Give me a thumbs up if you're feeling comfortable," Dad said. Marny and I returned the thumbs up. "Lay back and slip your arms into the sleeves. Try to keep your hands and arms relaxed and don't clench your fists; that will cause the suits to close. If that starts to happen, it's not the end of the world, just relax and the suit will stop." I wondered how many people he'd trained to operate a mechanized infantry suit in his life.

"Okay, wait one. Both suits are coming online. You should see a prompt in your HUD. That's me asking for command control. You need to agree."

I saw the prompt and agreed to it. He continued to walk us through a customization process. We set up security protocols and finally closed the suits by clenching our fists. As the suit closed, a membrane surrounded me, shrinking tightly over my vac-suit, fitting the interior to my body. It was a little intimate and I had to remind myself that the membrane was just an inanimate object.

"Before you stand up, you need to verbally ask the suit to report weapon status, then report that status back to me," Dad ordered. After another fifteen minutes of instruction and status checks he finally announced that we were ready to take our first steps.

Standing up turned out to be more difficult that you might imagine. While the suit bent neatly at the waist, the normal mechanism of pulling my legs beneath me or rolling over to my knees didn't work well from the crate I was in.

"Lesson number one. The suit is capable of doing a lot of work - let it. Push your arms back and keep your waist stiff, the suit will recognize your desire to come to a standing position. Your AI has a lot of learning to do, might as well get started now. You first, Marny." Pete positioned himself at the end of her crate.

She popped up a little too quickly and started to over-rotate. Dad had anticipated this and gave her a little nudge backward. "Good. You do that next time and I guarantee you'll catch yourself just fine."

He stood in front of my crate and nodded at me. I pushed my arms back to get a feeling for how much power I had available. The feedback made me feel like I was pushing on something very light. I popped my hands down and came flying up out of the crate, clean over the top of Big Pete. Having flown a lot in a vac-suit, it didn't concern me too much, but I knew I needed to adjust. I tucked into a ball, straightened out behind him and landed on my bent knees.

"Sorry," I said, as I turned around to face him.

"You mean to do that?" he asked.

"Not initially, but once I was up and going, I just kind of rolled with it," I said.

"That was quite a maneuver, for a maggot." He sounded a little impressed. "How about you take it easy on that sort of thing for a while?"

Now that we were upright, walking was possible. Nick identified crates he wanted us to place in the container. To start out, walking was difficult, mostly because my legs were used to a particular stride. In the suit, my legs were now about half a meter longer.

We took two hours to load the container, a task that could have been accomplished by stevedore bots in twenty minutes or less. It had been a good exercise, though. The maneuvers involved had helped us learn to control the suit for basic tasks.

"Believe it or not," Big Pete said. "The mechanized infantry probably still spend more time moving equipment than fighting. In my day, the extraordinary power of the suit, combined with the fine controls of a skilled Marine made us invaluable in relocating camps."

"We need to get going and I don't think there's enough room to bring the suits down to the surface with us this time," Nick said. "Maybe tomorrow?"

"Unnecessary," Big Pete said, "we can do a high altitude insertion."

"Are you nuts?" I asked.

"Not at all. While the first time is a little exhilarating, the suit actually does all the work. We'll bring it in nice and easy. We can even follow Nick in," he said. I could tell he was loving every moment of being in charge.

"Marny?" I asked.

"Aye. I'm in, Cap. It's something I've always wanted to try," she said.

"Every Marine has suit envy. It's to be expected." Pete was smiling widely.

We formed up on the pod-jumper, holding onto the container

as Nick sailed towards Mars. At an altitude of two hundred kilometers, our suits disengaged from the pod-jumper and we spread out, separating by a kilometer. At ninety kilometers, the suit started to shake and I noticed that the external surface was starting to glow red, but I kept falling directly at the planet, head first.

Exhilarating was the wrong word. Terrifying was the right word. It looked like the entire forward surface of my suit was on fire. I kept expecting the heat to reach into my suit and burn me up, which of course it didn't.

At fifty kilometers the suit flipped over so that I was falling with my chest pointed toward the surface of the planet. If I hadn't been so terrified, I might have found the view to be amazing. I tried to express this to Nick. As it turned out, Big Pete had muted me because, apparently, I was screaming all the way down. When I reached eight kilometers the suit rotated again, feet down. Arc-jets started firing and my descent finally slowed to a reasonable rate.

The ground came up toward us unbelievably fast. I couldn't imagine how I wasn't going to smash into the surface and bury myself twenty meters beneath the dirt.

Incoming emergency hail, my AI announced.

Accept, I heard Big Pete say. He was in command of our suits and would need to answer for the three of us. We were all falling within fifty meters of each other.

"Unidentified craft. You're about to enter a secure area, alter trajectory or you will be considered hostile."

I saw a grid outlining our landing location. I didn't think we had a lot of choice about the matter until my suit rotated forward and small foils appeared between my legs and in the space between my arms and chest. We veered violently off to the side. In my opinion, we were too close to the ground to execute such a maneuver and live. The ground rushed up to meet me and at the last moment the suit forced me to curl up into a ball just before impact. Since I had a significant amount of horizontal movement, I skipped across the ground, finally rolling to a stop.

"Liam. What happened," Nick's panicked voice asked. He was behind us considerably, but I had no doubt he'd been tracking us.

"We didn't let Tali know we were coming and tripped one of her security protocols," I said.

"Everyone okay?" Big Pete asked on the squad's channel.

"Aye," Marny replied.

"Roger that." I rolled over and popped my hands back with less force than I had in the warehouse. I came up with only a little over rotation and caught myself easily.

"I'm afraid I must have entered the wrong coordinates," Big Pete said. "Sorry about the landing, but it's better than being fired on."

"Good news and bad news Dad," I said. "That was the right location, we just neglected to tell our landlady that we'd be dropping in on her."

"Form up, shoulder to shoulder. We've got incoming. I'm not unlocking your weapons unless we're fired upon, but something's coming in fast," he said.

A riderless grav-bike roared over the top of us at twenty five meters.

"What in the…" Big Pete started.

Incoming communication request, I heard on the squad comm channel.

Accept, Big Pete replied.

"Identify yourselves. You're trespassing." It was Tali's voice.

"Dad, that's Tali. Give me an open comm," I said. The squad controls didn't allow me to communicate as long as Big Pete was in charge.

"You're open. Go," he replied.

"Tali," I said quickly. "Don't shoot, it's Liam and Marny."

"Who's the third?" she asked.

My HUD outlined her as she walked up over the hill. She was carrying a large blaster rifle.

"It's my Dad," I said. By now she'd have received my ident signal.

"You might let a girl know you're going to practice high

altitude drops. That was a heck of a maneuver you all took there at the end. Anyone hurt?" she asked.

"Do you count being queasy?" Marny asked.

"Sorry, my friend. Where in the world did you get these suits?" she asked.

I exhaled a sigh. "Long story."

"Always is with you, Liam. Sorry about all that, I thought we were under attack," she said.

I introduced her to Big Pete, who'd been watching the exchange dumbfounded.

"Nice to meet you, Miss Liszt," he said. He'd opened up the suit and reached down to shake her hand. I wasn't sure I could do the same without falling over. "What is it with you boys and all these beautiful women?" He looked at me, genuinely baffled.

"Don't let her fool you, Dad, Tali's every bit the fighter Marny is," I said.

"That'd be an understatement, Cap," Marny added quickly.

We accompanied Tali over to where her grav-bike had landed. Apparently, she'd jumped off early and used it to cause a distraction.

Big Pete wasn't about to miss a training opportunity and challenged us to jog back to the habitation domes. His superior skill was evident, as Marny and I both fell several times when we misjudged the uneven terrain. Each time we got back up, however, it was a little bit easier. I could see how it would take a Marine several months to excel in the suit, but it also seemed to me that we were learning the basics quickly.

Nick and Tali were waiting for us at the habitation domes. We stepped out of the mech suits and I grabbed my civvies from the pod-jumper. For several minutes I found it difficult to walk with my now, overly short-feeling legs.

"I think we should have a barbeque," Tali said. "Any chance you could talk Tabby into coming over for that?"

"She's not overly mobile yet," I said.

She tilted her head and gave me a look that I could only interpret as sympathy. "She will be. They'll kick her out of that hospital sooner than you'd think."

"I'm seeing her tonight. I'll ask."

"Be patient, it's a big adjustment. I've a lot of friends who've made it through. It's too early, but when she's ready, I'd like to introduce her to them," she said.

"Thank you," I said. It was time to go see her. "Nick, any chance I could get a ride.

"Actually, I'm going that way. I can drop you at the MAG-L if you like," Tali said.

DEAL WITH THE DEVIL

For the next week, days pretty much repeated themselves. I'd spend nights with Tabby, only to get kicked out in the morning by the physical therapist. During the days, I spent time playing mech-warrior with Marny and Tali. We'd even been able to convince Nick to train with us. Originally, I'd been worried about causing the suits to lose value, but Nick reminded me that we'd likely be giving them back to Mars Protectorate once someone actually read through the inventory.

I discovered that a person's personality outside of the suits translated directly to their personality within them. Marny was just as undefeatable in hand-to-hand combat with a suit as she was without it. She easily anticipated my moves and more often than not, it turned into a lesson in combat. Similarly, she had a difficult time keeping up with Tali.

"Tomorrow, I'm starting on the arc-jet chair," Tabby announced at the end of the week. She sounded upbeat, which made sense since she'd be gaining a substantial amount of mobility.

"Have you looked into different models?" I asked.

"Of chairs? I guess I hadn't thought about it. The Navy will supply one for me."

"Maybe they're all the same," I said, not believing it for a minute.

"One thing at a time," she said.

"Speaking of… Mom and Ada will be back on Tuesday and Tali invited us out for a bonfire and barbeque. Would you be willing?" I asked.

The color drained from Tabby's face and her eyes opened wide. "I… I… I'm… I don't think I'll be ready for that."

"No pressure, if it doesn't work out, no big deal. Let's talk on

Tuesday and if you're not in for that, I won't push you. Sound reasonable?"

"I suppose." She looked down at the back of her prosthetic hand. I was impressed with how much mobility she'd gained with the arm and hand. It wasn't as good as her normal arm, but she'd become proficient.

"Cards?" I asked.

"Sure," she said.

The next morning started earlier than most. Tabby woke me up and said, "Liam. Patricia's going to be here early today and I don't think she likes you very much."

"I don't care," I said sleepily.

"Get up," she said. "I asked her if she could start early today. Did you know she stays late every day and doesn't even get paid for it?"

"Why is she so grumpy?"

A familiar harrumph came from the doorway. "Because *she* has important work to accomplish and boyfriends just get in the way. Now off with you."

I rolled out of the bed, put on my prosthetic, grabbed my holster from the chair and swung it over my shoulders. I gave Tabby a warm kiss and refused to make eye contact with troll breath. It was a no win situation and I knew when I was beaten.

I stopped at a corner coffee shop and pulled up my queue. A priority comm from Mars Protectorate was at the top. I opened the message and discovered that Nick and I had been summoned to a meeting in Coolidge at 1400 this afternoon. The location wasn't very far from where I was drinking coffee.

"Nick, you up?" I asked. It was 0600 local time.

"Am now," he said.

"And he's not getting out of running this morning," Marny said into his comm unit.

"Check your queue," I said.

"Okay, give me a second," he said. After a few minutes he summarized, "It didn't say much, did it?"

"Any ideas?" I asked.

"Sounds like I'm coming your way this afternoon," he said.

"Do you think we need a lawyer?" I asked.

"No. There's no legalese in the message. If they were charging us with something, we'd have received a much different type of summons and it would have come from the judiciary," he explained.

I found myself oddly frozen in time, not wanting to trek all the way over to our compound just to come back in the middle of the afternoon. I met Nick at the MAG-L terminal an hour before our meeting.

A four-seater shuttle dropped us off in front of a twenty story white building. Stone steps led up to a wide apron. The lofty atrium was separated from the elements by soaring transparent panels. Initially I didn't think there were doors, but when we crossed over the threshold it was clear we'd passed through an energy barrier.

"Any idea where we're going?" I asked.

"No. I'd have thought when we entered the building it would allow us to register, but I'm not getting an interface," Nick said.

"Maybe we need to check in?" I nodded to an oval shaped counter, behind which stood two Marines in dark gray service uniforms, complete with sidearms.

"May I help you?" The taller of the two asked.

"We were summoned to a meeting, but we're not finding any instructions on where to go," I said.

"Are you sure you have the right building?" he asked.

"Pretty sure," I said.

"Perhaps I could look at your summons?" he asked.

"That won't be necessary."

I turned to see the approaching figure of Lieutenant Gregor Belcose. He was dressed in dark blue slacks and a neatly pressed, collared khaki shirt. I'd never seen him in anything but a uniform vac-suit. From my perspective, however, he might as well have been wearing a uniform. His bearing was all military.

"If you'd follow me," he said without pleasantries.

We followed him to a door on the atrium's back wall, one that my eye had skipped over previously. It wasn't specifically hidden, but was designed to blend in with the wall décor perfectly and was almost invisible.

"What's this about, Gregor?" I asked.

"Not yet," he said.

He led us down a hallway and ushered us into a service elevator. He held up a small disc and pressed it against the security panel. The elevator started dropping, but there was no indication of floor progression as we descended. Finally, the doors opened to an unadorned hallway. The floor and walls were made of cement and the lighting was bright and industrial. Wherever we were, it was obvious no one was trying to impress visitors.

We wound our way through a labyrinth of halls, finally ending up in front of a steel door. Gregor pressed his security disc onto a panel. The only indicator of success was a thunking sound and a centimeter of space at the jamb.

The room we entered was barren with the exception of a table and a crate sitting next to it. On the opposite side of the room was another door.

"What's going on, Gregor?" I asked. The room looked like an interrogation chamber from an old vid. It suddenly occurred to me that no one knew where we were or how to find us.

"One minute and we'll explain everything. Please place your weapons and communication devices in the crate," he said.

I was suspicious, but we complied. He placed the top on the crate and picked up a black wand that sat on the table.

"What's that about?" Nick asked.

"I'll tell you once we're done," Gregor said and looked at us for approval.

Nick shrugged, which Gregor took as a sign of assent. He swiped the wand up and down our bodies on all four sides. He spent extra time scanning my prosthetic foot, but in the end he was satisfied.

"This way," he said and walked to the far door. His disc once again provided entry.

This next room was much nicer than any we'd just walked

through. It was carpeted and held a long, wood-grained table in the center. I was surprised to see Commander Sterra rise from her seated position at one end. A second man also stood as we approached. Unlike Belcose, Sterra and the stranger were wearing gray service uniforms. I'd learned to read the uniforms in the last several months and I was surprised to see the single silver-star on the man's collar. My eyes flitted quickly to his shoulder epaulettes and it confirmed that we were meeting with a rear admiral.

"Mr. James, Mr. Hoffen, welcome," Commander Sterra said. Her tone was formal but her smile was warm. "May I introduce you to Rear Admiral Brock 'Buckshot' Alderson?"

"Gentlemen," Admiral Alderson's deep voice filled the room. He stepped forward, holding his hand out.

I shook it. I'd never actually met an admiral before, so I might have been a little dumbstruck.

"Please, have a seat." He swept his hand over the table generously. "LaVonne, how about you get us started."

Curiously, I looked at Commander Sterra. Once, she'd confided in me that only friends used her first name. I couldn't read her face as to whether the address bothered her or not.

"Thank you, Admiral," she said. "Gregor, are we secure?"

"Yes, ma'am," he replied curtly.

"Very well. First, let me apologize for the clandestine nature of this meeting. I'm obligated to inform you that Mars Protectorate considers the information we're about to share to be a secret at our highest level. Sharing what we're about to discuss with anyone outside of this room will be considered treason and will be prosecuted to the maximum extent of the law. You may leave now, if these terms are not acceptable to you," she said.

Nick stood up from the table. "Liam, I don't think we should be here."

I stood with him, surprised at his immediate reaction. Sterra nodded her head slightly in understanding.

Alderson put up his hands and said, "Hold on, gentlemen. I hate it when we lead with all that legal mumbo jumbo. The fact is Mars Protectorate needs your help and I'd take it as a personal favor if you'd listen to what the Commander here has to say. If you don't like it, you just need to keep it to yourselves."

Nick looked back to me. "Do you want to stay? So far, the only thing we're doing is placing ourselves at risk. There's no upside."

"Let's listen to what they have to say," I said.

"For the last five years, Mars Protectorate has been gathering intelligence on the rising threat of the Red Houzi," Sterra started. "Until recently, the clan has limited their attacks to hit and runs, never staying in a single location for more than a few hours. The raids that culminated in the battle for Colony 40 and the destruction of our rapid response fleet, show a substantial change in their stance. We believe that the entire series of attacks that began at Anaimalai and ended at Colony 40 were orchestrated for one purpose. Would either of you care to hazard a guess as to what that purpose was?"

"Simple. It was a trap," I said.

"That's right, Mr. Hoffen. It was a trap," Admiral Alderson said, unable to contain himself. "The bastards wanted to make the statement that they could wipe out a Mars Protectorate fleet. Once word spreads to the other colonies, widespread panic will ensue. We can't possibly defend all of the colonies at once, and we have nothing to strike back against. In short, aside from reacting, we don't have a move."

"How can we possibly help? You're the Navy," I said.

"That's precisely why you can help. Believe it or not, your crew has a reputation for getting the job done. Your work at Colony 40, Baru Manush and most recently Jeratorn, show you to be just the sort of people who can help us," he said.

As a born negotiator, I knew when someone was buttering me up and he was laying it on thick. Whatever they had in mind was going to be a doozy. I might as well move us along, so I took the bait.

"What do you have in mind?"

"On Jeratorn, our intelligence assets discovered that the Red Houzi have constructed a base. We currently believe it to be in the Trojan or possibly Greek asteroids of the main belt," he said.

He might as well have said he was looking for a grain of sand in either Coolidge or Puskar Stellar. The Trojans stretched out for a distance that was longer than the distance between the Sun and Jupiter.

"Those are some big regions," I said.

"That's true. But we believe we have an asset that knows exactly where they are located," Gregor said.

"If you know where they are, why wouldn't you form up a fleet with the North American, Chinese, Indians and every other space-borne country and go get 'em?" I asked.

"Well, that's the rub. This particular asset won't work with anyone but you," he said flatly.

My stomach sank. I could think of only one person he could be talking about.

"You can't trust her. She'd say anything to get out," I said.

"We don't believe that Xie Mie-su actually has any real intelligence. Most likely the information she has is old and the Red Houzi have moved on. The problem is we can't afford to leave any stone unturned," Alderson replied.

I was shaking my head. This was a bad idea. "Last time, she tried to kill us all. I don't see why we'd get involved in this, Admiral. I don't believe for a minute she's on the level."

"Commander Sterra anticipated that you'd feel this way. I don't suppose I could get you to do this as a matter of civic duty?" he asked.

Nick practically growled. He wasn't happy with any of this. "I think you used up all of our civic duty on Jeratorn."

"The way I hear it, you made out pretty well on that trip. You claimed a mostly operational frigate, if I recall," Alderson said.

"Respectfully, Admiral, we more than risked our lives on that job. And if *you'll* recall, Mars Intelligence substantially misrepresented what we'd be getting into when we agreed to it. If given the chance to do that again, I doubt we'd agree," Nick said.

"Tut, tut. I didn't mean to offend. I only meant to point out that your dealings with Mars Protectorate have been plenty profitable," he said.

"No profit is worth the life of any of our crew," Nick said.

"How about if you could avenge the death of your mother? Prevent others from losing their mothers?" Alderson asked.

This was over the top. "That's not fair. You can't put that on him."

"No? What if we could arrange to restore Cadet Master's left arm?" he said.

"What would you have us do?" Nick asked.

"Nick, no. Tabby would never accept that," I said.

Nick ignored me. "What's the mission?"

"It's straightforward. You sail to wherever Xie Mie-su directs, scan the area and let us know what you find. If you find the dreadnaught, contact us and stick around until we can scramble a fleet to take it down," Gregor said.

I crossed my arms and leaned forward. I didn't trust a one of them to be completely up front with us. "Why don't I think you're telling us everything?"

"It really is that simple," he said.

"And you'll agree to pay for Tabby's surgeries and regrow her arm?" Nick asked.

Alderson's eyes lit up. He smelled a deal. "Only if you locate the dreadnaught."

"You've admitted that you're sending us on a wild goose chase with a psychopath. There's no upside. Why would we do that?" I asked.

"Because I'll be revoking your Letter of Marque if you don't. Carrot and stick, Mr. Hoffen," Admiral Alderson said.

I sat back. I couldn't believe he'd stoop to this. Names that I would never say out loud swirled in my mind as I looked the man in the eyes.

"Our ship's armor was damaged in the battle and we've lost a good deal of our stealth capabilities. We need intellectual property for that armor," Nick said.

"Anything else?" Alderson asked.

Nick didn't miss a beat. "Supplies - ammo, fuel, that sort of thing."

"Done. You can work out the details with Lieutenant Belcose. I want you underway by the end of the week," Admiral Alderson said. As he rose, Sterra and Belcose stood with him. He walked out of the room without acknowledging us further.

"Liam, Nick, I'm sorry that we had to meet under these circumstances," Commander Sterra offered once Alderson left the room. "Off the record, I don't like what we're doing here. I think it lessens us all. I understand the urgency, but I can't escape the morality of horse trading on Tabby's misfortune to achieve our ends."

PRIMED AND READY

When I got to the hospital, Tabby was back in bed working with her prosthetic arm, trying to pick up a variety of objects on the sheet in front of her. The prosthetic wrist and fingers were clumsy, but she was making progress.

"How'd chair training go?" I asked.

"Patricia said I was doing really well. It's a lot like AGBs," she said.

"Can I see?"

"I need a lot of help getting into it. I'm not ready for you to see that," she said.

"We could go for pizza if you did."

She thought about it for a minute. "Okay, here's what I need you to do," she said.

The arc-jet chair was pretty straightforward. A custom fit L-shaped seat came just under her bottom and two straps held her chest firmly to the chair. There were no arm-rests and she controlled the flight with both vocal commands as well as gestures she'd been working out with troll breath. Currently, she only had the basic commands, one of which was to maintain a level flight and orient her body next to another person.

"We take a lot of things for granted when we walk with other people. For example, when you are in a hallway and there's not enough room, we compress into single file or even turn sideways slightly. It's all very natural for us. The problem is, you need to anticipate these things when you're in a chair," Tabby explained.

"You're doing really well. I'm not even thinking about it," I said. "I'm not sure why they call it a chair, though."

"You'll see," she said.

"Megliano's?"

"What?"

"That pizza place I took you to last time," I said.

"I don't know, it's a lot of people. Could we stay in Coolidge?" she asked. It made sense. There would be a lot of military types in Coolidge and they wouldn't think twice about a veteran in an arc-jet chair.

"We have to walk," I said. The cool air of Mars had me pulling my gloves on, but I'd grown to appreciate breathing the non-mechanically processed air of the planet.

Find nearby restaurants, Tabby instructed. "What's Mexican?" she asked.

"Provence of the North American Alliance," I said.

"Not where. I said what?" she retorted.

"No idea. Let's do it."

The arc-jet chair settled easily into the restaurant's chair. Small legs extended from the arc-jet chair, locked to the back of the seat and allowed Tabby to sit in a normal position. I helped slide her into the table.

We discovered that our favorite part of Mexican food was the margaritas. It's not that the food wasn't good, it's just that the drinks came first. By the time the food arrived, neither of us was in any position to taste anything.

If not for our AIs, we'd have had a difficult time getting back to the hospital, though it wasn't more than a few blocks away. The next morning I awoke to a stubby finger poking me in the chest.

"Wake up, slacker. You're going to need to learn to take care of this equipment. If you think the Navy is going to replace this just because you're too drunk to put it away, you've got another think coming."

I opened my eyes to troll breath looking down at me. I rolled off the bed, but landed more gracefully, having had a few mornings to practice the maneuver now. I looked around the room and noticed that we hadn't left the room in great shape last night. My prosthetic foot was in a heap right next to Tabby's arc-jet chair. I vaguely remembered helping her get out of it before passing out.

I knew it wouldn't do any good to defend myself, so I hopped over to the pile and pulled on my foot. If I thought troll breath would give me a break because of my disability, I was wrong.

"Do you ever clean that thing? I'd better not find that's how you're treating the chair," she said.

I picked up the arc-jet chair and hung it back on its rack, next to the bed, feeling proud of myself for not knocking the woman back a few steps. Tabby was up and moving, looking as bleary eyed as I felt. I leaned over and kissed her on the forehead.

"Tuesday's the barbeque. Can you let me know if we're going - sometime today? I need to tell Tali," I said.

"Oh, she's going," I heard from over my shoulder.

I winced. I should have known better than to say anything in front of this woman. Tabby rolled her eyes at me and I suspected we'd be talking about that later.

"Don't be rolling those eyes at me," Troll breath continued. "You're going if I have to drag you there myself."

"Sorry," I whispered and scooted out of the room.

I found Nick and Marny seated at the mess table in the central habitation dome. They looked up expectantly when I came through the door.

"You want some eggs, Cap?" Marny asked, as I walked through on my way to the head. The very thought of eggs made me nauseated. I mumbled "No," shut the door, and stripped out of my civvies. I dropped my suit-liner into the freshener and stepped into the shower. The hot water made me feel better - if not substantially.

After showering, I grabbed a cup of coffee in the mess. Nick had a bemused look on his face and Marny couldn't stop from asking the obvious question.

"Cap, you hung over?"

"Margaritas turned into shots of tequila last night. My head is pounding."

Marny opened a cabinet, pulled out a med-patch and handed it to me. "You need to drink more water," she said.

With the patch applied and a few minutes sitting with my head in my hands, the cacophony finally subsided.

"Nick tell you what's going on?" I asked.

"I wasn't sure if you wanted to read your dad in or not," Nick said.

"Where is he?"

"Visiting some friends. Said he'd be back in a couple of days when your mom and Ada got back," he said.

"Have you talked to the shipyard?" We were past the planning stage and needed to get on with our preparations.

"Belcose sent me the pattern for the *Hotspur's* armor last night. They'll be done by Thursday."

"Navy's not getting their hands on it, are they?" I asked. Last time our ship was at the Navy's shipyard they'd installed all manner of spyware on it.

"No, but maybe we should ask Bit to sweep it before we take off," he said.

"Any ideas on how we're going to keep track of Xie Mie-su?" I asked.

He gritted his teeth. This wasn't going to be a fun trip. "She'll be restrained, we're putting her in cuffs."

"We won't need a brig?"

"The ship will monitor her and if she gets close to any person or control surface, her movements will be substantially restricted or she'll receive a shock. Apparently, they're pretty effective," he said.

"Can we up the voltage?" I quipped, causing Marny to chuckle. "Marny, can you work out what we need to get those suits fully operational? M-Pro said they'd provide ammo and I think we need to take advantage of it."

"Aye, Cap. Can do," she said.

"Tabby's being released from the hospital at the end of the week," I said. "I was thinking she could come along. We could modify one of the pilot's chairs.

"Is she recovered enough?" Nick asked.

"I think so and we could use help with watches. I don't want to tell her about any surgeries until it's certain. I'll talk to her about it tonight, if you're good with it. I also think there's a pretty good chance she'll come to the barbeque on Tuesday."

"I'd really like to see her," Nick said.

It was early afternoon when I got back to the Veteran's Hospital. Tabby had pinged me to let me know her physical therapy had finished early, but Patricia (aka troll breath) was requiring her to go out again. Apparently, I'd earned brownie points by taking Tabby to the restaurant last night. Unfortunately, I'd lost a lot of those points by getting her drunk.

Tabby was seated in a chair, working on picking up small items with her prosthetic when I walked in.

"How'd it go today?" I asked.

"We spent a lot of time working on getting in and out of the chair, it's really frustrating. Patricia says I need to spend more time working with my prosthetic arm."

"So, about the barbeque tomorrow. I'd really like us to go. Jack will be there. He's had a rough time with it all. I think he'd really like to see you."

"What about Nick?"

"Of course, he'll be there."

"Okay. You have to promise you'll bring me back right away if I ask, though." Tabby wasn't scared of much, but her eyes told me this trip might be too much.

"You have my word," I assured her. "Have you thought much about where you'll stay after they release you?"

"I have a stipend for housing. I figured I'd get an apartment here in Coolidge," she said.

"Would you consider taking a trip with us? M-Pro wants to send us on a wild goose chase."

"Let me think about it, okay?" she said. I couldn't wait until she regained her confidence. Tentative Tabby broke my heart.

"Of course," I said. "But, one more thing."

"Seriously?"

"Yeah. We're going shopping this afternoon. I thought it might be a good warmup."

She looked down at the table and sighed.

"I'm sorry. I can cancel it. You've already agreed to the barbeque. Let's leave it at that," I said.

"No, it's okay. I know you're doing it for the right reasons. It's just hard, Liam. I've always been large and in charge, and now I'm... well... I don't know what I am," she said.

"You're the same person you've always been, Tabby."

"That's not true. I'm not. I can't do the things I used to. I'm not whole."

"Maybe I'm looking at this too simply, but we'll get through it," I said. "So, are you ready to get going?"

"Now?" she asked.

"Trust me," I said.

I hailed a cab and it took Tabby a couple of tries to get in successfully. She could have allowed the AI to do the work, but she was more interested in gaining skills.

The cab dropped us off in the Open Air District.

"Where are we going?" Tabby either loved or hated surprises, I wasn't sure which it would be in this case.

"This way," I said.

The brick streets of the Open Air District were lined with small shops, all with colorful awnings to shade shoppers from the afternoon sun. The shop we approached had a simple sign that read 'Kathryne's Boutique.' An elegant, middle aged woman sat outside in a comfortable chair and watched us approach.

"Are you sure this is right?" Tabby asked.

"Of course he's not," the woman answered for me as she stood up and approached. "Such a beautiful girl, you remind me of Natalia when she was younger. I'm Kathryne. Please come in."

Initially Tabby resisted, but in the end it became obvious that Kathryne wasn't to be trifled with. I wondered who won arguments between her and Tali.

"Hold this." Kathryne handed me a bag after she emerged from a back room that I'd been banished from for the better part of an hour. "Come on out dear," she called. She back-handed my shoulder, "Stand up in the presence of a lady."

Tabby glided out. She was wearing a blue dress with a v-neck that plunged deeply, but still elegantly. Her long copper colored hair had grown back and sat braided over one shoulder. I gasped involuntarily. I'd been so worried about survival, missions, and everything else, I'd forgotten how beautiful she was.

"You're gorgeous," I said. Tabby, for the first time I could remember, blushed.

"It's not my hair," she said.

"Hush, child, of course it is, I matched it perfectly. Do not ruin the moment," Kathryne scolded gently.

"I don't know how to thank you, Kathryne," I said.

She winked at me. "Well, financially, of course."

I swiped the signature pad. "Thank you for this."

The next day started like every other, with troll breath barging in before I was ready to wake up.

"Up and at 'em," she said. "Today's the big barbeque, we need to get started early." I wasn't sure why she was so focused on this barbeque, but I appreciated the help.

Nick kept us busy the entire day, picking up supplies and delivering the crates we'd brought back from the outpost to the auctioneer. We'd originally thought we'd have time to sell the stock more slowly, but as usual, we were rushing on to our next mission.

I picked Tabby up from the hospital that afternoon. Troll breath, aka Patricia, had worked with Tabby to get her dressed in her new clothing.

"I'm totally overdressed for a barbeque," Tabby worried out loud in the cab. I smiled. She was worried about what she was wearing and it was great.

Tali met us as we walked from the cab.

"We're over at the pit," she said. "And don't you look beautiful?"

"Thank you," Tabby replied. "Kathryne is so nice."

"That has to be the first time I've heard that," Tali said, laughing. "Boys. Get over here and meet a real hero."

Tali introduced Tabby to her team; Ben 'Jammin' Rheel and Jordy Kelti. Like Tali, Jammin and Kelti were both in amazing physical shape. Where Jordy was tall and athletic, Jammin was average height, thickly muscled and, though he was quiet, he had a quick smile.

One of the great things about ex-military was their understanding of disabled vets. Instead of treating Tabby as a fragile doll that would break at any minute, they accepted her as one of their own. It was a bond I was jealous of, but grateful for all the same.

By 2300 the fire was dying down and we'd all drunk more than our share. All in all it had been a great night.

"I'll go with you," Tabby said. She'd been dozing on and off, giving into the warmth of the blankets we'd been snuggling under.

"Perfect," I said.

"What time is it?" Tabby asked, rousing from her nap.

"It's getting late, how about we sleep in my bed tonight." I said.

"Patricia will be pissed."

"It'll be worth it."

ALL DRESSED UP

Early Thursday morning I received a comm from the shipyard, they'd finished work on the *Hotspur*.

"So this is it?" Tabby asked.

"Are you ready?"

"I'm scared, Liam," she said.

"I've got a surprise for you," I taunted. I missed playing with her.

"What? You have to tell me."

"You'll see," I said.

I grabbed the large case holding her medical attendant robot. It was heavy enough that there were arc-jets in the case to keep it aloft.

"Nick, the ship's ready and we're on the way to grab her," I said.

"Yup, we'll be waiting for you," he replied.

We grabbed a four-seater to the Coolidge terminal and I changed into my vac-suit, strapping my flechette into its chest holster. Kathryne had manufactured a vac-suit for Tabby. It was a big step that she could put it on with help from the attendant bot. While Tabby hadn't said it, I'd suspected that if that process hadn't gone well, she would have backed out of the trip.

The space elevator was busy, so we waited twenty minutes for a car and then rode up with a group of what I suspected were local manufacturing workers. Their suits were well worn with an unfamiliar logo.

We grabbed a shuttle over to the shipyard and were met by Priyanka Lanka, the original rep who'd walked me through the changes. It surprised me a little, as I'd expected he was more of a front man than someone who would be able to walk us through the work that had been done.

"Welcome back, Liam Hoffen. Who's your friend?" he asked.

"First mate Tabby Masters," I said.

He shook both of our hands. I was impressed that he didn't even bat an eye at Tabby's arc-jet chair.

"We've had good success with your repairs, better than I'd originally promised." He led us down a hallway and through a blue energy barrier into a repair bay.

I was taken aback when I looked at my girl, sitting in the brightly lit bay. The light absorptive armor made it difficult to pick out individual details, but the dark gray outline stood in sharp relief against the bay's white walls. The turrets had been retracted beneath their protective cowls. Her stubby wing, no longer a kludged mass of welds, had been restored. She, once again, aggressively bragged and begged to be let loose.

"That's better," I breathed.

"My crew does fine work," he said. "You know, we'd be interested in licensing that armor recipe from you."

"I'm not sure we have enough ownership for that."

"It'd be worth a lot," he prodded.

"I'll take it up with my partner."

We walked around to the back of the ship after inspecting the bottom side of the wing. The change to the cargo hold was immediately obvious as we walked up the open ramp. A long rectangular bump-out spanned the back wall with a new door a little right of center.

"We converted your old exterior hatch to a single portal style. The airlock there, was no longer necessary. Think of the new hallway as an extended airlock," he explained, sliding the new door open. I heard the door lock with a click.

"Why the lock when the door is open?" I asked.

"Stand back a moment," he said. A blue film illuminated the doorway.

"Is that a… "

"Pressure barrier. That's right, Mr. Hoffen," he said.

"I thought those weren't practical on a ship."

"Not for reasons of expense. They're actually quite reasonable to manufacture. The issue is their power consumption. But, as Mr. James pointed out to us, your *Hotspur* has an excess of available power. Unless, of course, you spend a lot of time with all of your turrets firing - which I trust you don't," he said, chuckling at the suggestion.

"Probably not while we need to use the door." I said.

He gave me a quizzical look, trying to assess whether I was messing with him or not. "We installed one in the berth deck door as well as the exterior door." The doors might not be expensive, but they were going to feel like luxuries. The barriers would make getting in and out of the ship as easy as walking around inside of it.

"That's quite an upgrade. What if we run low on power?" I asked.

"While I can't imagine that happening, since this old girl has more joules than any ship we get through here, the metal doors would slide closed," he said.

"Have you done a signature analysis? Is the new armor as good as the old?"

"We did a full scan and ended up replacing three older panels. The new armor is identical. Whatever your source, it looks like it's the original recipe," he said.

We walked through the rest of the repairs. As charming as Priyanka was, I was glad to sign off and get out of there.

"You want to see your surprise now?" I asked Tabby once we were by ourselves.

"Yes, you twit. Show me."

"This way," I led her up to the cockpit.

"And?" she asked, unimpressed.

"Try sitting in the chair," I said.

"What?" Even though she asked the question, curiosity had already won and she jetted up the stairs to look at the seat.

"Go ahead, sit on it," I said.

"Yeah, I don't know how well that will work," she said.

I just stared at her, not giving in until she obliged. Finally, she spun her arc-jet chair and hovered over the pilot's seat. Lowering herself slowly, Tabby instructed her AI to extend the locking clamps that would hold the chairs together. A satisfying clunk let us both know the chair was secure.

"What do you think?" I asked.

"I love it!" Her face beamed. She was back.

"You want to sail us out of here?" I asked.

"Frak, yah!"

"Pull up the checklist first and then we'll get out of here," I said.

We ran through the checklist and I wasn't surprised to see that everything, once again, was green.

Engage accessibility controls, Tabby instructed.

"What's that?" I asked.

"Most people don't know it, but almost every system has these controls that adapt to different disabilities. It'll interface with my AI and learn about what I have problems with and even correct things for me," she said.

"Perfect."

Tabby had always had a very precise flying style and she smartly spun the ship around with ease. I'd worried about her prosthetic right arm not having enough sensitivity, which would translate to poor directional control, but soon found I had nothing to worry about. She glided into the busy local space of the Coolidge terminal and followed the navigation path that I'd negotiated with the local harbor master. Within a few minutes, we were dropping into Mars' atmosphere, the ship slicing cleanly through. Before I knew it, I was a few kilometers from Tali's homestead and dropping fast.

Open Comm Tali Liszt.

"What's the word, Captain?" she asked.

"I'd like permission to enter your sovereign airspace," I said, only half joking.

"You are permitted to enter," she said dramatically.

"Roger that," I said and closed the comm channel.

We were coming in hot and Tabby put us down a hundred meters away from the compound and then used the arc-jet thrusters to close the distance. She spun the ship around, lowered the landing gear and set us down gently.

"Nicely done," I said, meaning every word of it.

"Jupiter, but that felt good," Tabby stretched her arms, as if she were attempting to take in all of the bridge.

I dropped the ramp and Nick, Marny and Big Pete met us at the bottom.

Big Pete strode forward to greet us. "Tabitha Masters, I can't believe you're still hanging around with these bums."

"Anything to sail a ship," she said.

"Don't let 'em see weakness. They're a bunch of capitalists."

"Too late," I said.

He'd slipped his arm through Tabby's good one as we walked down the ramp. "What are you all up to?"

"We picked up a job. Should be back in a couple of weeks." I wondered if Marny and Nick had been avoiding telling him that we were headed out.

"Need any help?" he asked.

I hated not telling him what was going on, but didn't feel right dragging him into my schemes. "I was hoping you'd stick around to meet Mom and Ada. I've scheduled them for a forty-eight hour leave and then back out again," I said.

He grinned and held up his hands defensively. "You don't need to make up work for me. I understand where you're at. I wanted to make my own way when I was your age too. Anyway, I'm headed into town."

"Can we drop you somewhere?" Nick asked.

"Nope, cab'll be here in five minutes," he said.

Nick and Marny had gathered most of the supplies we'd need for our trip using the rented pod-jumper. Once Big Pete was gone, we donned the mechanized suits and moved everything into the hold, including the crates that would store the suits. Nick had convinced me that we needed to bring them along, just in case we ran into trouble.

"What's with all of the cases marked ordinance?" I asked. We'd carried in no less than ten cubic meters of cases marked this way.

"Loadouts for the mech suits," Nick said.

"Why would they let us have that?"

"Alderson signed off on supplies and ammo. He wasn't specific on the ammo so I improvised. At some point some clerk is going to bust us, but technically we're allowed."

"You really are a capitalist," Tabby said.

I just laughed. "You have no idea. You guys ready to jet?"

"Just need my go-bag, Cap," Marny said as she stepped out of the center of the mech suit, now lying in its crate on the floor of the hold.

"We're low on fuel. Where are we picking up Xie?" I asked Nick.

"We'll need to take on fuel once we're in orbit. The prison is twenty thousand kilometers out," he said.

"Roger that. Tabby and I'll be on the bridge," I said. We'd already stowed our gear in the captain's quarters.

A few minutes later Nick and Marny had loaded up and joined us on the bridge.

"What do you think of those pressure barriers?" Nick asked.

"Coolest thing ever," I said. "I'm not sure why you'd ever turn 'em off."

He nodded at me. "I've programmed the ship to require face shields if you approach the berth deck door. Also, it'll close the hard door if you're not wearing a suit. It's not foolproof, but it should keep us safe."

"You're always a step ahead of me," I said.

"So nothing's changed?" Tabby asked.

"Laugh it up." Man, it felt good to have us all back together.

All stations, report status, I said. Nick, Marny and even Tabby reported our readiness.

"Nick, what are you doing with Jack?" I asked.

"Lena said she'd watch him while we're gone."

"Roger that," I said.

"Tabby, the helm is yours," I said.

Once we escaped the atmosphere, I set a navigation path to a nearby fuel depot and we took on a much needed load of fuel.

"Nick, can you give us a nav path to the prison?" I asked.

"Navigation path Charlie-two," he responded.

I nodded to Tabby.

Engage navigation path Charlie-two, she instructed.

The throttle and flight sticks retracted from the arms of the pilot chairs as the ship took over. With only twenty thousand kilometers, we wouldn't be sailing long, but it was enough that fuel conservancy was useful.

Approaching Kar'kel prison. Security checkpoint required, the ship's AI said.

"Hold up here," I said to Tabby.

She zeroed out our Delta-V with the prison, which had grown quickly in front of us. The prison had been cut out of an irregularly shaped iron asteroid, wider than it was tall. If approached from the wrong side, you might not be aware of its function. From this side, we were able to see a flat, steel face set back two hundred meters into the rock. Tabby rotated the ship to align our orientation with that of the prison.

Hail Kar'kel, I said.

"Department of corrections. Please state your business." The torso of a woman in a light gray uniform appeared on the forward holo.

"We're here to pick up the prisoner Xie Mie-su," I said.

She was all business and her voice flat. "Please transmit identification."

I sent her an encrypted burst with the ship's identification, something I didn't do very often.

"That checks out. You're cleared for landing bay three. It is critical that you don't stray from your approach lane," she warned.

Execute landing sequence, I requested. I wasn't about to have Tabby or myself sail in manually. I'd never seen such a concentration, nor variety, of blaster turrets in one location. The ship brought us in and set us down neatly on the well labeled BAY-3 pad.

"Marny, you ready?" I asked.

"Aye, Cap," she said.

I stopped in my quarters, pulled on my armored vac-suit and met her in the new hallway that led to the exterior hatch.

"You'll need to leave your flechette in the armory," she said.

I placed it on the table and we exited the ship through our new energy barrier on the starboard hatch. We climbed down the metal stairs to the asteroid's surface. I didn't know what to expect, but I was a little surprised there weren't any guards on the apron in front of the prison. The path we were to follow was illuminated by glowing ribbons embedded into the asteroid's surface. The door we approached was a standard air lock and we cycled through, finding ourselves in a small, grimy alcove.

A rough looking man in a gray uniform, sat behind a glass panel on the far wall. I approached and waited for him to acknowledge my presence.

"Liam Hoffen and Marny Bertrand to pick up prisoner Xie Mie-su," I said when he looked up a few minutes later.

He nodded to a long steel bench. "Have a seat. She'll be right up."

Apparently, 'right up' was a figure of speech. It took nearly an hour before the door next to the glass panel opened. It had only been a few months since I'd seen Xie, but those months hadn't been kind to her. She'd always been thin, but now looked like she'd lost at least ten kilograms - mass she didn't have to spare. Her long black hair was short and uneven and it looked like she hadn't showered in a long time.

"You have a vac-suit for this one? Or are you just spacing her right away?" the guard asked with a chuckle.

"I'll get one," I said and turned for the door.

"No need. We'll provide a transport suit. Prisoner will kneel," he said. Xie caught my eye and then looked away as shame colored her face. She complied and knelt on the ground.

"Jerta, get me a suit," the guard said. A few moments later, the door opened and a thick woman handed him an orange suit I assumed was a vac-suit. He threw it on the ground in front of Xie. "Put it on then. We don't have all day."

Xie struggled to her feet, sat on the bench and started working to pull the suit on. It fit so poorly that she slipped into it easily. I hoped these clowns hadn't given her a leaky suit.

"Just sign there." The guard behind the glass gestured to a permanent reading pad on the wall.

Analyze agreement, I said. I assumed that Nick would have already worked out the language of anything we'd be signing.

Agreement is an acknowledgement of the transfer of Xie Mie-su from the custody of Crano Industries Corrections, Incorporated to Loose Nuts Corporation. This language has been approved by Nicholas James, my AI informed me. I swiped my signature onto the pad.

"She's all yours." The guard pushed Xie toward Marny, who caught her just in time to keep the woman from falling as her feet got tangled in the over-sized, sagging suit.

Marny helped her through the air lock and I followed behind. Once outside, Marny held up for a moment and waited for me.

"Cap, we need to drop the cargo ramp. She'll never make it up the stairs in that suit."

"I don't understand. I know it's big, but what's the problem?" I asked.

"Those suits have a weighted hobble in them. The guards gave her an oversized suit made for a much heavier, stronger person. She's having trouble moving her feet." Marny started moving toward the ship again, helping Xie.

"Got it," I said. I arc-jetted my way to the back of the ship and signed in, recycling the air from the hold. Marny and Xie had arrived before the air had been reclaimed, so we waited a few minutes. Finally, the ramp was down and I lowered the gravity in the hold to .2g.

As soon as we popped through the barrier into the hallway, Xie stumbled and fell.

"Marny, we've got a problem."

"Frak. Help me get her suit off," she said.

I tried, but the suit appeared to be locked on. "I can't get it."

Marny pulled a finger-length cylinder from her belt and flicked her wrist. A thin, red, nano-blade extended from the end and she carefully cut into the correction's suit, peeling it away from Xie. I helped remove the material, still not sure what was going on.

"She's freezing. That bastard gave her a dead suit," Marny said.

Emergency medical diagnosis, I said. I stepped into the armory and pulled out the medical kit.

Hypoxia and mild hypothermia. Apply medical patch 1032 and place affected in warm shower to restore body temperature.

My HUD outlined the correct patch in the medical kit. I pulled it out and applied it to Xie's chest, just below her collarbone.

"I'll clean her up," Marny said.

"Thank you, Marny. I'll replicate a suit liner for her and leave it outside the door."

"Aye, that'll work." Marny knelt down, scooped up Xie's limp body and carried her through the door to the berth deck.

I took the lift to the bridge deck and changed back into my normal vac-suit.

"Everything okay?" Nick asked. Tabby had come down from the cockpit and was hovering next to his chair.

"Xie's in really bad shape. They gave her a faulty suit and she didn't have enough O2 to get to the ship. Marny's helping her," I said.

"Is it safe to leave Marny with her?" Nick asked. He had a good reason for the question, as the Xie we both knew was very capable of deception.

"You should see her, Nick. She looks bad. Prison has been hard on her," I said.

"We still need to be careful. She's clever," he said.

"Agreed. How about we get out of here?" I didn't want to be near this awful place any longer than necessary.

"Can do," Tabby jetted nimbly up the stairs and strapped into her pilot's chair.

I joined her and we walked through an abbreviated check list.

Negotiate exit corridor with Kar'kel prison, I said.

A moment later a navigation path appeared.

Engage.

THE DEEP DARK

With nowhere to go, we simply glided along without power to the engines. Thirty minutes later, Marny accompanied a barely conscious Xie to the bridge and helped her onto the couch. I walked back, grabbed the aft station chair and brought it over to the table. For as badly as Xie had been treated, I wasn't about to sit next to her on the couch.

"Thank you," she said. Xie still looked pathetic even after Marny had cleaned her up and straightened out her hair with our hair cutting appliance. It was hard for me to imagine that Xie could be faking all this as part of some big master plan. Although if anyone could, it would be Xie.

"That's criminal to give you a broken suit. Those guards could have killed you," I said.

"Welcome to a Crano run prison."

"That's not right."

"Don't be naïve," she said with disdain. "No one cares. That's why M-Pro contracts out to Crano who then hires low cost thugs."

I shook my head. It was frustrating to think that people could be so cruel.

"Where are we headed?" I asked.

"I need access to an AI and comm equipment," she said.

"Sure… 'cause, what could go wrong with that?"

"You can't possibly believe I have this information memorized." Xie shook her head in disbelief.

"I've got it," Nick said. He knew I was getting frustrated.

I slid into the cockpit chair next to Tabby.

"You get kicked out?" Tabby asked.

"Sort of. I have trust issues with that one," I said.

"Isn't she the one who shot Nick?"

"That's the one."

Marny had come to sit between our two chairs. She had a good view of Nick and Xie, but apparently wanted to say something.

"Nobody distrusts that woman more than I do, Cap. Especially considering she both shot and vamped my boy there, but they brutalized her in prison. I did a full scan and she's had multiple bones broken and mended in the last few months," Marny whispered.

Another twenty minutes passed until Nick finally approached.

"I've got it, but you're not going to like it," he said.

"What now?" I asked. If Nick thought I wasn't going to like it, this was going to be an interesting conversation.

"She won't tell us unless we let her go when we're done. She'd rather die than go back."

"We can't do that. If we cross Alderson he'll revoke our Letter of Marque."

Nick grimaced. "What's the value of that Letter if he's willing to use it against us?"

"We could just take her back to prison."

"But then Alderson will cancel our deal."

"You think Xie knows this?" I asked. I wasn't ready to underestimate her.

"No. But, she's willing to gamble everything. According to her, she's got nothing to lose."

"You're in, aren't you?" I asked.

"I am. Think about it. It doesn't matter. If we turn around now, we get nothing and Alderson takes our Letter. If we actually deliver, nobody's going to care about Xie after that."

"Marny, Tabby, you want to weigh in on this?" I asked.

"Don't look at me," Tabby said.

Marny just shook her head. "I'd have a hard time taking her back to that prison."

"Fine. Let's do it," I said.

"She wants your word, Liam," Nick glanced back at Xie.

I nodded and stood up. Nick and Marny moved away from the stairs where we'd all been huddled.

"Feels like we've been here before," Xie said when I approached her.

"Be funnier if you hadn't shot Nick."

"Not my best day. I was in with some bad people and that seemed like a good way through it. It was my decision and it was a mistake."

"Well, this might turn out to *not* be my best day, but we're in."

"I need your word that you'll let me go after we're done."

"You have it," I said.

"Hand me the reading pad." Xie nodded at the pad on the table. I slid it across to her and she punched up a destination.

I took it and looked her in the eyes. "While you're on the ship, you're not to attempt to use any communication devices, approach any weapons or enter the hold. You should know that the restraints you're wearing will initially warn you, but if you persist, they will incapacitate you. Don't attempt to remove them. That said, you have free reign of the berth deck. You are also allowed to visit the bridge as long as you confine that to sitting on the couch. Bottom line is we don't trust you, but we're not interested in making you miserable, either. Marny will show you your bunk room and after that you can set your own schedule."

"Why wouldn't you just lock me up?"

"I guess I'm a romantic. I don't believe everyone is just bad or just good. I'm hoping if I show you respect, that someday you'll decide to show that respect to someone else."

"You want to reform me?" Her face was hard to read, but I swear I saw a flicker of something that gave me hope.

"Nah. It's really just how I'd want to be treated," I said.

Marny interrupted. "Come on. I'll show you where the mess is." I hadn't realized she was standing behind me.

It was difficult to watch Xie walk back to the lift. Even without the heavy prison suit, she shuffled.

"You really are hopeless," Tabby said as I sat back in my cockpit chair.

"I know. Let's see where we're going."

I swiped the top of the reading pad and flicked the data that

Xie provided to the navigational system. The forward holo immediately projected a location in the Hildas region of the main asteroid belt. It was a good location, on the edge of North American controlled space and so far out that likely nothing but probes were sent there. If this really was the location of the dreadnaught, it was also on the opposite side of the solar system from where the Navy believed it to be.

"That's on the edge of The Deep Dark," Tabby said. The Deep Dark was a term spacers used to describe the vast emptiness of space once you got past all of the asteroids and planets. Although, in this case, we'd still be in the orbital path of Jupiter, but I understood her point.

Calculate navigation plan with a twenty degree dogleg above the ecliptic at a million kilometers, I said.

"Why the dogleg?" Tabby asked.

"We've run into our fair share of problems out here and I don't need anyone anticipating where we're going. We'll sail above the ecliptic, then straighten it out," I said.

All hands, prepare for hard burn.

"Nick, are you ready?" I asked.

"Yup."

Engage.

"Now what?" Tabby asked.

"Cards?"

"Seriously?"

"For the next four hours we need to keep a close watch, just in case. Soon, we'll be far enough away from Mars that we can relax. There shouldn't be much out there, especially once were above the ecliptic plane. After that, we'll just need to keep someone either in the cockpit or on the bridge. That's not normally a problem because we tend to hang out up here anyway."

"You don't have jobs to do?" Tabby asked.

"We do, but it's not a lot. My girl here is in pretty good shape." I leaned forward and patting the console in front of me. "There are a few maintenance chores, but Nick and I will split them up. The big deal is getting exercise every day. It's easy to ignore."

She gave me a wry grin. "Patricia would kill me if I neglected my PT."

"Four hour watch work for you?" I asked.

"I think so."

"Good. You'll be going four-four-two. I'll schedule out the whole trip that way, but if that doesn't work, we can talk about it."

"Four-four-two?"

"Right. Sorry. You'll be on for four hours for your first watch, four hours for your next watch, then two hours for the following watch. Nick, Marny and I will also have the same four-four-two schedule," I said.

"Why is it uneven?"

"Mostly for variety. Monotony is the thing we struggle against the most out here."

"Hard to imagine this getting boring," Tabby said.

"Yeah, I get it. That feeling won't wear off for a couple of trips. I still love it, but some watches can get long. You're just lucky Ada isn't on board. She'd have you working on your pilot's license."

"I'd do that," she said.

I just shook my head. Of course she would. "Shoot a message to Ada. She'd love to work you through it."

"I will."

"We also have a change of watch formality that I need to run you through. Currently, you have the helm. So when I'm taking the watch I ask 'Anything to report?' to which you respond with any changes to system statuses. After that, I'd say 'I relieve you' and you respond 'I stand relieved.' Overall, it's pretty simple, but the ship is keyed into those phrases, so we always know who's got the helm," I explained.

"Simple enough."

"Anything to report?" I asked.

After I relieved Tabby, she popped out of the chair and hovered down the stairs. "I'll be back," she said.

I hardly noticed the change from .6g to 1g when the engines reached their full burn, but Tabby struggled on the stairs. She was independent enough that she wasn't about to mention it.

I had a lot of work to finalize before we got too far out of the system. Mom, Ada and the *Adela Chen* would be back on Mars by the end of week and I only had them scheduled for one more trip. It would take at least three similar-length runs for them to stay busy for the entire time we were gone. I was starting to get a feeling for the types of jobs that were available and filtering out the stuff I didn't like became a lot easier. By the end of my shift, not only were we clear of Mars, but I had two more loads scheduled, as long as they weren't spoken for by the time we dropped out of hard burn in about eight hours.

"Anything to report?" Marny asked from behind my chair. We exchanged the rest of the formality that had become second nature to us.

"How's Xie doing?" I asked. I couldn't believe how quickly I'd moved to thinking of her as a victim.

"She's sound asleep and has been since I took her down to the aft bunk room," Marny said.

"How can you be sure?" I asked.

"I'm monitoring her. Just because she's been abused doesn't mean I'm going to trust her."

"I could use some shuteye too."

"I'll have breakfast in six hours."

"What time is it?" It felt a lot more like afternoon than the middle of the night watch.

"We're back on universal time. By the way, you're scheduled for exercise after breakfast."

I sighed but didn't say anything. I knew better than to fight it. I found Tabby asleep on the bed. It seemed ironic that she was able to use up most of the bed, but I didn't think I'd be pointing that out any time soon. I snuck in beside her and lay my head on the pillow after setting an alarm for five hours. I wasn't about to miss breakfast if Marny was cooking.

I woke Tabby after my alarm had been going off for way too long. Intellectually, I knew that the sound of the alarm was transmitted directly to my ear through my earwig, but it seemed like the noise should also have disturbed Tabby.

"We've got forty minutes before breakfast and you've got watch in a little over two hours," I said.

She blinked at me, trying to come awake. "Okay. Take a shower and let me get ready in private."

"I'd like to learn how to help you."

"Not yet, I'm not ready for that. The assistant-bot can do it just fine for now," she said.

"I'll be in the mess." I turned to go.

"Don't be mad, Liam. This is hard for me," she said.

"I know. We'll go slowly," I said. I popped a mouth freshener and leaned over to give her a kiss. She grabbed me, causing me to fall back into the bed. We wrestled around. My mind had a lot of conflicting emotions. To say that it wasn't weird that she was missing limbs wouldn't have been a fair statement. It was totally weird. On the other hand, this was the girl I'd fallen in love with and couldn't imagine living without. It took some effort, but I pushed out the thoughts of weird and simply embraced the moment.

When we finally came up for air it was 0600 on the dot. Marny's breakfast would be ready and I'd feel bad if we didn't show up. "We gotta go. Marny's got breakfast."

"Go. It'll take me ten minutes, but I'll be right there."

As I stood up, she somehow grabbed a handful of my rear end.

"Hey," I said and scooted away.

"Best not to turn your back on me," she said.

"I guess not."

I skipped the shower and saw that Nick was at the helm. "Hey, you want me to bring you some breakfast up?" I said loudly, across the bridge.

"Sure. Something light though. I'm headed to bed in a couple of hours."

"Roger that."

Xie was seated at the mess table. She'd chosen the corner with her back against the wall.

"I wondered if you sleepy heads would be getting up," Marny said.

"Tabby will be down in a couple of minutes. Sleep alright, Xie?" I asked. I'd told myself that I was going to try to treat her like any other crew member.

"It was okay." She looked at me warily.

Marny gave her a concerned glance. "If you need something to help you sleep, I think we have some stuff."

"Maybe," Xie said.

"You mind running this up, Cap?" Marny asked as she handed me a plate loaded with eggs and toast for Nick. Wordlessly I took it and jumped on the lift, returning a minute later.

"Here you go," she said and slid a pan of cinnamon rolls onto the table. Like I said, I didn't like to miss her breakfasts.

Xie didn't take a roll, but looked at them suspiciously. I pulled one off, put it on a plate and slid it over to her. "Just take a bite. If you don't like it, you might keep that to yourself. Marny's also in charge of our physical conditioning and you don't really want to be pissing her off," I said trying to keep things light.

"What's the catch?" she asked.

"What do you mean?"

"Last time you locked me in a cell," she said.

"You've got to eat, Xie. And let's be clear; last time you tried to kill me and my entire crew and *then* I locked you in a cell. I'm willing to put most of that behind us if you are."

"What about the restraints?"

"What do you think?"

She nodded as if she got it. She also pulled the plate over and ate the cinnamon roll like it was the most precious gift she'd ever received.

"Cap. You're scheduled to work out after breakfast, so you'd better take it easy on those rolls," Marny said just as Tabby arrived and I'd grabbed a second roll.

"Where do you work out?" Tabby asked with interest.

"You passed right under it when you came in the hold. Marny set up a ring for boxing and it has a cardio bike and running track," I said.

"I'll go. I've got two hours before my shift, and I've got some exercises I need to work on. I could even use your help," she said.

"Great, I'm in," I said.

We cleaned up the dishes and started to head back toward the hold.

"Xie, if you want to come along, you can. As long as one of us is accompanying you, you won't get stopped at the back door," I said.

A tiny smile showed on her face. I wasn't quite sure how to interpret it, but I wasn't willing to think dark thoughts this soon after having had Marny's cinnamon rolls.

The four of us trooped into the hold and I pointed at the three meter wide square attached to what we considered to be the ceiling.

"Local gravity up there is .6g. It extends for most of the ceiling. If you climb the wall, you'll find the flip-over point at three meters off the ceiling," I explained.

Before I could say anymore, Tabby arc-jetted upward and neatly rotated just before impacting the ring.

"We'll have to climb," I said. I'd made the climb dozens of times, so I just pulled myself up along the rib of the ship that sat exposed in the hold. "Do you still do yoga?" I asked looking at Xie.

"Not for a long while," she said.

As expected, my workout hit muscle groups I'd neglected while we'd been on Mars. I'd swear that Marny had some sort of spyware that plotted my activity and found the most trying activities.

Tabby had an entire routine of exercises she was to work through. We weren't able to get through many of them, as her muscle tone had been badly compromised by lying around in the hospital bed. At the end of two hours we were all a sweaty mess and ready to be done with it.

"Is it always like that?" Tabby asked after we were out of earshot of Marny.

"I'd be lying if I said that wasn't Marny's favorite activity," I said.

Over the long trip, Xie slowly started to come out of her shell.

She was nowhere near the confident thug I'd met on Colony 40, but she was taking a more active role in ship life. I knew her to be an expert at hand to hand combat and as she regained her strength and agility we started working out together more and more. It was good to work out with Marny, but our fighting styles were considerably different. Most of my finesse moves were lost when used against Marny's much larger mass and superior strength. With Xie, however, I was able to practice more subtle offensive moves that relied less on brute strength. Before I knew it, we had fallen back into a comfortable pattern of training.

"You're much stronger and faster than you were," Xie admitted after one particularly exhausting session.

"You've regained your speed," I returned. We'd had to remove her restraints while working out because they punished her for moving too quickly.

"You're a strange person, Liam Hoffen. I don't know why you're treating me so well," she commented.

"Maybe that's just the world I want to live in," I replied.

"Maybe..."

PLAN B

In the main asteroid belt, the farther away from the Sun you got, the more spread out the asteroids were. The Hildas region of the belt was about as far out as you could go without actually crossing the orbital path of Jupiter (which I was disappointed we weren't even remotely close to). This feature made mining in these sparsely populated regions a very expensive proposition.

We were approaching a cluster of asteroids that could be contained in a box no more than a hundred kilometers on a side - about a tenth the size of Colony 40's original claim. In my mind, I thought there was a better than fifty percent chance that Xie was lying to us and had no idea where the dreadnaught would be located. I'd never sufficiently discovered how high up in the Red Houzi command chain she'd been, so I had no good way to judge the value of her information.

For the last four days we'd crept forward in stealth mode, our passive sensors not picking up any local activity. I'd decided to play it safe and not arrive too close, the Houzi would no doubt have sensors to warn them of enemy approach. That is, if they were actually there.

On the fifth day, we'd come close enough to tell that there was, indeed, no ship, no base, nothing.

"There's nothing here," Nick declared.

We were seated at the table on the bridge. For the last few hours, it had become increasingly clear that something large had been here, given the amount of garbage. Whatever it had been, it no longer remained.

"How about it, Xie. Was this just a wild goose chase? Or did Red Houzi just move on?" I tried to keep the anger out of my voice. This woman had betrayed me the last time we'd sailed together. My mind, naturally, ran through the different reasons she might be doing it again.

"No. They're supposed to be here. Don't get too close, though. We always left traps behind. The alarms will let Red Houzi know that someone has found one of their abandoned bases," she said.

"So what? We're done? Twenty-four days of sailing and nothing?" I asked.

"They had to move somewhere," she said.

"You're out of the loop. This mission is a bust," Nick said.

She took a breath. "Wait. There's another spot."

"Why should we believe you," Nick asked.

She placed her hand on his arm and Marny visibly stiffened. I could see this going very badly in a short period of time.

"You're right, Nick. I used you and Liam. I know trust needs to be built and I haven't done that. If it means anything to you, I'm sorry for how I behaved - for using you, shooting you, and for trying to take your ship. I'm not expecting forgiveness - you have no reason to forgive me. I just needed to say that."

"This feels manipulative," Marny said.

"No, I get it," Xie said, retracting her hand from Nick's arm. "Let me put this out there though. The other location isn't that far, another eight days, plus a stealth approach. I'd bet you have enough fuel to try one more location. What's the harm?"

Nick slid a pad over to her, "Give me the location."

"Thank you," Xie said.

"I didn't say we were going."

Xie nodded demurely. I was just paranoid enough to feel like she was playing Nick perfectly. I caught Marny's eye and saw that she was thinking the same thing.

"We'd only just have enough fuel. If we got into any combat, it'd be a long ride home," he said. He was referencing a well-known idiom and romantic theme in space travel. The 'long ride home' being a reference to using your last small amount of fuel to send you back home, even though you'd run out of O2 and food well before you got there.

"You can't trust her, Nick," Marny said.

"The Navy will be interested in this site, either way," I said.

"True," Marny agreed.

"It's another week. If she'd wanted to pull us into a trap, she didn't need to bring us here first," Nick said.

"You're right, of course," Xie said. "I've not been trustworthy. It's also possible there won't be anything there, but we were developing the location. It wasn't supposed to be up and going for another year."

"We'll look," Nick said.

"Thank you," she replied.

Four days later at the midpoint, I decided that I'd give Sterra a heads up. I'd been assured that the quantum crystals were untraceable and the Navy had been expecting some word from us.

"Belcose, come in, are you there?" I said into the handheld receiver that actually had a cord connecting it to the main comm device. I repeated this call once a minute for ten, which was our protocol.

"Belcose here, what's your status, *Hotspur*?" he asked. It was interesting that he specifically knew it was me, given I hadn't identified myself.

"Negative contact. But we're headed to a second site," I said.

"Coordinates?" he asked.

"Not yet. We'll check it out and once we're clear of the area, I'll share. We did, however, find an abandoned base. Our prisoner assures us it was recently active," I said.

"Status in system has changed. There's been another attack," he said.

"Did our target show up?"

"Negative."

"How long ago?"

"Eighteen days. When will you know about your second site?"

"No more than a week. We're not that hopeful, though."

"Understood. Anything else?"

"No. Hoffen out," I turned the set off and placed it back in its box.

It was easy to slip back into our normal routines, but with a growing sense of apprehension. We'd seen the enemy's lair and it was reasonable to expect they were in the area. Xie had grown withdrawn, nervous even, and that added to my own sense of foreboding.

Finally, we arrived near enough to a new group of asteroids still in the Hildas region of the main belt. The navigation plan called for us to creep in the final four days using our stealth capabilities. Each day we got closer, we further limited the use of anything that might generate a signal.

"Liam, you need to see this," Tabby said. She was on watch and I was back in the hold working out with Marny. Out of a need to release our frustration, we'd been sparring more and more as the days wore on.

Show on HUD, I told my AI.

Our passive sensors were finally able to resolve the thirty kilometer ring of asteroids. More importantly, I was able to just make out what I believed was the dreadnaught. If we turned on our active sensors, we'd know for sure, but the consequences could be dire.

"Tabby, slow our approach and bring us to a Zero Delta-V," I said.

"Aye, slowing approach with maximum stealth, to Zero Delta-V," she responded. Repeating commands apparently was something they taught at the Academy because it was something she frequently did.

"Xie was right. We're needed on the bridge," I said to Marny.

On the way past Xie's bunk room I knocked. She spent most of her time in her room, only joining us for our one common meal of the day. She opened the door and looked up at me, her face was drawn with worry.

"You were right. We found it," I said.

Unexpectedly she jumped and hugged me. She'd startled me and I almost treated her hug like a grapple. At the last moment, I accepted it. She felt my response and pulled back suddenly.

"I'm sorry. That wasn't appropriate. You've taken a big risk on me," she said.

"Nick is the one who approved this leg of the trip."

"We both know that's not a hundred percent of it. If you hadn't advocated for me, this would have gone the other way."

"Let's talk on the bridge."

Tabby projected the asteroid field onto the small holo sitting on top of the bridge table. The passive sensors were constantly refining the image. There was no doubt we were looking at the dreadnaught. It was nestled next to three rectangular structures, which were in turn attached by long catwalks.

"Have we seen any other ships?" I asked.

"We're too far out. The only reason we're able to see the dreadnaught is because there is so much external work being done on it. The AI is filling in details for us, making guesses. We'd have to get closer to detect anything smaller than a destroyer," Nick said.

"So, that's good news," I said.

Everyone looked at me, mystified.

It made sense to me. "There aren't any destroyers."

"We don't really know that for sure," Nick said.

"What are we waiting for? Why aren't we just calling the Navy so they can come out and get these guys?" Tabby said.

"Good question. Nick?" I said.

Nick raised his eyebrows and tilted his head to the side. It was his, 'that's probably what we should do,' look.

"Marny?" I asked.

"Aye. It's a sound idea," she said.

I looked to Xie. She looked like she was busting to say something, but to her credit, she was keeping it to herself.

"Xie. You have something?" I asked.

"It's stupid," she said.

"What?"

"Where's the fleet?" she asked.

"Their fleet got destroyed by the Navy on Colony 40," I said.

"Yes. That was their first fleet. They have two fleets though, where's that fleet. It should be here, protecting that dreadnaught," she said.

"About three weeks ago the Braryth colony was sacked by a pirate fleet," I said. I hadn't shared that information with Xie.

"Don't you see it? They're vulnerable," she said.

"What could we do against a dreadnaught? Even more, what if we got it, what would we do with it?" Tabby asked.

Nick was on it. Just like he always was. "Leverage. The Navy's got us over a barrel. If we had control of that ship, we'd have leverage."

"Are you nuts?" Tabby asked looking first to Nick then to me to get my support.

"It takes a lot of people to man a ship that size," I said.

"If they lost their first fleet, they're already short of manpower. There can't be anything more than a skeleton crew on that dreadnaught and most of those workers are press-gang and won't provide any real resistance. The key is getting control of the bridge. Red Houzi Captains are afraid of the crew and as a result the bridge controls everything. The only problem is, it's also the most heavily armored part of the ship," Xie said.

My mind spun with options. We could escape right now, Tabby would get her arm replaced and we'd get the Navy off of our backs. The target was tantalizing, though. What Xie was saying was easy to understand and believe. Unfortunately, those were hallmarks of a good deception.

"How do you propose we get command control?" Nick asked. Straight to the point. If we couldn't sail the ship, then all was for naught.

"We bluff. I bet I outrank anyone on that station," Xie said.

It was almost too ridiculous even for me. "You want me to believe we could walk in there and just take it?"

"No. It wouldn't go that way," she said. "Whoever the captain is, he won't be giving control to anyone of any rank. But if we can get to him, I'll get the command turned over to you."

"Let me guess, you'd need to be in charge? What'd stop you from just turning on us once we're inside?" Marny asked.

"What if I could get us on the ship? Could you get us to be recognized as friendlies for long enough to make it to the bridge?"

I asked.

Xie was having trouble with that. "How would you do that?"

"They can't possibly have patched that thing up entirely. When we saw it last, there were three hundred square meter sections of missing armor. We could just sail in."

"That'd never work. They'd see us coming," Tabby said and she pointed at the holo. "And this ship looks patched up."

"No, that's just the AI filling in details. The missing sections wouldn't really light up that well. I'm with Liam on this. We could probably get on board," Nick said.

"There's no way to know if their systems will recognize me," Xie said.

"I'm not sure if they need to. We're talking about pirates here," Marny said. "How much inter-factional fighting is there?"

"Competition between the franchises is pretty fierce," Xie said.

"Fierce enough that you might see a power play while the fleet's away?" Marny asked.

"Of course," Xie answered.

Marny gave us a frightening smile. "I've got a plan,"

Like most of our plans, this one wasn't particularly complex. The first part was simple. We had to get close enough to see if we could actually land the *Hotspur* inside the big ship.

Xie knelt on the stairs between the two pilot's chairs. It gave her a good look through the glass in front of us, which was all we'd have since we were totally blacked out.

"They'll have a lot of defensive guns. You don't have to worry about them, though, because if they see the ship, we'll be dust before we know it," she said. I didn't find the comment to be overly helpful.

I held my breath as we passed the outer ring of asteroids. If our armor was leaking energy we'd know it shortly. We were strapped in and prepared for a combat burn, but I agreed with Xie on this. We'd have to be extremely lucky not to get tagged by their defensive systems if they saw us.

I breathed more easily as we sailed, apparently unseen, beyond the outer ring and approached the dreadnaught. Then, my heart fell as we passed along the flank of the giant ship. Somehow, they'd reskinned the missing sections of armor. It wasn't armor, but it might as well have been, because there wouldn't be any stealth landing.

"I'm backing off," I said. Everyone was listening intently on the crew's comm channel.

"I think we're down to Plan-B," Marny said.

I released a breath. "I've always been a big proponent of Plan-B."

BLITZKRIEG

"I hate this," Tabby said.

"Of course you do," I said. "You're a warrior at heart. The thing is, there are a lot of lives that are counting on the Navy knowing where this base is. If we're unsuccessful, you have to make that call. People are depending on you."

I gave her a lingering kiss and made my way down to the hold. Marny and Nick had already powered up their mechanized suits and Xie, tiny in her armored vac-suit, stood next to them holding a blaster rifle. I hopped into my mech-suit, still dormant in its crate. I think I'd always known it would come down to this.

I thought back to a couple of weeks ago when I'd first been introduced to the suit and how difficult it had been to even stand up. It didn't feel like a second skin yet, but I was more comfortable with it than I had been. I raised easily to my feet and did a few turns to make sure everything was limber.

"Cap, run through the checklist I just sent you," Marny said. I ran through the mostly familiar list that Big Pete had taught us. Marny had added a few additional ones that included the weaponry.

She continued, "I'm setting you both on three shot for your primary weapon and you'll have door breaching grenades as secondary. I've programmed that as Alpha. Beta setting is auto fire and heavy grenade loads. Be careful with that. You can run out of ammo pretty quickly that way."

"Roger that," I said. I cycled through the weapons interface. It was a little overwhelming.

Beta, I said. I heard a positive chime and noticed the HUD's indicator showed AUTO where previously there'd been three bullets.

Alpha, I said. It changed back to the three bullet display.

"I think I've got it," I said. "Marny, I'm taking tactical for the EVA. Once we're on board, it's all you."

"Aye, Cap," she acknowledged.

I cycled the atmo from the hold. We were too big to go back through the hallway to the hatch on the side of the ship.

"Tabby, we're ready for approach," I said.

I watched through my HUD as she carefully sailed us past the outer ring again and approached the same starboard flank where the new skin had recently been patched in. I lowered the cargo bay's ramp just enough for us to exit, hoping that the puff of residual atmo wouldn't draw any attention. From this point, we were on communication blackout.

I was the last to push off from the ship and I pressed the interior panel causing the ramp to retract. It was Tabby's signal to clear the area. She gently nudged the ship away. We were completely exposed, adrift next to the enemy behemoth.

With mere whispers from our arc-jets, we drifted, more than sailed toward the ship. So far, we either hadn't been seen or they were deciding what to do with us. I could imagine Marny chastising me to simply stay in the moment. If it wasn't something I could control, then I needed to put it out of my mind. Distractions would get us killed.

We landed on the side of the ship. It was easy to see how the decks were laid out from the welds stitched across the otherwise pristine metallic surface. The next step would be critical to our plan.

Nick placed the welder/cutter against the hull of the ship. Our gamble was simple. The material the pirates had stretched across the large wound would only be thick enough to hold atmosphere. They were, no doubt, still manufacturing armor. Without the ability to hold atmo however, they wouldn't be able to repair the interior systems damaged in the fight. There was no way to know what was behind the skin.

My suit's visor dimmed when Nick's cutter fired up. The light was extremely bright light and it made me nervous, but there was nothing to be done. His first cut wasn't deep and we were careful to stay away from the meter-radius hole he etched in the surface. His goal was to weaken the metal and allow it to blow out if there was atmo built up behind it. When Nick finally cut through, no atmo escaped. A few minutes later, the panel finally came loose and started to slowly flutter away from the ship.

I grabbed the metal disc before it could go too far, and held it in place while Nick tacked a small hinge in place. The plan was to pull the piece closed behind us, covering our tracks. The deception wouldn't last long and the crew would know we were here soon, regardless.

Marny jumped through the hole and I followed. All of our training in teams would pay off here. It didn't matter that we were in mechanized suits, the rules still applied. I knew Nick would be right behind me and we'd instructed Xie to stay between Nick and myself as much as possible. It would be the safest spot for a squishy.

We entered a vast open deck on the ship and clung to the side. Overall the ship was shaped like a huge shallow V. This deck was littered with debris and stretched across what looked like the entire two hundred meters width of the ship. It also extended forward a hundred fifty meters which was about ten percent of the ship's length. It wasn't hard to understand why we'd gone undetected so far.

Nick grabbed the metal disc he'd cut out and pulled it down, bending the metal, so that it sort of covered the hole. It would be discovered at some point. We needed to move.

My AI started mapping out the interior space, relating it to what we knew about the overall dimensions of the ship. It would continue to build out the map as long as more area was explored.

"Let's move," Marny said. Once again we were communicating using only line of sight transmitters. It made everyone's voice sound tinny, but it was better than announcing our arrival. She'd also assumed tactical command now that we were inside the ship.

Marny pushed away from the wall and slunk forward, sinking to the deck. My HUD showed that there was .1g. It was enough to hold items to the deck but wouldn't take much ship's energy to maintain.

We stayed close to the outer wall and moved forward, finally arriving at a large airlock that was big enough to move equipment between these large lower decks.

"It's locked," Marny said.

"We could bust our way through," I offered.

"No. They'll be on to us right away," Xie said. "Stand against the wall. Let me try to get us through. If that doesn't work, you can blast your way in. Stand back so they can't see you through the airlock."

We pulled back around the corner and Xie took Nick's welding unit from him and stood in front of the airlock door.

"*Bakunawa* command, this is Captain Mie-su. I need an unlock on the airlock in front of me," she said.

"Mie-su, I thought you were dead. What are you doing on my ship?" a voice came back.

"Identify yourself," she said.

"Captain Jakab. I'm sending a squad your way. I'm taking you into custody," he replied.

"Don't be an idiot, Jakab. I was sent to infiltrate your ship and I've done just that. Don't make it worse on yourself."

"Pardon me if I don't believe you," he said.

"Up to you, but you better send more than a squad. I'm feeling frisky," she said.

"Are you nuts?" I asked.

"No. I'm trusting you to come get me, Liam," she said.

"What? I don't understand."

"Jakab will drag me up to the bridge so he can humiliate me. I'll transmit everything I see along the way, you'll get a map of the ship. It's the only way," she said.

It was already in motion and there was nothing I could do about it. I had to decide who she was playing. If she was playing us, we were in for trouble. If she could get us a path to the bridge, it would be worth a lot.

It took a few minutes for a group of armor vac-suited pirates to show up. Contrary to her bluster she lay her blaster rifle on the ground in front of her and knelt on the floor with her hands behind her head.

"Not so tough," the lead pirate said, taking the opportunity to club her with the stock of his gun. It took all I had not to leave our cover at that moment. They'd sent six pirates, all men, after one single woman. Impressive.

As promised, Xie was transmitting as they drug her down the hallway and to a lift. It took nearly five minutes to drag her to their destination, but she finally stood in front of a red-faced man. The bridge was nestled deep in the center of the ship.

"So what is this about?" he asked.

A crew member approached and said something to Jakab that we were unable to hear, but it became quickly obvious what the conversation was.

"She's transmitting?" Jakab asked.

"Secure her," he screamed. "We've got intruders. Sound the alarm. Lock down the ship."

"Cap, we've got to move," Marny said.

I cut off the stream of information coming from Xie. It would distract me. I just hoped she'd make it through.

"Go!" I said.

Marny erupted from where we'd hunkered down. The end of her left arm sent a stream of explosives towards the airlock. We were in a vacuum so we didn't hear anything, but the lock exploded and atmosphere boiled across the deck. Marny, not waiting for the chaos to subside, charged into the fiery tumult.

"We've got to move, they'll be locking down that bridge," she said, sprinting forward.

The lift was a hundred meters directly forward, but two doors slid down, triggered by the sudden loss of pressure. We wouldn't be able to clear them both, but we successfully got under the first one before it slammed shut behind us.

"Blitzkrieg," Marny said. It was a tactic we'd discussed. Essentially, we would overrun enemy lines and not stop to engage, striking at the heart of the target.

"Go," I said.

She fired an ordinance at the bulkhead that had slammed down, blocking our path. The atmosphere had already started to return to this end of the hallway and no explosive decompression occurred when the door blew.

Marny charged through the opening. Before I was even clear of the smoke, I heard blaster fire and red targets appeared on my HUD. Marny wasn't stopping, however. I moved just to the left of her and raised my left arm, firing a grenade down the hallway.

Beta, I yelled, doing my best to keep up. The hallway was only a meter taller than we were and the two of us, not to mention Nick, filled all available space. We simply ran through the first group of defenders who'd hastily set up.

"Blow the lift," I said. We'd covered the hundred meters in short order and the remaining pirates in the hallway had taken cover, poking out to take potshots at us. Nick, who trailed, kept them busy by firing back, but so far their weapons were unable to penetrate our armor.

Marny accepted my recommendation and fired a salvo of explosives. The fascia of the elevator exploded shortly after, exposing the open shaft.

"Cover me," she said.

We'd come to a 'T' in the hallway. I spun down, taking a knee, covering ninety degrees to the port side which included looking back down the hallway. Nick had either taken care of our initial attackers or, more likely, they'd gotten smart and weren't trading rounds with a superior, mechanized force. I knew he'd be oriented just like me on the starboard side. I heard him firing, but didn't spend any effort to see what he was into. If he needed help, he'd say something.

"Got it," Marny said.

"What?" I asked.

"Had to blow the elevator cars," she said. "We're Oscar Mike," and she stepped into the shaft.

She disappeared upward, arc-jets pushing hard. I jumped in behind her and followed her up.

"Move now, Nick," I said.

"On your six," he replied.

Marny hovered for a moment several decks up and pushed her way through the un-armored elevator doors.

"You overshot," I said to her. We were two decks above where the bridge would be.

"Aye. Let's go."

I followed her out. The hallways were empty.

"In here." She pushed her way through a closed door.

"It's like there's no one on this ship," I said.

"Aye. They're short staffed. It's not like pirates grow on trees. Mars Navy took out a whole fleet of 'em. If the other fleet's on patrol, you can bet they took the biggest and meanest," Marny said.

"Trees?" I didn't get what she was saying, but the biggest and meanest thing made sense.

"Never mind. Stay on target," she said. "Blow the floor, I've marked it for you."

I wondered what she had in mind, but wasn't about to ask. We were in combat and speed was important. My HUD showed the location and even showed a suggested explosive load. I raised my left arm and the grenades blooped out in a circular pattern.

"Clear," I said and we all ducked out into the hallway, at least as much ducking as you can do in a two hundred kilogram mechanized infantry suit. Three seconds later, the explosion ripped out most of the walls causing me to stagger, but I didn't fall. The suit held up just fine.

"Same again. Nick, we'll need your explosives too," Marny said, having re-entered the smoldering room.

I followed her and looked into the hole, she'd marked the floor in the next room down. I finally understood her plan.

"This time we'll need more cover," she said and jumped out of the room into the hallway.

I leaned over the cratered floor and dropped the recommended spread as Nick did the same. By my estimation she'd nearly quadrupled the amount of ordinance. Again, I wasn't going to question it, but it seemed excessive.

"Clear." We sprinted back to where Marny had knelt down.

A massive explosion rocked the ship, at least in the vicinity where we were. Black smoke roiled up through the floor.

"Go!" Marny said. I followed her toward the raging fire and jumped through the hole. We fell down, landing on a hard surface.

I looked down and the outline of a large, armored, circular room became evident. It had to be the bridge. We were screwed. All we'd successfully accomplished was to burn away the decking around the bridge on the top and the sides, but it stood intact in front of us.

"Frak," Marny said. "That's no good."

Heavy automatic fire started stitching the air around us and we backed around the corner. They'd brought up some bigger guns.

"Stay down," Marny said. "Those babies can get through the suit."

"Retreat?" I asked.

"Not sure that'll work, Cap. It was a good try. We'll have to fight our way through those guns."

"Frak." The blasters they were firing at us ripped up the walls like they were made of paper. It was only the bridge that was giving us cover.

I peeked my head around the corner to see the advancement of a well-armored squad. They'd anticipated our destination and had set up for us. I sprayed automatic fire down the hallway and launched my remaining grenades.

"Outta grenades," I said.

Nick stepped around me and fired down the hallway. A lucky blaster shot caught his shoulder and it spun him back into the wall behind us. I grabbed him and pulled him back to cover while Marny unloaded automatic fire in response.

"I think this is trouble, Cap. No matter what happens, it's been a good run," she said.

"No time for that, Marny," I said. "Stay in the moment."

Big Pete had told me how to transfer munitions between suits and I locked into Nick's suit and vamped half of his remaining load. I spun and fired down the hallway. The pirates had stopped advancing, waiting for us to run out of ammo.

I switched to three shot and lobbed a smaller grenade at them. Unfortunately, it was batted down and exploded harmlessly in the hallway between us. I pulled back behind the corner.

"Nick, how are you doing?" I asked.

"Okay." It wasn't true, he was hurting. I could hear it in his voice.

We were in big trouble. We sat for a few minutes, which was a terrible thing to do, the pirates would be better able to organize. We needed a new plan, and now. At least Tabby would get away, I thought.

"Liam, honey, can you hear me?" A soft voice asked. It was soft enough I wondered if I was hearing things.

"What?"

"I was wondering if I could convince you not to fire if I opened this bridge door." It was Xie's voice, transmitting over the ship's public address. I was hearing it through my helmet.

"Okay," I said hesitantly. We really had no other options.

The armored exterior of the room we stood next to started to slide around, exposing a more normal looking door. The door opened, but it wasn't big enough to fit through with a mechanized suit.

"I need you to come in here," she said from around the corner, still not visible.

"Don't trust her," Nick said. "It's a trap."

"I don't see a choice, buddy," I said.

I turned my back to provide the best cover, opened the chest of the suit, and climbed out. Free of the suit, I skulked over to the door, trying to stay clear of the line of fire from the front line of pirates.

"See? I told you I could end this," Xie said to the man I recognized as Captain Jakab.

She was seated comfortably in a chair, unbound, with her legs crossed. She didn't appear to be under any duress.

"This is the famous Liam Hoffen?" he asked.

"And you captured him. What a hero that makes you," Xie said.

"You bitch." I couldn't believe she'd successfully played me. Again.

"Now, now, lover, don't be mad. I needed a ride home. Maybe I'll keep you as a pet," she said.

"Hah, that'd be funny. Close the bridge," Jakab said.

"You have another problem, though. Their ship is out there, just beyond the ring. The pilot's going to transmit our location if we don't get her," Xie said.

"Don't," I said, my eyes filling with tears.

"Don't be sentimental, lover. It's not personal."

END OF AN ERA

"Where?" Captain Jakab asked.

"I can locate it, but they have very strong stealth capacity. I need access to the sensors. And, lover, tell your friends to stand down. I'd hate to have to kill them, especially Nicholas." Xie's voice was silky smooth.

"Ensign Cagnina, provide Captain Mie-su access to the sensor station," he ordered.

"Sir? She's not in our command structure," Cagnina said.

"Ensign. That was an order. Captain Mie-su is a well-respected member of Red Houzi command."

"Yes, sir."

Xie pushed the ensign out of her way, pulling his pistol out of its holster as she did. She shot him in the head, killing him instantly.

Jakab fumbled with his side arm, finally pulling it out and levelling it at Xie, who'd placed her pistol on the station next to her.

"Tut-tut, Captain. That little bastard questions my captain in front of me? It's my duty to put him down," she said.

"That's cold." He put his weapon away, but I noticed that his hand shook as he did.

"Now, Liam," she gushed. "I *said* have Marny and Nick stand down. If they do, Captain Jakab will no doubt allow me to take them as my trophy."

"Of course," Jakab nodded, trying to sound magnanimous.

"There she is," Xie said. The outline of the *Hotspur* showed up on the vid screen in front of her.

"Don't, Xie," I said.

"Captain, would you allow me?" Xie asked.

"To?" Jakab asked.

"If you'll give me your code, I'll send a salvo of rockets off to send her along her way. It'd really mean a lot to me."

"0AB55AEC," he said.

Xie punched in the code.

"Captain, we have a problem," one of the three remaining crew said.

"What?" he asked, crossing to look at the vid screen.

Xie winked at me and lithely snaked her way out of the chair, drawing a nano-blade from the waist line of her suit. In a single, fluid movement she deployed the blade and ran it through the surprised Captain Jakab. In that same movement she also picked up the gun in front of her and levelled it at the remaining crew.

"My friends. You have only a few choices here. I've just destroyed the entire base and the *Bakunawa* is now under the control of my franchise. I've removed the head of my rival, in the best tradition of the Red Houzi, and rightfully claim what is mine," Xie said.

"Yes, Captain," they each replied and turned back to their stations.

All hands, she commanded. "We've quelled the incursion and I'd like to welcome you all to the Blue Heron Franchise. As of this moment, you'll record your loyalty to this clan. We've got a mission of the utmost urgency and will be underway within the hour, please make necessary arrangements."

Xie turned back to me.

"Well, Admiral Hoffen. Your plan worked flawlessly. I hope you'll allow your humble servant to continue to serve," she said bowing.

"Seriously?"

"Well, to be honest, I thought some of the plan was a little rough around the edges, but it seemed to work out like you'd planned overall," she said, smiling widely.

I gulped back a breath. "You're scary."

"True enough," she replied.

"Nick, Marny, you need to come in here," I said after

instructing the crew to open the bridge door.

Marny helped the limping Nick through the door, which we promptly closed again.

Xie explained that she knew the bridge would be well fortified. Promotion in the ranks of the Red Houzi was often accomplished by simple assassination. Without a strong show of force, the crew would never follow her. She fully expected there would be attempts to unseat her, but by controlling the bridge, we had a safe place to hunker down.

Safe passage had been granted to the *Hotspur* by Xie and Tabby had been escorted by Nick and Marny, both in their recharged mech suits, back up to the bridge. They'd brought along a crate of food and water at Xie's recommendation.

After a short period of recovery, one of the crew - we'd come to know him as Rhees - alerted us, "Captain, we have a problem."

"What's that?" Xie and I asked at the same time.

He looked between us and decided it was safer to simply answer us both.

"The fleet has returned and we're being hailed. Apparently, Admiral Batista would like an answer as to why the station has been destroyed," he said.

"Tell him there was a mishap with an arms load and that Captain Jakab is overseeing the cleanup," she said.

"But…" The crewman looked to Xie and then reconsidered. He conveyed her words.

"Admiral Batista would like a conference with you as soon as possible," he said.

"Absolutely. Put him on the comm," she said.

"What's going on, Captain? I authorized no change in leadership," he said.

The fleet had returned and consisted of a single destroyer, a corvette and five frigates. Ordinarily a fleet of terrifying proportion, but they looked puny on the holo projector when compared to the *Bakunawa*.

"After Captain Jakab blew up the outpost, I couldn't simply stand by anymore. I am at your mercy," she said, simpering.

"Heave-to and prepare to be boarded," he said.

"Aye, aye, Admiral." She closed the comm.

"What do you think, Liam? We could simply run. They can't do a thing to us."

"I want to end this," I said.

"By your command," Xie said. "Get me a firing solution on that destroyer."

"Sir?"

"Do it or I'll replace you with someone who will," she said.

"Aye, aye," he said.

All hands, battle stations, Xie said.

I wasn't sure what to expect next. "Will they follow your commands?"

"They have no choice. Once I take provocative action, that destroyer will attack us with everything it has. They'll die if they don't," she said and turned to Rhees. "Fire when ready."

"Captain, they stand no chance. The *Teumessian* can't possibly withstand the barrage," he said.

"Good to be on the winning side, don't you think?"

"Yes, sir. We'll have a solution in twenty seconds," he said.

In all, the battle lasted less than ten minutes. Two of the frigates slipped away, but the other ships were completely destroyed. There was nothing to be done about the frigates, as they'd bolted at the first signs of aggression from the *Bakunawa.*

"Well, Admiral Hoffen. Do you have other orders? I believe the Blue Heron Franchise is the last standing franchise of the great Red Houzi," Xie asked deferentially. Somehow, I'd become the leader of the very organization I despised.

"Yes. Lay in this course," I said. Nick had worked up a careful navigation plan that would allow us to skirt North American and Chinese territories and slide down the edge of the neutral zone between Mars and Chinese space. Essentially, we were headed directly toward Jeratorn.

"How quickly would you like to arrive?" she asked.

"Make all possible haste," I said.

It would take fourteen days and we would burn an

unimaginable amount of fuel. On board we were operating with a skeleton crew of two hundred and ten. Many were hardened criminals, others simple slaves who had been pressed into service. Separating one group from the other was a duty beyond our capability so we remained locked on the bridge, except for Tabby who preferred the solitude of the *Hotspur*. I suspected it had something to do with the privacy she needed to deal with her disability. Unfortunately, I couldn't leave the bridge of the dreadnaught as it felt we were in a very delicate situation.

If the pirates on board got wind of what we were doing, there would be rioting and we might never make our destination. Xie had done a good job of whipping them into a frenzy about the next colony we were going to sack. She'd explained that Jeratorn was our target and revenge was our goal. We'd suffered our only defeat there and would wipe them from the history books.

At mid-point, Nick and Marny accompanied me back to the *Hotspur* to make the all-important call to Mars Protectorate.

We wouldn't be fulfilling the letter of our agreement with Mars Protectorate and I wasn't sure how they'd handle it. But, I didn't care. They'd pushed us too far, using us to do their dirty work. They had leverage and used it. It was now our turn to use the leverage we had. In my mind, M-Pro differed from Red Houzi because they had laws they upheld. But in this action, they'd been little more than thugs.

"Belcose, come in, are you there?" I asked.

I waited a minute and tried again.

"Belcose, come in, are you there?"

"Belcose here. What's your status, *Hotspur*?"

"Gregor, I need to talk with Commander Sterra," I said.

"What's your status?" he asked.

"We're up, but we've got a change in plans."

"Please communicate," he said.

"I need to talk to Commander Sterra," I repeated.

"Understood."

The four of us sat in my office, waiting. I felt the pressure of the situation.

"Commander Sterra here," came a familiar voice.

"Commander, we've got a situation."

"I see. How might I be of assistance today?" she asked.

"Commander, I'm sorry for putting you in this position, but honestly you're the only one at the Protectorate that I trust."

"This sounds pretty serious, Liam. What's going on?"

"I need you to take command of a dreadnaught filled with pirates," I said.

"Are you joking?" she asked incredulously.

"No, certainly not. But, I have some terms that have to be fulfilled first."

"Are you saying you've located the dreadnaught and you want to change your deal with Alderson?" she asked.

"No. I'm saying we've captured the dreadnaught and I want to change the deal. I don't trust Alderson."

"Liam. He's a good man and is under a lot of pressure."

"Be that as it may, will you negotiate with me?"

"Are you sure you want to do it this way?"

"Yes. Terms are pretty straightforward. We'll deliver the dreadnaught to the neutral zone. The Judiciary will pardon Xie Mie-su for all crimes. The Navy will pay to restore all of Tabby's limbs and let her have her spot back at the Academy once she's healed. And we want to be held harmless for all actions up to this point and be kept anonymous." Nick had given me most of the terms.

"That's it?"

"Yes."

"And if we refuse?" she asked.

"Don't," I said. "What we're asking for is fair."

"I thought Mie-su was your enemy."

"Things change. Also, you might be interested to know we destroyed the Houzi's second fleet," I said.

"Say again?"

"As well as their outpost," I said.

"Please repeat last," she said.

"The Red Houzi's second fleet, consisting of one destroyer, two corvettes and several frigates, was destroyed. We have data streams we'll share with you once we come to an agreement."

"Give me an hour," she said.

"Roger that."

"You didn't need to put me into all of that. I'm just glad we got out of there alive," Tabby said.

"It's not enough for me. Mars needs to pay their debts to the veterans. I can't make 'em do it for everyone, but I can at least make them pay for you."

"I can't say I haven't dreamed of it," she said.

"I know."

Marny disappeared for half an hour and came back with a tray full of steaming food. We'd been limited to ration bars for the last week and it smelled delicious.

It was hard to enjoy the food, as my stomach was nervous. I had too much riding on this. The Navy could treat us as the enemy. If they did, I wasn't sure what we'd do.

"Captain Hoffen?" It was Admiral Alderson's voice.

"Speaking," I said.

"This is Admiral Alderson. I understand you've got news for us," he said.

"Yes, sir. We've captured the dreadnaught *Bakunawa* and would like to deliver her to the Navy for safekeeping."

"I understand you have some conditions," he said.

"We do."

"It feels like you're going rogue on me here. You realize I could declare you an enemy of the state and throw you in prison for the rest of your life."

"Yes, sir. I do," I said.

"And you want to proceed with your demands?"

"They are hardly unreasonable conditions." This man infuriated me, but I just needed to get through the next few minutes.

"Wouldn't do you much good from prison," he said.

"I would hate to need protection from my own country. But if I do, it seems that the North Americans or the Chinese would love to get their hands on this ship. If you ask me, I'd like to see Mars

Protectorate come out on top here. Are you sure you want to go down this path?" I asked.

"No, probably not. I like to test the mettle of the men I go up against and I like that you haven't caved. I took a big risk trusting a group of mercs like yourselves, but Commander Sterra was right about you and Mars needs this win," he said. He clearly couldn't see the sweat dripping from my face. "I accept your terms."

"We're sending coordinates now. We'll be there in a week," I said.

"We'll make sure to provide a warm reception," he said and signed off.

I looked around at my crew and friends. "Do you think we can trust him?"

Marny was looking at me, face ashen, and eyebrows raised.

"What?" I asked.

"Do you realize you just threatened an Admiral in the Navy? That was Buckshot Alderson, for frak sake," Marny said.

"So, you think he's good for his word?" I asked.

"That was a recorded conversation. You can't get a more binding contract. And he might be a hard-ass, but I've read about him. He's as honest as he is scary," Marny said, shaking her head in disbelief.

EPILOGUE

Even with Xie's frequent updates, the crew was restless. And, for good reason. We barely had enough hands to keep the ship going, feed everyone and perform necessary maintenance. It was obvious to the veteran pirates that we weren't on the up-and-up with them and we ended up repelling a couple of mutiny attempts. Fortunately for us, the fortress design of the bridge, as well as the overwhelming force of the mechanized infantry suits, made the few ill-conceived assaults short-lived.

A day from our destination, our thoughts turned to what we'd do next and I realized that it would be our last chance to load up on supplies before the Navy took over.

"Nick, can you see if you can find some missiles? We should load up the *Hotspur* while we're here," I said.

The *Hotspur* had two launch tubes and room for six missiles in total. If you could find them, missiles sold for seventy-five thousand and you could pay two or three times that amount if you weren't close in to Mars.

"Good idea. There are two pallets on the starboard flight deck," he said.

Marny and I equipped the mechanized suits and tromped our way down to the flight deck. Under normal circumstances the deck should be filled with twenty fighters. A single fighter, apparently not operational, sat abandoned and alone on the otherwise barren deck. The missiles weren't difficult to find, held in a rack that was designed to hold thirty such pallets.

Once I saw the pallets, it wasn't difficult to convince Marny to help me load them into the hold. Originally, I'd just thought to grab six and arm the *Hotspur*, but twenty four missiles were hard to ignore. We were careful to strap them tightly to the floor of the hold. It would be the only booty we'd take. I was a little disappointed to discover the pirates didn't have a treasure trove, but two dozen missiles wasn't nothing.

Once loaded, I pushed Tabby to take off in the *Hotspur* and meet us after the exchange was complete. Initially, she'd resisted, but the very real possibility of the Navy coming at us aggressively changed her mind - especially with a hold full of missiles.

A significant design difference between a naval ship and a pirate ship is the ability to control just about every function directly from the bridge. On a naval ship, there is a reasonable expectation that competent men and women will perform their jobs, better than any commander or bridge crew could possibly do by themselves. On a pirate ship, there's no reasonable assumption of loyalty. As a result, every aspect of the ship had to be controllable directly from the bridge. Operating this way was not something that could be done well, but at a minimum, every system could be shut down or frozen.

Under Xie's command, the *Bakunawa* came to a halt at our pre-ordained coordinates at exactly the time we'd arranged. I felt a certain amount of letdown when there was no Navy to be seen. Over the last twelve hours we'd been shutting down major systems throughout the ship and closing off bulkheads, slowly at first, with the goal of segregating the crew. Shortly before arrival, we'd shut down all major systems and movement throughout the ship was extremely limited. Marny, Nick and I had spent the last six hours of our approach hunkered down outside the bridge in the mechanized suits. We'd anticipated a final rush on the bridge, but none came. I had to remind myself that the crew we had on the *Bakunawa* had been rejected by not one, but two different fleets the Red Houzi had organized.

One moment, we were sitting in empty space, a million kilometers from Jeratorn, barely poking our toe into Mars Protectorate space. The next moment, a giant fleet of M-Pro Naval ships appeared, virtually from nowhere. They'd executed combat burns, arriving neatly, formed up five kilometers off our bow. In space combat terms, they'd landed on our head.

This was no quick reactionary force, but rather the biggest collection of ships I could imagine. There were three battleships, seven destroyers and more corvettes, frigates and cutters (although I admit to not even looking for them) than I cared to count. In short, if they wanted to make an example of us, there would be little we could do about it.

All hands, "This is Captain Xie. If you look at your monitors, you'll see that we've run into a small snag. I've overridden all systems and have no desire to go down in a blaze of glory. If you would be so kind as to patiently wait for a friendly boarding party, I'm sure we'll be back about our business shortly."

"Having fun?" I asked her.

"Something about having a shiny new record has put me in a good mood," Xie replied.

"You know, that's only for past sins, right? You have to straighten up now," I said.

"It's certainly something to consider," she said. "By the way, the boarding parties are only two decks away. I recommend you disarm those suits, I doubt you want to appear too provocative."

"Aye, Cap. I think she's got a point there," Marny said.

We stripped out of our suits and joined Xie on the bridge. We'd bound the remaining bridge crew, more for their safety than ours. Under different circumstances, they seemed like they might be decent enough people.

Admiral Alderson swaggered onto the bridge, leading two of the burliest Marines I'd ever seen, who were desperately trying to get in front of him.

"I admit to being a little disappointed you didn't put up any resistance," he said.

"I like to keep my word," I said biting off what I really wanted to say.

"I appreciate that, but it would have made quite a recording," he said.

"Any chance we could get a shuttle to our ship? It looks like you have this more than under control," I asked.

Admiral Alderson was magnanimous, directing a cutter to take us wherever we requested. There was a tense moment when we loaded into the mechanized suits, but he apparently preferred to have us out of the way and stood his guard down.

I was relieved when we finally loaded onto the *Hotspur* and watched the cutter speed away.

"Xie, where can we drop you?" I asked.

"Where are you headed?"

"We'll probably burn for Jeratorn - we're short on fuel - then on to Mars."

"I wouldn't mind visiting an old friend on Jeratorn," she said.

"Hollise?" I asked.

"How could you possibly guess that?"

"Are you sure you want to go into business with her?"

"What. Beth-Anne? She's mostly harmless. Smuggling is much less dangerous than being a pirate."

Two weeks later we finally arrived at Mars, having dropped Xie off at the Welded Tongue bar on Jeratorn. I wasn't sure that Xie was making a great life choice, but it was certainly hers to make. News reports from the Navy were incredible, not to mention completely fictitious. The news outlets had been buzzing about the end of the Red Houzi pirates and how the Navy had gloriously captured a previously undiscovered dreadnaught and destroyed all traces of the once mighty opponent.

In the end, I didn't really mind how it was being spun, just as long as our names were left out. Even though the Red Houzi had been wiped out as a group, it would be a lot safer for us to not be associated with the events. Who knew how many sympathizers might still be out there.

Two days from Mars, Tabby received word from the hospital, scheduling surgery in a month. They'd already started growing tissues and manufacturing her new skeletal limbs. She'd opted for the nano-crystalized alloys in lieu of actual bones. She'd become enamored by the idea of the additional strength they'd provide. She also received a formal invitation to rejoin the next class of cadets.

"It's everything I could hope for," Tabby said. We were on the bridge couch, just holding hands enjoying the quiet of an early morning watch.

"Will they let you back into the fighter school?"

"I'd probably have to requalify, physically."

"You've got almost eight months. I bet we could get you into shape before that."

"I don't know if I'm going back."

"But it's your dream. It's what you've always wanted."

"That's true. It was, anyway."

"So what's the problem?" I asked.

"I don't think I can go back. I guess what I'm saying is, I want what's in front of me, right now."

"I don't get it."

"Don't be dense, Liam. I'm saying I want to stay with you. I want to be part of all of this," she said, sweeping her prosthetic arm, indicating the ship.

I leaned in and kissed her.

"I'd like that too," I said.

Two days later we arrived on Mars.

Open comm, Tali Liszt, I requested as we broke through the Mars atmosphere.

"Hoffen, are you back in town?" she asked. A week previous, I'd sent her a comm, letting her know we were on our way, giving her a rough time of arrival.

"Roger that, requesting permission to land," I said.

"You're clear, but there're some mighty anxious people down here. You might start getting your story together," she said.

"Roger that," I said.

Up to this point, I'd been able to push off thinking about my family's reaction to our return. We hadn't let anyone in on what we were doing and it was time to pay the piper.

"I think Tabby should exit first," I said.

"You'd throw me to the wolves?" Tabby asked.

"In a heartbeat."

We landed near the compound and glided in on arc-jets. It was 1600 local and the sun was shining brightly over the purple-hued grassy plains. I opened the hatch on the starboard side of the ship and the sweet smell of planet-borne atmosphere gently welcomed us.

I helped Tabby down the ladder and the four of us approached the compound. To our surprise, just about everyone we knew was there: Mom, Dad, Jack, Ada, Tali, Jenny, Lena, Jake, Bit, Jammin and Jordy. They were all milling around a group of new picnic tables. The tables were covered with a meal that looked to have been finished a few hours ago.

Instead of reproach, my extended family did something that I'd never have expected. They stood and applauded us as we approached. Dozens of hugs and claps on the back later, we joined them around the table, finding the beers to still be cold enough to enjoy. Somewhere along the line, they'd put two and two together.

"What's next?" I asked, mostly joking. Personally, I was hoping for a nice long vacation.

"Funny you should ask. I ran across this advertisement for mining claims in the Tipperary solar system," Big Pete said.

"Now, Pete," Mom said, patting his leg. "Let them relax. There'll be plenty of time for that later."

"Sure. I'm just saying it's something to look at."

But, that's another story entirely…

BIG PETE

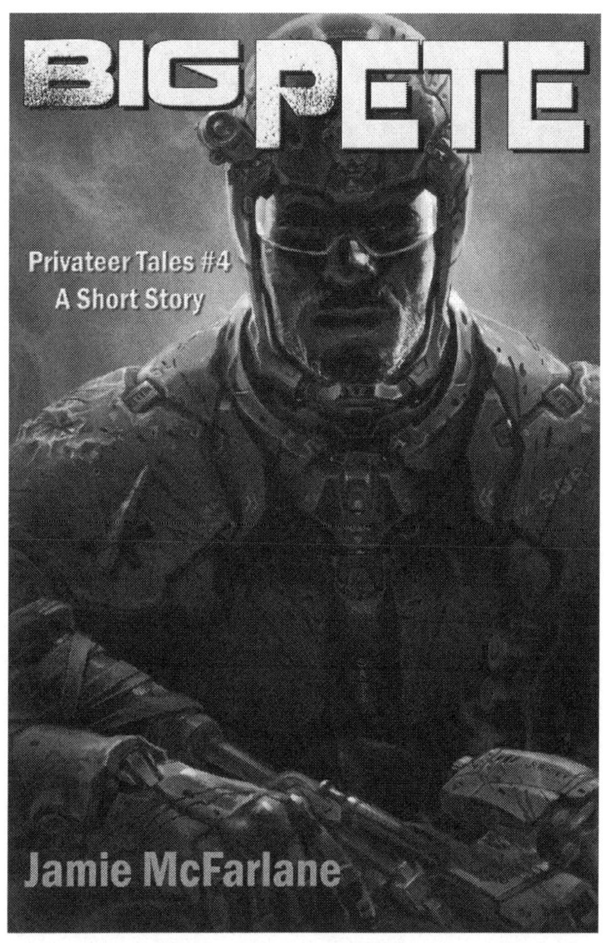

IT'S THE SUDDEN STOP

Our two squad transports slipped quietly across the besieged city. The pilots had been given orders to fly as low as possible. Lieutenant Irawan, the pilot of my squad's ship, had taken the orders quite literally, flying no more than a dozen meters above the buildings, juking and jiving around the tallest structures. In the last month alone, Charlie Company had lost three transports to SAM (Surface to Air Missile) equipped patrols while out in the bush so I for one, wasn't complaining.

Each transport was configured with drop rails that held a full squad firmly in place. In combat we could be, and had been, dropped from just about every height. Personally, I didn't care for stealth insertions, where we were dropped from high altitude and not allowed to fire our arc-jets until the last minute. I was all about flying low.

Charlie 12 or the One-Two, as we referred to ourselves, was on the way back to base for some downtime. Four empty hangers on the drop rail were the only testament to the team members we'd lost over the last month. The entire platoon had been dropped into a shitstorm and our squad's casualties weren't as heavy as others. I guess we'd been lucky, although it hadn't been lucky for Padre, Benny, Scratch and Giggles, who weren't making the return trip.

"Aren't you out in a month, Sarge?" Patch asked. I was one of the few members of the team without a nickname.

"Can it, dickhead," Mulehog fired off before I could respond. Jason 'Mulehog' Mueller was the most intimidating member of our team, if not our whole damned company. At two meters tall and a hundred-thirty kilograms he was imposing without armor. Put him in a hundred fifty kilos of mechanized armor and he looked like a tank with long legs. It also didn't hurt that his weapon of choice was a SAW (Squad Automatic Weapon) slug thrower which added fifty kilos to his normal load-out.

Patch had only been with the squad for the last month. He'd

earned his nickname only a day after he'd arrived, by getting shot up while on patrol. The damage to his suit had been extensive enough that the field-techs applied several obvious patches. The armor had since been repaired, but the nickname stuck.

Mulehog was pissed because it was an unwritten rule that we didn't discuss our end dates. Most of us believed it was bad karma, especially since we'd all known guys who had one day left and hadn't made it out.

I wasn't about to respond. It turned out that Mulehog was pretty easygoing as long as you didn't get him too fired up. And in reality, the only guy on the team who was stupid, or brave enough to mess with him was his smaller buddy Mark 'Methane' Metzner. Where Mulehog was a spray and pray guy with his machine gun, Methane was a triple shot, precision shooter. As squad leader, I'd learned that together they complemented each other very well.

"I'm just wondering if he's going to re-up," Patch complained.

It was a question I hadn't answered for myself yet. I didn't really have anywhere to go to, but I'd been a Marine for five years and seen way more than my fair share of combat. I was a good Marine and a good team leader, but I'd recently started to question if I was really a career type of guy.

I didn't have a chance to answer as my helmet's clear visor snapped shut and the floor of the transport dropped away.

"Taking fire, prepare for drop," the pilot's steady voice said over my helmet's audio. I'd gotten a look at her when she'd picked us up. Killer curves and a fresh, bite-your-ass attitude for a lieutenant. She'd flown us before and there'd been more than a little talk about her - but that's about as close as a grunt would ever get. A little idle chatter was okay with me. Many of the men didn't make it back and a little fantasy wouldn't hurt anyone. That is, as long as they didn't cross the line.

She'd broken protocol by skipping a convo with me, so I knew we were in for trouble. Normally, it was my responsibility to communicate the drop. There could only be one explanation.

The first missile hit the back of the transport just as I felt the familiar release of the drop rail. The explosion tore through the transport and instantly vaporized several members of my squad. Worse yet, the transport was pitched to its side and the shattered hull caught us before we'd fallen clear.

I'd been in some pretty bad scrapes in the past but this rapidly jumped to the top. If we'd had more altitude, escaping from the badly damaged transport wouldn't have been quite as critical, but we were fast losing altitude and if we couldn't get clear of the transport we were done for.

In my experience, luck and situational awareness are the two most significant factors in surviving any engagement. You might argue that getting struck by a missile was bad luck, but you'd be looking at it wrong. It certainly was bad luck for my squad mates who'd been vaporized. For me, it was simply the beginning of the engagement.

I looked over at Methane and Mulehog, who were positioned directly across from me. Neither had successfully deployed from the transport either. More troubling, however, was that Methane had his grenade launching rifle aimed right at me.

One reason Methane was still alive in this war was that he completely rocked at situational awareness. A split second of eye contact and I knew he'd correctly assessed our predicament. The ship was slowly rolling over, and blowing out my side of the transport might be our only escape route.

I grabbed Patch and fired my suit's arc-jets so that we hurtled directly toward Mulehog. One second later, Methane fired a grenade at the position we'd just been occupying. Releasing Patch, I flipped over and planted my feet on the transport wall above Mulehog's head. Counterintuitively and hoping my timing was right, I jumped out toward the explosion from Methane's grenade. I could feel shrapnel pelting me from the blast and hoped my armor was heavy enough to withstand it.

Mid-jump I noticed that Patch hadn't figured out what was happening yet, only I was too far away to do anything about it. Frak ...

"This way, maggot," Mulehog's gruff voice said over our team channel as he grabbed Patch, spun him around, and followed Methane out of the transport.

The wind pulled at me as I exited and just like that I was dropping like a rock.

Emergency drop. My AI (Artificial Intelligence) had finally figured out that we were in free fall. *Prepare for impact.* I'd checked my altitude and we were still a good eight hundred meters above the ground. I twisted around to see what I was about to collide with and before I could figure it out, I'd crashed through a glass window and was tumbling over desks and chairs. The AI contracted the artificial ligaments of the mech-suit and I took the shape of a large armored ball.

I punched through more than a few walls, but fortunately didn't fly out the other side of the building. The AI relaxed the suit's ligaments and I lay there, splayed on the floor. I slowly pulled myself into a seated position and scanned the immediate area. My HUD (Heads-Up Display) didn't show any hostiles or civilians nearby. I was glad we'd dropped at night. Even with a war going on, these buildings were still occupied during the daytime.

I stood up and ran back through the holes I'd created in the walls and looked out through the side of the building. The wind was whipping through the opening, but it didn't bother me much. Between me and the suit, I weighed in at over two hundred and twenty kilos. It'd take a lot of wind to move me.

I could have asked the AI to locate the transport ships, but it was clear where they'd gone down. Irawan had successfully cleared all of the largest buildings and her ship lay broken and burning, several kilometers from my current position. The other ship had run into a tall building and appeared to have exploded on contact. The fire lit up the night sky like a giant torch.

Open comm. Corporal Earnest, I said to the AI.

Corporal Earnest is deceased.

Frak. She'd been on the tail end of the transport where we'd taken the most damage.

Try Corporal Yeong.

Corporal Hwa Yeong is deceased.

Frak. *Open comm with remaining squad.* Finally, I heard the reassuring chirp of communication being established.

"Charlie One-Two report in," I said.

"Mulehog, Methane and Patch on ground. Good to hear your voice, Sarge," Mulehog responded.

I sighed in relief, knowing they were together. "What's your sit-rep?"

"Patch is pretty busted up and I'm not going to be doing any dancing anytime soon. We got bogies on top of us. Any chance for an extraction?"

"Roger that. Hunker down. I'll call it in."

Establish comm with transport one-two pilot.

Lieutenant Irawan is not available for communication.

That was interesting. If there was one thing the AIs were good at, it was being precise. Irawan was alive but incommunicado, which could mean anything. She wasn't in armor so she'd have been in a light vac-suit. Good enough for the vacuum of space, but crap for bullets.

Get me a location on Irawan.

A translucent, blue, three-dimensional arrow popped up, superimposed onto the scene in front of me. It flew away from my current location to where I'd seen the transport ship go down, a contrail of blue smoke left in its wake.

LIMITED COLLATERAL DAMAGE

I pulled up the controls in my HUD and sent a SITREP back to the Platoon Commander, complete with the combat data streams from each of our suits. We'd lost six, including my team leaders, Corporal Earnest and Corporal Yeong. I requested immediate danger close fire support for what remained of Bravo Fire Team.

Almost immediately, I received a response from a very unhappy Lieutenant Stick-In-The-Ass (this might not have been his name). Fire support was denied and we were to make our way to an exfiltration zone and were under strict orders to limit collateral damage. I wondered if Lt. Stick-In-The-Ass (SITA) had reviewed the part of the combat stream where I'd installed fresh air ventilation on the hundred fortieth floor of this office building.

I was still looking out at the crashed transport when I heard automatic fire and explosions a kilometer away. Frak!

Show tactical display from Mulehog.

My HUD showed two dozen lightly armed enemy combatants trying to close in on my men. We always traveled with a full load-out, so unless some real armor showed up, it would be a stalemate and some of these locals were going to bleed. I needed to change the geometry of the fight, but I was a hundred forty stories and three city blocks away.

Establish squad comm, "Take defensive positions, immediate fire support denied, I'm en route."

"Copy that," Mulehog responded.

If we were lucky, I figured we had less than twenty minutes before the Skampers, the bastards we were tussling with over this god-forsaken city, rolled out some armor. At that point, things were gonna get real ugly. A couple dozen squishies (non-armored combatants) were something we could deal with. A squad of armored Skamper grunts would open us up like so many cans of tuna.

One thing at a time. Right now, I needed to get over there without attracting any new attention. I ran over to the elevator bank and saw what I was hoping for. The building's elevators were an anti-grav design which meant there were no cables. I looked into the shaft which was painted bright white with large black numerals. The closest set read one-thirty-six.

I pulled the grenade tube off my leg armor and snapped it in place beneath my slug-thrower's stock. The reassuring clunk of my suit's auto feed assured me an explosive round had just been advanced into the tube. I stood back as far as I could, but I wasn't messing around. I needed to get going right now.

A grenade flies slowly enough that if you're expecting it, your eye can trace its path. The transparent doors to this elevator were made of a steel lattice that was not only strong, but stayed almost perfectly clear at all times. It was expensive material, someone obviously had money to burn. Well, if it was burn they had in mind, I'd be happy to oblige. My helmet blanked on impact and I instinctively raised my left arm to shield my face. It was a stupid move, but mostly involuntary.

Debris from the doors and surrounding walls pelted me, ricocheting off every surface. I'd chosen a smaller load than Methane had when he'd blown out the armored wall of the transport and I was confident my suit could handle it.

I lumbered forward and jumped into the shaft, hoping the anti-grav car wasn't directly below me as it would slow me down. My AI had already predicted my maneuver and adjusted my attitude in the shaft as I fell by firing off small arc jets burst from my boots and other strategic locations on my suit. I'd come to trust the AI's competency, so I didn't even think about it. Everyone had their job to do and keeping me from being a pancake was definitely not my problem.

I saw the elevator car beneath me, somewhere around the fiftieth floor. That was pretty good luck since I had time to fire off two more grenades. By the time I got down there, the car would be long gone. This was definitely the fastest way down without attracting attention. I wasn't sure how I was doing on the collateral damage front, but frak him, I'd count it as a personal achievement if I lived long enough to get chewed out by that pencil pushing, chicken-neck Lieutenant.

When you're falling at forty meters per second, even with AI assist, shooting an exit hole in an elevator shaft at a precise location is something of an art. Turns out, I'm not actually much of an artist, so I wasn't overly surprised when the AI informed me that I'd exited on the third floor instead of ground level. The mind of a Marine is a flexible thing and we don't get overly hung up on details. So much for an easy exit.

Show me the nearest hallway terminating northeast side. My AI had already downloaded the building's floor plan and instantly popped up a map, highlighting a path. I fired a minimally charged grenade into a door, charged through the rubble and ran down the hall. One final grenade into the wall at the end of the hallway and I had open air. *Hold on men, I'm on my way.*

The unenhanced human in incredible physical shape can run at a top speed of ten meters per second for a hundred meters, at which point their body is done. A Marine in full combat armor can sustain twenty meters per second over rugged terrain for hours if it's called for. Unfortunately, I was close to top speed when I burst through the hole and angled toward the ground. I immediately regretted not paying greater attention to the exterior details of the map. The tall steel fence seemingly came from nowhere and captured me pretty neatly. I tumbled with it wrapped around me and I would have been in trouble had there been any baddies watching. As it turned out, I just looked like a jackass for the instant replay.

I disentangled myself, ripping the fence away from my body. *Display combat HUD.* My position showed up as a blue dot, as did Methane's, Mulehog's and Patch's. I was glad they were still up. The main concentration of enemy forces were located on the second floor of a building between our two positions. I charged down the desolate street, a plan forming in my mind.

Between the four of us, we had a terrifying load-out. The armored suit actually manufactured rounds on-the-fly for both the slug thrower and grenade, allowing an armored Marine a nearly infinite variety of detonation choices.

"Snap on your bang-sticks men, and dial it up to a hundred. I'll give you the spread in ten beats," I said over the squad comm. I could see their ammo loads and we could afford two salvos at a hundred percent. It'd be enough. I quickly marked off tactical locations on the building where the Skampers were holed up. The plan was simple. If we couldn't hit them, we'd blow the frakking building.

A positive chime sounded for each team member and their icons pulsed green, indicating they'd successfully changed their load-outs and received the coordinates for their targets. *Fortunas audentas juvat,* or luck favors the bold. Words to live by in combat, especially if the baddies are about to roll up on you with armor.

"Methane, count it off and then fire," I directed. "I'll provide a distraction."

Even with all the sophisticated views of the combat space that I had, I still preferred to let whoever was sitting in the shithole make the decision on when to pull the trigger.

I fired three - one hundred percent rounds into the backside of the thirty-story building. I'd targeted three exterior supports. I didn't have any reason to expect that I'd bring the building down, but I'd get a good portion of the fascia to slide off on my side. If that wasn't enough to distract the squishies, I didn't know what would.

"Three... Two... One..." Methane's voice came over squad communication.

Did I mention that a Marine in full armor is a terrifying beast? I should have.

LEAVE NO ONE BEHIND

Some say that demolition is a science. Most of my squad would find this statement laughable. More accurately: precision demolition is a science. To that statement, we'd all nod our heads sagely and agree. I wish I'd had time to stand around and watch the fireworks, but the best time to go Charlie Mike (continue mission/get moving) is when big shiny objects are blowing up.

"Go! Go! Go!" Methane's voice cut in over the squad communication channel. I'd provided a rendezvous location and was currently sprinting toward it. My route would take me next to the building into which we'd just fired a crap-ton of explosives. I was carefully watching for surviving squishies who might gain line of sight on us. Turns out, I didn't have anything to be concerned about. Whoever was inside seemed to be busy dealing with the disintegration of the building. With a few horrific groans and screeches, the detritus-spewing structure slid over a few yards and sank into itself. I later learned that we'd overdone the explosives by a factor of two or three. Meh! Why have 'em if you can't use 'em, was always my theory on that sort of thing.

Mulehog and Methane had gotten out of the courtyard where they'd previously been pinned down, dragging Patch with them. I was pleased by the lack of return fire, but we were in a hot-zone and needed to make sure we cleared the area quickly. At some point, the battlefield lines had changed. Up to this point the city had been a neutral zone but that had obviously changed recently. I suspected this was news to Cent-Comm (Central Command), otherwise we wouldn't have been given the go-ahead to fly over. None of that crap meant anything at this point. Three of my men were alive and I had a ten-minute-old location on our missing pilot, Lieutenant Irawan. Everything else was noise.

Command, give me an update on Lieutenant Irawan.

"Sergeant, you are ordered to make your way directly to the extraction zone. Lieutenant Irawan is down, and we can't afford any more collateral damage." The Lieutenant's reedy voice grated on my last nerve. Man, I disliked this guy. I actually hadn't met my new Lieutenant yet, as we'd just been reassigned. I couldn't believe he'd just compared damage to a building and a Marine's life, as if they had the same priority.

"I have no confirmation on Irawan's status. Frak! She's in a flight suit, her comm gear could just be busted. We need eyes on her."

"You have your orders, Sergeant."

"Bullshit!"

"Sarge, I think Patch is going into shock." Methane's voice cut in on my conversation.

The pavement in front of us exploded, throwing us to the side. I adjusted easily since I wasn't carrying anyone, but Methane and Mulehog couldn't, with Patch between them. Frak! How many things could I deal with at a single time? Time to simplify.

Combat HUD. My AI immediately switched my comm to squad-only and pulled up an overlay view of the immediate area. We'd run into a nest of bogies. My HUD projected a contrail of the rocket's path from a nearby building.

"Return fire!" I jammed my foot into the pavement and used the momentum to spin me around. I brought the A3 up to my shoulder in one fluid movement and switched to full auto. There is no better way to limit the effectiveness of someone who is firing at you than to send a bunch of rounds back their way.

"Frak! Outta frags," Methane complained as he faced the target. It wasn't completely necessary as I could see his ammo level, but I was busy and he wanted to give me a warning.

If you've ever heard the sound of a SAW machine gun firing, you won't forget it. Mulehog's load-out was different than ours in that he carried the much heavier X203, and the requisite additional ordinance load. Like a sewing machine from hell, he opened up on the side of the building which I'd marked as our primary. I had to mute his audio feed. The man really didn't have the ability to limit his verbal stream of expletives and manic cackling. God help the dumbass who'd fired on us.

With Methane and Mulehog up, I worked on the situation. We were five kilometers from the extraction zone and could cover that distance in twenty minutes since I'd be carrying Patch. I needed Methane and Mulehog available to return fire. We'd been lucky only one grenade had been fired and that it hadn't hit any closer.

I found Patch lying face down on the pavement, so I stowed my A3 and picked him up. The armor suit was actually designed so we could mount a soldier on our back. It's quite a load, but for twenty minutes I could endure it. Lieutenant Irawan would have to wait. I had to focus on what I knew: Patch was going down if he didn't get help.

I looked through Methane's visor at the now-ruined building. There were no signs of the bogies who'd ambushed us. "Cease fire." I only had to say it twice as Mulehog's blood lust had fortunately abated. "On my six, we're Charlie Mike." With a younger group I might have worried someone in the squad could miss the command, but not these two guys. Either one could have run the squad just as well as or better than I. Hell, they'd already anticipated our next move.

Now, I might have overstated the ease with which you can run carrying another Marine on your back. It's one of those things we train for, hoping it'll never come up. My lungs were ready to explode by the time we were ten minutes out. We'd seen a few signs of squishies, but apparently these were new-and-improved squishies who were able to recognize an armor signature. They didn't challenge us.

It's hard to describe the joy that fills a soldier's heart when they first catch sight of a transport in hostile territory. When we reached the open doors, Mulehog and Methane pulled the unconscious Patch off my back. It was an incredible relief. We quickly boarded the ship, dragging Patch through the door as the transport lifted off.

The transport was a small drop ship with armor rails inside.

We pushed Patch up into position on the rail and locked him in. The ship's AI immediately started diagnostic and supportive care.

"Snap in, men," I ordered.

"What about the pilot?" Methane asked.

"Cent-Comm says she's down," I answered. I had to be careful. Methane could sniff out a lie at a hundred meters. I helped push him up on the rail as he was a little shorter than Mulehog, who only had to raise up on his toes to get snapped in.

"You aren't buying that shit, are you?" Methane asked.

I pulled up the jump-master on my HUD and activated the lock, ensuring my men couldn't self-release without my command or through pilot override.

"Nope." I moved over to Patch and removed his ordinance load-out and snapped it on top of my own, transferring the contents. It brought me back to about half a load. It would have to do, as I didn't want anyone getting wise to my plan. The transport was already lifting off, but the doors were still open.

"Sergeant, you're going to need to get strapped in there," the corporal who was manning the door gun instructed.

"Frak you, Pete!" Methane knew what was coming.

I walked up next to the perplexed gunner and looked down. It was only two hundred meters. "Sorry corporal, nothing you could have done about it. We don't leave people behind." I jumped from the transport and plummeted toward the ground.

The way I figured it, I'd followed orders and gotten my wounded to the extraction zone. The remains of my squad were safe, Patch would no-doubt get fixed up. I couldn't give a rat's ass what my CO thought about weighing damage to the city vs. the unknown status of Irawan. I wouldn't be able to live with it if I found out she'd been alive and I'd bugged out.

The great thing about the transport ship taking off, was that anyone tracking us would think we were gone. I'd directed my suit to make the jump with a minimal signature. I'd land hard, but well within the range of my skeleton's capacity to survive without broken bones. I still dreaded contact with the ground, as I well knew what that was going to feel like.

Give me a direct route to Irawan's last known location.

I took off at an easy jog, choosing stealth over speed. I'd move at about half speed but with about a tenth of the noise signature. It was refreshing to not have Patch on my back and my legs settled into the comfortable rhythm.

The transport had gone down in an industrial part of the city, just a couple of kilometers out of the downtown district. I bounded up on top of a low, one-story building and crept up to the edge of the roof, surprised to see no Skampers near the downed craft.

The transport was completely wrecked and lay crumpled next to a building half a click from my position. The cockpit was completely intact and my heart rate quickened. It was very possible that the Lieutenant had survived the crash. I couldn't imagine what it must have taken to get the ruined vehicle onto the ground.

I was suspicious about the lack of Skamper activity, but there was nothing that I could do about it. Irawan's last location perfectly lined up with that cockpit. I had to get a look at it. If it was a trap, I'd be given a clear path to the transport and they'd spring the trap when I was inside. If it wasn't a trap then I needed to get in and out as quickly as possible. I couldn't see any scenario where trying to sneak into the area made any sense. Then again, I'm an armored Marine and the idea of stealth is a little fuzzy to me.

I jumped from the roof down to ground level and spun the intensity of my sensors up to full power. The transport was rolled onto its side. The bottom was extremely well armored and I wasn't going to get through it, so I jumped up onto the closed cockpit door and snapped off an articulated pry bar that is built into my calf armor. It would give me a meter of nearly impervious nano-crystalized steel that I could use to work the door open. One end had a wide flat surface, the other a point. I jammed the point into the locking mechanism and pulled with all the strength the suit provided.

The door peeled back like the skin of a banana and I jumped

down into the narrow hallway behind the chairs. The transport's cockpit had room for two pilots, although HQ could rarely afford to send two anymore.

Both chairs were empty and I saw what I hadn't seen from the outside. The lower, armored-glass panel, had been popped outward and lay on the ground. She was alive. I knew it.

CAPTURE

Proximity warnings blared in my ears. Frak.

My HUD showed several dozen red blips surrounding the transport ship. *Trap it is,* I thought.

Incoming communication from enemy command. My AI would normally have screened the message, but it had changed protocol based on my predicament.

"Release your armor and step free of the craft. Will you comply?" a heavily accented woman's voice insisted. It was a standard requirement when capturing an armored Marine. I'd captured a few Marines in my time and understood the desire to limit additional casualties. I had to make a decision. Go out in a blaze of glory or get captured. I'm sure Lieutenant SITA would prefer the former, but I was only twenty-five years old and had no desire to punch that final ticket.

"I'll comply," I replied. SOP (Standard Operating Procedure) was to brick the ship and then the suit. I didn't think that was necessary with the transport ship, it had flown its last mission. My armor, however, was another thing. It wouldn't do to have some Skamper killing men with my suit. I set the self-destruct, which would fry all of the components and effectively turn it into a brick.

I directed the armor suit to release and wriggled up and out of it. I was wearing a suit-liner in bad need of a cleaning and it wasn't completely lost on me how bad I smelled. Without HUD, AI or communications, I pulled myself up and out of the side of the transport ship. I stood figuratively naked in front of an enemy host.

"You guys sure know how to throw a party," I said with humor I didn't feel.

"Secure the prisoner," the squishy Lieutenant directed. She was wearing the gray and maroon officer's uniform of the Skampers. I suppose it wasn't fair for me to think of her as squishy anymore. I was just as squishy, something they were about to prove to me.

I didn't take it personally when the soldiers fell on me more heavily than was required. My team had taken quite a toll on their forces tonight. I felt grateful that at some point one of them was magnanimous enough to knock me unconscious. After that they had a simple decision to make: kill me or keep me alive. It wasn't that I didn't care, it was just beyond my ability to control and the adrenaline of combat had long since faded.

When I woke up in a cell with a handful of med-patches covering my body, I took it as a good sign. I estimated I'd been down for no more than an hour. My body was plenty sore and the patches hadn't had much time to do their work. An inventory of my limbs revealed no broken bones, save for a few cracked ribs. My head hurt like the dickens, which wasn't surprising after having been knocked unconscious. All in all, I'd made the transition from enemy combatant to prisoner quite successfully.

My cot was in a temporary cell which led me to believe they hadn't been expecting visitors. I was probably in a temporary command center, which meant someone wanted to talk to me. As if I knew anything. Surprisingly, I was only bound by my wrists.

When the door opened, the same squishy Lieutenant who'd captured me walked through the door. It was a bold move since I could have easily jumped her. It was probably some elaborate ruse to put me off balance. I grunted a laugh. It was working.

"Sergeant Hoffen, you've had an interesting evening, I'm Lieutenant Peralta," the woman was older than me, but not by much. Her black hair was cut short, like most female officers I knew, and her skin tone was the light brown of most of the Skampers.

"Yeah. It's been lovely," I said.

"The damage you and your team did to the city of Manaus is considerable. What was your mission?"

"Just trying to get home, ma'am," I replied.

"You knocked down a thirty story building and took out a company of the army of Soledad de Charus. Explain to me how you were trying to get home? What was your mission, soldier?"

"Seriously? You Skampers knock down a transport ship full of armored Marines and then complain about damage to your city? We had no mission. We were headed back to the FOB to pick up some maggots and take a couple of days of R&R, hopefully not in that order."

She stepped up and slapped me with an open hand. "You'll keep a civil tongue while addressing an officer," she reprimanded. I'd forgotten that Skamper was a derogatory term that loosely implied these guys were still tribesmen from the jungle.

"Yeah. My bad," I replied.

"What was on the ship that you wanted to recover?"

It was a common interrogation technique. She'd ask me a bunch of different questions and cover a lot of bases. I could expect to hear these questions a few hundred times over the next several hours, most likely with little to no sleep. She'd keep moving the questions around, chipping away at me until I gave up something useful. The fact was, I didn't know anything useful. War hadn't changed a lot over the last dozen centuries. We poked each other with pointy sticks until someone went home.

The city of Manaus was at the center of a long running war over mineral resources in the Amazonian basin. My team and I were ultimately just the pointy end of the stick. Someone else had all of the brilliant ideas and it's not like any of that brilliance ever trickled down to me. My guess was she already knew that - otherwise a more sophisticated interview team would be handling me.

"Nothing on the ship that I could see," I said.

"Where's the pilot?" she asked.

I tried to hide my interest in her question but it took me off guard. She picked up on it. We were both crappy at this game. She'd told me something valuable and I'd turned right around and told her something even more valuable. Now she knew that we hadn't recovered Lieutenant Irawan. I was more than a little pleased that they hadn't either.

The Lieutenant suppressed a smile and stood to leave. No doubt she was going to send out a search team for Irawan. Peralta fired off a series of orders in a language I didn't understand. It sounded like Spanish, but in this region it could be any number of different dialects. My AI would have translated, but I wasn't wearing any intelligent clothing. Just before the door closed, I caught a glance of the connecting room. It wasn't a normal military base. I was being held in an office building.

AVENGING ANGEL

My head was screaming, so I lay back down on the cot. I was looking forward to letting the med-patches do their work. Frak, what I wouldn't give for a glass of whiskey. The Skampers had left the lights on, I supposed to keep me awake. If they thought that'd prevent me from sleeping, they were nuts. Find me a grunt who can't sleep in the middle of a crowded room of monkeys singing the *Hallelujah Chorus* and I'll show you a grunt who hasn't seen combat.

I wasn't sure how long I'd been down, but I estimated no more than two hours. When you sleep in a room, you get a sense of the rhythm of sounds around you - from the ventilation system to the opening and closing of doors. I didn't sleep with one eye open, so much as with one ear open, so when I heard the change I knew it was time to get up and pay attention.

Something was out of place, but I couldn't immediately identify what that something was. My eyes stayed closed and I placed my hand against the wall. For ninety seconds nothing happened and I was about to dismiss my feeling as just nerves. Then I heard a low rumble and the wall shuddered beneath my hand. If you weren't paying attention you would likely have missed it. In my cell, I had nothing else going on, so it got my full attention.

It made no sense. If Command wasn't willing to send in a team to rescue Lieutenant Irawan they certainly wouldn't send anyone after me. But no one uses explosive charges on a building they control. No, the Skampers had an uninvited party guest and I was all about turning up the music. What's the worst that could happen?

"Hey! I need to talk to the Lieutenant! Open the door!" I

banged on the door with my fists, as if it was a drum, and repeated myself as loudly as I could. I kept it up for almost a minute and wondered if my voice would go hoarse, when finally the door was thrust open.

Three squishies piled into the room with their rifles. First through the door was a big boy with a bigger attitude. He brought the butt of his gun up in an attempt to catch me in the gut. I'd been in enough scrapes to see it coming and stepped into it. I spun around and brought the back of my elbow into his head. The dumbass should have been wearing a helmet, should have used a stun weapon - lots of should haves – but all of them were moot. I felt him crumple. These guys definitely weren't pros. They obviously thought three against one would be enough to shut me up.

My timing was pretty good. A loud explosion blew into the adjacent room, sending debris billowing into my cell. It was a perfect distraction for my remaining two guards. I was expecting it and they weren't. Involuntarily, they jerked their heads around to discover the source of the explosion.

Lethal combat is the name of a class we take in Basic. There are twenty-two ways to kill a person with your bare hands. Personally, I like to keep things pretty basic as I'm a big guy, which is why they call me Big Pete. And if I could avoid killing someone, I was okay with that. My wrists were bound, so I just brought them around, smashing 'em into the nearest nose I could find. Lights out, Betty Joe. Two down and one to go.

Unfortunately, I was more of a brawler than anything else and the third guard figured out what was going on in plenty of time to drop me like a sack of potatoes with the butt of his rifle. It wasn't enough to completely knock me out, but I was stunned and fell to the ground. I heard the tink, tink, tink of something small and metallic bouncing on the floor and then recognized the marble-sized objects that skittered in front of me. It was all I could do to put one hand on an ear and roll into the guard who'd dropped me. I had to get clear of the doorway. A second later a loud explosion and a bright flash confirmed the flash-bangs I'd seen.

You can close your eyes and cover your ears all you want, but when flash-bangs go off, you know it. The design is simple and has been around forever. A really loud noise and really bright lights do a fantastic job of stunning a person's ability to react. The fact that marbles were being used let me know that I wasn't being rescued by an armored squad. We didn't have any use for marbles. Small discs imbedded in our armor could generate both the lights and the noise.

Stunned as I was by the rifle butt and the near miss with the flash-bangs, I knew the last standing guard was having a much worse time. I pulled up to my knees and saw him stagger away from the door. He had his rifle half raised and was firing into the wall, slowly turning toward the open door. A lucky bullet will kill you just as dead as a well-aimed bullet and whoever had breached the room didn't need the crossfire. I figured the guard and I were operating at about the same level and I've always thought fifty-fifty were acceptable odds.

I staggered to my feet and lumbered into him, while at the same time, tripping on the two bodies cluttering the floor. I was going down either way, as I was still too stunned to keep myself upright. The bodies just made it a lot less elegant. The guard didn't see me coming and I threw my bound arms over his head and drug him down with me. I almost felt guilty, as the guy just wasn't that big and I had thirty kilograms on him. I choked him, all the time hoping he'd make it. It had long ago stopped being personal for me. I had a job to do, and I'd do it, but I'd sure had enough of the killing.

A quick motion caught my eye and I squinted up through the haze and saw a Skamper guard take a thin black combat boot straight to the solar plexus. He stumbled and waved a blaster pistol back toward his attacker. Shock barely described my emotions when the transport pilot, Lieutenant Irawan, stepped into view and fired two blaster rounds into the man's chest. She turned, looked straight at me and took aim.

"No..."

She fired and the shot whizzed over my head. I swiveled

around to see the big guard, who I'd dropped first, fall back.

"Shit..."

It's impossible to look cool when you're lying on top of another person, with your wrists bound and wrapped around their head. Moreover, removing yourself from that position makes you look quite a bit more ridiculous. I wasn't sure why, all of a sudden, I cared about that...

Check that. Of course I did.

ESCAPE

"How'd you get here?" I asked, crawling over the bodies in the doorway. Again, there's just no graceful way to do this with your hands bound.

"A simple thank you would suffice," she replied and crouched down next to me. She was holding a pistol in one hand and flicked open a nano-blade with the other. I pushed my wrists towards her and she cut the simple but effective band-style restraints.

"Right, thanks. Did you come alone?" I picked up weapons and discarded them for the junk they were. The Skampers were fighting a war and they were radically underfunded.

"Yes. We need to get out of here," she said peeking nervously around corners.

"Give me a second." I found a decent, medium-sized hand blaster with a quarter charge. It would be a bitch to aim without an AI interface but it'd have to do. "Where'd you get the flash-bangs and breaching charges?"

"They were in my go-kit. We need to move, Sergeant." Her voice took on an air of command.

I smiled grimly to myself. *That didn't take long,* I thought. "Yes, Ma'am. Right behind you."

"Don't get pissy. You know as well as I do we can't hang out here."

"Agreed, but if I don't get something on my feet, it'll slow us down. What floor are we on?"

"Second," she answered, "and I've only got one breaching charge left and no flash-bangs."

"Perfect." I looked over the four fallen Skampers in the room and chose the big guy I'd originally dropped. I was pulling his boots off when we heard the sounds of people running. "Is that door unlocked?" I indicated the one in the opposite direction of the noises. While she was checking, I dragged a Skamper soldier forward, setting him up so that he looked like he was peeking around the wall with a rifle, guarding the hallway.

Irawan ran to the door and was unable to open it. "Want me to blow it?" she asked.

"Nope. Help me with this guy," I said. We pulled the big guard over to the door. Since this guy had been first in the room, I was hoping his palm print would open all the doors on this level.

Semi-automatic blaster fire lanced the room, just over the head of our dummy guard. Fortunately, we weren't directly in line with the hallway anymore, but it wouldn't be long before we had company.

I heard the lock click and Irawan slipped through the opening. I quickly followed, pulling the guard through behind us, shutting the door and using the guard's hand to lock it.

"One sec," I said. She was already half-way down the hallway. The guard had been through a lot. He was still breathing, but not too lively after taking blaster rounds to the chest. Hopefully, he wouldn't come around and let anyone through the door for a while. So far, we'd escaped cleanly. I caught up with Irawan and we ran to a corner and peered around. My ruse wouldn't last long. They'd figure out the guy in the doorway wasn't returning fire and that we'd found another way out. A few minutes could be a lifetime for us, though.

"Here," I whispered harshly and jumped into an abandoned office. I closed the door behind us and looked out the window. It was raining which wasn't unusual since the city was surrounded by a tropical rainforest. We needed a way down. My eye caught the branches of a tree brushing against the window and it gave me an idea.

"Put your charge on the window. Time to get out of here," I said.

Once again, Irawan got right to the action and did as I asked. I hunkered down behind the old desk and pulled my borrowed boots on and laced them up. She waited for me to tie them off and then blew the window.

"We jump into the tree and climb down," I said. "We're only on the second level, so you'll survive if you miss."

I was floored. She didn't even hesitate, but walked up to the opening, hopped up on the ledge and jumped into the tree. I suspected she'd had martial arts training because she made it easily and started climbing down. My jump wasn't as elegant, but I made it and met her on the ground.

"There's a curfew and they'll no doubt have drones patrolling once the rain lets up." I almost had to shout to be heard above the din.

I turned for no reason I could imagine and barely missed being hit by a blaster bolt. "Go!" I yelled and we both took off down the street at a sprint. It was complete luck that I hadn't been hit and it wouldn't happen twice. The rain obscured our flight, but any decent AI could pick us off.

"Trust me!" I demanded. She had no good reason to trust me, but I could feel the pursuit dialing us in. I didn't give her much of a chance to decide and wrapped my arm around her shoulder and dove for the storm sewer, pulling her down with me.

So the good news is that the civil engineers of Manaus know how to build storm sewers. With more than twenty three hundred millimeters of rain each year, their very survival depended on the quality of their sewers. Turns out, so did ours. I also knew that we were in one of the driest months of the year, which just might save us from drowning.

We slid down a slimy ramp and then fell into the rushing water of the storm. My feet hit the bottom and I estimated we had fallen into about a meter and half of water. We accelerated quickly as the stream caught us and carried us along. The force of the water made standing up impossible and Irawan surfaced two meters ahead of me, sputtering. I hoped she was a decent swimmer.

For a few minutes there wasn't much we could do other than fight with the water and try to gain equilibrium. Most of my life as a Marine had been spent in combat in and around large urban cities. I'd spent my fair share of time in sewers. I was grateful this was a storm sewer and not made for transporting sewage.

I maneuvered myself up next to Irawan. The roar of the water was significant but the enclosed tube echoed. "This should flatten out and slow down when it joins with a larger branch," I explained.

"A little warning would have been nice." She didn't sound overly upset and I couldn't blame her for the sentiment.

"Yeah, sorry. It happened pretty fast."

Any response she might have had was cut off by the sound of approaching falls.

"Frak. This could get interesting." I grabbed her hand.

For the second time that night we were in free fall in the dark. If I'd paid attention in physics class, I'd have had some idea how far we'd fallen by counting off the seconds. But it's hard to count under those circumstances and I didn't know the calculation anyway. We landed in a pool of water in a larger room, by the sound of it.

"Was that part of your plan?" she asked, annoyed and coughing water.

"No. We need to find the ladder. There'll be at least one of them bolted to the wall. Swim away from the current. We don't want to get further into the system."

"You don't say," she said without humor.

I swam away and found the edge of the basin. The concrete side was straight up and down and it was difficult swimming alongside it, but the current wasn't quite as intense any longer.

"Over here," she said. I was fatiguing and glad she'd found the ladder. The boots that I'd so desperately wanted were weighing me down. I found her holding onto the edge of a ladder that I knew would run the entire vertical length of the room. I locked my feet into it below hers and grabbed the edge. The water wasn't overly cold, especially given our recent exertion, but the warmth of her body wasn't lost on me. I don't care how tough of a soldier you are, having company in a stressful situation can make all the difference.

"Well, that went pretty well," I said.

"Where do you think this ladder goes?" she asked, ignoring my glib assessment.

"Probably street level, I'll go up and get an idea of where we are. You okay here?" I asked.

I felt her body relax before she said, "Yes."

We shifted so that I could climb up. Forty-two rungs later I reached a small alcove I suspected was directly beneath ground level. It would be a good place for us to dry off as long as no maintenance workers showed up. I sat for a moment and regained the strength in my arms and then climbed back down.

"There's a dry location at the top, you good for a climb?" I asked.

She didn't answer but started climbing. I followed. The alcove was a little tight for two of us, but it sure beat sitting in the water.

"I lost my go-kit and pistol," she said. There was no complaint in her voice, but I recognized frustration when I heard it.

"Yeah, my blaster's gone too," I said. We were facing each other although there wasn't enough light to see. It wasn't the most comfortable position, but for now it would do just fine while we recovered.

"You really know how to show a girl a good time," she said.

"Why'd you come back?" I ignored her good natured flirting. The question had been burning a hole in my mind since I'd seen her breach the room, commando style.

"You first. Why did you come back?" she responded in a softer voice.

"It's what we do. We don't leave anyone behind. There are only a few things a Marine can hold on to in a scrape, one of those things has to be that someone's coming for him," I answered.

"You were ordered to evac, but you came anyway."

"How do you know that?"

"I heard Lieutenant Bentrod give the order. My comm was busted, but I could hear the squad command channel. So why'd you come back? You know they could court martial you for that?" she asked.

"The way I figured it, I had evac'd my squad, just like I'd been ordered. The thing is, I knew you were alive because the AIs have nearly a hundred percent accuracy on reporting casualties. I really didn't have a choice. I had a Marine down behind enemy lines and there was something I could do about it. So what went through your head?"

"Honestly, I didn't have a plan. I saw them set the trap on the transport and I was hunkered down in a building. I wanted to warn you, but couldn't without giving away my position," she explained. "Once you surrendered, I followed you. You pretty much know the rest."

"Thanks," I said simply.

"Silver," she said. I couldn't for my life figure out what she was saying.

"I don't follow."

"My name is Silver Irawan. Thought you should know."

"Pete Hoffen, most people call me Big Pete."

"So, Pete, buy me a drink after we get out of this?"

Straight and to the point. I knew it was probably the adrenaline talking, especially considering the problems she could get into as a Lieutenant having drinks with a Sergeant. Nothing like being knee deep in crap to bring people together though. I didn't know where this friendship was heading, but if I wasn't motivated to come up with an escape plan before, I certainly was now.

COMING HOME

We dozed for a couple of hours, listening to the rain fall on the disc that separated us from the top side. It would be best to move while it was raining, but I had no idea where we were, so that was a real problem.

"I'm going to see if I can get a peek at our surroundings," I said.

"Careful," she said. I couldn't agree more.

I pushed the heavy disc up and peered into the street. I didn't get a great view, but I could tell we were in some sort of slum. There were a few slums in the large city and my best guess was we had ended up east of downtown. That area was closer to the headwaters of the great Amazon River and it made sense that the rainwater would drain in that direction.

Our FOB (Forward Operations Base) was on the southeastern side of the city, so this was probably as good a place as any to end up. We'd need water, food and transportation if we were going to get out of here. I'd take the latter over the first two if we could find it fast. I explained the situation to Irawan after replacing the disc.

"No doubt the drones will be covering the slums," she said. "It'd be the first place I'd look."

"It's still raining, probably going to be our best chance," I said.

"Did you see any transportation?" she asked.

"Nothing obvious, but with the curfew, I don't think we want to be moving at night."

"So, what? Break into a house and hunker down?"

"That's what I was thinking," I said.

"Great. Okay. Lead on."

I pushed the big disc away from the opening and the rain

started pelting us again. On this street, there were stores on the lower levels and apartments on the upper levels. The stores all had retractable grills and looked to be pretty much burglar proof. I jumped up into the street and saw an alcove that looked like it could provide us some shelter. I pointed and Irawan ran for it while I slid the cover back in place.

"Anything look promising?" I asked when I joined her.

"I think we can climb up on that roof over there." She pointed to a low-hanging eve. There were lights on in the apartment. "Someone's awake though."

"Ready?" I asked.

"Sure," she said.

I ran across the street, jumped and grabbed the overhang. I pulled myself up, lay on the edge and dropped an arm down for Irawan. She ignored me and kicked off of the adjacent building, allowing her to get both hands on the roof and easily climb up to join me. At this point, I wasn't sure who was rescuing whom, and I sure appreciated having her at my side.

I crawled up the roof to the dormer window where we'd seen the light. Music filtered out from under the open window. Someone was making this easy on us. I twisted around so that I was on my knees but still below the sight line of the window. I popped up, raised the window and slid into the room.

A young woman standing at the opposite end of the room turned and screamed as she saw me enter. She couldn't have been more than seventeen years old. There was nothing to be done about it, I couldn't have her screaming, so I ran toward her. She tried to run, but panic had frozen her in place. I clamped my hand around her mouth.

Irawan slid in through the window and closed it behind her. She slid her hand down the side of the window to activate the privacy shield.

The girl struggled against me, but she couldn't have been more than forty-five kilograms. I felt like such a heel.

"Clear the apartment," I whispered hoarsely to Irawan. The girl tried savagely to break free.

Irawan looked at me and the girl and nodded. There was only one other room.

"Frak," I heard her say. I dragged the girl with me to the doorway. A small boy, no more than three years old, sat on the edge of the bed, looking at us with wide eyes.

"Can you understand me?" I asked the struggling girl. "Stop struggling. If you promise not to scream, I can let go. We don't want to hurt you or your family."

She stopped pushing against me. "Will you promise not to scream if I take my hand off of your mouth?" I asked.

She nodded affirmatively. I kept hold of her arm, but let go of her mouth. She spoke to us in her native language, but I had no idea what she was saying.

"We don't have our AI and can't understand you," I said.

She nodded and pointed to a drawer, saying something else I didn't understand.

"I think there's a pad or earwig in there," I said to Irawan. The girl nodded her head, indicating I was right. She also talked to the little boy, who seemed on the verge of crying.

Lieutenant Irawan opened the drawer and pulled out a reading pad. She was still wearing her jump suit and I knew it would take over the functions of the small device.

"If I let you go, will you keep calm? We don't want to hurt anyone. We're actually in trouble and running from the officials." I wanted to be ambiguous about which officials we were running from.

She replied and the pad started translating for us. "Yes, please don't hurt us. We won't say anything."

I wasn't dumb enough to believe she wouldn't turn us in, but I also believed she'd behave for the time being. I let her go. "Just don't make any sudden movements and we should be okay," I said.

"What do you want," she asked.

"We're on the run and need to get out of sight. We'll be out of your way as soon as we figure out how to get some transportation."

"My brother has a vehicle. He could take you," she said.

"He'd get in trouble for helping us," Irawan said. "Don't be so quick to involve your family. What if we stole his vehicle? I have money." She unzipped her jumper, reached in and produced a card and handed it to the girl with the reading pad.

The girl waived it over the pad, gasped and asked, "This much?"

"Twice that," Irawan said and took back the card. "If you get us to safety, I'll give you two of those."

"Let me call my brother," she said.

"Not until morning, after the curfew, when we can actually leave. Would you make us something to eat?"

Morning took forever to arrive. We'd had only two hours of sleep in the last thirty-six, but we had to wait for daylight.

"I'll leave one chip with you," Irawan explained. "This way your brother will know we are on the up and up. If he gets us to within two kilometers of our base, I'll hand him the other chip. If he turns us in, I'll be sure to mention how helpful you've been."

The girl blanched at Irawan's naked threat. "I'll call him," she said hesitantly.

Half an hour later, a small blue hauler pulled up in front of the shop beneath the apartment with its door open. We'd wrapped scarves around our heads to avoid identification, although the drones wouldn't need much. Once in the hauler, we pulled a heavy, smelly blanket around us and hunkered down.

"Thirty minutes," he said. "It'll be safer if I take back streets."

He drove like a madman, careening through the streets with his low flying anti-grav hauler. The principle of the vehicle was simple; it floated a meter above the streets and was powered by small arc-jets to push it in one direction or another. It was an extremely inexpensive vehicle, not to mention a little slippery to navigate.

"We're as close as we can get," he said. "There's a Soledad checkpoint up ahead. I can go no further."

"Two chips to buy your vehicle?" Irawan replied instantly.

"Let me see them," he said. She handed them over. He didn't

even turn around, just hopped out of the vehicle and walked away.

Irawan handed me the reading pad and said, "Set up a secure channel with Cent-Comm. Tell 'em we're coming in hot." She jumped into the driver's seat and took off at the vehicle's max speed. At this point, I was more concerned about our side shooting us than theirs. I doubted that the checkpoint we were approaching had ever seen action, I was certain our base had seen plenty.

"Well. They know we're coming. It didn't sound like they believed me," I said.

"Get down." She swung the back end of the hauler around. Two men had jumped out of a temporary building which was their guard post. The hauler punched through the temporary shelter and bounced down the street away from the guards. They picked themselves up off the street and pulled their weapons into firing position.

"Hold on," Irawan said as she swung us around again. We'd lost quite a bit of speed running into their shelter and now we were accelerating again. A fusillade of blaster rounds whizzed past us, some hitting the back of the vehicle. We were out of range too quickly for the rounds to cause much damage.

Through the forward window of the hauler I saw the checkpoint leading into our base. We weren't looking at two guards and a temporary shack. It was a fully defended, completely modern base. There would be no shortage of armor and firepower - all feeling itchy about our approach.

Irawan slowed and when we got to five hundred meters she stopped entirely. "Best we do the last bit on foot," she said.

I handed her the pad and she established communication with the base. Someone must have believed her because ten minutes later a heavily armored transport landed in front of us, doors wide open. A full squad of Marines hopped out with guns drawn.

We sank to our knees and interlocked our hands behind our heads. I didn't blame them, we were coming home in a pretty unconventional manner.

PANEL OF INQUIRY

Half an hour later I was cooling my heels in the brig. I hadn't expected to be welcomed back as a hero, but I thought the brig was overkill. If Lieutenant Harold Bentrod wanted to be a pain, he could bring me up on charges. I had, after all, ignored a lawful, if not stupid order.

I had to be honest. Being locked up was the easiest duty I'd ever experienced: three squares a day, air conditioning, a full night's sleep and there was absolutely no chance I would have to jump into the middle of a firefight. For the love of god there was even a mattress on the bed! If Bentrod's goal was to punish me, he really sucked at it.

I also didn't hold a grudge. Bentrod had given me a legal order and I'd absolutely chosen to ignore it. That's one of those things that pisses me off. People break rules and get all whiney when they get called on it. Not me.

On the third day of confinement I got a visit from a young naval lawyer on loan from Mars Protectorate.

"Lavonne Sterra," she said, holding her hand out as she entered the room. I shook her hand, which was stronger than her small spacer build suggested. She was a pleasant looking woman, if not a bit thin. I was confused by her uniform, though. It was definitely not North American.

"You're a fair piece from home," I said.

"It's part of our training. We get a chance to participate in low level court-martials and panels of inquiry," she answered.

"I'm getting court-martialed?" I asked.

"No one has talked to you yet?" The surprise on her face was evident.

"I've heard some gossip, nothing official, though," I said.

She wrote on the tablet she'd brought with her and then said, "I imagine that's right, and no, you're being brought in front of a Panel of Inquiry. One Lieutenant Bentrod has filed two charges that we'll be exploring. The first is that you've been accused of willfully disregarding a lawful order under section 192A.465." She paused and looked at me.

"True enough," There was no reason to argue. It was true.

She continued, "And the negligent destruction of civilian structures under section 192A.545."

"That little shit," Now I was annoyed. That was another thing that pissed me off. Little rule followers who would do anything to prove a point to someone they were jealous of.

"Pardon?"

"Oh, Lieutenant Bentrod's full of himself. That last one's a pile of crap. The first one, not so much. He told me to come home. I had the opportunity and I didn't. He's right," I said plainly.

"There's good news and bad news. The bad news is the city of Manaus wants your head for the mess caused and so the Lieutenant's charges are being heard."

"And the good news?" I asked.

"The Marines aren't likely to bend to political pressure."

"What's the worst case?" I asked.

"Recommendation for a special court-martial," she said.

"When can we get to it?" I asked.

She checked her pad again. "Don't you want to talk about your defense?"

"Will my company commander be there?" Captain Raffe was the real deal. He'd worked his way up through ranks and had the respect of his men, including me.

"Yes. Captain Raffe was selected to be part of the panel."

"Then no, I don't want to talk about my defense. Raffe has seen his share of combat. He'll do the right thing."

"Understood." I'd expected her to be a little pissed off, but she wasn't anything of the sort. "I admire your faith in your commander."

"When?" I asked.

"This afternoon if you're amenable. Personally, I'd like to have more time to prepare and review the combat data streams," she said.

"Let's do it," No sense waiting. Bring the pain.

"Alright, Marine. I'll be back in a couple of hours. Get cleaned up. I'll meet you there."

The room they led me into wasn't all that impressive. There was a table with three comfortable chairs behind it and a small desk in front of that with two less comfortable chairs. Sterra was already seated at the desk when I arrived.

A few minutes later three people entered. Captain Raffe was the only person I recognized. I'd risen to attention, which was simple protocol when an officer enters a room. Once they'd been seated and the proceeding was called to order, Colonel Alma Pertino introduced herself and the other members of the panel, Captain Raffe and Colonel Rostermel.

The charges were read out loud for the panel to hear. I had no doubt that they'd already been through them but we were the Marines and we had formality that had to be observed.

"Before we get started," Pertino said, "Lieutenant Silver Irawan has asked to be allowed to give a statement."

I'd never seen Irawan in anything but a flight suit. When she walked through the door in her dress uniform, I have to admit that I was thinking about anything but the proceedings. She nodded at me, gave me a guarded smile and snapped to attention.

"At ease, Lieutenant. You have a statement?" Colonel Pertino prompted.

Irawan spoke for about ten minutes, mostly outlining the details of our escape. She was light on the details where she'd saved me and emphasized where I'd done a decent job. She didn't step over the line and say anything untrue, but it was uncomfortable to hear her rendition of it.

"May I ask a question?" Captain Raffe asked once she'd finished. It was rhetorical, as he was her superior officer. She recognized it as such and nodded. "In your opinion, would you have made it out of Soledad-controlled Manaus without Sergeant

Hoffen's aid?"

"No, sir."

Captain Pertino dismissed Irawan and waited for her to leave the room. "Sergeant Hoffen, would you like to make a statement to this panel?"

"Yes, ma'am," I said and stood up straight.

"I know there's a lot of formality that goes into proceedings like this. But I also believe that we're in a room full of Marines. I may not be right, but I believe the reason we have a court-martial system is because war brings about unusual events. If you haven't experienced it, you really don't have any damn idea how crazy things can get. I also don't believe you'll hang me on my words and that I can speak Marine to Marine here. Does that sound about right?" It was do or die at this point.

"Please continue," Colonel Pertino prompted. "But continue respectfully, and know your words have meaning here and once said they cannot be unsaid."

"Thank you," I said. "The way I see it, the destruction of property thing is ridiculous. The Skampers…"

"Sergeant!" Colonel Pertino interrupted.

"My apologies, Ma'am." Frak, I'd forgotten 'Skampers' was a bad thing to say. "Well, like I was saying, the enemy blew up both of our transport ships and ended up dropping a platoon of armored Marines into the city. They then occupied a building in order to gain a tactical advantage. Methane, Mulehog and Patch were pinned down. My intent hadn't been to knock down the building. That said, I absolutely wanted to distract them long enough to get my squad out of there. I think the data streams pretty clearly show this."

"I see. Anything else?"

"As to the disregarding of a lawful order, I agree. I did that. Lieutenant Bentrod gave me a perfectly valid order. However, I also knew perfectly well that the odds of Irawan being alive were very high. You see, AIs do a great job of counting the dead and the AI told me that it had lost comm with her, not that she was dead. For me it was simple, we don't leave our people behind. So yeah, that one's on me. You want to know the most embarrassing part of all that?"

Pertino looked at me like a schoolmarm addressing a rowdy student. "Certainly."

"I didn't save her one bit. Lieutenant Irawan had to save me."

"Is that all?" Pertino asked.

I tried to think if there was anything I had missed. Nope. "I think that's about it."

"Sergeant, your term is up. Have you decided what you'll do?" It was an unexpected question from Captain Raffe.

"Honestly, sir. I think I'm done. I love my men and I love the Corps, but I've seen too much."

"I find that disappointing, but I understand. You'll be missed," he replied, looking down at his pad.

There were more questions and more talk, but nothing of real significance and the panel excused themselves after half an hour.

"How do you think we did?" I asked Sterra.

"I might have been a bit more subtle, but your honesty was compelling," she replied.

The panel returned and I stood at attention to hear their judgment.

Colonel Pertino surprised me by starting almost casually, "Sergeant Hoffen, were you serious about leaving the Corps?"

"Yes, ma'am. I believe I've served with dignity and to the best of my ability."

"This panel agrees with that statement and commends you on your honesty. You will be missed as a leader. As to the charges, we are dropping the count of destruction of property. We agree with your assessment. As to the charges of disobeying an order, we find you guilty. The order was lawful, although in the view of this panel, also poorly considered. Your actions, regardless of your view of them, ended up in the safe return of Lieutenant Irawan. The problem is that you are still guilty, which I believe you understand."

"I do ma'am. Might I add that it is not a sacrifice if there is no payment required," I said.

"Well said. It is the judgment of this panel that you should be released from active duty immediately, with an honorable discharge. A disciplinary note will be added to your jacket. If you should desire to re-enter the service this might prove to be a roadblock, but not insurmountable. These proceedings are closed."

RETIREMENT

I shook Sterra's hand and thanked her for her time.

"It was my honor, Sergeant. You're a remarkable man and I wish you all the best."

I was happy to find Lieutenant Irawan waiting in the hallway. She stood as I walked up to her and quite unexpectedly gave me a hug. It was outside of protocol, but I appreciated the gesture. If only we didn't have the whole Lieutenant / Sergeant thing going on. It wasn't until much later that I realized we didn't. I'd missed my opportunity. We released and I stepped back. We both tried to start talking at the same time.

"You go first," I said.

"How'd it go? It's good you're walking free, right?" she asked.

"I think it went like it should. I've been given an honorable discharge," I said.

"They're kicking you out?"

"It's expedient. I'm at the end of my tour and was done either way. I don't want to be a warrior anymore," It was hard to look at those eyes in front of me. For a moment, she seemed sad.

"So what do you want?" she asked.

"Thank you," I said quietly. I wasn't really one for talking about myself. I must have changed gears too quickly because she looked at me in confusion. "You didn't have to make a statement at my court-martial. I know they'd already interviewed you. You made me sound like a hero."

"You *are* a hero, Pete. It's okay for me to call you that now, isn't it?"

"Sure. I'd like that and I'm no more so than you, Silver," I'd never said her first name out loud. It was a beautiful name.

"I wasn't being grilled. So where will you go from here?"

"Back to Iowa," I said.

"Iowa, really?"

"My dad's a tenant farmer, he always needs help. I hated working for him when I was a kid, but after all this, I can't wait to get back there."

"Sounds peaceful," she said.

"It's short term though. I've got my eye on an asteroid."

Silver laughed like I'd just told an inside joke and when I didn't join her, she raised her eyebrows and glanced away, cheeks flushed.

"No, I'm serious." I wanted her to understand. I needed her to understand. "I know it sounds crazy, but it's not that different from what my dad does. You rent out a claim and work it. Nobody to tell you what to do. Unlike farming, though, there's a decent chance you'll hit it big eventually. But even if you don't, there's a good living to be made." I'd never told anyone about my big plan and saying it out loud, on that day of all days, cemented it in my mind.

"Well, good for you. It sounds like you're really going places."

"I still owe you a drink," I said.

"Don't think I won't hold you to that. Good luck, Pete." She gave me a final hug and walked down the hallway. I stood there looking dumbly after her. It seemed like I should have done or said something, but for the life of me I couldn't figure out what that'd be.

...Three years later...

Iowa, in late September, is the most beautiful place a person can be. The air is clean, the weather is getting cooler and it's time to bring in the crops. The hard work is done by machine, but there is no shortage of errands to be done. This particular day I'd taken the grav-hauler over to one of the bigger fields we worked. The combines were bringing in the corn and it was my job to haul the giant green bins back to the co-op.

"Pete, where're you at?" my dad asked over the comm. I'd tried to convince him that he could just ask the AI, but he didn't want anything to do with that.

“I'm down on the old Jennings stead,” I answered.

“Hold up, I'm coming over.” He knew that I couldn't leave while the hauler was being loaded. I figured he was bringing dinner out. It was early, but then he was old. After a few minutes I saw his familiar beat-up, old farm-hand runabout bouncing over the already harvested field. I waved and was surprised to see both doors of the vehicle open.

I couldn't take my eyes off of her. There she was, standing in a cornfield in the middle of Iowa. I'd thought of her often since I'd left the service, but had never worked up the courage to contact her.

“Is this who you been pining for since you came back?” Dad asked after I got within hearing distance. He was never one to play it close to the vest.

“Good to see you, Pete,” Silver said to me. She looked good.

“How'd you get here?” I asked. Stupid question. I'd lost any ability to make sense.

“Is that the only opening line you know?” she asked, amused.

I don't know whether Dad saved me or made it worse, but he said, “I've got the hauler, Pete. Why don't you take Miss Irawan here back home so you can get cleaned up? She isn't hooked up, so I reckon you still got a chance.”

“Dad,” I reprimanded.

“Stop your whining and get on about it.” He walked over to the hauler and then called over his shoulder, “Nice to meet you, Miss Irawan.”

“You too, Mr. Hoffen.” She turned her attention back to me. “I think you owe me a drink…

ABOUT THE AUTHOR

Jamie McFarlane is happily married, the father of three and lives in Lincoln, Nebraska. He spends his days engaged in a hi-tech career and his nights and weekends writing works of fiction. He's also the author of:

Privateer Tales

1. Rookie Privateer
2. Fool Me Once
3. Parley
4. Big Pete
5. Smuggler's Dilemma
6. Cutpurse (coming April 2015)

Guardians of Gaeland

1. Lesser Prince

Word-of-mouth is crucial for any author to succeed. If you enjoyed this book, please consider leaving a review at Amazon, even if it's only a line or two; it would make all the difference and would be very much appreciated.

If you want to get an automatic email when Jamie's next book is available, sign up on his website at fickledragon.com. Your email address will never be shared and you can unsubscribe at any time.

CONTACT JAMIE

Blog and Website: fickledragon.com
Facebook: facebook.com/jamiemcfarlaneauthor
Twitter: twitter.com/mcfarlaneauthor

Made in the USA
Columbia, SC
11 August 2019